MINDWORKS

Also by Neal Shusterman

Novels
All Better Now
Bruiser
Challenger Deep
Chasing Forgiveness
The Dark Side of Nowhere
Dissidents
Downsiders
The Eyes of Kid Midas
Full Tilt
Game Changer
The Shadow Club
The Shadow Club Rising
Speeding Bullet

(with Jarrod Shusterman)
Dry
Roxy

(with Debra Young and Michelle Knowlden)
Break to You

Arc of a Scythe Series
Scythe
Thunderhead
The Toll
Gleanings

The Accelerati Trilogy
(with Eric Elfman)
Tesla's Attic
Edison's Alley
Hawking's Hallway

The N.O.A.H. Files
(with Eric Elfman)
I Am the Walrus
Shock the Monkey

The Antsy Bonano Series
The Schwa Was Here
Antsy Does Time
Ship Out of Luck

The Unwind Dystology
Unwind
UnWholly
UnSouled
UnDivided
UnBound

The Skinjacker Trilogy
Everlost
Everwild
Everfound

The Star Shards Chronicles
Scorpion Shards
Thief of Souls
Shattered Sky

The Dark Fusion Series
Dread Locks
Red Rider's Hood
Duckling Ugly

Story Collections
Darkness Creeping

Graphic Novels
Courage to Dream: Tales of Hope in the Holocaust

MINDWORKS

AN UNCANNY COMPENDIUM OF SHORT FICTION BY

NEAL SHUSTERMAN

SIMON & SCHUSTER BFYR

NEW YORK AMSTERDAM/ANTWERP LONDON
TORONTO SYDNEY/MELBOURNE NEW DELHI

SIMON & SCHUSTER BFYR
An imprint of Simon & Schuster Children's Publishing Division
1230 Avenue of the Americas, New York, New York 10020

Package design by Chloë Foglia and Max Löffler

Interior design by Hilary Zarycky
The text for this book was set in Bembo.
Manufactured in China
First SIMON & SCHUSTER BFYR edition November 2025
2 4 6 8 10 9 7 5 3 1
Library of Congress Cataloging-in-Publication Data
Names: Shusterman, Neal author
Title: Mindworks / Neal Shusterman.
Description: New York : Simon & Schuster Books for Young Readers, 2025. |
Audience term: Preteens | Audience: Ages 12 up | Audience: Grades 7–9 |
Summary: This collection of horror stories features bizarre worlds,
forces that can bring back the dead, eerie creatures, and more.
Identifiers: LCCN 2025012867 | ISBN 9781665990783 (hc) | ISBN 9781665939799 (pbk) |
ISBN 9781665939782 (deluxe POB) | ISBN 9781665939805 (ebook)
Subjects: CYAC: Horror stories | Short stories | LCGFT: Horror fiction |Short stories
Classification: LCC PZ7.S55987 Mi 2025 | DDC [Fic]—dc23/eng/20250407
LC record available at https://lccn.loc.gov/2025012867

To the teachers and librarians
who made a difference in my life,
from Hertha Paustian to Deanna Fleischer,
Judith Shapiro to Laurie Aguera-Arcas,
Gilbert Weatherby to Randy Perazzini,
and dozens of others.
You are seen,
you are remembered,
you are loved,
and you've changed not just one world,
but thousands!

MINDWORKS

CONTENTS

Introduction ix

Forces of Nature 1

A Unity of [Purpose] 3

I, of the Storm 14

Smells Like Kafka 26

Obsidian Sky 42

Ralphy Sherman's Bag of Wind 56

The In Crowd 65

The Living Place 85

Angels, Demons, Monsters, and a Tree 101

Non-Player Character 103

Midnight Michelangelo 113

Boy on a Stoop 131

Butterball 142

The Bob Squad 143

Special Deliverance 158

Ralphy Sherman's Jacuzzi of Wonders 163

Terrible Tannenbaum 169

The Wheel of Destiny 181

Dawn Terminator 183

The 💩 on Our Shoes 194

Number Two 221

Fear-for-All 223

Bad Fortune at Richard Yee's 241

Pea Soup 254

Majority Rules 270

Opabinia 278

Presumed Destroyed 295

Attics, Basements, Windows, and Walls 307

Caleb's Colors 309

Retaining Walls 323

Open House 338

Mr. Vandermeer's Attic of Shame 346

Dark Alley 371

The Living, the Dead, and the Undecided 387

Dead Letter 389

Resurrection Bay 392

Perpetual Pest 420

Yardwork 430

Deadliner 441

Loveless 453

I'm Not Myself Today 461

The Body Electric 463

Mail Merge 472

The Elsewhere Boutique 480

Ralphy Sherman's Inside Story 488

The Soul Exchange 497

Clothes Make the Man 510

You Reap What You Sow (The World of *Scythe*) 521

None More Beautiful Than I 523

The *Scythe* Interviews 560

INTRODUCTION

When I was fourteen, during the single unstructured hour we had at summer camp called "free play," I would race down to the waterfront, get a canoe before they were all checked out, and paddle out to the middle of Anawana Lake with a copy of *Isaac Asimov's Science Fiction Magazine*, where I would read until the scratchy recording of a bugle sounding "Recall" blew from the camp's loudspeakers.

I loved those stories! They inspired me to write stories of my own, which I would then submit to *Isaac Asimov's*, *Ellery Queen Mystery Magazine*, *Analog Science Fiction and Fact*, and, dream of dreams, *Omni*.

Never sold a story. I did get some nice rejections, but rejections were all I received.

It wasn't until after I was a published novelist that I began to get asked to contribute short fiction to various anthologies, and was even allowed to write some story collections of my own. My first story collections were the two volumes of *Darkness Creeping*, which have since been combined into a single collection and is still in print with Penguin Random House. And then there were four collections I did with Tor Books: *MindQuakes*, *MindStorms*, *MindTwisters*, and *MindBenders*.

This compendium includes most of the stories from those four collections, along with hard-to-find stories that appeared in multi-author anthologies, as well as some stories that are brand-new—including two visits to the world of *Scythe*.

There are, of course, some stories I left out. . . . "Pacific Rim" comes to mind. I love the story—it's about the largest cruise ship in the world falling off the edge of the earth. Fun stuff—but I decided that I didn't want to further feed the ridiculous fires of flat-earthers. Then there's "He Opens a Window," which became the basis for the first piece in my Holocaust-themed graphic novel, *Courage to Dream*. As it had a new life of its own, it didn't feel right to include it here. And then there are some stories that I won't mention because—ugh! Really? Did I actually write that? Well, just like Madame Thornhill in "Perpetual Pest," some things are best left buried. . . .

Not all the stories here were solo ventures. A number of them that were written for other anthologies I cowrote with my son Brendan. And a couple I cowrote with my friend, award-winning TV writer Terry Black.

I have revised all these stories to some extent. Not just to keep them relevant and technologically current, but also to reflect social changes. We as a society have evolved over the years, and there definitely were some cringeworthy moments in some of my earliest stories that I was more than happy to change.

In reading through and reworking the stories, I found that they fell into seven distinct categories: Fate and destiny. Strange and terrifying beings. Nature out of control. The dead and undead. Doorways, windows, and walls. Personal transformations. Just deserts. But each story, regardless of where it falls, is eerie, or surreal, or mind-melting, or darkly absurd, or all of the above. A reminder that the abyss is always staring back at you. Although sometimes, it winks.

I hope you enjoy this little cabinet of shadows. And if these stories happen to keep you up at night, don't say I didn't warn you!

Neal Shusterman
November 2025

FORCES OF NATURE

There are some places that draw you to them.
They grab you so deep in your soul that you find
yourself drifting toward them, even in your dreams.

—from "The Living Place"

A Unity of [Purpose]

I long to sit at the Resolute desk. To bring a firm fist down upon the well-worn oak, and feel it resonate like a drum. That desk! Which has witnessed declarations of war, and countless State of the Union addresses. Oh, to preside over the machinations of government from the Oval Office. Preside! President! Presidential! How I wish my mouth could speak those words! But, alas, I must be satisfied with translation.

"Good morning, B. Are you ready for today? It's a full schedule."

Georgina! My campaign manager. My handler. My everything. She is beautiful inside and out by anyone's standards. I vigorously nod my approval, and she smiles.

"Then let's get you ready!"

Ah, but first a morning swim!

I am escorted to the brackish waters of the Hudson. It is brisk this early in the spring, and less buoyant than the sea, but it makes for an invigorating workout, and gives me time to get my head in the game.

Yes, the Resolute desk is well within my reach! But, alas, I will never actually sit behind it. Because I lack the ability to sit. Nor do I have a fist to bring down upon its smooth lacquered surface. But these are mere technicalities. At times it may weigh on me—but not today! Half an hour in the mighty Hudson, and I can take on the world!

With the help of a slinged winch, I am loaded back into my travel tank, and we roll!

• • •

My travel tank is a modified tanker truck. State of the art. Eleven thousand gallons kept at a constant sixty-seven degrees. Waterproof screens for communication with the team, and various floating diversions to ease the stress of overland travel. A morning rally in New York, afternoon in Philadelphia, and an evening fundraiser outside Pittsburgh are on the day's agenda.

The team confirms that the venues are all set. "The oratory tanks are in place," the event coordinator tells me, in his own little Zoom window, which looks like its own little tank. "Clear polycarbonate. Completely bulletproof."

It pains me that the tanks from which I present my vision for the nation must be impervious to ballistics, but these are the times we live in. There are those naysayers who would question my capabilities. Insist that I am defined by my physical limitations. Backward thinking. Besides, a great leader knows how to play to their strengths. My cool manner. My smooth movement. How I cut through liquid space like the most graceful of Olympians; the envy of any species sentient enough to comprehend so complex an emotion. And managerial skills? Please! I can balance a budget as easily as balancing a beach ball on my snout.

"Any questions, Mr. Breacher?" asks the event coordinator.

"Eeek eeek e-e-e-e-e-eeek!"

Georgina translates for me.

"As long as the tank is set to the proper temperature, I'll be fine."

Next, the team discusses accusations and attacks by the opposition, who have questioned my ability to sign official documents without opposable thumbs.

"Thumbs?" a loudmouthed pundit proclaimed on some partisan news station. "It doesn't even have hands—why are we talking about thumbs?"

But before I can say anything, Georgina jumps in. "That's exactly that kind of insensitivity that we need to call out at every turn."

"EEEK EEK eeeeee EEEEEEK!" I say to defuse the tension. *"As acerbic as it is, he has a point."* I wait for them to settle down before I continue. *"I cannot ignore the truth. Fin and flipper are not suited to traditional human instruments. The solution is to bypass the question entirely. Install a six-foot touch pad in my tank, and I will be able to deliver snout-written signatures with flourishes worthy of Hancock."*

"Which means it's a nonissue," adds Georgina.

"Precisely," I say. *"You're making an ocean out of an estuary. Now, what's next on our agenda?"*

The team goes on to discuss how the Oval Office might be sealed and lined with a polycarbonate coating, turning it into a worthy habitat. I like that they're thinking ahead. My mind goes once more to the Resolute desk, which will not fare well submerged. Perhaps it should be moved to my presidential museum, once one is established, for I suspect it will never be used again.

There is a sense of claustrophobia that must be overcome when traveling in a tanker truck, even one as well-equipped as this one. It's not just the limited space in which to frolic, but the terrible perversion of sound. One's primal brain panics at the slightest attempt at echolocation. The walls themselves seem to press down upon one's soul. It is a terrible way to travel, and if I am elected, I shall mandate the creation of great canals that will traverse the continent to advance the cause of accessibility.

But for now, it must be overland tanks that will travel deep into dry land—deeper than I've ever been. But I can handle it. I pride myself on my adaptability. An orca or a humpback could never handle such a rigorous campaign. They'd lose their minds after just a few minutes in the tanker truck. Lightweights, even with all that tonnage.

The stadium buzzes with excitement and curiosity. Chants of "Breacher! Breacher! Breacher!" build and crescendo as the curtain drops, revealing me in the oratory tank, its surface—slightly convex, like a lens—making me appear larger than life.

Everyone in this troubled electorate hangs in anticipation of something new. I am the Hail Mary of a system that has brought nothing but vitriol and self-interest and divisiveness for years. After what this nation has suffered under human rule, no wonder they've sought leadership elsewhere.

"Hello, New York!" I eek out, and Georgina delivers her translation from the diaphragm, all power and grace. *"I hope Jets fans don't mind a dolphin in the house!"* Cheers all around. It's a good day. At least it starts that way.

The speech goes perfectly until Georgina makes an unfortunate gaffe. I try to push through it, but it overshadows the entire event.

Once I'm back in my travel tank, we discuss how to address the situation.

"We need to get ahead of this," says the image-maker. "So they're laughing *with* us, instead of *at* us."

"I will not throw Georgina under the keel!" I eek out.

"I'm not saying we have to," he explains—I'm surprised that he understands me without translation. "But we need a response."

The unfortunate foible happened in the last five minutes of the speech. I was extemporizing, going off script, which is always a risk. *"We, the sentient, all want the same things for ourselves and for our loved ones,"* I proclaimed. *"I promise you that we can achieve it! All it takes is determination, and a unity of purpose."*

And then poor Georgina slipped in her translation and said, *"A unity of porpoise."*

She corrected herself, but the damage had been done. Nothing I said for the rest of the speech was taken seriously. It's already trending on every media outlet.

"I agree we need to do damage control," my media liaison says, "because I guarantee you the other side will run with this."

"Let them!" I declare. *"Georgina merely misspoke—but to intentionally call a dolphin the* P *word is so offensive, it's bound to backfire."*

I storm like a Caribbean squall at the very thought of it. To be compared to a porpoise! Porpoises are provincial and petty. Not only do they refuse to see the big picture, they refuse to admit there even is one. My son dated a porpoise once. Needless to say, it ended badly.

"What if we treat Georgina's error like it was gentle ribbing?" suggests the image-maker. "Like it was an intentional wink rather than a mistake."

I tell them to do whatever they need to do to make this go away. I have more important things to worry about. This afternoon's rally in Philly. I can't let this push me from my current.

But Philly is a disaster.

There is an air of derision in the crowd that's palpable. Applause, yes, but not as hearty as I would like. And the occasional shout of "porpoise" from opposition infiltrators. But what bothers me more are the shouts of "shark killer," which I've been hearing more and more often, rising like a bottom-feeder's murky cloud.

On the drive to the Pittsburgh fundraiser, the team asks for another meeting. I'm tired, and just want to lap my tank, preparing myself for the social niceties required for the evening's event. All those heavy gowns and tight tuxedos. I do not envy those who must cover their natural selves in vestments.

The meeting was called by the specialist in opposition research. The team assembles. A grid of faces on my screen.

"I have some sobering news," he begins.

"I am always sober," I inform him. Which is true. Alcohol is not a vice of my species. Of course, there's puffer-fish toxin abuse, but that's a discussion for another day. *"Tell me—no need to mince words. I'm a dolphin, not some fragile seal crushed by heavy tidings."*

He sighs. "The other party has put forth a new candidate."

I can tell from Georgina's expression that she's already heard this. And that it's bad. I take a moment to do a quick lap of the tank to prepare myself. Perhaps I'm more seal-like than I care to admit.

"They're putting their full weight behind Ling-o."

"I'm afraid I'm not familiar with this 'Ling-o.'"

"Yes, you are," Georgina says. "You must have seen the video—it's been viral for weeks. A little boy falls into the panda exhibit at the San Diego Zoo. A panda nuzzles him and protects him from the other bears. Then she flips him onto her back and brings him to a zookeeper."

"Ling-o is a zookeeper?"

"No. Ling-o is the panda."

The rest of the staff seems to melt before my eyes, and everyone starts talking at once.

"This is a disaster."

"How do we fight this?"

"Can we play up the association between pandas and China?"

I can't believe what I'm hearing. *"Aren't we avoiding the elephant in the room?"*

"Wait, now there's an elephant?" someone says. I think they might actually be serious.

"Pandas are a nonverbal, non-sentient species."

"Doesn't matter," says the opposition researcher. "Ling-o was verifiably born in this country, making her eligible. When it comes to being nonverbal, low-information voters don't really care what a candidate says, it's all about appearance and presentation—and every poll gives pandas a *much* higher adorability rating than dolphins. The cuteness quotient is off the charts."

"And then there's your smile," says the image-maker, blindsiding me like a swordfish.

"What's wrong with my smile?"

"Focus groups seem to feel your smile is sarcastic."

"Not just you, Breacher, but dolphins in general," says Georgina, dripping with sympathy.

"We're born this way! People can't make judgments based on that!"

"And yet they do."

"That being the case," says the opposition researcher. "You may want to consider a running mate with higher social approval. . . ."

The tank is strategically set in the center of a ballroom that will soon be filled with political power brokers—each one angling to make sure their interests will be met before they commit to a campaign donation.

"I much prefer the rallies," I tell Georgina before the doors open.

"Of course you do," she replies. "They have a much greater scope."

"Yes," I tease. *"A single word reaches thousands in a rally."*

I had meant it as a playful barb, but she reddens, and I immediately regret it.

"Breacher, I'm sorry about earlier today. It was unforgivable."

"It's already forgotten," I assure her. But we both know that's not true—because as much as I might want to forget it, the world outside my tank won't allow me to. We both let it go, but the tension remains.

"A word of warning," Georgina tells me as they begin letting people in. "The barrier reef incident is looming large. If you're asked about it, don't engage."

Throughout the evening, people are mostly polite and deferential. Some are content to sip champagne and talk amongst themselves, but there are plenty who get in line to talk with me.

"Can I speak directly to him," one woman asks Georgina, "or will you need to translate?"

"He'll understand anything you say," Georgina assures her, "but I'll have to translate his response."

Most are the expected questions; policy inquiries and details of the platform I'm running on. However, some questions are of a more personal nature.

"How can you claim to know what we need when you've never walked in a human's shoes?" one man asks, smoking a cigar that he's not allowed to smoke indoors.

"Empathy and understanding are the hallmarks of my kind," I tell him. *"I don't need to wear shoes to know how sore your feet get."*

My favorite is a question from a child, who's so adorable it makes me wish I could sport my own little red bow tie.

"Can you teach me to echolocate?" he asks.

"Yes," I tell him. *"But it takes a lifetime of study. Are you ready to commit?"*

He nods enthusiastically, then leans in close and whispers something that is an omen of things to come.

"*I* know you're not a porpoise," he says. "And I know you're not a shark killer either."

It's toward the end of the gala, when my guard is down, that I am approached by a man with a large hat and a fair amount of walrus blubber. He's been eyeing me for most of the evening—circling, even, like an ocean predator—so I already know what the subject of his conversation will be.

"So, I hear a bunch of your buddies did some killing off the Great Barrier Reef," he says. "Do you think it's really the right time to be supporting a dolphin?"

Georgina looks to me sternly, but I choose to answer him.

"It was a pod of Australian dolphins that killed that shark. I have not met them, nor do I condone their actions."

"Then why won't you publicly condemn it?"

I try to give a measured response. *"My dear sir, dolphins and sharks are natural enemies. To condemn a foreign pod for engaging in perfectly natural behavior would be, to say the least, hypocritical."*

"Yes, but it was a whale shark. They're gentle giants—my grandkids love them. How can I tell them I'm supporting someone who kills them?"

"I am not now, nor have I ever been, a shark killer. Frankly, I've never even met a shark."

And he latches onto that. "Yes—because you were raised in privileged captivity. You have no idea what it's really like out there in the big blue, do you?"

"I'm not running 'out there,' I'm running right here, you bloated bipedal ass!"

Wisely, Georgina does not translate that. Instead she says, "I'm sorry, but that's all the time we have for questions."

"We've gone through quite a few options for potential running mates," says the image-maker, "and we think we've nailed it." He shares the image on his screen. "This is Mr. Cuddles. He hits all the benchmarks for public approval and mass appeal."

I stare at the image, trying to wrap my sizable brain around it. *"You can't be serious."*

"All our research points to him as our best overall option."

"It's a gerbil!"

"Hamster."

"Be careful, Breacher," says Georgina. "Confusing them could be problematic for you."

"Oh, the way you confused me with a porpoise?"

"That's not fair—you know that was an accident."

But now I'm not so sure. Could it have been intentional? Could my Georgina have betrayed me? I don't know who I can trust in my entourage anymore.

"My God, look at it! IT RUNS ON A WHEEL!"

"Ooh, ooh!" says the image-maker. "Campaign slogan! 'Runs on a wheel instead of a platform! Living the rat race, just like you!'"

I do a flip out of frustration, hitting the low roof of the tanker truck, and it just adds to my indignation.

"No! Absolutely not! I will not have it."

"Ling-o is gaining in the polls," says the opposition researcher. "And after the barrier reef incident, you need to raise the ticket's adorability factor. This could tip the scales in your direction."

"And what if I were to die in office? A hamster will be president!"

"Well," says the image maker. "We've certainly had worse. . . ."

As the days go by, the crowds thin, and the catcalls become ever more hateful. My dread evolves into a sense of impending doom. The team engages with me less and less. There's talk of canceling appearances. I hear indirectly that none of the remaining campaign stops will have an oratory tank. Because I won't be speaking.

"We thought the shark-killer thing would be a speed bump," Georgina says, in one of the rare moments that she bothers to speak to me anymore. "But now we think it might be a campaign killer." She sighs, but it feels false, and I wonder if her concern, her enthusiasm, her connection with me has always been calculated. A fair-weather friend, fickle when I flounder.

"You might want to consider going home," she suggests. "You could take some time to rest and regroup."

But I already know that the decision has been made. Because our campaign caravan has turned south, heading back toward Florida. And SeaWorld.

"Look at him! He's so adorable on that wheel."

"Athletic."

"He'll look like a star projected on a jumbotron."

Run run run. Nibble nibble. Run run. Dig.

"He certainly is proactive. Industrious. We can play on that."

Dig dig. Thirsty. Lick water. Lick lick. Dig.

"After all, the executive branch is all about who you surround yourself with."

"How about I arrange a photo shoot? Some glamour shots. A series of well-placed billboards, paired with some strong anti-panda messaging. I see a blood-covered graphic of Ling-o in a restaurant with a gun. 'Eats shoots and leaves.'"

"Great angle! I love it."

Run run. Lick. Run.

Food? Food? FOOD!!

"He does seem sophisticated from a certain angle. Reminds me of the dramatic chipmunk."

"Yes—we could play on that."

Run. Stop. Sniff.

Other? Other!

Mount!

Mate! MATE! MAAAAAATE!

"It's settled, then. I think we have a winner."

I, of the Storm

A late afternoon wind ushered in the sudden downpour. I could see the courtyard of the museum beginning to flood, while up above, lightning volleyed angrily across the clouds.

"Rainy season," Mom said. "It rains for an hour or two most afternoons this time of year."

"It's a good thing," Dad added. "It cleans up some of the smog."

I watched through a fogging window as the dark cumulus clouds slid past one another—and it seemed to me that they were closer than the storm clouds back home in Florida. I asked my parents about it.

"I suppose it's the altitude," Dad theorized. "Mexico City's a mile and a half above sea level—much closer to the clouds."

A wind swooped down and rattled the window. I backed away, and Dad chuckled. "Aisha, this museum's stood through countless earthquakes. You don't have to worry about a little wind."

He turned and glanced at the gallery behind us. Giant Olmec heads with no bodies sat on pedestals beside sandstone sun wheels and weathered Aztec statues. The museum was filled with gallery after giant gallery of massive carved stones.

"Where's your brother?" Dad asked me. "Weren't you keeping an eye on him?"

I heard my brother Karson's giggle and the pattering of feet somewhere deep in the gallery.

"Don't play games, you two," Mom said, as if I was an accomplice to Karson's mischief. "We have to get through the whole museum before five." Dad took a last look over the room to see if there was anything he'd missed, then he and Mom went on to the next gallery. Our tour schedule only allowed us three hours at Mexico City's National Museum of Anthropology. And my parents were all about schedules.

Unfortunately, my life had been ruled by a very different clock lately. One that measured time in tantrums. It was a sugar-powered clock named Karson.

Three years old, and about as disagreeable as a human could be, my brother Karson lived by no schedule but his own, and right now, following Mom and Dad was not part of his agenda. He was nowhere in sight.

"Karson?"

I heard him giggle again—farther away this time.

"Karson, c'mon. Mom and Dad already left."

"Come and get me!" His voice echoed around the stones, and I couldn't tell where it came from.

"Fine. I'm leaving," I threatened, and turned, pretending to head off toward the next gallery. But I couldn't really leave him because Mom and Dad would be furious with me—as if it was my purpose in life to take care of Karson.

"Aisha, take Karson to the park."

"Aisha, tie Karson's shoes."

"Aisha, make sure Karson doesn't get hurt."

And when his endless tantrums drove them up the wall, I would always be the one who had to stop him from screaming, and kicking, and fighting, because I was the only one who could calm him down.

Not that he's like that all the time. There are times when Karson is so sweet and so loving that he makes you forget how unreasonable he was just five minutes before. And then there are the times like this, when he just makes you want to pull your hair out.

"Karson, you'd better come out now, or I swear I'll—"

"You're not playing right," said Karson. "You gotta play right. You gotta look for me."

Outside, lightning struck, bathing the solemn stone heads around me with a cold light that cast their eyes deep in shadow. We were the only ones in the gallery now. All the other tourists had moved on.

"Come find me, Aisha. You have to!"

"You better hope I don't!"

I ducked past a statue of a plumed serpent, and around the chiseled face of a Mayan god. Finally I found Karson standing on an altar behind a sign that said, DO NOT STAND ON ALTAR in both Spanish and English. His fists were at his waist like the Jolly Green Giant.

"Look at me!" he said. "I'm a statue!"

"Mom already told you not to climb! Now let's go!" I pulled him off the ancient altar, and he struggled against my grip.

"No, I wanna stay here. I wanna play hide-and-seek," he said. "And I'm hungry, too. I want a corn dog."

"You can't have one!" I shouted. "You're in Mexico. I don't think corn dogs are a thing here."

"You're lying. You're just being mean!" He was beyond reason, and I was beyond patience. Mom and Dad were probably halfway through the museum now, and I was getting a headache from Karson's voice and the city's thin air. So I grabbed him and carried him off, kicking and screaming.

"No! I won't go!" he wailed. "I won't, I won't, I won't!" He bit me on the arm, I dropped him, and he ran—

—right into a dark stone slab.

Karson bounced off it and fell to the ground. "You did that on purpose!" he insisted. "You pushed me!"

The leash on my temper was fraying, but I held on to it, figuring that maybe now he'd come along calmly. He turned to the figure carved into the stone slab; a young warrior.

"You stink," he told it, still holding the spot on his forehead that had rammed the slab.

"I wouldn't say that to him. Says here that this is Tezcatlipoca—the god of the night wind. It says he could become an angry wind that sweeps unwary travelers away. I wouldn't mess with a guy like that!"

I looked around and noticed that this slab wasn't on a pedestal. In fact, it was right in the middle of an aisle. No wonder Karson ran into it. I tried to remember if we saw it when we first entered the huge gallery, but for the life of me I could not remember seeing that face before.

Lightning struck somewhere far away. The light played off Tezcatlipoca's carved lips. I couldn't tell whether he was smiling, or grimacing.

"If he's supposed to be so mean," said Karson, "then how come he winked at me?"

"Don't be silly," I said, and pulled him away.

There are mistakes we make that seem tiny and unimportant at the time, but turn into monster regrets. The kind of regrets that shred your dreams into nightmares over and over again.

What happened next, well, that's my monster regret, and no one else's.

I headed out with Karson to find Mom and Dad, but they weren't in the next gallery, or the one after that. We weaved quickly through the maze of ancient civilizations: Aztec, Olmec, Toltec, and Mayan. And somewhere along the way, I let go of Karson's hand.

Finally I rounded a corner to find Mom and Dad studying the features of a fertility statue.

"There you are!" said Mom, not even realizing how far behind we had been. "Where's Karson?"

"Right here . . . ," I said, but when I turned, he wasn't there. "Oh, great!"

"You were supposed to keep an eye on him," chided Dad.

I just boiled at Karson's continual ability to get me in trouble.

"Karson, c'mon!" I called. "No hide-and-seek!" I felt dizzy, and a bit off-balance. I thought I was light-headed from the altitude, but an instant later I realized the ground was moving.

We were having an earthquake.

It wasn't what I expected an earthquake to feel like. It didn't grind and make lots of noise. Instead it kind of just sloshed back and forth, like we were standing on Jell-O.

It wasn't big. It didn't last long. And somewhere far away, I heard a deep, heavy boom as something fell.

"Karson?" called Mom, her worry slowly building.

The tremor was over, and I glanced outside. It was darker, and although the rain had stopped, a night wind blew a flock of twisted papers through the museum's courtyard.

"Karson, this is not funny!" said Dad in his sternest voice.

Karson didn't answer.

And suddenly I knew where he must have gone. He went to take one more look at the stone face of Tezcatlipoca—to see if it really had winked at him.

"Oh no!" I raced back through the winding corridors. Whatever had fallen, it was back that way, and I kept trying to tell myself that Karson was nowhere near it. We'd find him, Dad would scold him, and we'd go back to our hotel and finish up our vacation.

But we couldn't find him.

Instead we found a two-ton granite slab that had fallen facedown in the aisle.

The image of Tezcatlipoca.

"Karson!" screamed Mom. She seemed uncertain whether to be angry or to panic. We all kept believing that he'd leap out from behind some other statue. But he didn't. We had security search the museum for hours, but no Karson.

Finally, long after closing, they brought a winch to raise the massive stone. We huddled together, Mom, Dad, and I, not wanting to look but knowing we had to. Inch by inch, they raised the slab, until the museum lights lit the space beneath.

And nothing was there.

Nothing but the chiseled face of the slab, and the smiling, scowling image of the god of the night wind.

It's easy to rebuild a house. I know because we had to do it after a hurricane once. But rebuilding a home—well, that's something different. Because how can you hope to make a home again, when one of the most important parts is missing?

We never found Karson. Mom and I stayed in Mexico for weeks, and Dad stayed for months, working with the authorities and chasing blind leads until there was nothing for him to do but come back to Florida and go on with life.

Although my parents never blamed me, I knew it was my fault, and that weight pressed on me like a thousand stone slabs. There were times I would look out from our beachside house, across the Gulf of Mexico. I would imagine I could see Karson still there, hiding behind a giant, fat-cheeked Olmec head. Waiting for us to find him.

We limped along, day to day, for almost a year . . . until the storm.

The news report called it a tropical depression—a slow swirling storm that was riding up the east coast of Mexico. Mom and Dad watched the TV with mild disinterest . . . which was the way they looked at everything these days. They had become way too quiet over the months, and surf pounding on the beach sounded almost deafening when we sat together.

"Do you think it'll come this way?" I asked Dad.

"What?"

"You know, the storm." I pointed at the screen, but the weather map was already gone.

I would have forgotten about it . . . but the next day that tropical depression was upgraded to a tropical storm, and the day after that it was a full-fledged hurricane.

Florida has always been a magnet for hurricanes, so the storm was on everyone's mind at school and throughout the neighborhood. We checked the storm apps, and watched the Weather Channel for days, soaking in the reports, as Hurricane Zelda pummeled Galveston, Texas, and continued hugging the Gulf Coast.

"It probably won't come this way," Mom said. But hurricane paths are hard to predict. They wander over ocean and shore until they finally die. No telling where they'll head.

It was the morning after Zelda hit Galveston that I got my first hint of strange events yet to come. Dad was sitting at the breakfast table, lost in his phone, and the morning news feed. Glancing over his shoulder, I saw an image of the hurricane's devastation.

"Wow!" I said as I studied the picture. "Looks like Zelda shows no mercy." There was nothing left of a beach house but a pile of wet rubble. I'd seen storm damage like that before, but it's still hard to comprehend.

"The news is making too big a deal of it," Dad said. "Actually only a few homes were destroyed." Then he tapped on a different image to enlarge it—the same ruined house, viewed from a distance. There were homes still standing on either side of the wreckage. Sure, they had broken windows and all, but had taken nowhere near the damage that the house in the middle had.

"Probably had termites to begin with," Dad suggested. "A storm can do lots of damage when the wood's weak."

I pulled up the article on my own phone and studied the close-up image of the ruined house again. This time I noticed something curious I hadn't seen before.

The wood of the ruined house was a pale blue, and a gray flap of shredded fabric hung from what used to be a window.

"That house was blue, with gray awnings," I told my parents. "Just like ours."

"It's a popular color scheme," said Mom, dismissing it. And although I wanted to talk more about it, I inadvertently swiped the article away, and couldn't get it back.

With winds peaking at 150 miles per hour, Zelda, now a Category 4, nearly took out the levees in New Orleans again. We watched in numb disbelief as the news showed communities devastated by the raging winds and rain. With the hurricane growing in strength, more homes were washed away by the storm's power. On TV, a reporter stood in the ruins of one of the worst piles of wreckage—and although they say seeing is believing, I wasn't ready to believe anything just yet . . . but I was getting close.

"Blue wood and gray awnings," I pointed out to my parents. They had no comment this time. From the look of this waterfront Louisiana community, it seemed to have taken a hard slam from this angry storm. But this blue house seemed to have taken it worse than any other.

"Spooky," I said as I stared at the screen. "Karson would have said that Zelda's favorite color is blue."

Dad left the room at the mention of Karson's name, and Mom slipped out afterward . . . but I couldn't leave. I suddenly found my mind fixed on those damage reports, awed by the power of winds that could raise oceans and hurl boats half a mile inland.

There was one boat wedged in the side of a truck. The image made me smile in spite of the destruction, because it reminded me of Karson and the way he loved to play demolition derby. Especially with trains.

It wasn't until I saw the next report that I began to get a funny feeling inside. Like the kind you get about a minute before you have to throw up.

Three derailed trains.

They were miles inland, but a stray edge of the hurricane seemed to have lashed out and whipped them off their tracks.

My brain told me that it was all coincidence—it had to be. But intuition was filling my arms with gooseflesh and making my heart just about explode out of my chest. *Karson didn't just disappear*, my inner voice shouted to my disbelieving brain. *He disappeared into thin air. . . . He disappeared into the wind.*

It was a thought I simply couldn't push away. Instead it built inside of me like a hurricane in my own head until I began to believe it . . . more than believe—I knew. I knew exactly what had happened to my brother so many months before—and exactly what was happening now!

My parents were already asleep, but I shook them awake. My breathing was shallow, and my eyes must have been panicked because they sat up right away and asked what was wrong.

I didn't know what to tell them. I knew what I was thinking, but how could I explain it in any rational way? How could I convince them that the hurricane wasn't destroying homes that looked like ours by accident? This storm was looking for something, and when it didn't find what it searched for, the storm tore everything to shreds, like . . .

. . . like a child having a tantrum.

The truth was, Hurricane Zelda wasn't a "Zelda" at all.

It was a "Karson."

"I think the hurricane's heading this way," I told them, because I couldn't tell them the rest of what I was thinking. We turned the news back on, and it confirmed what I already knew in my heart. The hurricane had abandoned Louisiana and was cutting a fast, furious path across the gulf, toward the Florida coast.

By dawn, the sea was already climbing the old grass-covered dunes just behind our back porch. An hour later, they gave the order to evacuate.

No one was ready—no one expected the storm to pick up speed and change its course the way it had. Neighbors frantically nailed plywood over their windows as police urged everyone to leave their homes.

Mom and Dad packed our car with whatever it would hold, and we joined the slow-moving line of traffic inland. I looked out the back window of the car at the dark, angry sky looming over the horizon, wondering what the storm would do, and where it would go when it found our house empty.

That was when I realized it couldn't find our house empty.

With the wind already whipping the trees around us, we got caught in an evacuation traffic jam. If I was going to do it, I had to do it now. Around me, random things had been collected by my parents. Memories, mostly. One memory poked out of a box beside me—the tattered ear of a gnawed teddy bear. It was Karson's Nighty Bear. It was missing a leg and oozed white fluff from a dozen holes—still, Karson would never sleep without it.

I grabbed Nighty Bear and opened my door.

"Aisha? Aisha, what are you doing?"

But I didn't answer. Instead I ran into the wind, and toward the approaching storm.

The ocean had already begun to swallow our neighborhood by the time I arrived. Waves washed through streets and alleys, while up above, roofs were shredded by the relentless wind. The hurricane had hit with its full fury, ravaging the town.

I fought the rampage of wind and water. Cold and shivering, I held on to Karson's waterlogged bear. I knew my parents must have been coming after me, but I wouldn't look back, for fear that I might get caught and be pulled away to safety.

The street was flooded waist-deep around me; an undercurrent pulled my feet out and I went down. I gulped a heavy dose of salty sea before a wave carried me back to the surface, and *bam!* I found myself coughing up water, on a tilted porch. A blue porch. I was home!

The house was shifting horribly, and it shuddered every time a wave crashed against it. It had already been washed off its foundation, and it would soon go down completely. Before another wave could wash me away, I climbed in through a broken window and fell to the flooded floor.

The TV and living room furniture were floating, like shipwrecks, half-submerged around the ruined room. Another wave came crashing through the kitchen window.

I knew what I was thinking was crazy. I knew that I would probably die—but I had to go through with this. I climbed the crooked stairs toward my brother's room.

Karson's room had been kept in perfect condition. His cartoon bedspread smooth and neat, his finger paintings tacked up on the wall. But now the wind and rain poured through his broken window, and the floorboards were beginning to buckle from the strain on the shifting house.

Okay, I'm here, I told myself. *Now what?*

There was a great gnashing noise, and the roof peeled off like the lid of a can, tumbling upward, and shredding to smithereens. Now the only thing above me was a screaming tantrum of violent skies. With both hands, I took the ruined bear and held it high above my head, toward the dark clouds.

"Karson!" I screamed. I couldn't hear my own voice above the wailing wind. "Karson, it's Aisha!" The wind ripped Nighty Bear from my hands, and it flew straight up until it disappeared. "Karson, you stop this!" I demanded of the storm. "You come down here now!" The wind changed its pitch; now it sounded like a voice, a frightened, angry voice.

I didn't pretend to understand a force that could turn a child into the wind. I could never understand that kind of power.

But I had some power of my own—because I was the only one who could calm Karson down. I held my hands up to the sky, swallowing my fear. "I'm here, Karson!" I called out, and I imagined my voice carrying over the winds and out into the ocean, my words reaching the far edge of the storm. "I'm here . . . and you're home!"

The wind tore at me so strongly that I could barely see. I could feel the clouds collapsing, compressing, squeezing between my outstretched arms until the sound of the storm had changed into the screams and sobs of a child.

What had once been wind tearing at me were now struggling arms and legs—kicking and fighting as I held him in my arms . . . as I held my brother. Soon his struggling weakened, and his screams turned to sobs, and then to whimpers as he clutched me tightly around the neck, gripping his Nighty Bear in his cold hand.

"It's okay, Karson," I told him softly. "It'll be okay." He dug his face into my shoulder and closed his eyes, relaxing at last. And that was how my parents found me—holding my lost brother and gently rocking him to sleep, to the sound of floodwaters washing back to join the sea, in a roofless house, beneath a clear, cloudless sky.

I know there will be lots of questions. Many will be left unanswered, and even more left unasked. But that's all right. And even though we stand in the shattered debris of our house, I am not sad at all. Because now that Karson's back, our home is once again whole. And a house can always be rebuilt.

Smells Like Kafka

Bettina Plinth was the victim of guilt parenting. Her father was a plastic surgeon—the best in East Renfield—and was constantly on call for emergency nips-and-tucks among the town's middle-aged elite. As for her mother, she was an iron social butterfly, which was to say that the parties she spent most of her life planning defined society in East Renfield, and woe be to anyone who fell out of her good graces. This left very little time for child-rearing, which was why Bettina lived on a farm on the outskirts of town with her great-aunt Sophie, who, having seen her own seven children to adulthood with minimal casualties, seemed best suited for the job.

While Aunt Sophie pretended it was a grave imposition, she really didn't mind, as Bettina's presence was a welcomed break from hot rum toddies and the Home Shopping Network.

Bettina spent her days at Ravenscroft Academy, her parents' own alma mater, and spent her evenings with Aunt Sophie, who always had a great deal to say, even when she didn't.

The family Plinth had been cornerstones of East Renfield for a hundred years, had a street named for them, and tended to wear their name like mink. No surprise, then, that Aunt Sophie's farmhouse was the only place Bettina felt free of the weight of her family name. True, Aunt Sophie had been born a Plinth, but she had escaped by marrying a farmer, going rustic, and shedding that mink for overalls.

"You won't find any streets named after *me*!" Aunt Sophie was proud to say. This was a sentiment Bettina shared, for she knew life was much more interesting as a footpath than a boulevard. Unlike her parents, she hoped no one would ever say that they had an office on Bettina Plinth.

As for her parents, they were not terrible people, only terribly self-absorbed, and overburdened by the magnitude of their lives. They did love Bettina, and would come visit every Sunday to shower her with affection and presents.

"So good to see you, dear!"

"We've missed you so much!"

"You're always in our thoughts!"

"Was that my phone or yours?"

Guilt parenting. They felt so terribly *bad* about not spending more time with their daughter, they showered her with every gift imaginable. This was how Kafka came to reside at Aunt Sophie's farmhouse.

Kafka was a 150-pound teddy bear that filled a corner of Bettina's bedroom. His thick brown acrylic coat was almost indistinguishable from the real thing, and his eyes were genuine amethyst gems. He hadn't come with the name Kafka—just a little tag above his tail that said MADE IN HONG KONG. The name was Bettina's idea. Once, at one of her mother's parties, her mother had been talking to friends about literature, and the many, many writers she didn't like.

"Kafka's the worst of them," Bettina had heard her mother say. "I could never understand a thing he wrote."

And so, when her parents presented her with the bear, she promptly named him Kafka, knowing there must be some merit to something her mother couldn't understand.

For most of his early life, Kafka would sit in the corner, his gaze fixed out of the window, staring at dazzling sunsets that would refract though his amethyst eyes. He would observe on the occasions Bettina brought classmates over, holding his silence as those children made snide comments, turning their noses up at Bettina's less-than-elegant lifestyle. He would say nothing as Bettina tried desperately to win the friendship of these privileged children who were used to having their friendship bought.

"You can't get friends by acting like you want them," Marla Korkel had told Bettina. Marla was a popular girl at school, who, Bettina had concluded, was exactly what her mother must have been like at that age. "You have to act like you don't care," Marla had said. "Then people will want to be your friend."

This tactic failed on every level, because the snooty kids at Ravenscroft Academy were content to be ignored by her. Kafka, however, was always there for her in those moments she felt so utterly alone. She would throw her arms around him and cry, her tears running down his Scotchgarded pelt. If she pressed deeply enough against him, his arms would rise from the pressure, and Bettina could imagine he was hugging her back.

Aunt Sophie often hugged her—in fact, she made it a point to hug Bettina as often as possible. Still, it wasn't the same, because Aunt Sophie's years of child-rearing had left her on autopilot. Although Bettina knew Aunt Sophie cared deeply, those hugs-by-rote were like multiplication tables.

"I look at myself in the mirror sometimes, and I feel like there's nothing inside," she would confide in Kafka. "Nothing but stuffing." And perhaps that was why she came to feel him as a kindred spirit, as they quietly passed the days waiting for something in their lives to change.

It was on the day her parents left for a long-anticipated Mediterranean cruise that Bettina's mother took her aside for a heartfelt talk among the clutter of knickknacks in Aunt Sophie's living room.

"Listen to me, Bettina." (Her mother always began her admonitions with the phrase "listen to me," much the way sermons and hymns always ended with "amen.") "You need to try harder to fit in at Ravenscroft. Your teachers say that you do well in your studies—it's clear sailing academically, but in the other areas . . . in the *personal* areas . . . you seem to run aground."

Bettina cast her eyes down at a snow globe that featured a horse within a glass ball, nursing a foal. She picked up the globe and shook it. Snow swirled within the ball, and she wondered what self-respecting mare would nurse her foal in a blizzard.

"Bettina, are you listening?"

"I'm listening, Mother."

"Let me see your face." Bettina looked up and her mother examined her. "There's nothing wrong with you that a smile and some eye shadow can't cure. Remember, it's not so much what you have, as how you present it."

Bettina was not an unattractive girl, but she knew her eyes were a bit too small for her face, and her hair defied the most determined of brushes. "Dad says I have good bone structure."

"So you do, dear. So you do." Her mother ended their talk with a long, sorrowful gaze and a sigh. Amen.

That night the moon shone brightly through Bettina's window, reflecting off Kafka's deep violet eyes as she lay in bed, unable to sleep. Her tears had long since frothed into anger. She clenched her fists until her knuckles went the pale color of her mother's makeup base.

Through all of this, Kafka watched. To say that an object as inanimate as a cotton-filled bear could be watching or listening might have been scoffed at by her parents, but Bettina was sure that he did, because she was not beyond believing in the impossible.

"There's magic hidden in life's secret corners," Aunt Sophie once told her. "But you kill it if you clean with Pine-Sol."

Aunt Sophie's wisdom often had to be taken with a grain of salt, and sometimes Tylenol, but her view on magic was something Bettina had taken to heart. Bettina was sure, for instance, that the eyes of some old portraits truly did follow you across a gallery, that cameras did occasionally capture a soul, and that the most deeply loved stuffed animals were aware.

"My mother wants me to be more like her, Kafka. But why should I want to be?" Yet there was a part of her that *did* want to be like her mother. As much as she hated her parents' world, she couldn't help but long for the perfect fit they made with it, like her mother's hand in a long satin glove. Bettina knew she was like a planet revolving around a distant but powerful sun. Either she would find the enormous energy she needed to break free from her mother's formidable gravity, or she would never reach that critical velocity, and would end up trapped in orbit, becoming nothing but a poor imitation of her mother, and not who she wanted to be. If only she knew who she wanted to be.

"What is it I really want?" she asked Kafka just before she nodded into sleep. His answer, as always, was silent meditation.

Bettina woke the next morning to find her face being slimed by a tongue the size of a trout, and smelling just as bad. She yelped, then screamed, when she realized she was not dreaming. Leaping from her bed, she cowered in the corner.

There was a bear in her bedroom.

There was a living, breathing bear standing between her and the door.

"Aunt Sophie!!" she screamed. "Aunt Sophie, help me!!"

But Aunt Sophie was not waking for all the world this morning. She was several REM states away from consciousness, having gone on a home-shopping bender the night before until three a.m. Nothing short of the apocalypse would wake her this morning, and even then, the Four Horsemen would have to wait until she had coffee.

With no help from Aunt Sophie, Bettina looked around for something to defend herself with, but her room was full of damnable soft things, because her parents did not believe in supplying hard objects like, oh, say, a baseball bat, to a girl. It did occur to her, however, that of all the soft things in her room, one was missing: a rather large one, which, until last night, had occupied the very corner in which she now cowered. The bear watched Bettina with curious, concerned eyes. Familiar eyes.

"Kafka?!"

The bear sat back on its haunches, the way he always did in his corner of the room. "Harrumph," said the bear as his rear hit the floor. The boards creaked beneath him—it seemed the entire house bowed from his weight. Somewhere downstairs, something fragile fell from a shelf and smashed.

Yes, this was Kafka! There was no doubt about it. There was no other explanation, and Bettina thanked her lucky stars for having been chosen for this glorious, if somewhat pungent miracle.

She went up to Kafka slowly, reached out her hand, and brushed his fur, so soft and dense. Then she led him out of the room and down the stairs. With every footfall, something else fell from one of Aunt Sophie's many shelves. A statuette of a sad child with oversized eyes. A plate with the likeness of John Wayne. A whiskey decanter in the shape of Frank Sinatra. Every step brought another casualty until Kafka sat in the same living room where her mother had lectured her on the importance of presentation.

"Well, what now, Kafka?"

The bear responded with silent meditation, so Bettina turned on the TV, then lay back into him like he was a beanbag, and they watched cartoons.

Aunt Sophie awoke at eleven, cursing the foulness of mornings, believing they were God's punishment to mankind for everything he was likely to do during the rest of the day. Gripping the banister, she came down the stairs, assuming the gamey odor around her was some new manifestation of old age. When she arrived in the kitchen, she found Bettina sitting there with something very large that refused to define itself in Aunt Sophie's mind without her glasses. She reached above the refrigerator, slipped on her glasses, and was faced with a bear eating kibble out of her crystal punch bowl.

Aunt Sophie sucked in a deep breath and held on to the door-frame to keep herself steady.

"Kafka was hungry," Bettina explained. "And we had plenty of dog food."

Aunt Sophie's dog, Geppetto, was a stubby little Lhasa apso that was several hundred dog-years old, and was so territorial that he would often attack Aunt Sophie's furry slippers. But right now he just cowered outside the doggy door, poking his nose through and barking, refusing to get any closer to the bear that was inhaling its kibble.

It was common knowledge that Aunt Sophie had been known to "nip at the NyQuil," as the neighbors put it. Thus, she was no stranger to unlikely animals wandering through her kitchen. Indeed, there was one time after too many vodka martinis that an entire zoo tramped through her house, singing selections from *West Side Story*. Usually those creatures didn't linger till the morning, however.

"You remember Kafka, don't you, Aunt Sophie? He's just changed a bit, that's all."

Aunt Sophie was also a conscientious hypochondriac, and was on a whole series of medications for ailments she no longer remembered. She clung on to that fact like a fine strand of sanity as she left the kitchen and returned to her bedroom to call her doctor, thoroughly convinced that this hallucination was brought on by the interaction of her medications.

When the bear did not vanish as the day wore on, she had to acknowledge that he was real, which begged more questions than she had years left to answer.

"That bear must have come from somewhere," she told Bettina as they watched it wander around the yard.

"He came from my room."

"He's probably a circus bear. Someone will come looking for him."

"Bet they won't."

"And what if he's dangerous?"

"Does he look dangerous to you?"

And actually, no, for all his size, it didn't seem like he would hurt a fly. There was no malice in his eyes, or in his ponderous body language.

For most of the day Bettina played with the bear in the yard, and Aunt Sophie watched dubiously from her favorite Adirondack chair, too distracted by the sight to even change out of her robe. Like Bettina, Aunt Sophie was also not beyond believing in strange occurrences, and had to entertain the possibility that this truly was Kafka transformed. Bears simply were not seen in the woods behind her home—or anywhere in the county, for that matter. And after all, just watching Bettina and the bear together made it obvious that their relationship went beyond the normal relationship between bear and child. She would pet him and he would purr. She would scold him and he would lower his head. She would praise him and he would stick his snout in the air, preening. She would open her arms to hug him and he would pull her into his fur, hugging back, but not with a heavy, leaden bear hug. His arms fell so gently over Bettina's shoulders, she could still stand on her tiptoes.

Aunt Sophie had been around the block enough to see a few miracles in her time. How her firstborn child had been pronounced stillborn, only to revive when she held him in her loving arms and prayed. She had seen her brother hit by a truck at seventeen and told he would never walk again, only to see him dance a soft-shoe at a family reunion a year later. And she had unmistakably seen her late husband's spirit shining back at her from a newborn babe she saw in a park not a month after his passing. If these miracles were possible, who was to say if Bettina's miracle might not also be true?

As for Bettina, she had quickly adopted this quirk of fate into her understanding of reality.

"I've made up a place for him in the barn," Bettina told Aunt Sophie.

"Well, that's all fine and good, but we're going to have to call someone to come take him away eventually, you know that, don't you?"

"No," Bettina proclaimed. "I'm keeping him."

"It's hard enough cleaning up after Geppetto. I'm not shoveling up after a bear!"

"I'll do it."

"You say that now, but my boys had hamsters, and who do you think had to clean up after them?"

Right about now Kafka came lumbering out of the barn and took an interest in Aunt Sophie's chair. They watched from across the yard as Kafka first sniffed at the chair, and then began to scratch at it heartily with his paws. Aunt Sophie ran toward him, screaming—and understandably so. This wasn't just any old chair, and Bettina knew not even to sit in it, lest its fragile wood give way. To hear Aunt Sophie explain it, the old Adirondack chair was the last of its kind—the only surviving relic from Hotchewanna Lake Resort, where she and Uncle Walter had met and were eventually married. When Hotchewanna Lake Resort closed down, the hotel was bought by an exotic religious cult that worshipped trees. Hence, all wooden objects short of the hotel's timbers were burned. Fortunately, Uncle Walter had stolen the chair a year before the terrible Hotchewanna bonfire. The sentimental value alone was just this side of the Hope diamond.

"You get away from that, you miscreant!" Aunt Sophie yelled. The bear lumbered toward her, rearing up on his hind legs. Aunt Sophie wagged a furious finger at him. "You go near that chair again and I'll send you back to wherever it is you come from!"

Kafka roared back at her, but then strode away with his head held low.

"You didn't have to yell at him!"

They went to the chair to inspect the damage. There were gouges all over the right arm of the chair, in strange crisscrossing patterns.

"Look at what he did! I'll never be able to repair that!"

Bettina turned her head slightly and took a long look at the gouges. She thought there were patterns there. "It almost looks like writing. Kind of like Chinese."

Aunt Sophie frowned and studied the gouges, brushing away the splinters. "Don't be ridiculous. It's not Chinese."

"It is so!"

"Bears don't write! It's a known fact. And besides, why would he write in Chinese?"

Bettina crossed her arms. "Didn't you ever read the tag on his back? He was made in Hong Kong."

Word spread quickly that Bettina Plinth was now the proud keeper of a brown bear who wrote perfect Chinese, and since the closest thing to a Chinese person in town was the Hawaiian woman who ran the local donut shop, no one could disprove the claim. People from miles around made pilgrimages to the farm to see the bear and his mysterious runes.

Later that week, Bettina attempted to bring Kafka into Ravenscroft Academy, only to be turned away at the gate. Still the appearance of Bettina walking a bear on a little green leash became grist for an overactive mill. The image alone was enough to make Bettina the center of attention. Add to that the mysterious Asian scrawlings, and Bettina became a star. By the end of the week, she would walk into the lunchroom and all the popular kids would sit with her, asking a million questions.

"How much does he weigh?"

"Did he ever bite you?"

"Does he like Chinese food?"

And although every day Aunt Sophie threatened to call animal control to haul him away, she never did.

For two weeks it went on, until the evening before Bettina's parents were to return from their trip. In the late hours of that night, the moon spilled a creamy glow across all it touched, as comforting as warm milk. While Aunt Sophie snored off her latest eBay binge, Bettina crept out to the barn and snuggled against Kafka's fur. The bear purred, the sound so deep it rumbled in Bettina's bones like a wave crashing on the beach. It should have been a perfect moment, but Bettina was still filled with an indefinable longing.

"They like me in school, Kafka," she told him. "Everyone's my friend." But it felt like a guilty confession more than anything else. The kids' interest was in Kafka, not in her; she was merely basking in his mysterious light, and while it was fun to bask, she knew the adoration of the kids at Ravenscroft Academy was a flicker that would soon die. Yet it didn't bother her, for she also discovered that as much as she longed for friends, those kids were not the friends she longed for. They were all cut from the same mold as her parents. Old money and new clothes. "Snobmongrels," Aunt Sophie called them.

She took a deep breath as she leaned against Kafka, filling herself with the powerful scent of bear and the musty aroma of hay that filled the barn. Her parents would not approve of Kafka, and she wondered what tomorrow would be like. No doubt her parents would arrive tomorrow morning with a carload of guilt-offerings from their cruise. On a normal day they would come and they would leave again, no big deal. Only tomorrow would not be a normal day. In the two weeks they were gone, she had grown into a different person. Witnessing Kafka's transformation had made her demand change in her *own* life, rather than just longing for it. Her spirit had been kindled by him, and she felt herself ready to ignite.

No, her parents would not approve of this at all, and she wondered if it was their approval she wanted. Was *that* what was missing in her life?

"What do I want?" she asked the bear. Even in this moment, where she should have been content, she felt needy. "I need your strength," she told Kafka. "Strength enough to figure out what I really, really want." She had always been manipulated and tossed by the forces around her, but here was this bear—this glorious beast—mighty and powerful, yet at her command by its own choice. He had been sent to her for a reason. She had to believe that, because fate and magic were two sides of the same coin.

"We're all victims of fate," Aunt Sophie once said. "Thank God for insurance."

If Kafka's arrival in Bettina's life was something destined, then it meant he was more than fur and stuffing; more than flesh and bone. He was a spark of something much greater than that.

"What are you, Kafka?" she whispered. "*Why* are you?"

Kafka shifted his big dark eyes, catching the moonlight glinting through the door. As she looked into those eyes, she began to feel as if she could fall into them. As if they weren't the eyes of a bear at all, but a window to her own soul. She stared deeply into the light of those eyes, until she finally understood what she truly wanted.

By the time Bettina's parents arrived the following morning, the crowds had thinned at the Adirondack chair to a couple of neighborhood kids who poked sticks in the dirt, trying to create their own bear language.

Bettina sat on the porch swing watching her parents get out of the Mercedes, their hands too full of international booty to open their arms for a hug.

"Darling, we missed you!"

"You would have loved the Acropolis!"

"We sat at the captain's table!"

"We thought of you in Venice!"

Bettina stepped down from the porch and opened the picket gate for them.

"Welcome, back, Dad. Welcome back, Mother." Her mother turned her face to the side for a kiss. Bettina obliged.

"High time you got back," Aunt Sophie shouted as she came out onto the porch. "It's been Animal Planet around here lately."

Mrs. Plinth beamed, mistaking Aunt Sophie's meaning. "You've been having friends over from Ravenscroft, then?" She noted the neighborhood children playing around the chair near the barn.

"Some," Bettina admitted, "but mostly it's just been me and Kafka."

"Oh." It was an "oh" weighty with disappointment. "Which reminds me, we need to have a word with you about Kafka."

Her parents gave each other a mind-reading sort of look like surgeons over a fading patient, then Dad put down his gifts and went to retrieve something else from the car.

Bettina took a deep breath. Her heart pounded with what she was about to do, but she did her best not to show it. "Mother, I've given it a lot of thought, and I've made up my mind about a few things."

Her mother deposited her load of gifts on the porch swing. "Whew! I'd forgotten the humidity here. It's a much drier heat in the Mediterranean."

"I know how you'll feel, but I will not take no for an answer."

"Of course, dear." She turned toward her husband. "Ah, here it is!" Bettina followed her gaze to see her father returning from the car with something large, furry, and very, very pink.

"Here *what* is?"

But as her father approached, she saw exactly what it was. It was another huge stuffed bear, but this one had fur the color of Aunt Sophie's artificial sweetener packets, and a smile just as artificially sweet.

"It's to replace Kafka," her father said brightly.

"But I don't want to replace Kafka!"

"That model was recalled, dear," her mother explained. "It was too realistic. Apparently it was frightening children to death."

Bettina could only stammer.

"Besides," her father said, "this one's better: it's programmable!" He squeezed the pink bear's paw and the bear said:

"Hi, I'm Candibear! Enter user name, please."

Bettina shook her head violently, trying to jar her resolve back into place. "No! No, you can't take Kafka! I won't let you! *He* won't let you!"

"What are you talking about?"

Bettina turned toward the barn. "Kafka!" she called.

The bear didn't come. Aunt Sophie sat on the porch swing, and Geppetto hopped into her lap. They waited to see what would happen.

"Kafka!" Bettina called again.

Her mother rapped her nails on the porch railing. "Bettina, stop this, you're being ridiculous."

And then Kafka came.

He slowly lumbered out of the barn, and the neighborhood kids playing near the lawn chair scattered.

"Is that . . . a bear?" Her father dropped Candibear with a thud, jarring loose an eye, which rolled off the porch steps.

Bettina turned from Kafka and locked her gaze on her mother, who was transfixed by the approaching bear.

"As I said, I've made a few decisions," Bettina announced. "I've decided that I want parents—*real* parents—and I believe you can make the transformation. So I'm coming home with you today."

No response from her parents, only frozen gazes over her shoulder.

"You have room for me at home, but you don't have time. So from now on, you'll *make* time."

By now the shadow of the bear had fallen over her own as Kafka reared up behind her, not so much eclipsing her shadow as merging with it.

"My God!" her father said, but made no move.

"I'm leaving Ravenscroft Academy. I'll attend a neighborhood school, and I'll play with neighborhood kids. We'll have dinner together, you will ask me how school was each day, and I will tell you, 'Just fine,' because it will be."

She felt Kafka's breath on her neck, and the softness of his fur as he wrapped his arms around her shoulders from behind and hugged her, gently.

"I'm your daughter, not an inconvenience. Is that clear?"

Her father nodded immediately. Her mother held out.

"I said is that clear, Mother?"

Kafka roared, nearly blowing Mrs. Plinth back through the screen door.

"Yes, yes, Bettina," she said. "Not an inconvenience. Aunt Sophie—do something!"

Aunt Sophie rocked gently on the porch swing. "Ain't my bear."

"And one more thing," Bettina said. "From this moment on, I refuse to call you 'Mother.' From now on I will call you 'Mom.'"

"You can call me 'Dad,'" her father offered, but then, she had always called him Dad.

"Well . . . *Mom* . . . what do you say?"

Her mother finally met Bettina's eyes. She might have been quite the iron butterfly, but she was no match for the bear.

"All right then," Mrs. Plinth said. "You'll come with us today, and we'll have Aunt Sophie send your things."

Bettina gently tapped Kafka on the paw, and he dropped from her shoulders. She knelt to him and gently rubbed his fur, then whispered into his ear so that only he could hear.

"Thank you, Kafka," she said. "You can go now."

The bear took a long look at her. Into her. Then he grumbled a bit and sauntered toward her father, who backed away. Kafka bowed his head, but only to clamp his teeth onto the arm of the pink bear on the ground.

"Hi, I'm Candibear," it said. *"Enter user name, please."*

Kafka swung around and dragged Candibear out of the gate. Together they disappeared into the woods.

"Well," said Aunt Sophie. "Don't that beat all?"

"What on God's good earth was that?" her father asked, still dazed by it all.

Aunt Sophie stood up. "I'm still not sure—but you owe me for two hundred and ten pounds of dog food."

Bettina felt no sense of loss in setting Kafka free, for she knew that she was taking quite a lot of the bear with her. But leaving Aunt Sophie would be harder.

"There will always be a room for you, dear," Aunt Sophie said. "Unless, of course, I put in that pool table."

She gave Aunt Sophie a kiss and a bear hug that almost pressed the wind out of the old woman—and the hug Bettina got back from her was anything but rote.

Her mother put her arm around her as they turned to go. It was the first time Bettina could remember her doing it. "For your information," her mother said, "I never insisted that you call me 'Mother.' That, my little grizzly, was *your* idea."

Then Bettina Plinth, good bone structure and all, triumphantly marched to the car with her parents, knowing that her family's transformation had already begun.

Obsidian Sky

"Watch," says the girl. "They'll be coming soon."

The sun rides low on the horizon, slowly dousing the South Texas plain into red dusk. I stand there, wondering what it is about this strange girl that makes me want to stay. She bothers me. Not enough to make me want to leave, but enough to tease my curiosity into wispy strands of wonder and fear.

"Who will be coming soon?"

"Not who," she says calmly, "but what."

People more judgmental—people like my parents—might take one look at the girl and turn their noses up at her, calling her ugly. But if you took a moment, you'd realize she's not. She just looks different and in interesting ways—ways that don't resonate on a simple spectrum of appearances. Not apples and oranges—more like apples and dragon fruit—so how do you even begin to compare? Well, to me, she's interesting in all sorts of ways, and my parents aren't around to bother me with annoying surface judgments. They're off on their second honeymoon, which is why I'm here spending two weeks at my uncle Mason's farm.

Uncle Mason and Aunt Eunice's kids are grown and gone. Even though it's just my first day here, I can already sense that there are very few kids around at all. The empty fields reek of "maturity." There's not a ball or bike or video game between here and San Antonio. I'm pretty sure this odd girl is the only other kid within ten square miles of this place. She's even got a strange name, too: Zephyr.

Well, I figure it might not be so bad, on account of Zephyr knows things. She knows how to find snakes and hold them so they won't bite. She can catch bugs in midair and never misses.

But now she's getting weird, standing here looking at the setting sun like it's gonna jump up and do a dance for us.

"Listen," I tell her, "it's been fun, but I've gotta get back for dinner."

"Shhh, Jack," says Zephyr, turning her face to me. I can't see much of her eyes because she wears dark shades. Each lens is in the shape of a valentine heart, surrounded by a bright pink frame. "Be quiet and listen," she says.

I listen, but I don't hear anything out of the ordinary, just the distant lowing of cattle beneath the shrilling of katydids. Then a new sound begins to swell and overwhelms those other noises. A fluttering, like sheets on a windblown clothesline.

Zephyr clears her throat—a raspy clicking sound, almost like a snicker. "Yes," she says, "they're coming."

Suddenly a swell of darkness obliterates the setting sun. The darkness rises in the distance like a black mushroom cloud. The fluttering grows more intense, and as I watch, to my amazement, I see that the cloud is not a cloud at all, but a swarm. Tiny dots of darkness fill almost every inch of sky, flitting madly in all directions. They draw closer, and I see the flapping of dark wings.

"Are those . . . birds?" I ask.

Zephyr shakes her head. "No, Jack," she tells me. "They're bats."

In an instant the swarm is over us, turning the twilight to night. I duck—I cover my head, expecting them to dive from the sky, to suck my blood, to tear at my flesh.

But Zephyr only laughs. "They won't bother you, silly," she says. "They're Mexican free-tails. They eat bugs."

I dare to turn my eyes upward to see the moving mass of bats, an endless stream of sinewy wings that beat past so powerfully they create a wind. The smell of bat guano is thick in the air, like a hot day at the zoo—but Zephyr takes a deep breath and smiles. "I love their smell," she says. "It's so . . . different."

The bats just keep flowing across the sky. I figure they have to stop eventually, but they don't. "How many more could there be?"

"It will take two or three hours for all of them to leave the roost. They'll feed, then flood the sky again on their way back home, just before dawn."

"There must be millions of them!"

"Twenty million," Zephyr quickly says, "but my momma says there's many, many more—more than anyone could ever count."

"That's impossible," I tell her. Now they've formed a blanket of night above us, as dark as coal. "Where do they come from?"

Zephyr smiles. "Come back tomorrow," she says, "and I'll show you."

"Stay away from that one," Uncle Mason says when I tell him about my afternoon with Zephyr. "The girl's touched in the head. So's her mother." He shovels his peach pie into his mouth, and takes his time before continuing. His thoughts are always well-measured, even if they are opinionated. "They're not right. They got funny ways. The mother's a recluse and never goes out. I think they're in some kind of cult."

Aunt Eunice serves me up another slice of pie. "Just because they got their own way of seeing things doesn't make them a cult," she says, but I can tell she's just saying it for the sake of argument. She doesn't like Zephyr and her mother either. "The poor thing is so homely," Aunt Eunice says. "You've got to have pity on a girl like that."

"I don't gotta have pity on no one," grumbles my uncle.

"That's because you don't have a charitable bone in your body!"

I can see that the two of them are working themselves up into a huff, so I try to change the subject.

"What about the bats?"

Uncle Mason puts down his fork. "So? We got bats round these parts, what of it?"

"Do they always come?"

"Yep," he says. "Every night, spring through fall, before they migrate south."

"They clear out the bugs, that's for sure," adds Aunt Eunice. "Don't even need to crop-dust the fields. Of course, there is that awful smell."

"Zephyr likes the smell," I tell them.

My uncle snorts. "I'm not surprised."

"There's nothing wrong with that," says Aunt Eunice, again taking whatever side Uncle Mason isn't on. "When I was a little girl, I liked the small of cow pies," she says. "In the winter, on the way to school, I would even stick my feet in them to keep warm."

"Oh, gross!" The thought of sticking my feet into a steaming cow pie makes me want to hurl.

"Now look what you've done, Eunice, you've gone and made the boy ill!"

As I think about it, I wonder which is weirder: cow-pie footbaths or a sky full of bats.

"So," I say, "the bats are a good thing then?"

Once again, Uncle Mason takes his time in answering, so Aunt Eunice answers for him. "Of course they are, Jack . . . but I do wish there weren't so many of them."

Uncle Mason shakes his head. "More and more every year," he says. "Can't be natural. Can't be natural at all."

Zephyr, heart-shaped sunglasses still fixed on her face, leads me across field after field the following afternoon, until I can no longer see any houses behind us. There's nothing but cactus and scrub brush around us, and the ever-growing aroma of bat. I begin to sense something strange—as if Zephyr isn't strange enough: now I sense something off in the world around me. It's like a premonition without words or thought, releasing itself on my senses instead of my brain. Gooseflesh rises on my arms and legs, sounds are hollow, and the afternoon light is somehow lessened, like a partial eclipse. The feeling is both disturbing and exciting; different—like the smell of the bats.

"We're here," says Zephyr.

We've stopped at the edge of what looks like a meteor crater. In the center is a huge hole, at least ten feet across.

"That's it," says Zephyr, a grin of anticipation on her face. "That's the entrance to Bracken Cave!" She brushes back her brittle hair and begins to descend toward the sinkhole mouth of the cave, but I hesitate. The mouth of the cave is speckled with bat droppings. Zephyr turns back and takes my hand. "Don't be afraid," she says. "I come here all the time. There's nothing to worry about as long as you're quiet. The bats sleep during the day."

I have to admit, I'm scared to go anywhere near the cave, and I begin to feel humiliated. Here I am afraid to go in, but Zephyr isn't scared at all. The truth is most other girls—most other people—wouldn't go anywhere near that cave. There are DANGER signs posted everywhere, and warnings not to disturb the bats. My brain goes into reverse, but my feet are like tires spinning in the mud—they simply won't move me back. Then Zephyr gets close to me and whispers something in my ear that really should frighten me away, but instead it has the opposite effect.

"I've never brought any other boy here," she whispers to me. "And I'll never bring anyone else here but you."

I don't know what it is about her words that gets my feet moving toward that hole. Maybe the feeling of being special. Being chosen. Still holding my hand, she leads me toward the gaping mouth. "Come on, I'll show you something amazing," she whispers, and she climbs down into darkness, taking me with her.

We reach the bottom of the cave, where I can see very little beside the fact that the walls are moving. I swallow my revulsion, and focus all my attention on Zephyr's calmness. If she's calm, then I can be too.

"They're everywhere," Zephyr whispers. "A hundred babies in every square foot. Soon the mothers will be nursing." She clears her throat again—that weird cackling noise—then she leads me forward into darkness. I want to resist but find that my fear, tired of being ignored, has finally slipped out of consciousness, leaving me numb and intoxicated by the acidic smell of bat droppings.

Beneath our feet, something crunches like eggshells.

"They're carnivorous dermestid beetles," she tells me, as if it's something every kid should know. "They cover the floor, eating dead bats. If you stood in one place long enough, they'd eat you, too, but it might take a while."

She moves sure-footedly through the darkness, so fast that it scares me, but we don't bump into a single wall. There are strange clicking sounds all around me.

"What are those noises?" I ask.

"The bats are echolocating," she explains. "They make those clicks, and use sonar to 'see' in the dark."

Every once in a while, I feel a bat brush past my face. It really bothers me at first, but I soon become desensitized to it. I think about summer camp, and how during the first few days I'm always freaked out by the size of the bugs and spiders—but after a week I couldn't care less. It's funny the things you can get used to.

Again, Zephyr clears her throat and changes directions. "This way!"

"Where are we going?"

"You'll see."

We walk for what seems like forever, turning every now and then, and I think about how long the walk back will have to be, with beetles below and bats hanging above. I wonder if my fear will suddenly wake up again and send me off into a berserk screaming frenzy.

Finally I see faint shades of light around us, gray on gray. "Okay. So, where are we?" I ask.

"We're home," she says, then she pushes open a wooden door to reveal something I never expected. We step into a farmhouse. Her house. First, I breathe an incredible sigh of relief that the ordeal is over. Then, it occurs to me how very odd it is that her house opens up into Bracken Cave.

"The cave leads many places," she says, as if reading my mind. "No one knows how deep it goes. My momma says it has roots that grow out the bottom of the world."

I chuckle nervously. "Your momma says a lot of funny things, doesn't she?"

"Would you like to meet her?"

"Not really."

But Zephyr has already gone to a back room—a dark room. I try to think of an excuse to leave, so I can hightail it across the field to my aunt and uncle's house, only a few hundred yards away. But before I can bolt, I hear a voice from the dark room.

"What is it, Zephyr?" The woman's voice is soothing and musical. Her tone seems to coat me like sticky sap, and I can't move. I have to see who belongs to that voice.

"He's here, Momma," says Zephyr. "I brought him, just like you told me."

"Come in, Jack," says the woman.

Again, that sense of unsettled excitement fills me—a curiosity that buries my urge to flee. Slowly, planting one foot in front of the other, I step across the threshold of the dark room.

The room is full of paintings—magnificent canvases, all of the same subject: bats escaping into a twilight sky. In the center of the room sits a woman, with eyelids half-closed.

"Come closer, Jack. I don't bite."

She's dressed like some sort of hippy, or earth mother, or something. Her long brown hair is tied into a rope-braid so long it coils on the floor around her like a snake. "My name is Gaia, but you can call me Momma too. Everyone does." The way she moves her head when she speaks, the way her small eyes don't track, makes it clear to me that she's blind. Yet she holds a brush, painting another black-winged portrait.

"But . . . but how . . . ?"

I don't have to ask the question. She knows what I'm about to ask. "You don't need to see what you paint," she says in that musical voice, "if you know every in and out of it."

She wipes the paint from her fingers with a towel and beckons me closer. I step over the coils of her braid, and she touches my face, moving her fingertips over my nose, cheeks, eyes, and neck. It tickles, but it isn't an unpleasant feeling.

"A strong face," she says. "Good bone structure. A fine man he'll grow to be."

"Uh . . . thanks," I say, not sure what else to say when someone compliments you on your bone structure. "Listen, it's probably getting late. I gotta get back for dinner." Although the last thing I have right now is an appetite.

"Not yet," says the strange woman. "There's something you must first see. Zephyr?"

Obediently, Zephyr comes to her. "Show him," the woman says, and Zephyr grabs a chair. Standing on it, she reaches up to the rafters and pulls down a single bat, handing it to her mother. "Here you go, Momma."

I shiver as I look up to see a small cluster of bats clinging to the ceiling. *These people live with the bats!* I tell myself. *Their house opens into Bracken Cave. Uncle Mason was right. They're weird—worse than weird! I have to get out of here!* I feel panic welling inside me, but instead of making me run, it locks me in place, like a deer on a highway. I can't escape this now. Whatever horror is bearing down on me, I can only watch it happen.

Gaia gently brushes the bat's fur, then stretches out its wing. "This isn't your ordinary free-tailed bat," she says. "This one comes from the new generation. The generation that will emerge for the first time tonight!" The skin of its wing is as dark as crude oil.

"Touch it, Jack," Gaia tells me. "Touch his wing."

Her voice is gentle, but it resonates in me like a command I can't ignore. Besides, a part of me wants to touch the bat; a part of me that seems to be growing stronger the more time I spend with Zephyr and her mother.

I move my finger toward the wing, which is so dark, I can't see any texture on the thin membrane. What happens next catches me completely by surprise. I reach for the wing, moving my finger closer, and my finger passes right through it. I gasp and draw back, thinking that I've punctured the membrane of the wing. But when I look at it, I don't see any hole in the wing. That's when I realize that the wing isn't really a membrane at all. It's not flesh, but rather an *absence* of flesh. A hole in space, the shape of a wing. I reach forward again, and my whole hand passes through into the darkness of the wing, as if I've reached through a small window into another place. I can feel my fingertips getting cold, and I pull my hand back, shivering.

I peer at the bat, trying to grasp what has happened. All I can see in that wing is obsidian darkness.

I slip to my knees, suddenly dizzy. I'm afraid. I'm confused. "I . . . I don't feel so good."

"Sit with me, then," says Gaia, "and I'll tell you a story."

I sit beside her, allowing her to comfort me. She starts to coil her heavy braid around me, and I begin to feel like a baby tightly wrapped in a warm blanket. Gaia rocks me gently.

"Forever and forever ago," she begins, "before time had a memory, a flock of bluebirds burst from a hole in the void and spread their wings across the chaos. They filled the space from yonder to yonder, until nothing remained but the blue of their wings, which became the blue sky above a new world of light."

Then she leans close to me; so close I can smell her breath. It smells like the depths of Bracken Cave, but somehow cleaner, as if the acid were washed away, leaving only a rich, organic aroma behind. "It's time you knew, Jack," she says, "that the age of the bluebird sky is over." That's when she touches my chin, turning my head to look at Zephyr—and for the first time, Zephyr reaches up, pulling off her dark sunglasses . . .

. . . to reveal that she has no eyes.

I gasp, but it comes out as a pained wheeze. I look away, not wanting to see, but Gaia gently turns my head back, forcing me to look at her daughter.

There are only faint indentations where Zephyr's eyes should be, covered by smooth skin. No lids, no lashes. No brow.

"It's all right," Zephyr says brightly. "Don't worry, I can still 'see' just fine." Then she opens her mouth and clears her throat, as she's done so many times before—only now I realize that she's not clearing her throat at all. She's sending out little sonar clicks, echolocating like a bat.

For a brief instant I come to my senses enough to realize the depth of the trouble I'm in. I am bound in the endless coils of a massive braid, looking at a mutant girl, and I can't escape.

All at once I hear a sound outside—sheets flapping on a clothesline. I know that sound. It is the bats! Millions of black-winged bats taking to the sky.

I struggle to pull myself free from the braid that ties me.

"It's no use," Gaia tells me, "and it's best that you don't see. Stay here, Jack, with me and Zephyr."

I don't even answer her. I fight to free myself from the cocoon of her hair. At last I uncoil myself, and, tripping over the knot of braid, I race out of the dark room and toward the front door.

"No, Jack!" cries Zephyr, but I don't care what she says anymore. I burst out the door to see the twilight sky disappearing behind a flood of obsidian-black wings. I know that if I could reach up and touch each of those wings, my hand would pass through them as well, into darkness. It's as if they are devouring the sky—and soon I see objects falling from up above. Dead birds. Bluebirds. They fall like hail, littering the fields around us.

"No!" I cry. "It can't be! This can't happen!"

Zephyr stand in the doorway behind me. She won't come out. Instead she turns her face up and clicks to the sky. "It's beautiful," she says.

The light around us is fading beneath the great membrane of a million black wings. And soon the bluebird-covered ground becomes speckled with bat droppings, as lightless as the bats themselves. They are like spots of black paint flung at a canvas, obliterating the world beneath it.

"Don't stand there, Jack," says Gaia from the door. "You must come here. You'll be safe here."

I would run to my aunt and uncle's house—but I know I would never make it. I would be buried under a fall of bluebirds and bat droppings. I can't even see their house in the distance anymore. Maybe it's already washed away. I hurry to the doorway, terrified of being struck by black droplets, for fear they might burn right through me. The three of us watch as the sky disappears into darkness and the ground dissolves beneath the rain of black.

"What about my parents? What about my aunt and uncle?"

"Everyone you know will be gone," says Gaia with sympathy and compassion. "When the bats stretch from yonder to yonder, they will be no more. They will fade peacefully with the world of light." She says it as if it is a wonderful thing. I feel sick to my stomach.

"Why won't it take us?" I ask. "Why are we spared?"

"There must always be a seed for the next world," she tells me. "You are young, but time will help you understand."

And then her words come back to me. *Good bone structure. A fine man he'll grow to be.* She said it as if Zephyr and I would be together for a long, long time. Me and that ugly, ugly girl with no eyes.

"There are only the two of you now," says Gaia. Earth Mother. Mother Earth. "Only the two of you, and me to pave your way."

Outside, the trees and fence posts, the grass and hills crumble to nothing, dissolved by rivers of black. Gaia closes the door, shutting out that world. She comes closer, dragging her endless braid behind her. I back up until I'm against the wall. There's nowhere for me to run. I can't get away, and if I screamed, there would be no one to hear me.

Gaia touches my cheek, feeling my tears. "You are in pain," she says to me. "If thine eyes offend thee, pluck them out."

Then both her hands shoot to my temples, I feel my head pressed between the vise-grip of her palms. She presses her thumbs against my eyes and I feel a fiery pain. I am about to scream out, but suddenly the pain is gone, replaced by a different feeling . . . a draining feeling, as if my sinuses are clearing. Something opens up deep within my mind. Then she takes her fingers away.

I reach up to feel my eyes, and find that they are gone. No blood, no holes—it's as if I never had eyes at all. There is only a faint indentation in the bone of my face where my eyes should be—but no sockets beneath that, only solid bone. Like Zephyr.

This can't be happening! I tell myself. You can't erase a person's eyes with the touch of a finger. Everything before me now is black. No, not black . . . *absent.* Not dark, not light, but simply not there. I have no sense of sight whatsoever, or even a memory of what sight was like.

Overwhelmed by it all, I have a sudden, uncontrollable urge to clear my throat, and when I do, it comes out in a series of hollow clicks. Echolocation! In a flash of echoes, everything around me becomes clear. It is more than sight, more than sound, but a sense that is completely new. I am blasted by a wave of incredible perception!

My terror is extinguished like fire drowned in water. I can "see" Zephyr and Gaia, their shapes formed by the echo. Not just their shape, but the density of their flesh, and the exact dimensions of the room around me. I can "see" things not just in front of me, but all around me!

It is Zephyr's face that catches my attention. I step closer to her and click again. It's amazing—the way the bones and flesh of her face echo back my signal. It's such a pleasing sensation, I want to echolocate her again and again.

"Zephyr!" I say. "You're beautiful!" for she truly is. What was hideous to my sense of sight is glorious to this new sense. I don't think I've ever experienced anything so beautiful—so perfect—as the echo of Zephyr's face.

"I'm happy you think so," she says. I can feel the smile on her face from where I stand.

"All is in tune for a new beginning, then." Gaia puts her hands on our shoulders and slowly moves us toward the wooden door at the back of the house.

Was I frightened a few moments ago? Was I mourning the loss of the world I knew? It's as if when Gaia took away my sight, she also took away all that sense of loss, leaving behind only excitement, and a feverish desire to go forward into this new unknown. Gaia swings open the door to Bracken Cave. I echolocate through the door and find a breathtaking expanse of caverns, the shape of their echo as pleasing and satisfying as a colorful landscape, although I can't even recall what color is.

It is now that I realize that there is light here—immense radiance all around me. It's not daylight, but the light of spirit, so much easier to see without the burden of eyes.

I "ping" the caverns once more. The echo shows me winding tunnels that stretch to infinity.

I want to go down there! I want to explore, to be a part of it, but I sense that something is missing. I raise my hand and feel the empty space beneath my arm. Yes, there is something missing. I turn to Gaia, and she cups her hand gently against my face, knowing what I am thinking. "Some things must be earned, Jack." Then she lowers my arm to my side. "In time, both you and Zephyr will earn yours. But for now you must go on without them."

Understanding, I take Zephyr's hand. We send our signals ahead of us into the bottomless depths of Bracken Cave; they resound together in perfect harmony, beckoning us downward into this new place. This new world.

Sometimes change catches us off guard. We fight it with fear and denial. We run from it, hide from it, until it envelops us, only to leave us wondering what there was to be afraid of. I'm ready for what comes now—whatever it is. And, so, together Zephyr and I race off into the endless labyrinth, holding our arms out wide as we run, hoping that soon, very soon, we will earn our wings.

Ralphy Sherman's Bag of Wind

The bag sat innocently on the library table between my sister Roxanne and me. A brown paper bag—the kind of sack you get at the grocery store. The kind you can cover your schoolbooks with. Just a plain brown paper bag. The top of this one was folded over, so you couldn't see inside.

Roxy and I had left it unguarded. We hadn't thought much about it. I mean, who was going to bother it in the library? But I guess when you leave a single brown paper bag alone in the center of a big round table and walk away, some bozo's bound to wonder what's inside.

We were racing stealthily around the aisles, playing one of our favorite games: Psychotic Librarian. The game involved misshelving books in unlikely pairs, while the librarian ripped her hair out, searching for us down the narrow, mazelike aisles. I had just shelved *Breakfast at Tiffany's* next to *Naked Lunch*, when the librarian made an exhausted lunge at me through the stacks, from the next aisle.

"I'll get you, Ralphy Sherman," she growled, "if it's the last thing I do," and it might just have been, considering the way she was huffing and puffing.

I slipped out of her desperate grasp, and took off down the science aisle, where I ran into Roxanne. She held a copy of *Moby-Dick* in one hand and was searching for a suitable match on the anatomy shelves.

That was when we caught sight of Marvin McSchultz leaning

over our table, his hands slowly trying to open the curled lip of our bag to get a look inside.

"Can you believe him?" I said. "Somebody oughta call pest control!"

We stormed out of the aisle to catch him red-handed. He turned to us, his beady little eyes trying to feign innocence.

"Oh, hi, guys."

Marvin McSchultz was what you might call "rodential." He was ratlike in every possible way. Always tattling on people, always poking around in business that wasn't his—and anytime there were germs being spread, you could bet Marvin was the vector.

Roxanne put her hands firmly on her hips. "Have my eyes deceived me, or were you daring to touch our stuff?"

"Who, me?" blurted Marvin. "No, I was just going to move your bag over. Yeah, that's it, I was gonna move it to the other side of the table—to keep *other* people from touching it."

"Well, it's a good thing you didn't open it," I advised him. "It could have been disastrous."

Marvin's ears pricked up. "Whaddaya mean, 'disastrous'?"

"Don't tell him," warned Roxy. "If you do, he'll blab to everyone, and we'll never keep it to ourselves."

"C'mon, please," said Marvin, taking the bait like a mouse at a trap. "Please, I promise not to tell."

I checked the aisles behind us. The librarian had not yet emerged, obviously still wandering the maze in search of us. I sat Marvin down, while Roxy began to read her copy of *Moby-Dick*.

"This isn't any old bag," I whispered to Marvin. "It's a receptacle for a supercell mesocyclone vortex."

"Huh?"

Roxy sighed, but kept her eye on her book. "I knew he'd be too dense to understand."

Marvin looked from me to her, and then to me again for further explanation.

"Okay . . . in layman's terms," I said, running my finger gently down the edge of the sack. "There's a tornado in this bag."

Marvin stared at me with uncomprehending reptilian eyes. "Whaddaya mean, a tornado? You mean one of those science kit things, where you can make a twister in a bottle? I seen those. It's just water pouring from one soda bottle to another."

"No, Einstein," said Roxy. "We don't go for cheap imitations. This is the real thing."

Then Marvin quirked his lips in disbelief. "Yeah, right," he said, "and I'm a green space alien in disguise."

Unruffled, Roxy tossed her hair. "If you are, then please tell your people to bring back our mother. It hasn't been the same at home since your people abducted her."

"You're just a couple of losers," he said. "You two can't even come up with something clever to say—like telling me there's a rat inside, or a tarantula, or some animal you found runt over in the road that your mom says you gotta bury or else you can't come home for dinner—" Marvin grimaced, recalling some unpleasant memory.

"Actually, Marvin, all those things might be in the bag, too," I offered. "You never know what gets swept up inside a tornado."

"I wouldn't be surprised," added Roxanne, "if there were a few farm animals swirling around in there."

"Ha, ha," said Marvin. "I don't believe a word you say!"

Roxanne raised an eyebrow, and turned a page. "Nobody believed Ahab when he first told people about the great white whale." She slammed the heavy cover of the book with an ominous thud and pushed it across the table toward him. "But he had the last laugh. Even as he died in agony." The book caught the very edge of the big brown bag, and it rocked slightly back and forth.

"And then again, maybe there's nothing inside the bag," I told Marvin. "Nothing . . . but air."

Marvin slowly turned his eyes to the sack, watching it closely until it stopped rocking.

"If you don't believe us, why don't you peek inside?" I suggested.

He called my bluff and began to reach for the bag.

"Of course," Roxanne added, "you might end up like something 'runt over' in the road—but don't say we didn't warn you."

Still Marvin refused to listen to us, and he poked his finger in the bag's folded edge, beginning to pull it up . . . and a breeze blew across the little hairs on the back of our necks.

"Did you feel that?" I whispered.

Instantly, Roxanne and I both dove off our seats, taking cover under the table. Marvin was a microsecond behind us.

"It was just the air conditioner," he insisted, his head beneath the table, and his butt sticking up into the air like an ostrich. "It was just the air conditioner, right? . . . Right?!"

"Are you certain of that, Marvin?"

By the tone of his voice, we could tell he wasn't certain of anything anymore. "It's . . . it's impossible," he blathered. "Wind can't stay in a bag!"

"It can if it's charmed," I said.

"Charmed?"

Roxy picked up where I'd left off. "Yeah. You know, like a snake?" She pulled on his collar until the rest of his body fell under the table to join his weaselly face. "You can control it, if you know the secret incantation."

"Incantation?" echoed Marvin. "It sounds spooky."

I peered out from under the table to make sure we were unobserved, then I leaned closer and whispered into Marvin's ear. "The twister was charmed into the bag a hundred years ago by some wizard, and as long as you say the incantation right, it will never harm the person who opens the bag."

"We got it last year from an old lady in a trailer park," Roxanne continued. "She told us that she spent the last forty years moving from one mobile home to another, and when she got tired of living in one, she opened up the bag, wiped the whole place out, and collected the insurance."

"Trailer parks!" shouted Marvin. "Is that why tornadoes always seem to hit trailer parks?"

"We took the bag on vacation with us," I told him. "We used it for skydiving."

"No way!"

"Have you ever skydived down the mouth of a tornado funnel?"

"It's a real trip!" said Roxy.

Marvin just shook his head as if trying to make it all go away. "No," he said. "No, no, no!" He crawled out from under the table, bumping his head on the way up. We followed. Around us, the library seemed even quieter than before. No one had noticed our little foray under the table, and no one noticed us come out.

"Forget you guys!" he said, dismissing us with a wave of his hand. He tried to leave but couldn't, for although his feet kept walking away, his eyes kept staring at the bag, pulling him into a weird elliptical orbit around the table. "Okay," he said, pushing forth his last question. "If it's in there, how come I can't hear nothing inside?"

I just shook my head. "Don't you know, Marvin? It's always dead quiet before a tornado."

"Before it comes roaring in like a freight train," added Roxy.

At last we broke through his thin wall of resistance, and he finally looked at the bag with fearful respect, and a flesh-searing curiosity. Curiosity enough to kill the largest of cats. We knew we had him.

"We've grown tired of it lately," I told him.

"Yeah, too much responsibility," said Roxanne.

"And too much to clean up."

"And it eats us out of house and home—literally."

"We were hoping we could get rid of it."

"For the right price, of course."

Then Marvin, eyes locked on the silent paper bag, shoved both his hands deep into his stuffed pockets and jingled them around.

"How much you askin'?"

I smiled. "How much you got?"

Five minutes later and twelve dollars poorer, Marvin left the library a happy man, with one extremely light brown paper bag in his hands.

"Remember," Roxy reminded him as he pedaled away, "don't open it until you're out in a field far away from here."

"Far, *far* away," I emphasized. "And don't forget to swing your Hula-Hoop while repeating the magic incantation."

"And if it doesn't work the first time," added Roxanne, "try it again in your underwear. That usually does the trick."

"I'll remember!" shouted Marvin, as he hurried off, steering his bike with one hand and holding the bag gingerly in the other as if it contained a small nuclear device.

We watched until he disappeared over the hill.

We thought we'd heard the last of it until dawn the next day. That was when the storm came. No one predicted it. It wasn't on any weather map. It just showed up on the doorstep of our town like an uninvited guest. I awoke to the sound of rattling windows, and Roxy frantically calling my name.

I stumbled out into the hall, where Roxy was standing in her nightgown. "Where's Dad? Where's Whatserface?" Whatserface was our new nanny. As we went through nannies too quickly to count, we rarely bothered to learn their names.

We heard the front door open as Whatserface went out to retrieve the morning paper. With umbrella held high, she stepped out onto the porch and was promptly pulled up into the skies by the wind, and we haven't seen her since.

"Ralphy, I think it's a tornado!"

"Here? We never have tornadoes here!"

And in response, the wind growled and hurled a minivan through the living room window. Well, that was enough to wake up Dad. He shuffled out of his bedroom and took a long, hard look at the beached car, its upturned wheels still spinning.

"Is that ours?" he asked.

"No," I told him.

"Oh. Good," he said, and returned to his bedroom, hit the snooze button, and vanished beneath the covers.

Then, as quickly as the storm had begun, the raging, roaring winds fell silent, and we heard a loud thump on our roof, followed by what sounded like sheets flapping in the wind.

What the—? But before I could finish the thought, our broken living room window became shrouded in a red flutter.

Something rolled off the roof into the fluttering fabric, with a clumsy-sounding *Oof*, as it hit the lawn. That was how we knew it wasn't a something, but a someone.

Roxy and I pulled open the door, which was almost off its hinges, and were met by a sight even stranger than the minivan in the living room. A lump bobbed and bumbled beneath the slick red fabric, like a rat under a rug. Finally the lump emerged. Beady eyes in a rodential face. Marvin McSchultz.

"Wow!" said Marvin, more hyped-up than I'd ever seen him. "Wow! That was great!" He struggled to free himself from his parachute harness. "It pulled me off the ground, spun me higher than the clouds. Heck, I thought I was on my way to Oz! But then it just dropped me down the middle! I was spinning, I was tumbling, then I pulled the rip cord, the chute came out, and suddenly I'm floating while the whole world's spinning all around me. It's true what they say—there's no wind in the middle of a tornado. Everything's nice and still. A'course I had to pull on these here steering ropes, to keep myself right in the middle. It was just like you said: the twister didn't hurt me, because I did the incantation, just like you told me, Hula-Hoop and all!" His eyes were wide with excitement. His hair, which was usually a greasy bowl on his head, was teased into wild tornado-twisted tufts. Then I noticed that in one hand, he clutched the brown paper bag we had sold him—making sure to keep it closed.

"Thanks, you guys," he said, shaking my hand so hard it almost pulled my arm right out of its socket. "You changed my life! Thanks for selling me this fantastic bag of wind!"

Roxanne's jaw had dropped so low, I thought it might fall off completely. "But . . . ," she began. "But it can't be! We made up the whole—"

I closed my hand over her mouth so quickly, it made a popping sound, but it succeeded in shutting her up. "Sold it?" I said to Marvin, keeping completely calm. "We didn't sell it to you—we *rented* it to you."

The smile began to drain from Marvin's red-cheeked face. "What?"

"You don't think we'd part with something like that for a mere twelve dollars, do you?"

Roxanne pulled my hand from her mouth and caught on, falling in stride with me. "That's right," she said. "You paid us the one-time usage fee, and now the bag comes back to us."

Marvin pursed his lips and tried to tame his wild hair. "No fair!" he said.

"Of course, we could go to the police and tell them who's responsible for all the storm damage," I said.

"Or we could keep it to ourselves," said Roxy.

Finally Marvin caved. "Fine," he said, handing over the bag. "Be that way." And he turned and left, dragging his parachute behind him.

When he was gone, we looked at the bag for a very long time. We put our ears up to it, and heard . . . nothing.

"What do you think?" I asked Roxanne.

"I don't know. What was that incantation you told him?"

"Owah . . . Tanass . . . Siam . . ."

Roxanne raised an eyebrow and shrugged. "Go figure." Then she turned and went back into our wind-blasted house in search of a broom, dustpan, and hydraulic winch, so she could clean up. As for me, I went straight down to the basement on a mission.

All things considered, I suppose there really are stranger things in heaven and on earth than we dare imagine. Maybe even stranger than Roxanne and me. Now if I can only find that Hula-Hoop . . .

The In Crowd

Alana was a boomerang, flying through her sixth foster home, doing maximum damage, and then heading right back to Harmony Home—the institution where she had spent most of her life. Although they euphemistically called it a "group home," that didn't change the fact that it was an orphanage. At sixteen, she was one of the oldest there. And although she could petition to be emancipated, she didn't do it. Because where would she go?

"Why, Alana?" the therapist would ask. "Why is it always the same with you?"

Alana could not—would not—look her in the eye. She could hear the stabbing anger and accusations in the woman's voice. She didn't have to see them in her face as well.

"The DiGiorgios are good people—but you just had to lose your temper, didn't you? You couldn't control it just this once. Didn't you even try?"

The fact was, Alana had tried. She had tried for three whole weeks, accepting the pitying way her new foster parents spoke to her. Enduring all those overly kind, bend-over-backward sort of gestures. She lived with the way they whispered about her at night, as if she was a pet that had to be house-trained, and she pretended to "belong," when all the while she felt outside of their double-paned windows, even though she stood inside their house. Then that morning, she just snapped. She couldn't say what caused her rage, but when it was over, everything that could break in the DiGiorgio household had been broken. The gentle couple wasn't too gentle when they hauled her back to Harmony Home and washed their hands of her.

"You're like a land mine," said the therapist. "Someone treads too close to you, and you detonate."

Still not looking up, Alana heaved a shrug. "I guess I push people away."

The therapist gave a bitter guffaw. "That's putting it mildly."

Dinner in the cafeteria. Silly gossip, petty cliques scheming against one another. Kids either preening, posturing, or fighting. It was like any other prison—and Alana had come to think of Harmony Home as a place of incarceration, for although the halls and grounds of the old converted mansion were more inviting than some other group homes, that didn't change its nature. She and at least a hundred others lived in its overcrowded rooms, went to school there, suffered through adolescence there. Now, as she sat with her regular friends, it felt as if she hadn't been gone for a month. It was as if she had never left—and that wasn't a good feeling.

"So, I guess you haven't met the new boy," Justine said over dinner.

"Of course she hasn't met him," said Missy. "She hasn't been here to meet him." Missy and Justine were permanent fixtures at Harmony Home. For whatever reason, the powers that be had deemed them unplaceable. Alana could never understand what made her friends even less placeable than herself, and she never asked because she really didn't want to know.

"I don't care about any 'new boy,'" Alana told them. She had seen her share of new boys come into Harmony Home, and they were nothing to shout about. Too many of them treated girls with contempt and disrespect—and they were always angling for the One Thing. Alana wanted nothing to do with them. "Not interested," she said, trying to shut it down.

"But this boy's different," insisted Justine.

"And he's good-looking," added Missy.

"And he's smart, too," offered Justine.

Alana gave her dry pork chop a decent burial beneath her mashed potatoes.

"But he's messed up," said Missy. "I mean, he doesn't *seem* messed up, but . . ." Then she leaned in close enough for her hair to dangle into the motley mess of Alana's tray. "They say he killed his family."

"Not just his family," added Missy, "but his entire neighborhood."

There was a windstorm that night. The kind that blew hot through the canyons, rattling windows, uprooting trees, and tearing up the roof. Alana could hear those orphaned shingles bouncing helplessly above her. When she was younger, she would hear the shingles and tar paper scraping past, and would think the sky was falling. She heard the phantom sounds of the wind in her dreams that night, jolting awake to flashes of heat lightning. Then, when morning came, she awoke to find herself alone in the oversized bedroom she shared with five other girls—Justine and Missy included.

"Rise and shine," said Ms. Zabel, the housemother assigned to their wing—but as she stepped into the room, there was only Alana to coax out of bed.

"Where are the others?" Ms. Zabel asked.

"Beats me."

Alana quickly dressed, figuring she would meet her friends at breakfast. Maybe they were waking up earlier these days. But they weren't at breakfast. In fact, a good dozen kids didn't show up for breakfast that day, and through Alana's classes, the empty seats screamed out in their silence. Every corner of the grounds was searched, from the furnace-blackened basement to the old storm cellar by the edge of the woods. All searches came up dry—but rumors ran rampant. According to what Alana had overheard from the teachers, the kids had conspired to run away—in fact, they had been planning it for weeks—and since teen conspiracy theories were big among the adults who ran Harmony Home, everyone figured that was what happened. Authorities were notified, and it was left in the hands of the police. Alana had to admit they were probably right. She had run off with various groups of friends many times before. But her boomerang spirit always brought her back. Perhaps Justine and Missy would be the same. Still, it troubled her that they hadn't told her what they were up to.

It was that afternoon, when she passed one of the private bedrooms reserved for special cases, that she heard someone crying. Alana stood outside the unlabeled door, listening for a full five minutes to a boy whose sobs sounded so agonizingly genuine that Alana wanted to cry as well. The sobbing didn't stop. It was as if his grief knew no bottom. An endless well of sorrow. What could possibly make someone cry like that?

Alana never looked into the room, but she instinctively knew that this was the new boy.

"You don't look so smart."

For Alana, first contacts were more like pokes with a stick, but at least it got his attention. It was two days later. The afternoon was bright and clear, and those who didn't have some trouble to tend to were out in the rec yard after classes. Alana found him sitting against a tree, alone, watching some other kids shoot some particularly brutal hoops.

"Who said I was smart?" he said, only throwing her the slightest of glances.

Alana stood above him, arms folded. "My friends did. Missy and Justine."

"Oh. Them."

"Don't you want to know my name?" prompted Alana.

"You'd be better off if I didn't."

"It's Alana. An *A* at the beginning, middle, and end."

The boy stood up, but not to greet her. Instead he turned his back to her, putting more of his attention onto the basketball game he was watching. It annoyed Alana to no end, but she fought the urge to say something rude.

"If you're so interested in the game, why don't you go play?"

The boy took a few moments before answering. "I don't know any of those guys."

Alana snickered. "How long have you been here? Weeks, right? And you don't know any of them?"

"Nope."

"What are you, the kind of guy who doesn't have friends?"

He turned to her sharply, stung by her words. "I have friends. They're just not here right now. That's all. Okay?"

Finally Alana understood. "So the friends you made here all ran away the other day, huh? Is that why you were crying?"

His expression hardened. He became guarded. Suspicious. But he didn't deny that those tears had been his.

"There can't be anything so bad that you have to cry like that," said Alana. "I don't even cry like that, and believe me, I've got plenty of reasons to."

He regarded her, stone-faced. It was strange—she felt as if his eyes were somehow invading her. Picking her like a lock.

"Anyway," continued Alana, "someone'll catch those guys that left and bring them back, so you won't be friendless for long."

He continued to regard her with that lock-picking gaze, and Alana refused to look away. If he was trying to intimidate her, she wouldn't give him the satisfaction. That was when he said something that chilled her in spite of the heat of the day.

"They're never coming back," he said, speaking so matter-of-factly it was all the more disturbing. "And if you're not careful, you won't be coming back either."

Alana felt anger rising to her face in a bright red flush. "Are you threatening me?"

"Not a threat," he said. "But a warning."

His name was Garrett. Garrett LeBlanc. Although Alana didn't believe what Justine and Missy said about what he had done, they were right about him being different. He didn't hang around with the other kids, and although Harmony Home was famous for its loners, he wasn't like the others. Most loners insisted on distance, and usually got it. No one much cared that they kept to themselves. They'd sit alone at a table, or wander off to a quiet corner, and they'd be out of sight, out of mind. But Garrett was never out of mind. When he was in a room, you could feel him there. You could feel his eyes boring into you, even when he was looking in the opposite direction. And it wasn't just Alana—other kids could feel it too. Too many conversations seemed to be about Garrett. Who was he? Why was he here? Why, once you started thinking about him, couldn't you get him out of your mind?

Garrett was right about one thing: those other kids didn't come back. Not one of them. They had made their escape. With Alana's closest friends gone, Garrett became a project for her. She would systematically break down his layers of defenses and find out what made him tick. And then she would find out if any of the dark rumors about him were true.

Day after day she forced herself to treat him decently, which proved to be a chore. Even though he excelled at ignoring people, she would talk to him until finally the cold reception he always gave her heated to lukewarm.

On a rainy Saturday she found him in the Multiuseless Room, which was really called the Multipurpose Room, but most of the kids had concluded that it served no practical purpose. In an attempt to "socialize" him, Garrett had been taken from his secluded little bedroom and forced to share a larger room with five other boys. Apparently, it hadn't worked. Garrett was sitting alone playing solitaire.

Alana slid in across from him, pushed all the cards together, and began to shuffle them.

"I was winning," complained Garrett. "What are you doing?"

"No one wins at solitaire," she told him, "because even when you do, you just end up dealing the cards again until you get even more bored. You play blackjack?"

"No."

"I'll teach you, so we can run away together and take Las Vegas for millions." He just stared at her again with that lock-picking gaze. Alana ignored it and continued to shuffle. When she heard the Ping-Pong ball behind her stop bouncing, she looked up to notice that most everyone else in the room was looking at them. Perhaps because no one had kept Garrett this close to them for this long. It was a grand victory for a girl who was famous for pushing people away, and she was happy to flaunt that in front of everyone.

"You get dealt two cards. Dealer has to hit to seventeen. You don't."

"This is twenty-one. I know how to play this."

"Good for you." She dealt him his first card. A one-eyed jack. Alana always found one-eyed jacks mysterious. Like Garrett.

"You know," she offered, "if you ever feel like talking about stuff with someone who doesn't have a PhD at the end of their name, I'm sure I can find the time in my busy schedule."

Garrett leaned away from the cards, obviously realizing this was just another ruse to get inside his head. "Suddenly I don't feel like playing," he said, then stood up and breezed out of the room. Alana tossed the deck on the table and followed closely in his wake, undaunted. In a way, he was like a game of solitaire himself. Alana's game, and she was determined to deal again and again.

"Don't you know when to quit?"

"No," answered Alana. "That's why I'm stuck in this place. How about you?"

She followed him up the stairs and through the door to the roof, which was supposed to be alarmed but never was. The roof was strewn with dead leaves and other debris, waterlogging in the rain. If Garrett thought coming to this uninviting spot would deter Alana, he was wrong. In fact, she decided to call his bluff in a major way. The door to the roof didn't close all the way unless you really closed it tightly, which was exactly what Alana did. Until someone noticed, they were locked up there. Garrett had no way out—no path away from her. *Fine,* she told herself. *If he wants to be out on the roof in the rain, he will be. For a good long time.*

"Oh, that was just brilliant," snapped Garrett.

There was a warped plywood shelter in the corner built to protect a bird hutch—but like so many residents of Harmony Home, the pigeons had flown the coop years ago, and the hutch had been scavenged for various arts and crafts projects. It was there, beneath the low shelter, that Garrett and Alana waited out the rain.

He could just scream like hell until someone came up here to let us in, thought Alana, *but he's not doing that. Perhaps he isn't as anxious to be free of me as he seems.* Knowing that made Alana even more bold. They sat watching the torrents pummel the roof.

"What really happened to your family?" Alana asked. "I promise I won't hate you—whatever you tell me."

Garrett laughed. It wasn't the response Alana expected. Anger, maybe, but she didn't expect to be laughed at. He brought up his knees, to tie his drenched laces. "I didn't kill them, if that's what you're asking."

Alana tried not to show her relief, but she knew it could be read in her body language. "That's good," she said, which she thought might have been the dumbest thing she had ever uttered in her life.

But Garrett didn't laugh again. He kept his eyes focused on his own shoes. "Do you ever get . . . close to people?" asked Garrett. "So close that you can't let them go, no matter how hard you try?"

Alana looked away from him. She knew what he meant, and just the thought of it made her suddenly feel that disconnection—that unbearable loneliness that all too often sent her into a rage.

"No," she answered. "No, I've never really felt close to anyone."

"I might not seem like it now . . . but I get very close to people. I've always had lots of friends. People always like me—they want to get to know me. Just like you."

"So . . . you're saying I'm just like everyone else."

The corner of his mouth turned up in a grin. "No—you try harder." And then the grin faded. "You know . . . they say you carry with you all the things that ever happened to you in your life—even the things you don't remember. They're all inside your head somewhere. It's like that with people, too. All the people you know—they're all rattling around inside your skull. You know what I mean?"

Yes, Alana did know. Her own father had vanished from her life when she was five—but she still heard his voice yelling at her. She still felt the slap of his hand on her face. Yeah, you do carry people with you.

"There are some people," Garrett continued, "who can't handle all those people telling them things in their heads. All those voices screaming at once, all out of control . . ." Until now, Garrett had kept his knees pulled up to his chin, but now he relaxed a bit, lowering one knee to the ground and turning his shoulders to face her. "I don't lose my mind like that," he said. "But I do have seizures."

"Seizures? What do you mean, seizures?"

"Doctors say it's a brain thing. Like epilepsy—only instead of my head getting all fuzzy inside, everything becomes super clear. Suddenly I see the faces of the people I know—the people I've gotten close to. I hear their voices, I sense their thoughts . . . until their thoughts are my thoughts."

A sudden gust of wind blew a spray of rain across their faces, and Alana couldn't tell if the wetness on Garrett's cheek was rain or tears.

"See, I have these seizures," Garrett repeated. "And when I come out of them . . . the people I know are gone. . . ."

Above them, the bowed plywood creaked from the weight of the rain—but Alana didn't care about that. She was locked on Garrett's eyes—those eyes that seemed so invasive, as if they could decode every ounce of her being. He was trying to tell her something major—something terrible—but her mind felt like a brick, unable to absorb what he was saying. She could only stare at him, her mind a blank. And then what few coherent thoughts Alana had in that moment were extinguished when he leaned forward and kissed her.

There had been other boys who kissed her before. Usually they forced their lips against hers when she wasn't expecting it, stealing the kiss rather than offering it. Usually she swatted those boys away like mosquitoes, flattening them against the wall. But this was different. The kiss felt huge and overwhelming, as if it would swallow her whole . . . as if she could disappear inside of it. But then he pulled away, and she was left looking into his eyes once more, feeling as if the rain would melt her like the Wicked Witch of the West.

"I really like you, Alana. And so I tried to stay away from you. Do you see now why I told you about the seizures? I've gotten too close to you . . . and now you've got to get away from here—away from me—before it's too late."

Suddenly the plywood above gave way, dumping on them its heavy load of rainwater. The deluge snapped Alana out of her trance. Surrounded by the here and now once more, she let the world around her take hold . . . and a familiar reflex took hold as well. The reflex to push away. The urge to put everyone and everything at an arm's distance. She felt the rage build in her, like her own peculiar seizure, and rather than spewing her fury at Garrett, she hurried to the door, pounding it, kicking it, bashing it until the metal dented, until the doorjamb fractured and the lock sprung open, letting her back into the stuffy air of the stairwell.

"Hate me, Alana," she heard Garrett call after her. "Hate me and run away. Get out of this place! Go as far and as fast as you can. Maybe that way it won't happen to you . . . the way it happened to the others. . . ."

Alana didn't run away . . . but she didn't seek out Garrett's company the next day either. Instead on that black-clouded Sunday, she snuck into the computer room, for although Harmony House didn't have much contact with the outside world, it did have Wi-Fi. Alana spent the day scouring articles, and probing databases. She had already snuck an unauthorized peek at Garrett's file in the main office—and although several key pages were missing, she knew he had come from the town of Cranston, which was clear across the state.

Finally she found the article she was looking for. It didn't have any direct links. In fact, every other reference to the town of Cranston on that particular day had been systematically deleted from the web, as if someone had done it intentionally. But this one article, from the local paper, had slipped through the cracks.

BLOOM STREET MYSTERY, the headline read. The story was more like the kind of thing you read in the cheap tabloids, next to stories of alien sightings and three-headed babies. Only difference was, this story was real.

Apparently, eighteen people on Bloom Street had vanished without a trace. All of them were neighbors. All friends. Even their pets were gone. In fact, only one person was left: a teenage boy. Although the article didn't print the name, Alana knew who it had to be. She reached over to turn on the printer, but a hand grabbed hers before she could touch it.

"What are you still doing here? Didn't I tell you to go?" It was Garrett. The expression on his face was between anger and desperate fear, but there was something else there as well. He was sweating something terrible, and his eyes kept trying to roll back into his head, as if he was fighting to keep control over something. *His seizures,* thought Alana. *He's about to have one of those seizures!*

Alana was caught off guard. Her voice quivered. "The gates are guarded ever since those other kids ran away—"

"You're smart, you can find a way out!" he insisted.

"Maybe I don't want to go!"

He grabbed her other arm, pulling her out of the chair so hard the chair fell to the ground behind her with a crack. In turn, she wrenched herself free and pushed him as hard as she could. "Get your hands off me!"

He hit a bookshelf, jostling it, and sent a dozen books cascading down around him. The books pounded on his shoulders and lay sprawled at his feet. To Alana he looked worn and beaten. He kept his distance. He didn't apologize, and neither did she.

"What happened on Bloom Street?" Alana asked.

"I don't want you to get hurt!"

"What happened on Bloom Street?" Alana demanded.

"I can't protect you from it!"

"WHAT HAPPENED ON BLOOM STREET?"

Silence from Garrett. He stared at Alana, reading her, grimacing as the sweat poured down his forehead. She swore she could see his temples pulse. And then he finally spoke. "When you were nine," he told her, "you snuck out of here late at night and went to see a movie."

Alana shook her head, trying to hitch herself onto whatever train of thought he had just begun. She swallowed hard when she remembered that she had never told anyone about the midnight movie trip. "How did you know that?"

"I know because Missy was with you that night."

"She told you?"

"She didn't have to. Just like Justine didn't have to tell me about the time she was six and got hit by a car. Or the time she and Missy hid in the old storm cellar so that everyone would think they were missing—but nobody noticed. Not even you. I could tell you a million things about a hundred different people, Alana. Things that no one knows but them."

"You read their minds?"

"No, I *have* their minds!" Garrett blinked hard to keep his eyes from doing those flip-turns in his skull. Then he took a step toward her. "I get too close to people, Alana. I get too close, and somehow they get pulled inside. They're not dead, but they're not really alive, either. My parents, my neighbors, all my friends from the last place I was at, and the first thirteen people I met here. I got too close to them . . . and now I carry them with me."

Alana could only shake her head, then her wall of resistance came crashing down. She was suddenly flooded by everything he was trying to tell her. Still, she couldn't accept it. She would rather have heard that he had killed them all. But to think that his mind had latched on to the people it knew—on to Missy and Justine and the others—to think that his mind was powerful enough to wrap around them . . . and swallow them whole . . .

The door flung open to reveal two men in dark suits, and two others behind them. They wasted no time. "That's him," one of them said. Then they grabbed him. "Garrett LeBlanc, you're going to have to come with us."

All of a sudden it became clear to Alana. Why all the articles were missing about the people who had disappeared. Why Garrett's file was incomplete. He had been under surveillance all this time. There were people watching, and waiting. Trying to piece together what he had done and how he had done it.

So that they could use him.

"No, you can't have him!" yelled Alana.

One of the men flashed a badge, as if she cared. "This is official business, miss, so why don't you let us do our job."

"Yes," said Garrett. "Take me away from here. Put me someplace that's safe."

One of the men laughed. "Oh, don't worry. We got a nice cozy place for you."

But Alana knew as well as Garrett what lay in store for him. Where would they put him? A chrome lab where they could run test after test after test? Even life at Harmony Home was better than that.

She kicked one of them in the kneecap and grabbed Garrett. One of the others pulled a gun. *Fine,* thought Alana. *I dare them to shoot.* They didn't, of course, and her momentum pulled Garrett out the door, with the agents right behind.

But halfway down the hall, Garrett dug in his heels and stopped. "It's too late," he whispered desperately. "It's happening."

Now Alana was certain she could see his temple throbbing. His teeth locked, his eyes began to roll again, and he forced his head to turn away from her to the four men, whom he had only just met. His body jerked once, as if he had been hit with an electric shock, there was a flash of light . . . and the four men were gone, leaving nothing but a *pop* as the air rushed to fill the space where they had been.

Alana could have stared in shock for a good hour, but there wasn't time. Not now.

Garrett fell to his knees. "It's going to get worse before it gets better."

"What do you want me to do?"

"Run!" he said. But Alana still wouldn't do it. There had been so many things she'd run from. So many people. And here, finally, was someone she didn't want to leave. No matter what happened to her. Even if his gaze turned her into little more than a thumbnail in his mind, she would not leave. He was too close to her heart now. Too close to run from.

"Quickly," she said to him, helping him up and moving down the hall with him again. Several people stopped to look at them suspiciously. Alana ignored them. "Quickly—tell me how it works. Do you have to be looking at them? Do they have to be in the room with you?"

"No. They can be anywhere nearby. I just have to know them. To have seen them, or heard them, or smelled them, or—"

Garrett groaned, his body jolted, there was a snap of light and a series of pops. A few of the people in the hallway disappeared, followed by the sudden pops of air. The others who hadn't vanished stood dumbfounded, voicing their shock at what they had just seen. Alana had to bite her own lip to make sure that she was still there.

"Okay," she said, keeping herself under control. "We just learned something. We just learned that it's random. And that it doesn't take everyone at once. Just a few at a time."

"They're so frightened," wailed Garrett, and it took a second for Alana to realize that he wasn't talking about the people around them; he was talking about the people who were gone. The ones he had just pulled inside. "They don't know how they got here. They don't understand where they are. They're so afraid. . . ."

"Don't think about that now!"

Another body jolt and another set of flashes. They were coming more quickly now, building in intensity. Would it take over his whole body? wondered Alana. Would he start convulsing right here on the floor, the air strobing around them in bright flashes until they were all gone? By now Garrett had met everyone at the home. When his seizures were done, no one would be left.

"What's its range?" she asked him. "If it only took eighteen people from your neighborhood, then maybe it only reaches a few hundred yards or so, right?"

"I don't know."

"Maybe if we got you out onto the street, away from here."

"No time."

Flash! Flash! Flash! Trays dropped to the ground in the cafeteria as the people holding them were drawn from their lives, sucked through the walls, captured by Garrett for all time.

They paused for a brief moment, and something finally clicked in Alana's mind. Through walls . . . The walls at Harmony House were practically paper-thin—but there were thicker walls nearby. Although Alana didn't know the strength of Garrett's soul-snatching seizures, she did know that the storm cellar had been turned into a bomb shelter many years ago, long before the mansion became Harmony Home. The man who had once owned this place was a doomsday prepper, and had lined the small underground bunker in lead, which was why it was off-limits. If lead could block radiation, maybe it could block other forces as well. All at once Alana knew where Garrett had to go.

"Let's go!" She pulled Garrett down the stairs. He didn't ask where they were going—perhaps he already knew. If it was true that he now owned Missy's and Justine's memories, he would know all about the lead-lined shelter.

She struggled with him out the back door, his body becoming stiff and rigid with each flash of hot, searing light. A basketball bounced on the court nearby. Instinctively Garrett looked over. A bunch of kids were playing a half-court game. Too late. The players and spectators were already beginning to vanish.

"Chaysen . . . Omar . . . Dani . . . Dawn . . ." Garrett could only recite their names helplessly as they passed that barrier between matter and thought, becoming permanent residents of Garrett's mind. Alana knew it was only a matter of time until one of his mental flashes struck her, turning her into a memory as well.

Garrett fell to his knees, and a security guard took notice of their panicked activity. Alana tried to pull Garrett through the thick, muddy grass. She was strong, but she couldn't move him fast enough.

The storm cellar was still a dozen yards away, on the other side of the basketball court.

"Get away from me!" Garrett gasped. "You have to go! Now!"

The burning flashes of light came one after another now, like a strobe, as Garrett fell to the ground, his limbs jolting, his back arching, and only the whites of his eyes showing through his fluttering eyelids.

She couldn't get him to the shelter, she couldn't stop his seizures . . . but there was something she could do. She could leave him. She could push herself away, as he had begged her to do. In so doing, maybe she could save the others.

She turned from Garrett just as the security guard approached. For an instant he stood in her way, but then he dissolved in midstride, and Alana could swear she felt him pass through her as he was sucked into Garrett's mind. She couldn't think about that now. She had a mission to accomplish.

She raced onto the basketball court, where kids were still reeling from the random disappearances. They all looked around, not sure what to think, not sure what to do. The younger kids who were watching the game all began to stand, confused and terrified, searching for someone older to explain what had happened. It was Alana who took charge.

"This way," she yelled, grabbing them, pushing them. "The shelter! Now!"

She managed to get nine of them moving, but there were only seven left by the time they made it down the leaf-strewn steps of the lead-lined shelter. She herded them into the dark, musty room and slammed the door, shutting out the outside world, and Garrett's inside world.

"What's happening?" one kid asked. But Alana didn't answer. Instead she held the door closed, as if an invisible hand might tear it from its hinges.

Then, as she stood there, she felt it. The room was dead dark, but tiny points of light came in from around the doorframe, which wasn't a perfect seal. One of those points of light had come for Alana. It latched on to her, tried to swallow her; she could feel her whole self being drawn through that tiny gap in the door, smaller than a keyhole. A part of her wanted to go—to be with Garrett—to be part of his crowded mind. But she fought it, asserting her will to be separate and apart, to be—as she always was—alone. Garrett's capturing light, robbed of its strength by the lead-lined room, lost the battle, and in a few moments the flashes of light shooting through the cracks came less and less frequently. Alana held the door closed, gripping the handle tight, feeling her knuckles grow numb and cold. Then, when she was absolutely certain it was over—long after the last flash—she released her grip.

The world had not changed. The trees were still there, the basketball court was still there. But the people weren't. The kids Alana had saved filed out of the shelter, not sure what to make of the silence, and for a long, terrifying moment, Alana thought that perhaps Garrett had pulled in the whole world. But no. She could hear traffic on the highway, full of cars and trucks between destinations. People whom Garrett had never met. No, everyone was still there. Everyone, that is, but the souls of Harmony House.

Garrett was gone too. She found his muddy footprints leading away from the spot where she had left him—a random, haphazard set of prints, as if he had stumbled away into the woods in agony. She wanted to go after him, but realized that he didn't want her to find him. The one thing he needed more than anything else in this world was distance from those around him—for he could only be happy if somehow he found his way, alone. And so Alana finally gave in to his lonely desire, allowing him the distance he so desperately needed.

She tried to imagine what it must be like inside his thoughts right now, where a crowd of frightened, furious people, crammed like sardines in a can, all fought to retain something of themselves. She could almost hear the dozens of individual voices struggling for the right to exist. How long would it be until they accepted their fate? How long until they all dissolved into one another, their thoughts, feelings, and memories becoming part of Garrett's? She supposed no one but Garrett and the people in his overcrowded mind would ever know.

As she stood there, looking down at Garrett's footprints in the mud, one of the younger children she'd saved—a girl about eight years old—came up to her.

"Where is everyone?" she asked, fear painted pale on her face. "Why did they leave without us?"

Alana felt the urge to ignore her—to just walk away and not deal with it. But she swallowed that urge, and offered the girl a slim smile instead. It occurred to Alana that she did not know this girl. In fact, aside from her own close circle of friends, she had known very few of the kids at Harmony Home. "What's your name?" she asked.

"Kimi."

"Well, Kimi, we're going to have to get along without the others."

Emotion welled up in the girl's eyes, and she began a steady flow of tears. Alana opened up her arms and folded her in, holding her, comforting her, and feeling a sense of compassion in herself that had always been absent from her heart . . . and she realized that Garrett had, in his own way, left her with a very precious gift.

I get too close to people, Garrett had told her—and here in his wake, Alana had somehow been given an ounce of that closeness as well. Nothing like Garrett's capturing light, but a warm glow that filled her own darkest corners. A blessing rather than a curse. For the first time in her life, Alana could feel herself caring, and it was a wonderful thing.

The next few days would be rough. The confusion, the questions from police and reporters. But eventually all that would fade away into memory, just as the strange passage of Garrett LeBlanc would fade into rumor.

I hope you find your peace, Garrett. I hope you find some far-off place where you can live your life alone with the crowds in your head, and in your heart.

Alana slowly rocked back and forth, feeling the child in her arms begin to breathe just a little bit easier.

"We're all going to be okay," Alana said, knowing that if she could only hold on to this gift of closeness Garrett had given her, she truly would be okay, and her life would no longer be a boomerang.

The Living Place

The old woman fills her porch rocker like it was built just for her, and she slowly shifts forward and back, forward and back. I think I might get seasick just looking at her. Her hair is as silver as a spiderweb on a dewy morning, her skin is as dark as a moonless night, and her glasses are thick, turning her eyes big and dramatic. Her name is Delilah. She's the first person we met when we moved in last week.

"Prime property you got there, Amber," she tells me as my brother Tyler and I sit on her porch, sipping sun tea sweetened with fresh comb honey. "Finest property in the county."

I turn around to look at our house across the street. It's not much to look at—gray shingles that have gone green from too much rain and a porch sagging in the middle from the weight of five generations. The place is old, filled with mysterious relics from vanished days—like the old coal furnace that no longer works, or the light fixtures, which have been painted over so many times they look like barnacles growing from the ceiling. The place is full of radiator coils like steel anacondas that groan and complain, then summon out legions of overgrown bugs from their depths every time they begin to heat.

"I hate our house," grumbles Tyler, who's seven and hates most everything. "I don't even know why we had to move here."

But he knows. We both do. It was living in the city that made Mom sick—all that stress. But she's better now. Total remission, the doctors said—sometimes it happens like that. She's putting some weight back on her bones, and her hair's growing back too. Life in the country is what she needs, so we bought this little house, and all the land behind it.

Delilah hurls a handful of seed out at the birds on her lawn, whose numbers grow with each handful thrown. "You can hate the house, but not the land it sits on," she tells us. "The land is something special."

Tyler flicks some birdseed off the porch. "I wish we could move back to the city."

Delilah shakes her head. "Cities!" She purses her lips as if the word were a sour lemon. "Cities are places that suck life away—just suck it away like a cat sleeping on your chest."

I feel a chill release itself on my spine, echoing through to my fingers and toes. Tyler looks at me, and looks down. I can hear his breath beginning to get raspy, and he reflexively taps the asthma inhaler to make sure it's in his pocket. It wasn't just Mom who lost bits and pieces of her life to the city.

Delilah looks up at the trees around us. "But this place is nothing like the city. This place is abundant."

"Abundant," I repeat, letting the musical sound of the word somersault off my tongue.

Delilah takes a long sip of her honey-sweet tea. "Have you been out back of your place yet?" she asks.

I shake my head. "Our parents won't let us. There could be rattlers, or gators."

"And ticks," adds Tyler. "Don't forget the ticks!"

"Nonsense," says Delilah. "Haven't been rattlers around here since I was your age, and we don't get gators—this place ain't exactly the bayou."

Back and forth goes her rocker. Birdseed crackles beneath its curved, blunt blades. Then she moves her chair as far forward as it will go without toppling over. Leaning toward us, she whispers, "You know . . . there are powerful places around these parts."

Now she's caught my attention. "What do you mean . . . powerful?"

"I'll show you."

We help her out of her chair and hand her a birch cane with an ivory handle. As we cross the lawn, the birds take wing, sweeping a frantic path toward the setting sun.

The field behind our house is huge. It's full of tall wheatgrass, windswept and wild like a mop of bed-hair, stretching for fifty yards. The property would have been big enough if it ended there, but it doesn't. Behind the field is a grove of oaks. "No good for wood, though," Dad said, as if everything had to be milled, distilled, or processed for it to be useful.

According to the real estate agent, the property goes back nearly half a mile; twenty-six acres in all. Mom and Dad had intended to survey the property with a notebook and a canteen, trekking through the woods like Lewis and Clark, cataloging everything our little Louisiana purchase had in store for us . . . but like so many things, real life came first. Unpacking before exploring. So our property was mostly unexplored by us.

Delilah leads us through the wheatgrass, toward the woods. "I knew the folks who owned the property before you. Nice folks, for a time."

"For a time?" I ask

Delilah takes a while in answering, as if weighing what she should say and what she shouldn't. "People get funny now and again. You see those signs?" She points at some trees around us.

"Yes," I tell her. To be honest, the signs are hard to miss: NO TRESPASSING in big red letters, on iron signs rusting around the edges. There's one on our front fence, and one on the tree in our side yard. Out back, those signs seem to be everywhere.

"And they meant it," Delilah says. "Nobody came onto their property, not for any reason under the sun." Then she sighs. "Of course, they weren't always like that. There were times I remember when I was a young woman, they used to have parties and picnics like the rest of us. Then one day they just shut the gate and put up those signs. I suppose they would have put up electric fences if they could afford 'em."

"But why would they do that?" Tyler asks.

"Got greedy, I suppose. Wanted all that beautiful land for themselves."

I think back to when we met the old man who sold us the property. His face was deeply cragged with wrinkles, and his limbs as gnarled as the branches of a juniper. When he signed the papers and handed over the keys to my dad, he said, "It's not my responsibility anymore," as if leaving the place took the weight of the world from his shoulders.

The grass flattens before us, leaving a green trench that betrays our path. We wear long pants to protect us from the swarms of mosquitoes, and the aforementioned ticks, but I can still feel the coarse grass brushing across my legs. A rich chlorophyll aroma is pressed out of the grass as we make our way toward the woods.

"I don't know about this," says Tyler, slowing down as we reach the tree line. "Mom and Dad won't like this at all."

But I remind him that Mom and Dad don't have to know; they're off buying wallpaper to cover the mildewed bedroom walls.

Delilah laughs when she hears that. "Nothing wrong with a little mildew," she says. "It's just one form of life changing into another. It reminds us that we're part of the circle. There, you see?" Delilah says cheerfully, pointing to several saplings sprouting from the moss-covered remains of a felled oak. "It's all recycled in the end."

Tyler continues walking, but not before double-checking that his inhaler is still in his pocket. Strange he would worry about that, because right now his breathing sounds clearer than it has in weeks.

We move deeper into the woods. The trees are thick and tall, and the light is dim. I wonder if it's getting dark, or if it's just the canopy above us. Birds call to one another. We hear something scurrying past in the brush and duck out of sight.

Finally Delilah stops. "Look here," she says, pointing to a moss-covered rock.

"Just a bunch of moss," says Tyler.

"No . . . look closer."

"Let me see." I bring my hand across the stone and flake away the thick layer of moss, to reveal something carved into the stone. "Wow." The markings are badly weathered, and appear to be very old, but I can clearly make out the shape of a circle, with swirls coming out of it.

"Who made them?" Tyler asks.

"No one can say," answers Delilah. "These marks are as old as time itself."

"Do you think this was some sort of ancient burial ground?" I ask.

"Cool!" says Tyler, thrilled and terrified by the thought.

"No," says Delilah. "Not a burial place . . . a *living* place."

Tyler and I look at each other, not sure what she means.

As I turn back to Delilah, I notice the boulder beside her is more than a mere boulder. It's a piece of stone carved into a wedge, like an arrow . . . and it points deeper into the woods, where a rusted barbed-wire fence cuts between the trees.

"What does it point to?" I ask.

Delilah seems a bit less sure of herself now. With her cane for balance, she shifts her weight from one hip to the other. "Can't be sure," she tells us. "When I was young and foolish, I came out here and found the stone. But something about it gave me the willies."

"You got scared?"

"Scared enough to turn and run. It wasn't long after that the fences and 'no trespassing' signs went up."

I take a deep breath. "Well, this is our property now, and no one can stop us from going on in." Now I lead the way instead of Delilah. Finding a gap in the barbed wire, we climb through.

The deeper we move into the forest, the more I understand what Delilah means by "a living place." The emerald green of the trees; the sounds of birds and insects filling the air; the rich smell of peat, like a spring garden—every inch of the place seems to be alive. I begin to feel light-headed and wonder if, like the rainforests, this air is rich in oxygen. This truly is a living place, where all life thrives and even my brother breathes clearly, without a hint of an asthmatic wheeze.

At last we come to a clearing within a circle of tall, straight oaks, and between each oak is another triangular stone pointing toward the center. The sky above is a patch of early twilight blue surrounded by shimmering green leaves, and the clearing is filled with wispy gossamer grass and wildflowers bursting with such powerful color you could swear you feel those blues, yellows, and pinks caressing your brain.

"Lord Almighty, will you look at this place!" says Delilah, her breath taken away. "What a wonder!"

Tyler lopes out into the clearing with an enthusiastic stride, instead of shuffling his feet like he usually does.

"Maybe it's like an ancient temple," he suggests, "like I seen on TV! People come secretly at night and make human sacrifices!"

"It's no such thing!" I tell him, and I instinctively know that I'm right. This is a place of life, not death. Maybe it was once a place of worship, but not of dark deeds. Not here.

Yet, as I look at Delilah, I can see that her wonder is quickly dissolving into concern, then fear. Her fear becomes contagious, and I can't help but to feel that we shouldn't be here—and that something terrible is going to happen.

"That's enough," Delilah calls out to Tyler. "I'd best be getting you two back home."

But Tyler is in his element, prancing around the grassy clearing, kicking up the rich scent of wildflowers and weaving fantasies.

"Maybe it's a pirate place," he says.

"We're nowhere near the ocean!" I remind him.

"So? Pirates can walk. Even if they got peg legs. Maybe pirates hauled their gold here and buried it right in the middle of this clearing!"

Then he takes off toward the center.

"Tyler, you get back here!" I yell, but he's not listening. "Tyler!"

And then suddenly he's gone. He just disappears into thin air—or so it seems to me—but old Miss Delilah, thick glasses and all, sees the whole thing better than I do. She drops her cane and goes running right to the center of the field, throwing herself on the ground.

"Amber, help me!" she cries.

I hurry to her and see Tyler's face looking up at me from a dark hole in the ground, less than two feet across. His hands cling to the grass at the edge of the hole, and I can only thank heaven that the grass is healthy and that its roots are strong enough to hold firm.

"Help," shouts Tyler. "Don't let me fall!"

"I got you, Tyler," says Delilah. Not bothering with his hand, she grabs him by his hair.

"Ow!" he yells, but with her hand snagged in his hair like that, there's no way he's going to fall. I grab his arm and pull, then pull again. Finally, between the two of us, we haul Tyler out of the hole. Lying there on the grass, he sobs for a few moments, but gets over it quickly, determined not to let us see his tears.

"I told you pirates were here!" he says. "It's a pirate cave!"

"It's no cave," I tell him flatly. "It's just an old well."

Tyler peers down into the well, disappointed. "So? It *could* have been a pirate cave."

Now that Tyler is safe, Delilah trembles with the fright of it all. "Lordy, we almost lost you down there."

I think of the stories I've heard about kids who've been trapped in wells. Someone digs the wells, then forgets them, or they board them up but the boards rot. Kids and animals fall in. Sometimes they die—especially when the well is hidden in tall grass, like this one. Tyler got lucky today.

He leans over the well, tempting fate. "Tyler!" I scold, gripping onto the waistband of his pants, just in case he loses his footing. He is consumed with curiosity. I guess I can't blame him.

"How deep do you suppose it goes?" I ask.

"To the center of the earth, I'll bet," says Tyler.

I look to Delilah, but her face is clouded with thoughts as deep as the well. She knows something—but it's not something she wants to share with us.

A breeze blows past us, and I can hear it whisper across the lip of the well, conjuring forth a raspy moan. "Sounds like something's down there," I say.

"Just the breath of the wind," says Delilah. Once more her fear lays itself upon me like a yawn. "You two come on now." She fishes her cane from the grass. "Got to get home while there's still some light left."

We leave together, but as we reach the circle of trees, I have to look back. From here the hole is hidden by the grass around it.

Delilah takes my arm. "Come along. Maybe it's best you keep to the other side of the barbed wire from now on."

We wind through trails and over logs and boulders until we're on our back porch once more. Only then do I hear that Tyler's wheezing has returned.

There are some places that draw you to them. They grab you so deep in your soul that you find yourself drifting toward them, even in your dreams. That's how it is with the Living Place. It isn't just that we're drawn there; things felt different there too. That first time out there with Delilah, we felt full of ourselves, full of life, and even as we left, I knew we would be going back.

We don't tell Mom and Dad about the well, or the stones, or the old barbed-wire fence. Our parents' boundaries have not yet reached beyond the tall grass in our yard—and even then, Dad has only managed to mow half of it. At this rate it will be months before they venture deep enough to find our secret little spot. We keep it to ourselves. We don't even talk to Delilah about it anymore.

The next time we go back, Tyler takes his soccer ball. It's a shiny one, still as smooth as the day Dad got it for him, because Tyler never uses it much. Not that he doesn't want to; his asthma just won't let him. One time he had an attack just running for the school bus, and ever since he's been too worried to play much of any sport. And yet it doesn't surprise me that he grabs the ball when we go back to the Living Place.

"You be careful out there," Mom calls to us from the back porch.

"Don't worry," I tell her, "we won't go far."

The second we cross from the tall grass into the woods, Tyler drops his ball and begins dribbling it around rocks and gnarled tree roots. The closer he gets to the Living Place, the faster he moves, and I have to jog to keep up with him. As I run, I can feel the pores on my face open as if I'm in a steam bath, and I know that being out here will even help my acne.

Tyler stops as we near the clearing that hides the well. He won't go into that clearing again. Neither will I. Instead we stay just outside of it, kicking the ball back and forth between the trees.

"You be goalie," insists Tyler, bouncing the ball from one knee to another, high-stepping like the leader of a parade, no sign of asthma or worry.

"Okay," I tell him, "but if you aim at my head, you're dead meat!"

"I won't aim at your head," he tells me, then takes a shot directly at my face.

I throw up my hands a moment too late—the ball painfully ricochets off my ear, and between two trees.

"Goal!" shouts Tyler, jumping up and down.

"Why you little—"

"Amber—the ball!"

I turn to see the ball bouncing into the clearing, over the brightly colored wildflowers. I know exactly where it's headed.

"Stop it!" yells Tyler, as if I have arms that could stretch out that far and bring the ball back. I race out, but it is too far away, and I can only watch as the ball disappears into the well.

"Oh, great!" says Tyler. "You owe me a new ball!"

"*You* kicked it!"

"It hit *your* head!"

I step up to the well and look down, seeing nothing but darkness. Then I hear something: a distant sucking sound. Then silence. Until that moment I didn't realize there was any noise in the air at all—I guess my ears just became accustomed to the faint rasp of wind across the well—but now that airy hiss is gone.

Instantly things begin to change.

At first, I think it's just my imagination. "Tyler! Look at the grass and flowers. Do they look funny to you?"

He looks around and shrugs. "No."

"See how they're lying? They're not as tall as they were before. It's as if the whole field has flattened out a bit."

"That's because we just ran across it," he says.

"But we didn't walk everywhere," I say pointing to the other side, where the flowers have definitely begun to wilt.

He furrows his eyebrows, the way Dad does when something confuses him. "That's weird."

Tyler looks into the hole again. Dark and silent. "What about my ball?"

"We'll get you a new one."

"You're paying for it."

"Fine," I say, just to get him moving. "Let's just get out of here."

By the time we reach the circle of trees just beyond the clearing, I notice some leaves have begun to turn yellow.

A summer blight, the neighbors call it. A new breed of weevil, or something like that. Trees, grasses, and shrubs brown and yellow around us over the next three weeks. At first it's just our property, but the blight spreads in twisting spokes like brown tentacles of death, following the banks of streams and the veins of canyons. Birds fall dead from their perches on trees. Worms crawl up through the earth only to bake and dry in the sun. From my window I can see the brown wasteland of our backyard. The dead grass blows away like chaff in the wind, leaving behind mud.

The town begins a slow simmer, boiling toward panic as the arms of the blight stretch toward farmland.

Tyler doesn't play soccer anymore. He barely gets out of bed. At night his wheezing keeps me awake—not because it's so loud, but because I'm terrified that it might suddenly stop.

And then there's my parents.

One morning, after a breakfast as somber as a funeral, I dare to ask my father a question that I've been afraid to hear the answer to.

"Dad," I ask, "when did your hair start going gray?"

He looks at me as if it's a forbidden subject. It's Mom who answers. "It's just stress, dear," she says. "That happens sometimes."

But it's not just Dad's hair and Tyler's asthma—there are other things. Like the way the food I eat doesn't seem to nourish me anymore. I'm losing weight. Now all I ever want to do is sleep.

"What's happening around here?" I ask them.

They sense the urgency in my voice and look to each other as if communicating in some sort of parental telepathy.

"Honey," Dad says, "you don't have to worry about Mom. It's probably nothing; the doctor said so."

I'm caught completely off guard. "*What's* probably nothing?"

They turn to each other again, realizing they've opened a can of worms. Now that I look at Mom, I can see the dark rings under her eyes and the failing expression on her face, like a hillside about to give way.

"I just have to go back in for a few tests, that's all."

"The doctor says it's probably nothing," repeats Dad.

I bolt from the room, not ready to hear any more, not wanting to face the possibility that the cancer is back, growing through Mom's body like the blight spreading through town.

But it's more than just a "blight." I know that. I've known it from the beginning, but I haven't dared to think what it's really all about. Now I have no choice.

As I burst out into the street, the despair is everywhere—I hear hacking coughs from windows down the road. I pass a bone-thin dog, its coat mange-torn and its eyes large and hopeless. The stench and sounds of slow death rise in the air around me—they fill the air within me. I can feel my own body winding down.

I burst into Delilah's unlocked door. She always keeps it unlocked. She says she trusts in the safety of the world. I wonder if she trusts in it now.

I find her lying on her bed. At first, I think she's asleep, but her head slowly turns to me. "Amber," she says. "I suppose you've been wondering about me. I've been tired, is all." She smiles and gazes at me through rheumy eyes.

"I need to know something, Delilah." I gently take her hand. "I need to understand. You know what's happening around here, don't you? Please, tell me."

She nods sadly, and takes a long moment before she answers.

"It's dying," she says.

"What's dying?"

"Everything. The birds, the trees, the land, and the sea. All dying. All dying."

"What should I do?"

"Nothing to do," she says weakly. "The Living Place is dead. No telling why."

"What *is* the Living Place?" I ask her, afraid to hear her answer, but more afraid not to.

She sighs and shifts in her bed, not even trying to sit up. "Every living thing has a breath of life, child," she tells me. "And everything that breathes needs a place to do it from." I sit back in my chair, beginning to understand what she is telling me. "I knew it the moment I saw it. I've heard tell of such a place, but never dreamed it was real."

I just shake my head, not wanting to believe it.

"I thought you understood. . . ." Her voice gets weaker with every passing word. "The world . . . has stopped . . . breathing. . . ."

And in a moment, so does Delilah. She just closes her eyes, takes one deep breath, then a shallow one, then a shallower one still, and she is gone.

I let go of her hand and it falls limply to the bed. I want to cry, but I know Delilah would not want me to cry. It's part of the circle, she would say. Flesh to dirt, to daisies, to flesh once more. I realize now that the best thing I can do for Delilah is to make sure the cycle doesn't end with her. That the renewal continues.

I leave Delilah's house, stepping into my own house just long enough to fish out my dad's Swiss Army knife from a junk drawer. Then I head straight out into the backyard, tramping through the mud toward the barren trees beyond. The abundance of life Delilah was so fond of talking about is gone. All the moss is brown and the rich smell of peat has turned bitter. The bodies of rats and rabbits litter the ground as I get closer to the Living Place. They are uneaten, yet they are undecayed. Even the bacteria has died here, I think, and I wonder which is worse: the indignance of flesh breaking down into dust or the crime of it not being returned to the earth at all. I push forward past the wedge of stone pointing toward the center of life.

The hole stands bare now; the grass and flowers have been blown away, like flesh torn from a skeleton, and the parched, hard earth is cracked and mottled in sickly shades of gray. I imagine the blight stretching out from this place; a slow shock wave of death enveloping the whole Earth, leaving it a voiceless, soulless rock drifting in silent space until time itself ceases.

I stand at the lip of the hole. How long has it been since Tyler's ball went down there? Four weeks? Five? "There's nothing to be done," Delilah had said—but she didn't know the ailment. I do, and if there can be a cure, it's up to me.

This is for Delilah, I say to myself, and for my brother, and my mom and dad. . . .

And although I am terrified, I know that my fear means little, for if I succeed, even if I die, the life I save will be well worth my own. Before I can change my mind, I dive into the hole headfirst, with my eyes closed.

Rocks scrape me, tearing my shirt and jeans as I fall, until I am tightly wedged in the hole. With my hands before me, I must wriggle deeper and deeper, slithering in the darkness, feeling the blood rush to my head, pounding in my ears, and finally, when I can fall no deeper, my hands come across something cold and round, blocking the tight hole ahead.

The ball is wedged in the hole too tightly to pull out, so I don't even try. Instead I find the knife in my pocket. I pull out a stubby little blade and stab at the ball with all my strength. At first the knife just bounces off the hard leather surface, but I try again and again until the blade sinks deep, and I hear the telltale hiss of air escaping from the popped soccer ball.

I grab the flattened ball, pulling it free from the hole, and as I do, I can hear the sucking of wind growing stronger and stronger. I push out my elbows and knees to keep from being sucked any deeper, and just when I feel that I can't hold on anymore, the air being drawn into the earth stops . . . and then it begins to reverse with such force that the ground around me shakes.

I feel myself moving up and up, with a blast of moist air! Suddenly I'm being coughed up out of the bowels of the earth at an impossible speed. The darkness gives way to light, I see sky, and earth, and trees. I am airborne, but only for an instant before I fall in a heap on the hard gray ground. A flash of light—I seem to see stars, like they do in cartoons—and then darkness, as I lose consciousness.

I wake to the sound of birds. Just one or two. It takes a moment for me to orient myself, remembering where I am and what I have done. I sit up, my head still spinning from what must be a concussion. Around me is the clearing, still gray and bare . . . but something is different. I hear the faint rasp of air slipping into the hole at the center, and the smell of the air is fresh again. A few feet away is the flattened soccer ball. It's covered in dark, dark mud. In fact, so am I—it covers every inch of me, as thick as tar . . . yet I don't feel dirty, for I know that this dirt is clean. I sit there for a few minutes more, then take the airless soccer ball and head out of the woods.

We spread Delilah's ashes out over the Living Place. I know it's what she would have wanted. And now in the clearing the wildflowers grow taller and brighter for it. In turn, they attract more bees, who take the nectar and turn it into honey for someone else to use in their tea.

The blight ended as quickly as it came, and now the Living Place is back to its full green glory. I go back to the clearing every once in a while, to lie out there in the flowers. I never bring a soccer ball, and always keep a respectful distance from the "well." Usually I just go there to think and to breathe in the sweet air, looking up at the fingerprint swirls of clouds above.

I took Mom here once. Of course, I didn't tell her anything about the place, but she was impressed by the flowers nonetheless. A few days later, her doctors informed her that her treatment was successful, and that she was back in remission again, just as quickly as Tyler's asthma had subsided.

Diseases, and blights and trauma—they come and go, I guess. Sometimes they take the best of us, sometimes they take all of us. But other times they visit just long enough to remind us we're alive.

ANGELS, DEMONS, MONSTERS, AND A TREE

He knew it was virtual. He knew it couldn't be happening, but it didn't stop him from reacting as if it was real. And he wanted more.

"I'll tell you a secret," she whispered in his ear, and he could feel her breath as she did. "Your mind wants to tell you that this is pretend . . . but you don't have to listen. And when you stop listening . . . that's when it really gets fun."

—from "Non-Player Character"

Non-Player Character

By Neal and Brendan Shusterman

It was not an alarm, but the incessant beeping of a microwave that woke Darion up. He could sleep through the sounds of battle and the wails of the dying—but a relentless microwave was hard to ignore. It was still dark outside, and the faint smell of burned food filled the entire apartment. He looked around. His mattress, which sat like a beached whale in the center of the kitchen, had a green energy drink spill near his feet that looked like toxic sludge, and beside it the refrigerator door was ajar. From the other room came the sound of swarming zombies, and the rat-a-tat-tat of gunfire.

"GET THE KIDS! SOMEBODY SAVE THE KIDS!" shouted a voice he didn't recognize.

He crawled up on his spindly legs, raising himself to his feet. There was no kitchen table, or at least, not anymore; what was left of it sat in a broken heap of tangled wood in a corner, a bedsheet draped over it as if it were a corpse. He carefully stepped across the floor, avoiding bugs of various species traveling from one Doritos bag shelter to the next. He kicked aside a half-eaten bowl of mac and cheese that had more larvae than mac or cheese, and made his way to the beeping microwave, which was smoking. Inside Darion found an inedible mélange of blackened foodstuff. The kind that comes frozen—the kind any idiot can cook. His mother or his father must have set it for fifty minutes instead of five, and had promptly forgotten about it. Eating, after all, was only secondary to them now. He pulled the remains of the TV dinner from the microwave and threw it into the overflowing trash. What time was it? It was dark, and the clock on the microwave was no help; it blinked a perpetual midnight. In this house it was always the witching hour.

From the other room came more gunfire.

"OH GOD! SOMEONE HELP! THEY'RE EVERYWHERE!"

"TAKE COVER!"

He found his parents in their usual spots in the living room. The springs in the sofa had long since given up their battle against gravity, and the two of them sank into the cushions as if rooted there. His father held a weapon that wasn't there. His mother moved her arms as if directing airplanes on a runway. Both wore immersive headsets that put them into the world of the game, but it also played on a huge TV screen above the web-filled fireplace, and on smaller screens in every other room, so they wouldn't miss a thing, even when they took bathroom breaks.

Ever since *Mantra of Madness* was launched six months ago, it had consumed his parents like a stomach slowly digesting a heavy meal. The game's previous expansion packs had cost them their jobs, their friends, their bank accounts. This one had consumed what was left of their lives. The apartment had been different before *Mantra*. Things were functional. Darion had a bedroom. But that bedroom had quickly become a storage space for all the stuff his parents didn't need anymore—which was everything. His parents had talked to him before. But now, snarls and gunfire had replaced their conversations. Anything that didn't involve blowing away satanic alien zombies wasn't worthy of their attention. They treated Darion like an NPC in the real world. A non-player character. Computer-generated and soulless.

"Mom? Dad?" The first intrusion. He knew they wouldn't respond until the third or fourth.

"Mom? Dad? Can you hear me?" They shifted their shoulders

uncomfortably, aware they were being summoned from somewhere outside of their current reality—but it probably only registered subconsciously.

"You burned your food, and you have to eat!"

"Did you wake him up?" his father said to his mother.

"No, another NPC must have woken the sleeper," his mother said. "Damn computer."

"That's why I hate this level. Too many civilians to protect," said his father.

Darion tried again. "Did you hear me? Your food is burned."

"There'll be rations at the next checkpoint," his father said.

And so Darion gave up. Only once their mission was complete, and they realized that virtual food could only satisfy virtual hunger, would they leave the game long enough to gorge themselves. Right now, they would only eat if he cooked it and put it in front of them. And as much as he hated doing that, he knew he would, because the only thing worse than watching them play was watching them starve.

He wanted to scream, he wanted to cry, he wished he could just bawl his eyes out at what his life had become, but the tears just wouldn't come. How had their lives come to this? The change had been gradual and insidious, like the weeds that had strangled their yard. Suddenly this was the new normal, and there was never a moment to cry. He figured someday he would, and it would feel good. It would make him feel better. He would cry himself to sleep and have dreams without the sounds of an apocalyptic war.

Darion shuffled back into the kitchen. He looked at the wall clock, which had fallen from the wall and was now a baseboard clock. Its plastic face was cracked, and the hour hand was stuck at five o'clock, although the minute hand still ticked around the dial, as if in denial that anything was wrong. It wasn't only the digital clocks in his home that had lost their sanity. He considered putting the broken clock back up on the wall, but then considered the rest of the mess, and realized that any cleaning he could do would just be large quantities of zero. Best not to demoralize himself by trying. So, ignoring the squalor, he found a pan that was only slightly crusty, scraped it off, and cooked some larvae-free mac and cheese for his parents.

Back in the living room, he gave them each the first forkful. Only after tasting it did they respond by taking the bowls from him. Then they would eat it in between the major action.

Before becoming entirely immersed in *Mantra*, his parents had gotten him his own headset. For his birthday. That was what they called it—a birthday present, even though his birthday had been two months before. He had opened the box. He had looked at it. He had thanked them.

"Now you can play with your friends," his father had said—as if the only way to play with one's friends was in a virtual RPG.

They had seemed satisfied. But he had never put the headset on. Seeing a window into that world on the TV was more than enough. Why would anyone want to be immersed in a satanic alien zombie apocalypse?

"Aw, crap! Holloway is down!" his father shouted, nearly dumping his bowl.

On the screen, one of their teammates had been taken out by something unthinkably evil. Darion had no idea who Holloway was in real life—this online game was global. The players could be from down the street, or halfway around the world.

"Damn good player," his mother lamented. "Gonna miss him."

"Maybe he'll find us in his next iteration."

Then on the TV, red-eyed rats flooded from a sewer and chowed down on Holloway like piranhas until there was nothing left of him but bones, armor, and weapons.

"Waste not, want not," his father said, and their characters scavenged Holloway's belongings. Such was the way of the game.

Darion was about to leave and fix his own dinner when he

chanced to spot something in the corner of the TV screen. A girl. Pale blue shimmering hair. Almost silver. A mix of multiple races, in a stunningly beautiful combination. She was looking out of a broken window of what should have been an abandoned suburban home. The weird thing about it was that Darion could almost swear she was looking at him.

Darion went to school the next morning. Darion came home from school the next afternoon. Darion avoided his friends, because what would be the point of engaging them? It would be too awkward. He had to take care of his parents. Keep them from starving, or setting the house on fire, or flooding the house by leaving the water on. You can't have friends with those kinds of things on your mind.

"Hi, Mom. Hi, Dad. I'm home," he said each time he returned. It was more like a joke than an actual greeting, because they never responded unless they were on their way back from a bathroom run, or had taken off their headsets for some other reason. Then they would look at him with bloodshot eyes and slur something like "OhHeyHowuzSchool."

"Good," was always his response.

On the TV was a long city avenue of high-rise apartment buildings. A different landscape from yesterday. Some skyscrapers had toppled, others were leaning into one another. His parents had split off from their team, or the rest of the team had died. They now walked down the street precariously, because death and dismemberment could be around any corner.

And from distant places, civilians wailed for help, or just wailed.

"OH GOD, LET IT END!"

"PLEASE! PLEASE DON'T EAT MY BABY!"

All part of the ambience.

But then, as Darion watched the scene, he saw her again. The silver-haired girl. How could she be in two different landscapes? This time she was peering out from behind a pillar. And she was beckoning to him. She wore a glistening gown that was tattered and shredded like everything else in that world.

"Mom, Dad—do you see that?"

"Keep your wits about you," his father said to his mother. "We could be walking into an ambush."

"The girl—do you see her? There on the left, with the shiny hair."

"Huh? What? Just an NPC. Stop distracting me."

But still she beckoned. So, Darion did something he had never dared to do before. He put on his headset and turned it on.

The effect was instantaneous. The retinal projector erased all visual cues from the outside world. He was immersed in the dark, fiery, terrifying world of *Mantra of Madness*. He felt dizzy and nauseated. He wanted out, but he fought the feeling. When he turned, he saw his parents. He had seen their avatars before but had never really paid attention. Now, in three dimensions, they were impressive. They looked like his parents, and yet not. His mother had larger breasts, a slimmer waist, and her hair, which had gotten tatty and mousy in the real world, now bounced like a model's. His father looked like a steroid-injected bodybuilder version of himself.

"Well, look who finally decided to join the party!" his father said proudly. "About time you checked out the character we made for you! I've been leveling him up for when you were finally ready to play."

"Stay behind us," his mother told him. "This place can be dangerous. We'll protect you."

It was the first time they had actually engaged with him for weeks.

He looked around. The girl was still there. She had moved to a different pillar farther away, but she was still beckoning to him.

Darion willed himself forward. The game obeyed his mental commands.

"No!" his father shouted behind him. "Don't go after that! You can't get points for killing an NPC!"

But Darion ignored him.

"If we have to come rescue you, I'll be really pissed off!" his mother said.

He rounded the corner to see the torn fringes of her gown slipping into a dark doorway. He followed. The doorway opened on a set of emergency stairs that led up and up and up, until finally he emerged on the top floor of a skyscraper. The view was startling. All around him a city was on fire. Non-player characters were hurling themselves from rooftops to keep from being torn apart by satanic alien zombies.

The girl stood at the edge, but there were no creatures on this roof, and she didn't look like she was jumping. She smiled at him.

"You came. I knew you would come."

"Who are you?"

"That doesn't matter. What matters is that you're finally here." She moved closer. He reached out to touch her face. Even though he knew she was just a projection on his retina, he could swear he could feel her skin. So soft, so warm.

"This is a horrible place," she said, a tear dripping down her cheek. "You can see that, can't you?"

"Yes . . ."

"That's why I need you to save me."

Darion laughed. He was amazed they put this amount of programming into an NPC. Unless of course she was the kind of NPC around whom the plot turned. Not just an extra, but a principal in the story. How ironic if he came across a key element of the game that his parents had missed!

"Save you how?" he asked, ready to play along.

She didn't answer him right away. Instead she leaned close and kissed him.

He knew it was virtual. He knew it couldn't be happening, but it didn't stop him from reacting as if it was real. And he wanted more.

"I'll tell you a secret," she whispered in his ear, and he could feel her breath as she did. "Your mind wants to tell you that this is pretend . . . but you don't have to listen. And when you stop listening . . . that's when it really gets fun."

And what she did to him next . . . He knew it wasn't happening anywhere else but in his head, but that didn't matter. Because it was far more real than anything that had ever happened to him in real life.

He was hooked—but in a very different way than his parents. Day after day, he would enter the game, leave his parents to fight monsters, and run off to find the silver-haired girl. He would even kill monsters himself if he had to—but only to protect her. He had to admit, though, that the most satisfying thing was killing off other players. They would see him there, in his armor and with his laser cannon. They would think he was an ally, but then he would turn on them with a blast to the head. He would watch their digital brains explode and splatter the scenery. Their avatars would go down, and the rats would come. He wouldn't even take their belongings. He wasn't there to scavenge. His victory was in their fall. It could have gone on like that if the girl—whose name he still did not know—hadn't stopped it.

"They come back," she told him. "You can kill them, but they always come back. And every time they do, the game creates a hundred new monsters to kill those of us who can't get out."

Then, around a smoky corner of Armageddon, two players came. Darion recognized them right away.

"What the hell are you doing?" his father shouted at him. "Are you still wasting time with that NPC?"

"So what?" said his mother. "He's not in the way, and he's enjoying the game. Leave him alone."

"He's not playing right!" said his father.

But his father's attention turned to a gaggle of decomposing attackers. His parents began firing on them, shouting orders to one another—and just like the girl said, more kept coming and coming.

"You see how it is?" she said.

When Darion looked at her again, her eyes were now as bright silver-blue as her hair. There was an intensity in her that he could only guess at. He wanted some of that intensity for himself. He craved it. He'd do anything for it.

"Save me," she said, as she had on the first day. "You know what you have to do."

Yes, he did know.

When he removed the headset, it took a few moments to adjust to the "real" world. How strange that there seemed nothing real about it at all. It was just a miserable shadow world compared to the world he had come to know. *Her* world. That was the only reality that mattered now. This one? It was tragic and pointless. Who'd want to exist here?

His parents were sitting there, immersed in their battle. He was almost startled to see how scrawny and malnourished they were. Without him feeding them, had they eaten at all?

While weapons were plentiful in the game, the "real world" wasn't so well equipped. Still, Darion was able to make do. In the end, his parents never saw it coming. How could they, when they were so completely consumed by the zombie attack?

In the game, his parents suddenly stopped fighting, the zombies killed their unmanned avatars, and they were quickly being devoured by rats. Their hard-earned weapons were now free for other players to scavenge.

Darion reached for his headset, ready to return to the girl, but her voice called out from the TV. "No!"

He turned to see the silver-haired girl peering out at him from the TV screen. She was only pixels now. He touched the screen, but couldn't get through to her. This wouldn't do. He longed for her to be injected right into his optic nerves. Why couldn't he? Why would she say no?

"They're not the only ones," she told him. "As long as there are still player-characters, I won't be safe."

"And when they're all gone?" Darion asked.

"Then it's just you and me."

He touched his fingers to the surface of the screen, and she raised her fingers to touch his. He could almost feel her fingertips. Almost. He looked at the headset in his other hand. If he put it on, he knew she would run from him. He'd spend a lifetime searching for her in that world. The only way to get her back was to take on this mission. He dropped the headset to the floor. There was work to do.

The night was chilly, so Darion put on a jacket. He could hear the reports of machine guns, laser fire, and commands being shouted in more than one home on his street. Those noises, he knew, would lead him to where he needed to go. Not just tonight, but tomorrow and all the days beyond. Funny how the knife, still in his hand, was a far more effective weapon than a laser cannon.

"PLEASE, FOR THE LOVE OF GOD, DON'T HURT US!"

"SOMEONE! ANYONE! HELP US!"

Tonight, in Darion's world, he'd be racking up the points.

And in the girl's world, the rats would be feasting.

Midnight Michelangelo

By Neal Shusterman and Terry Black

With the sounds of traffic far below and the dark sky above, sixteen-year-old Micah Andrus hung suspended between the sky and the angry city. He didn't think about how high he was; he thought only about the task at hand: his masterpiece.

Silver paint hissed out the tip of a spray can, leaving a dazzling streak on the metal surface. *Just a few minutes more,* Micah told himself. *Just a few minutes more and I'll be done.* He had to remind himself not to look down, or he might lose his balance and fall in front of the cars that shot down the freeway. His work on the overpass was almost done; just a few finishing touches.

"Micah!" shouted a voice just out of view. "Micah, we've gotta get out of here!" It was Samira. His lookout. He could hear the panic in her voice, but figured it was probably nothing major. She simply wasn't used to this sort of thing. But an instant later, Micah heard the sirens.

"Micah, hurry!" Samira shouted. "They're coming!"

"One sec!" he shouted back. He couldn't stop when he was this close. He had to risk it. Blue and red lights began to play off the colorful work of art in front of him. He clipped the can of silver spray paint onto his mountain-climbing harness and grabbed the blue paint can. Quickly he filled in the blue iris of an eye that was two feet high. Below him he heard the slamming of a car door.

"That's enough, Picasso!" The voice of a policeman, bellowing through a bullhorn. "Get down here!"

But Micah wasn't about to be caught. Not tonight. He rappelled from the steel face of the freeway overpass and swung in a wide arc to the right. He stopped at the edge of his great painting and sprayed the initials *M. M.* in bright red. It was a tag that was getting to be known around the city, as great masterpieces of spray-paint art appeared overnight.

Nobody knew who M. M. really was. But everyone knew what it stood for: Midnight Michelangelo. As mysterious as Banksy—and soon to have the same renown, if he had anything to say about it.

Two policemen climbed the girder of the overpass to get to him. He rappelled once more, his harness holding him tight as he swung, a human pendulum, to the left. Then he unhooked himself and scurried down a fence to freedom, leaving the police confounded.

Samira was waiting for him. "Were those initials really worth getting arrested for?"

But Micah only smiled. His head was pounding. It was the fumes from the spray paint that gave him his headaches, he was sure, but his art was worth any amount of pain.

They were many blocks away by the time dawn began to break, and Micah had to turn back and look at his creation. The sun told a truth about his talent that the stark streetlights could not.

His work was a high-tech futurescape, filled with swooping monorails, bottomless steel canyons, glass skyscrapers reaching beyond the heavens, and sleek, silvery robotic faces. It covered the metal span of the overpass, looking down at the dull, urban sprawl around it. "It's incredible, Micah," said Samira.

"It's my best yet." As the sun grew brighter, the streaks of silver paint turned to gold.

"Every color has a voice, every texture a soul. . . ."

In art class that day, Micah sat at his desk half-asleep as Ms. Boyle spouted forth her philosophy of art. Few kids in class were listening, and the ones who were really had no clue anyway. Micah dozed off. He was startled awake by Ms. Boyle's tapping him roughly on the shoulder. She pointed to his blank canvas. "Working in white today?" she asked.

"Uh . . . I'm waiting for inspiration," answered Micah.

Ms. Boyle smirked. "Inspiration requires consciousness, Mr. Andrus."

Snickers erupted around the room, then a voice behind him whispered, "Guess you can't paint unless someone's filling out an arrest warrant, huh, Micah?" It was Dion Holt, of course. To Micah, Dion was everything bad about the world. He was handsome, arrogant, and brainless. The poster boy of privilege. He was also Samira's boyfriend. Sure, Samira might love Micah's artwork, but it was Dion who had her attentions in every other way. Somewhere along the line, Samira had let it slip to Dion that Micah was the Midnight Michelangelo. Ever since then, Dion taunted Micah with the information—always threatening to announce it to the world. It was just one more frustration in a life that was anything but a picnic—but Micah had learned to live with it. After all, lots of artists lived tortured lives, and Dion Holt certainly qualified as torture.

Micah tried to slip out quietly when the bell rang, but Ms. Boyle caught him and insisted he stay after class. He heard Dion snicker as he left the room, with his beefy arm slung over Samira's shoulder.

"Someone oughta spray-paint 'loser' on his forehead," Dion said.

Samira threw Micah an apologetic look, as if it was her job to apologize for Dion, and then they both got lost in the crowd of students filing out of the room. Micah continually wondered how Samira could like someone like Dion—but then Micah figured it was that same poor judgment that made her hang around with him as well.

When everyone was gone, Micah turned to Ms. Boyle. "I can explain about sleeping in class," he said. He was prepared to make up any and every excuse, except the truth, but Ms. Boyle would have none of it.

"I'm sure you can explain," she said. "You have a great imagination. Have you ever thought of putting it to good use?"

Micah shrugged. "I have been."

"Yes," Ms. Boyle said with a frown, "but you can't make a living breaking the law . . . Michelangelo."

Hearing her say the name made him flinch, and he was sure she saw it. Samira knew about who he was, and so did Dion. There were other kids in school who suspected, but for a teacher to know—that meant trouble. The dull ache in his head began to pound with the fury of a jackhammer.

"I've got a headache, Ms. Boyle. I really have to go." He tried to slip out of the room, but she stood in his way.

"Your work is great, Micah," she told him. "I can spot it anywhere. I especially like the robot ninjas on the side of the unemployment office." Micah thought she would make a move to get the principal, but she didn't. Could it be that she genuinely liked his work?

"You mean you won't tell?"

"I'm not the art police," she answered. "But I hate to see talent like yours going to waste."

That hurt. "Thousands of people see my stuff," Micah said proudly.

"But they condemn it as trash," insisted Ms. Boyle. "That's the difference, Micah—no one ever sandblasted the Sistine Chapel's ceiling."

Micah looked down at his paint-stained shoes. "So?"

"So your work should be shown in galleries, winning awards. You should earn respect, not handcuffs."

Micah scoffed and looked away, pretending he was bored, pretending he didn't care. But in truth, he was savoring every word she said. He closed his eyes and let the compliments sink in, hoping that maybe they'd drive his headache away.

"Your work has a soul, Micah," she said. "It has a life of its own."

And neither of them knew how very true that was.

That afternoon, Micah met Samira at *The Martians*. It had gotten to be a habit, meeting in secret, because neither of them wanted Dion to know. *The Martians* was one of Micah's best works. Red faces and bright, luminous eyes stretched the entire length of the wall. But today these Martians would die.

"I tried to stop them, Micah, but they wouldn't listen. They won't even admit it's art!" Samira said to him as he arrived. "I'm sorry, Micah. There was nothing I could do. They had already started when I got here. . . ."

"Started what?" Micah rounded the corner to see workmen with paint rollers covering Micah's Martian masterpiece with dull gray paint, the same color as the rest of the city. His heart sank. What had taken him days in preparation and planning to create was thoughtlessly being destroyed in a matter of minutes. He winced at the sight. It felt as if they were painting the walls of his skull. He could feel the pain in his head swell with his anger . . .

. . . and that was when he heard them. It was hollow and distant, but he heard them just the same.

The Martians.

He could hear their muffled, wailing cries as they died, suffocated by the thick, greasy paint. But there was something more—for as he took another look at the Martian faces, he could swear he saw them scowling darkly. He hadn't painted them like that. Their expressions had been glorious, not sinister.

"I . . . I didn't paint this," Micah said.

"What? What do you mean?" said Samira.

"These faces, they're all wrong." He moved closer to one of the twisted faces of the Martians, and in the shadows of the painting he saw a hulking shape. It was dark, painted in deep burnt umber. The shadow had strange, serpentine coils and eyes like smoldering embers.

"What is that?" mumbled Micah. But before he could have a better look, a workman painted it out of existence.

Micah's mom wasn't an artist. Nor was she an art collector. Unless of course, you counted all the tacky paintings she had bought from Amazon. She was a single mom working two jobs, which didn't leave her much time for things like art. As for Micah's dad, he had a new family in another city, and only came to gather Micah for a Christmas visit—more out of obligation than anything else. "'Tis the season to feel guilty," Micah had sung to his father when he picked him up last Christmas Day. The man had not been amused by the truth.

But Micah had his art—and that was something he could always count on. And so, while Mom dozed in front of the TV each night, Micah sat in his room, lovingly sketching the early drafts of the next great paintings he planned. Tonight's sketch was another alien landscape, this one full of tall, graceful creatures, chocolate-brown, with silky, gossamer wings. They swooped and soared around crystalline towers. But tonight, Micah couldn't keep his focus. Maybe it was the voices of the Martians and the strangeness of their faces. It had to be his imagination, he decided—sleep deprivation could do weird things to the mind. Still, he couldn't stop thinking about it.

Even in the privacy of his room, there was something that didn't quite feel right. He kept imagining that some hideous, tentacled beast was just behind him, ready to grab him. But when he turned, there was nothing there but the pack of his rappelling harness hanging on his closet door. He tried to ignore the feeling, but he knew it was there, just like he knew he had seen a creature in his painting of the Martians.

Four a.m. The brick wall of the building turned bloodred and pale blue, then bloodred again.

"Micah, it's the police!" shouted Samira.

The flashing light from the squad car painted the entire night red and blue. Micah quickly hooked his spray cans onto his harness, ready to make a quick exit—but something was different tonight. His hand was shaking, but not from fear. It was trembling in a way he couldn't control. Samira, standing on the fire escape beside him, reached out to him. "Come on, Micah," she said desperately. He reached out to her, puzzled by his trembling hand. Why had his hand started shaking like that? And why now? He pulled the emergency release of his harness. But in his confusion, he pulled too soon. Micah slipped out of Samira's hand and fell three stories into a pile of trash bags, and right into the arms of the Los Angeles Police Department.

He wouldn't call his mother—she didn't need this kind of trouble. Instead he gambled and called the one person he felt he could trust. Luckily, she showed up. Somehow, he knew he could count on the support of another artist. Ms. Boyle arrived at the police station less than half an hour after Micah called.

"Are you the mother?" asked the cop on duty.

"His parents couldn't make it," said Ms. Boyle. "I'm his teacher."

The cop rolled his eyeballs.

"What is he supposed to have done?" demanded Ms. Boyle.

The cop crossed his arms. "You might say he painted the town red." Then he threw a nasty glance at Micah. "Do you know how long we've been trying to catch this 'Midnight Michelangelo'?"

Ms. Boyle was too smart to ID Micah to the police. "Are you kidding me?" she said.

"It's no joke," said the cop. "He's defaced half the city."

Ms. Boyle laughed. "Officer, you've seen those murals. Do you really think that a high-school kid could do that?"

The cop, who a moment before had seemed so sure of himself, began to stutter just a bit. "Well, we caught him at the scene of the crime with a spray can."

Ms. Boyle shook her head and looked at the cop as if he was an idiot. "You caught him tagging, Officer. That's all."

Tagging? Micah bristled at the suggestion. "I'm not a tagger," he said, insulted. But Ms. Boyle threw him a warning glance, and he shut up.

She turned back to the officer. "I think you've sufficiently traumatized this boy for a first offense. You can rest assured that his initials will go nowhere but on his homework from now on." Still the cop seemed unconvinced, until Ms. Boyle laughed again. "The Midnight Michelangelo! Are the police so desperate to find this guy that they have to pin it on a kid?"

That did it.

"All right," conceded the officer. "Considering the kid's age, we're willing to cut him some slack. But I don't want to see him here again."

Ms. Boyle grabbed Micah and escorted him out.

They talked a lot on the drive home: about his talent, his troubles, his potential. But there was one thing Ms. Boyle asked that seemed to ring in his aching mind even after she had dropped him off at home. She asked him how often he painted.

"Whenever the inspiration hits me," Micah told her.

Ms. Boyle frowned. "Inspiration is a fine thing, Micah. But if it hits you too hard, sometimes you've got to hit back."

The next morning, Micah noticed the vein.

He had woken up to another horrible headache—the way he had almost every day for the past month. He doused his face with cold water. Then, dragging a brush through his matted hair, he saw it. On his temple. A single vein. And as he looked at it, it seemed to spread, as if it was growing, pulsing, thick and purple. He gasped and snapped his eyes shut. Then, when he dared to open his eyes and confront his reflection, it was gone.

It's my stressed-out imagination, he told himself, *like the creature in* The Martians. Playing it safe, he brushed his hair over his forehead where the spot had been. *It'll be all right,* Micah told himself.

And everything *was* all right, until he approached the front steps of school. That was when he was confronted by a smiling Dion Holt and his entourage of varsity lettermen and other assorted goons. "Micah, I'm glad to see you're here," Dion said in a falsely concerned voice.

"Why wouldn't I be here?" muttered Micah.

"After last night, I thought you might be in juvie or something," said Dion, loud enough to get the attention of just about every kid who was within shouting distance. They all turned to stare at Micah.

"I don't know what you're talking about," mumbled Micah. He tried to edge around Dion, but Dion's goons kept him from going anywhere.

"Sure you know what I'm talking about," said Dion. "Samira told me all about it. I'm just glad you didn't get her arrested as an accomplice." There was a circle around them now. The same circle of kids that always seems to arrive before a fight.

"Excuse me. I've got class."

"Obviously not much," snorted Dion. The few kids around them who got the joke laughed out loud. Micah could feel his head beginning to throb. He could feel that thick vein pulsing and wondered if everyone could see it.

"You don't want to mess with me today, Dion," Micah warned.

Dion chuckled. "All right, tough guy," he said.

Micah's headache continued to pound. "Just get out of my face. Why don't you go smash some beer cans on your forehead, or whatever you do for intellectual stimulation."

"You know why Samira hangs out with you, don't you?" Dion said with a nasty hiss in his voice. "She feels sorry for you."

Meltdown. Micah lost it. He pounced on Dion, like a rabid,

snarling dog. Dion clearly wasn't expecting it and was knocked down by the force of Micah's pounce. They both crashed to the pavement. Micah wasn't much for fighting, but few people had ever gotten him this angry. He windmilled his fists as hard and fast as he could, smashing them into Dion over and over again. And then, from the corner of his eye, he saw it. A tentacle suddenly appeared and coiled around Dion's neck. It squeezed tighter. Dion's face turned red. He was gasping. Far away, as if through a thousand layers of cotton, Micah heard a voice.

"Micah, stop it!" It was Samira. He turned to look at her. She was standing next to him, screaming down at him, but he could barely hear her voice. "I said, stop it!"

When Micah turned back to Dion, it wasn't a tentacle but his own hand that was squeezing Dion's throat. Shocked, Micah pushed himself off Dion.

"Are you out of your mind?" screamed Samira.

Dion staggered to his feet, clutching his throat and gasping for air. "Your charity case just turned into a basket case!"

Samira went over to Dion to make sure he was okay. Micah couldn't stand the sight of the two of them together. But he had to accept that Dion was right—Samira just hung out with Micah because she felt sorry for him.

"You two deserve each other!" Micah shouted. Then he ran off. He was cutting school, but he didn't care. What did it matter now?

"Micah, wait!" Samira called to him, running. Finally she caught up with him, and he turned on her.

"Why don't you just write it all over the walls, Samira? 'Micah Andrus just got arrested.' Here, I'll lend you a spray can."

"It wasn't like that," insisted Samira. "Dion's dad's a lawyer. I told Dion because I thought he might help."

"What makes you think I need help?" shouted Micah.

"Well, just look at you. It's not just what happened last night.

You—you don't look right, Micah. You've been acting weird." She grabbed him by the shoulder, forcing him to look her in the eye. "Something's wrong, isn't it?"

Almost as an afterthought he reached to touch the vein on his forehead, but it was gone.

"Micah," she said. "Tell me what's wrong."

There was genuine concern in her voice. But the fact was, he didn't know what the problem was, or how deep it went.

Then Micah's world grew one shade darker.

There was a commotion ahead of them. Crowds of people were huddled in front of an electronics store. They were all looking up at an outside wall—the same wall Micah had started working on the night before . . . before he was taken away by the cops.

"That is, like, so cool," someone said.

Micah looked up and had to grab a lamppost to keep himself from falling. It was impossible. There, before his eyes, was an immense horrorscape that covered the entire six-story brick wall. What was supposed to be beautiful winged creatures had morphed into cruelly misshapen predators with steel fangs and flesh-shredding claws. Instead of a metropolis of delicate crystal spires, the raptors flew over a blighted ruin of a city. And there, even larger than the hulking shape he had seen lurking in the mural of the Martians, was a tentacled creature looming in the shadows of this painting too.

A policeman spoke with the shop owner.

"Don't worry," said the policeman. "We'll catch him sooner or later."

The shop owner laughed. "Catch him? I want to hire him. You can't buy this kind of promotion."

"Who do you think this guy is?" someone asked, after the cop had left.

"I don't know," the shop owner shouted to the crowd, "but anyone who brings me this Midnight Michelangelo gets half off any item."

Micah stood there, feeling his eyes begin to glaze over. Samira nudged him.

"Why don't you tell him? Maybe he'll pay you to do another one."

"But that's not what I painted," shouted Micah. Then Samira turned to the crowd. "Hey! He's here. It's the Midnight Michelangelo!" Suddenly Micah was the center of attention, and the owner of the shop stormed through the crowd.

"You? You're gonna tell me this kid did that painting?"

Micah shook his head. "No, no, it's a mistake. I didn't do it!"

"He goes out every night," explained Samira. "He did the Martians at the bus depot and the robots by the river—I was with him when he did those. Are you going to hire him like you said?"

Micah turned to Samira. "You were with me," he said. "You saw what I was painting, and it wasn't that!"

Samira looked at the mural and shrugged. "I was up close. I couldn't see the whole thing."

Micah began to panic. There had to be a way to prove what his painting was supposed to be. Then he realized he did have proof. He had his original sketch! He reached into his backpack, pulled it out, and unfolded it, showing it for everyone to see. "See! This is what I was painting last night, you see?" The crowd pressed forward to look at it and murmured in admiration. Some people applauded.

"I'll hire you for another one," said the shop owner. "We'll work out the details later."

Samira looked at the crumpled piece of paper stretched between Micah's shaking hands and gave him a half grimace, half smile.

"It certainly is . . . impressive," she said, "in a twisted sort of way."

Confused, Micah turned to look at the paper himself. His hands, as badly as they were shaking, began trembling even more violently.

Because his sketch reflected the same bleak and awful mural in front of him.

"That is so cool, man," said someone behind him.

"You know, most people don't want the cops to catch you," said an old woman, then she grinned and whispered, "My favorite is the werewolves on the federal building."

"Werewolves?" said Micah. "*What* werewolves?"

He walked home alone, but by the time he reached his block, he realized he was running. When he got to his room, he took every last sketch off his wall and out of every drawer and threw them away. Then he took every spray can he could find and tossed them into the trash. He wasn't satisfied until the trash was dumped down the garbage chute, bound for his apartment building's compactor.

All the while, he could hear the sounds in his aching head. A mocking laughter, the screech of far-off predators, and the wet, slithery sound of a tentacled creature moving closer.

The next morning, there was a mural on the lockers at school. Not just one locker, but spread across an entire hallway. It would have been bad enough if the mysterious mural was just your typical nightmare. But this one had a very special guest star: Dion Holt.

In this mural, Dion was being mauled by a horrible clawed monster—half lobster, half human—but that wasn't the worst part, because in the mural's background a multitentacled beast looked on, eating popcorn. The creature, painted more clearly than before, looked like a cross between an octopus . . . and a human brain.

Samira glared at the mural, and then at Micah, with an anger and disgust she had never shown him before. "Micah, what is wrong with you? This is sick!"

"I had nothing to do with it!" screamed Micah. "It wasn't me." But there in the corner were the initials, just like there always were. *M. M.*

Dion stood before the perfect likeness of himself and, amazingly, held his temper. His friends quickly gathered in front of the mural, yelling, "Hey, man, kick his ass!" And more kids arrived on the scene, joining in on the group rage, just wanting to see a fight. But Dion shook his head.

"What a wonderful 'work of art,'" Dion said with a bitter smile. "I want the principal to see this. I want the cops to see it." Then his million-dollar smile widened. "Thanks, Micah," he said. "I couldn't have done a better job of getting you expelled."

Ignoring Dion, Micah turned to Samira, pleading. "I swear I didn't do it. I threw all my paint away yesterday. See! There's none left." He zipped open his backpack all the way open to prove it—but as he did, half a dozen spray-paint cans clattered out. Samira turned and stormed away, leaving Micah alone with his paint and his awful, awful mural.

Samira didn't stick up for him. Ms. Boyle didn't stick up for him. Micah was on his own this time, as he faced the principal.

"You trespassed after school hours, defaced school property—and look at the disruption you've caused! We have zero tolerance at this school—it's one strike and you're out. Do you know what that means, Mr. Andrus?"

Micah knew what it meant. "It means I'm expelled." He held his throbbing head. It felt as if it would blow apart any second.

"You and your mother will meet with the school board, and we'll go from there. . . ."

Suddenly Micah closed his eyes against the searing pain in his brain. He could feel the vein throbbing in his head. It felt as if something in his skull was trying to bang itself out. When Micah opened his eyes, there was a tentacle rising over the chair behind the principal. He wanted to warn the man, but Micah was frozen. He began to breathe in deep, sharp gasps.

"Are you all right, son? What's wrong?"

Tentacles loomed behind Principal Crenshaw, and one of them

reached over, grabbed a pencil, and drew a ghoulish caricature of the principal on his own desk blotter. The tentacle signed it, and the beast let loose a deep, wet, slithery laugh.

But the principal heard nothing—saw nothing. Even when he turned and looked straight at the awful gray tentacle, he didn't see it.

Micah got his breathing under control as the tentacles slithered away and disappeared. He knew what he had to do now—everything had suddenly become very clear. The principal turned away to call his mother, and the second he turned, Micah slipped out the door and into the hallway.

A line of silver spray paint trailed down the empty school hall, and Micah followed it. He tracked it to a doorway and down a creaky set of stairs, into the dank basement of the ancient school. It was a place littered with broken-down desks, battered shelves, and mildewed textbooks. Down here, every surface, every wall, every square inch, was covered with graffiti. Micah heard the laughter again—the laughter of the beast.

"Where are you?" Micah screamed. "Come out so I can see you." Something touched his face. He whirled to catch it, but there was nothing there. Nothing but a wet trail of slime on his cheek.

Micah found a fire ax. It was mounted on brackets behind a glass barrier labeled EMERGENCY USE ONLY. Well, he thought, this certainly was an emergency. Micah kicked the glass until it shattered, reached in, and took the ax in both hands.

"Hey, slimeball!" he shouted. "I've got something for you!"

In the dark recess he could hear the tantalizing hiss of a spray can. He inched forward, looking from side to side, searching for the beast that had grown in the shadow-painted corners of his own head.

"Come out, come out, wherever you are!" he shouted. Micah laughed at his own ridiculousness. The furnace came on and shuddered violently, then let out a deep rumble.

Something moved! Micah turned and swung, knocking over a pyramid of paint cans. They spilled a rainbow of colors across the floor. Again, he heard the laughter. It only made Micah angrier. Too angry to hold back his fury. He swung the ax in every direction, splintering a desk, cleaving a filing cabinet in two, smashing an old chalkboard until finally he found the monster standing against the round tank of the rusty boiler.

It was awful. A gray mass of throbbing brain tissue, and from it grew thick tentacles—nerve endings that thrashed and flailed like snakes. But worst of all were its eyes. Two pinpoints of red light in a cloud of gray matter.

"Don't do it, Micah," the creature taunted. Micah raised his ax. "You'll be sorry!" said the creature. But Micah couldn't stop himself. He swung the blade in a high arc and brought the ax down with all his might. The blade embedded itself in the boiler with a hollow clang and a blast of white steam.

The creature had tricked him. What little sanity Micah had held on to was gone. The mocking laughter in his head was now unbearable. He pulled the blade from the boiler.

"You missed me!" the creature screamed in his head. "Accept it, Micah, you'll never kill me!" He saw it there again, in the shadows, and he raised his ax to strike it . . . but then he had a better idea. He threw his ax down, opened his backpack, and pulled out a spray can for each hand.

"Oh, you're going to paint me?" taunted the creature. "Be sure to get my good side." The creature turned to show its profile and smiled that slimy brain smile.

"Hold that pose," said Micah. Then he let loose from both spray cans, dousing the creature in a blue-black fog. It laughed again, unbothered by the paint dripping down into the crevices of its cortex—not caring about the jumble of smashed paint cans and spilled enamel that it stood in. But Micah continued spraying. He sprayed a line of paint from the monster to the hot furnace, like a fuse, and as soon as the wet paint touched the furnace, it caught fire.

The creature realized the danger too late. "No!!!"

The flame raced down the paint-fuse toward the puddle of flammable enamel, and instantly the creature burst into flames. It let out an awful, dying wail as it burned, and finally it dissolved into the swirls of burning paint. That was the last thing Micah remembered before he lost consciousness.

He woke up in a hospital room with his mother beside him, holding his hand, and Samira on his other side. His head hurt something awful. "Is it gone?" Micah asked weakly.

"You're going to be all right," Samira said. "They got the tumor in time." Micah had to think very slowly and clearly about what she was saying. Only now did he realize that his head was tightly bandaged.

"Tumor?"

"Yes," said a doctor looking down at him, smiling as doctors do. "One nasty brain tumor," he said. "The good news is that we got the whole thing, and we took it out without damaging any of the surrounding tissue. You're a very lucky young man."

Micah's mom burst into tears.

"You're going to be all right, Micah," she said. "You're going to be all right."

"In a way," said Samira, "you tried to tell us. . . . Going out and painting those 'things,' then not remembering you did it. The doctor said it was your subconscious trying to warn you."

Micah took a deep breath. He supposed he could wrestle with himself forever, trying to figure out whether the creature was real or just a hallucination brought on by a tumor. But thinking about that was a sure way to madness. The important thing was that the monster was out of his head, and out of his life for good. It was a memory he was happy to paint over, and lose forever.

Samira gently held his hand. "I'm sorry about those nasty things I said to you."

Micah smiled. "Hold that pose," he said, never wanting this moment with Samira to end.

Meanwhile, deep down in the hospital basement, a med student tended to the pathology lab. With a sandwich in one hand and a medical instrument in the other, he studied a small, fleshy mass that had settled at the bottom of a jar of formaldehyde. It was a lump of brain tissue, with spidery, tentacle-like dendrites. The label on the jar read: M. ANDRUS.

"So that's a brain tumor," the med student mumbled to himself. "That is one ugly sucker."

He put down his sandwich to clean up the table and then picked it up again on his way out. He didn't notice that the jar of formaldehyde was now empty. He didn't notice that there was something moving between the slices of his bread as he took a bite of his sandwich.

But a few minutes later, he did notice a sudden headache coming on.

Boy on a Stoop

A row of abandoned tenements rots on a neglected city block where few people have reason to tread. There are a million ways to get where you're going without passing down that ruined street; nevertheless, Olivia takes that path to school every day. The buildings have been that way for years, and Olivia feels a strange sort of affinity toward them. In many ways, they are like her: ignored . . . forgotten . . . friendless. Nothing, not even a row of buildings, deserves to be that unloved. So she limps her way down the broken, weed-choked pavement of the condemned street every day.

That's where she sees him.

He sits on the stoop of one of those empty buildings, halfway down the block. It's the only one without a board nailed over the entrance. There's no door, just a dark rectangular hole, rimmed in chiseled plaster. Like her, the boy on the stoop seems about fifteen. He has jet-black hair and features so handsome she can't help but stare at him out of the corner of her eye. She can feel his eyes following her as well, and it embarrasses her—because no boys look at her. More often than not, they just look away. Olivia's glasses are thick, and one eye is slightly clouded from a childhood accident involving a neighbor boy and a stick. Then of course there's that horrible leg brace she's forced to wear on her weak right leg. She has been self-conscious about both her eye and her leg for as long as she can remember, keeping to herself and shying away from other kids. She prefers sticking to her books and her many collections.

So naturally, when she notices this handsome boy looking at her, her face goes red, and she moves out of his sight as quickly as she can.

He is there again as she walks home from school, still sitting on that porch as if he has nothing better to do than calmly watch life pass on the city pavement before him—and he is there the next day too, and the next. Each time he follows her with his eyes as she passes, like a portrait that always seems to stare at you, no matter where you stand. It's easy to deal with being invisible, but being noticed—that is something entirely different.

Does he look at everyone like that or is it only me? wonders Olivia.

Her parents are not problem solvers when it comes to talking through Olivia's troubles. Her father, who works two jobs, is rarely home, and when he is, he's too exhausted to take much time for her. Olivia's mom, who works at a day-care center, is always frazzled, and the last thing she wants to hear at the end of the day is another voice—even her own daughter's.

One night she approaches her mom, who sits up in bed, reading a sappy romance novel. "Mom, am I a good person?" she asks.

Her mother answers without hesitation, "Of course you are, honey."

"Then why don't more people like me?"

This time her mother does hesitate and begins to rub her forehead as if the question has given her a headache. "It's not that they don't like you," she answers, "it's that they don't know you. If you let people know you a little better, then they'll like you a whole lot."

It's easy for her mother to say, but it just doesn't work that way at school. There's a cruel pecking order, and once you find yourself at the bottom, the other kids won't let you rise above it.

But the boy on the stoop isn't a classmate. He doesn't know her place in the pecking order.

Olivia knows these are dangerous thoughts, because they fill her with the kind of hope that could be her ruin. So she returns to her room and tries to drive thoughts of the boy out of her mind. She reads a book, re-catalogs her various collections—rare coins, stamps, even exotic insects, pinned and labeled in a glass case. But not even her insect collection can keep thoughts of the boy away. In the end, she gives up and closes the case on her tiny impaled bugs, locking it with a shiny silver key. She wishes she could lock away her thoughts of the boy as easily.

The following Monday, a wind blows through the city, marking the arrival of fall. The leaves have already turned and are dropping to the pavement, where they will soon dry into brittle brown shells crunching underfoot. Olivia wears a coat that is too heavy and out of style as she leaves for school.

When she peers down the boy's street, she can see him sitting on the porch again, leaning back on his elbows, relaxed and calm—such a stark contrast to the tension of the city. She approaches him at a slow, steady pace, trying to hide her limp as best she can. Then, when she is in range, she turns to him—looking at him directly, rather than sneaking a glance. He smiles at her and she feels trapped in his deep green eyes. Her heart pounds a mysterious rhythm in her chest—a rhythm of fear and wonderful anticipation—because she knows that today she will say something to him.

But instead she gags on the gum she is chewing and launches into a coughing fit.

"Are you all right?" he asks, getting up and taking a step closer to her.

Feeling like an imbecile, Olivia clears her lungs with a strong, solid cough. The gum flies out and becomes one with the rest of the muck on the broken sidewalk. "I'm fine," she says.

"Good," says the boy. "I wouldn't want you to die. Not here on the sidewalk, anyway."

There is an uncomfortable moment, so Olivia tries to fill it.

"Don't you ever go to school?" she blurts out, and immediately realizes how nasty she must have sounded.

She thinks he might make a nasty comment back to her, and that would end it forever. But instead he just keeps smiling. "I'm homeschooled," he answers.

Now that she has the chance to study his face, she can see how irresistibly perfect it is. It should be illegal, she thinks, for a face to be that perfect. He seems smart, too. Not just smart, but sharp. Sharp as a blade.

"What's your name?" he asks her.

"Olivia."

"I'm Forest." He holds out his hand, and as Olivia reaches forward to shake it, she drops her books. They clatter on the cracked stoop and lie splayed and limp, like accident victims, on the sidewalk.

Olivia tries to kneel to pick them up, but her brace doesn't afford her such quick movements. Forest helps her, and when the books have all been collected, she finds herself sitting beside him on the stoop, like it's the most natural thing in the world.

"Why do you sit here?" she asks him.

Forest shrugs. "It's where I live."

Olivia looks up at the ugly tenement. Five floors of windows, either broken or boarded over, graffiti scrawled on the soot-stained bricks—and if she listens, Olivia imagines she can hear the scuttle of rats. "I'm sorry," says Olivia.

He gives her his strange, enigmatic smile again, and it penetrates her like a sudden blast of radiation. "It's not what you think," he says. "Would you like to see?" He gestures toward the entrance.

Olivia turns to look into it. It's a dark cavity, and the wind echoes inside it, making it sound as if it's breathing. A heavy vine grows out of the darkness disappearing off the edge of the stoop, and she wonders what could possibly grow in a place like that.

"Uh . . . I'll be late for school," she answers, suddenly afraid of his friendship and the place in which he lives.

He grabs one of her books before she hurries off. "Maybe I can read this," he suggests. "And the next time you come, we can talk about it together."

She nods, feeling her familiar shyness closing up her throat so she can't speak. Then she turns and hurries down the street and around the corner to school.

As luck is no friend of Olivia's, it turns out the book he borrowed, *Oddities of Nature*, is the subject of an oral report she is supposed to give that day. Still, she is glad that he took it, because it is one of her favorites, and when she works up the nerve to walk down his street again, they'll have a lot to talk about.

"It doesn't make sense," she tells her mother over dinner that night. "He's living in an abandoned building—I think all by himself—but he says he's homeschooled."

"Maybe we should talk to the police about him," her mother says, trying to hide the suspicion in her voice. "He could be a runaway."

Olivia fiddles with the spaghetti on her plate. "If he's a runaway, he wouldn't be sitting out there like that, for the whole world to see."

"Well, whatever he is, I'd leave him alone if I were you."

Her mother's words linger for the rest of the night. Her mom has always pushed Olivia to make more friends, but at the same time injected her with a heavy dose of paranoia. Here is someone who seems to welcome her friendship. Is she going to throw that away?

As Olivia prepares for bed, she studies her face in the bathroom mirror and wonders what the boy on the stoop sees when he looks at her that could possibly make him smile.

"It's a really interesting book," says Forest as they sit together after school the next day. Always on the stoop—never moving from the stoop. Together they flip through the pages of *Oddities of Nature*. "It's full of weird things."

"I know, isn't it great?" Olivia flashes him a rare smile.

They turn to a page that features a bird with both of its eyes on the same side of its head, then Forest points out his favorite—a frog that can freeze solid as a rock, but comes back to life when defrosted. Olivia turns to a dog-eared page toward the back of the book.

"This is my favorite," she says. "The anglerfish."

The picture shows a strange-looking thing with small eyes, sharp teeth, and a wormlike stalk growing out of its forehead. "It hides behind rocks, or in the dirt," Olivia explains, "so passing fish only see its stalk. The fish think it's a worm and try to munch on it, then the anglerfish jumps out and munches on them."

Forest takes a long look at her. "You really like strange things, huh?"

"Yeah," she says excitedly. "I collect them—strange coins, strange stamps—I even have a whole case full of strange bugs."

"You're not like the other girls," says Forest, never taking his eyes off her.

Olivia looks away. "Are there lots of other girls that you talk to?"

"A few," says Forest, "but you're the most interesting."

Olivia can't look at him. She blushes. It's as if he knows exactly what to say, exactly what she wants to hear. When she dares to glance up at him again, he's grinning mischievously.

"I'll bet I can show you something weird you've never seen before!"

Olivia closes the book. "What?"

He stands up, takes her hand, and moves her toward the dark, peeling hole of the dead tenement building. Olivia grabs the rusting iron railing of the stoop, not letting herself be dragged in.

She thinks of all the things her mother has told her about strangers—and all the warnings she's heard in school, ever since a girl vanished a few weeks before.

"It's okay," Forest says in the softest of voices. "You can trust me."

Somehow she feels certain that she can—that this boy would never do anything to harm her. And besides, everyone was sure that missing girl had just run away.

Olivia loosens her grip on the rusted iron railing and lets herself be led into the dank, decaying building, following the trail of that long, thick vine that grows out the front door. Around her, mildewed paper peels in thick layers, and termite-eaten wooden floors feel soft beneath her feet. Then he leads her through a back door, into paradise.

In the city, most low-rise buildings are built back-to-back, and between them one can sometimes find a courtyard. Those narrow brick courtyards rarely see the sun and are usually filled with weeds and trash. This hidden courtyard, however, surrounded on all sides by condemned buildings, holds a garden.

Olivia has read a book called *Lost Horizon* about a beautiful, magical place in the midst of snow-covered mountains. If there could be such a place in a concrete-and-steel city, then this is it. She has never seen trees and plants so beautiful—wide leaves dense and green, flowers blooming with every color of the rainbow. They all seem to sway in the breeze. They seem to gently reach toward her. Everywhere else in the city, leaves are turning, and trees are dying for the winter, but not here. This is a lush urban jungle. Barely able to catch her breath, she touches a large purple petal that feels like silk.

"But . . . how?"

"Must be an underground spring," Forest suggests, "or maybe just a broken hot-water pipe. Anyway, it's here."

She explores the dense garden with Forest, and he explains the many plants: one that only opens up in twilight and lets off a rich blue light; another that has large round seeds embedded in its branches, which look like eyes, the same shade of green as his. Olivia could swear she saw one of them opening and closing.

It's then that Olivia finally begins to feel just a bit apprehensive. It's getting late; the courtyard has fallen deep into shadow. The afternoon has quickly become dusk.

"I'm glad," Forest says, "that you're not afraid. The others were all afraid."

There are too many things wrong with this picture. Olivia knows just about all of the oddities creation has spat out—but none of the plants here are familiar at all.

And then there's the vine.

Down every path, that singular vine grows, ropy and dense. She follows it with her eyes to find where it ends, for it no longer grows through the door and into the tenement. Now it loops back into the garden, as if someone has moved it. At last she traces a path to its end. It only takes a moment for her to realize the truth—and exactly what it means.

With the sun gone from the sky, a huge leafy pod, two stories tall, has opened up in the southern corner of the garden—and inside is a flower a perfect shade of ocean blue, with a dozen soft petals each as large as her hand.

"Would you like to pick it?" Forest asks.

Olivia looks at him sadly. "Are you my friend?" she asks him.

"Yes, Olivia," he answers. "We're friends to the end."

Olivia looks at the beautiful flower, and at the beautiful boy, then she reaches down and lifts up the heavy green vine. As she holds it, she can clearly see how it grows right into the base of his spine, like a tail—or more like an umbilical cord.

"I knew you were special," she says to him, her voice barely a whisper. "But I didn't know how special."

The truth is, there is only one plant in here; it just has many different faces. Whether it evolved from the slime of the city, or whether it came here from someplace else, it thrives, like an anglerfish.

This handsome, charming boy is merely the worm to lure its prey.

She's terrified now, but tells herself that she doesn't care—that her fear doesn't matter. Something as beautiful as this garden, as beautiful as him, deserves to live . . . even if it means that she has to die. There is almost something soothing and comforting about being devoured by this strange, exotic creature. Becoming a part of it.

Forest takes her cold hands in his. "I need you to pick the flower, Olivia . . . please."

Gently he guides her toward the large, lovely leafed pod in the corner of the garden, which looms like a giant cavern. As they draw closer, she can see thick black thorns, like jagged teeth, hidden beneath the leaves.

"We'll be together forever," whispers Forest, "and you'll never feel lonely ever again."

She would have let him throw her inside—she's not afraid to die. But she *is* afraid of pain. In the end it's that fear that drives her to action. Those thorns would hurt more than the teeth of a shark.

Just as Forest gives her one final push toward the open mouth of the cavern, Olivia digs in her heels, reaches up, and tears off one of the cavern's tooth-thorns. With a rush of air, the giant mouth snaps shut on the hem of her dress.

"No!" she screams. The green cavern opens its mouth once more, baring its black teeth, and the entire thing lurches closer. It clamps down on her leg—she can feel the pain shoot up her whole body. Forest backs away, his vine trailing into the thick underbrush.

"I'm sorry," he says. "I'm sorry, Olivia." The giant jaws open once more and chomp down again, getting more of her.

But it's not over yet. The thorn in her hand is sharp as a carving knife. She knows she can't fight the thing trying to eat her, so she reaches out and grabs the vine—Forest's vine—and she slices into it.

"Don't!" screams Forest, in a sudden terror more powerful than her own.

She feels the jaw behind her loosen its grip on her leg. She slices into the vine again. Around her all the leaves, all the flowers, begin to rustle and shake. She pulls on the vine, and Forest falls over. Then at last she finds the thinnest part of his umbilical cord, jams the knife into it, and slices through it again and again, until she has cut it in two, separating Forest now and forever from the plant.

The boy-thing screams, and his chilling wail echoes off the brick walls of the condemned buildings around them. Then she feels the pressure on her leg release. The leaves around her wilt and drop, the flowers disappear into their buds, and in a moment all is silence.

She pries open the jaws of the cavernous plant. She's bleeding, but not as badly as she thought. It's her leg brace that's saved her. The thing couldn't bite through it! She pulls herself free, and the dead green jaws close with a sickening *thwump*.

She goes over to Forest, who lies on the ground, as still as the rest of the garden, not breathing. But then, he never breathed in the first place, did he?

She cradles his head in her arms, brushes his dark hair out of his face, and with tears in her eyes, she kisses him. Then she grabs him by the arms and drags him across the dark ground of the dead garden.

A few weeks later they tear the whole block down and find just what they expected to find in the courtyard—the dry, crumbled remains of dead city weeds, although the weeds here seem to have grown much thicker than most other places.

Olivia always leaves for school early these days—but she doesn't go straight to school. Instead she goes to the basement of her apartment building. There is a storage room down there, a room that few people know about, and no one—not even the building manager—ever visits. It is one of the many forgotten places of the city.

Inside the claustrophobic room sits a beautiful boy with sparkling green eyes. His eyes stare up fearfully at Olivia as she enters.

"So you're finally awake," says Olivia. "You've been unconscious for over a month."

Beside the boy is a ceramic planter filled with rich potting soil, and above him hangs a fluorescent grow-light that makes his soft skin look blue. He is very thin, but Olivia knows that will be only temporary. The boy shifts to reveal the knotty vine growing from the small of his back and into the planter, where it has taken root. Olivia pours in a pitcher of water spiked with a healthy dose of Miracle-Gro. Then she takes a hamster from her pocket and releases it on the ground.

"You're going to be fine," Olivia tells him calmly. "I have a green thumb, you know. I'll nurse you back to health."

A small tuber has already grown from the pot, and at its end is a fist-sized pod. The hamster sniffs at the pod; the pod opens and snaps closed around the hamster without a sound. The boy barely seems to notice. Eating is an automatic response.

"Eventually you'll need larger things," Olivia whispers, "but I'll take care of that, too. I'll take care of everything."

The boy opens his mouth to speak, but his voice is raspy from his many weeks of sleep. "Why?" he asks. "Why have you done this?"

"Because you're my friend," she answers, happy and in control. "You're my friend . . . and you'll talk with me, and you'll play games with me, and we'll have good times together for the rest of our lives, won't we, Forest?"

And as she says it, she brings out a huge pair of gardening shears and sets them gingerly on a shelf as a warning.

Forest shudders at the sight of the shears. "Yeah," he says in weak but terrible dread. "Anything you want, Olivia . . . Anything you want."

Olivia smiles again as she gazes lovingly at him, then she turns and limps out the door. With a shiny silver key, she locks all three dead bolts behind her.

Outside, the day is cold, but that doesn't matter, because now something warm and wonderful fills Olivia's heart. How good it is to be blessed with a friend like Forest!

Butterball

Like the slow, blood-chilling creak of a rising coffin lid, the oven door fell open. Out of a wave of heat it rose, slithering off the rack, onto the open oven door, then finally dropping to the floor with a splat. It stalked forward, its juices sizzling on the faded linoleum tile. It had no feet, only raw knubs of bone. It had no head, and yet it seemed to know exactly where it had to go.

The woman stood at the sink peeling potatoes. She had no idea. She thought the pressure around her leg was just her five-year-old giving her a hug—and when she turned to see what was truly there, it was too late to do anything about it. All she could do was scream as it gripped her apron and climbed, shimmying higher and higher until it reached the counter, where it flopped, excreting a steaming dollop of stuffing. Then it grabbed the utensil. It knew the object's purpose—it knew exactly what it was doing. The woman could only stare in horrified disbelief as it raised the utensil high over its head, squeezed down on the rubber bulb, and soaked its own bloated body in the cloudy liquid that had been boiled from its flesh. Then, in a single bound, it leapt from the counter to the oven, landing square in the pan.

The woman, her wits finally gathered, raced to the oven and slammed it shut, trapping the infernal fowl in an inferno cranked to 325 degrees.

Her husband came up behind her. "What was that?" he asked.

The woman took a long, slow breath, and a swallow that forced her terror back down to the hungry pit of her stomach.

"Self-basting turkey," she replied.

The Bob Squad

"This is highly irregular," said the visitor at the foot of Bobby Jarvis's bed. Actually, it was one of seven visitors, standing there peering down at Bobby as if they had nothing better in the world to do but watch him sleep. None of them should have been there at two o'clock in the morning.

Just a moment ago, Bobby had been dreaming of scoring the winning goal for his hockey team. Bonnie Hermosa (whose very name meant beautiful—both of them!) was in the audience, blowing him a kiss. It was the finest dream he had ever remembered having—so vivid and real that it hardly seemed a dream at all. Then all at once he found himself back in his bed with seven strangers scrutinizing him.

"Huh? Am I still dreaming?" he asked, only halfway out of sleep.

"I'm afraid it's no dream, Bobby." The man who spoke was tall and slim, with a shock of cotton-white hair. "I wish it were a dream, but it's not."

Bobby briefly wondered if he was in a hospital ward—after all, these men and women were all in white suits. But this was his room, not a hospital; and besides, these visitors weren't wearing doctor's coats—these were tailored white business suits. Their shirts and blouses were midnight blue, and in them, Bobby could swear he saw stars.

"Who are you?" Bobby pulled his knees up under his covers. "Mom!" he called. "Dad!"

A hand clapped gently over his mouth. Startled, he turned to see that the hand belonged to a wise-looking woman, tall and matronly. "You shouldn't speak now," she suggested. "Not until you understand."

"Yes," said the white-haired man. "Don't make this any worse than it already is." Another woman, plump with a grandmotherly smile, pushed the door to his room closed.

Bobby pulled the hand away from his mouth. "What are you all doing in my room?"

No one spoke. The visitors just looked to one another, as if no one wanted to be the first to explain. Bobby had to admit this group didn't look very threatening, but anyone who mysteriously appeared in someone's room was highly suspect.

The white-haired man shook his head. "This won't do. This won't do at all."

A short, bespectacled man with a clipboard leaned in close to Bobby, studying him like a specimen in a petri dish. "Perhaps," he said, "he should go back to sleep."

"Quite right!" said the white-haired man. "Go back to sleep, Bobby. Maybe we'll be gone by morning."

"But . . ."

"No buts!"

"He never listens to anyone!" complained yet another one—this one with dark, spooky eyes.

"Close your eyes immediately!" insisted the white-haired man.

Bobby did as he was told, but opened his eyes only a moment later to find all seven of them still staring at him intently. All but the short one, who was jotting things down on his clipboard.

"Mom!" Bobby screamed. "Dad!"

The white-haired man motioned to the plump woman. "Could you see that the parents' slumber is undisturbed?" The plump woman smiled and walked through the door. Not out of the door, not around the door, but *through* it, as if the door was not even there.

Although Bobby Jarvis had never been accused of being the sharpest tool in the shed, he could put two and two together. He knew that odds were, when someone walked through a solid door, something out of the ordinary was going on. Bobby gasped, then groaned, feeling his dinner rising from the unspeakable depths of his gut.

The white-haired man raised an eyebrow, and the bespectacled man shook his head and made more notes on his clipboard.

Then a lithe, graceful woman stepped forward. "I'll ease his way," she said, then produced from behind her a harp—a huge thing much taller than she was, and much too large to ever fit through the door of Bobby's room, much less hide behind her all this time. He opened his mouth to ask how it had gotten there, but the moment she began to play, Bobby felt his jaw relaxing, along with every other muscle in his body. She played a soothing tune that lulled his concerns, and drew down the lids of his eyes. His mind began to drift, and soon he found himself sailing across the ice again, dreaming of hockey stardom.

"Rise and shine!"

Bobby's mother snapped open the curtains with a brightness in her voice that made Bobby want to crawl deeper under his covers. There ought to be a law against "morning people," he thought. Especially when that morning person was your mother.

"Upski and outski!" she shrilled. "It's a beautiful day, and you don't want to be late for school."

Bobby opened his eyes. His mother stood by the window. His seven visitors stood around her.

"Aaaah!" screamed Bobby. He suddenly remembered that odd dream—but it hadn't been a dream, had it?

"What's wrong?" asked his mother.

He pointed to the unwelcome guests. "Don't you see them?!"

His mother looked at him, then glanced around the room, then out of the window. "See who?"

The short, bespectacled man shook his head. "This is bad," he said.

"Yes, exceptionally bad," said the white-haired man.

The one in the back with spooky eyes and crazy hair pushed his way to the front. "What a waste of life you are, Bobby," he said, but almost instantly the plump woman came forward.

"Don't listen to him! You're special, Bobby. If you can see us, that proves you're very special."

"There!" said Bobby, turning to his mother. "Don't you hear them?"

He bounded out of bed, grabbed his mother by the shoulders, and turned her to look at the seven, who just sighed and folded their arms. "Do you see them now?"

His mother shook her head. "Pleading insanity will not get you excused from school." Then she left to get breakfast ready.

When she was gone, the plump woman closed the door. "It will be all right, Bobby. You'll see."

"It's the end of the world," announced the spooky-eyed guy.

"It's nothing of the sort," said the white-haired man, taking charge. "Now see here, Bobby—"

"No! You see here!" Bobby yelled. "This is my house, my room, so take all your ghosts and go haunt somebody else!"

The white-haired man burst out laughing. "Ghosts? You think we're ghosts?" The rest began to chuckle as well.

Bobby frowned, not sure what to think anymore. "Aren't you?"

The white-haired man took a step closer. "Why don't you take a better look?"

And so Bobby did. As far as he could tell, they were still wearing the same white suits from the night before, but then he noticed that their shirts and blouses were no longer midnight blue. Now they were a brisk morning blue, speckled with puffs of gray and white, mimicking the clouds just outside his window. Then as Bobby took in each of their faces, it occurred to him that there was something familiar about each of them. The white-haired man's decisive eyes; the plump woman's soft smile; the shifty stance of the spooky one; the gentle movements of the harp player's hands; the scrutinizing gaze of the bespectacled man; the whispers of the tall woman. Even the pretty, silent girl who sat in the background as if waiting for a time that had not yet come seemed familiar.

"I know you," Bobby said, confused. "All of you . . ."

"Yes," answered the white-haired man, "and no."

Bobby noticed something odd about the fabric of their suits. It wasn't like anything he'd ever seen before. He reached out and ran his fingers along the white-haired man's sleeve. It was smoother than velvet, and finer than silk. "What is it?" Bobby asked.

"Watch," he said.

All at once their suit coats lifted open, as if from a billowing breeze, and they stretched outward until Bobby could see that they weren't tailored suits at all. They were wings.

Bobby gasped in astonishment.

"Allow me to introduce myself," said the white-haired man. "I am Bartholomew, and we . . . are your guardian angels."

Bobby heard it, but he was still too dazzled by the spectacle of their open wings to say anything.

"You see," explained Bartholomew, "every human is attended to by a host of seven angels."

"We monitor you," said the bespectacled one.

"We advise you," said the tall woman.

"We caress your moods and emotions," said the harp player.

"We tend your inner fire," said the patient, pretty one.

"We comfort you," said the plump woman.

"We put obstacles in your way to challenge you," said the creepy one, with an even creepier little laugh.

Then Bartholomew gestured to the others and the fluttering of wings ceased. Bobby watched, entranced, as the wings folded over them, becoming simple white suits once more. "There are over fifty-six billion of us," Bartholomew said, "seven for every human, and we travel unseen within the lives of humankind."

"But . . . I can see you."

"Yes, you can." Bartholomew thoughtfully rubbed his chin. "Now you can understand our problem."

Bobby sat back down on his bed, trying to come to grips with what he had been told. He had always thought—hoped—that there were such things as guardian angels, protecting him, guiding him. But hoping for such things—even believing in them—was very different from seeing them standing in his room taking notes. He suddenly found his bladder several sizes too small.

"I gotta use the bathroom." Bobby slipped out the door and across the hall to the bathroom, glad to be away from them. But to his horror, he found all seven of them waiting in there for him. The bathroom was small even for one person, but now it held Bobby and seven angels. Three stood in the bathtub, two stood on the toilet tank, one hovered above the sink and another hung from the shower curtain rod.

"Do you mind?" asked Bobby. "Can't I even take a leak by myself?"

"Not a chance," said the bespectacled man, busy scribbling. "We're with you everywhere. We see every pick of your nose, every scratch of your butt, every cookie you steal from the cookie jar."

"Even the things you don't want anyone to see," said the spooky one.

"But we don't mind," said the plump woman. "It's our job."

"Now go ahead and do your business," said Bartholomew, "or we'll be late for school."

Bobby failed his math test that day, even though math was his best subject. It wasn't that he didn't know the work, he just couldn't concentrate. How could anyone concentrate with an entourage of seven angels hovering around you, taking notes, looking over your shoulder, and constantly telling you what to do?

"Do the easy math problems first," one suggested.

"No, do the hard ones first; get them out of the way," suggested another.

"Don't do any of them, run out the back door."

"Copy the answers from the kid next to you."

They were like a living multiple-choice test. So many voices, so much advice, and not all of it good.

Hockey practice was a crash and burn. Although their voices were mostly drowned out by the action around him, they were still there, gliding across the ice around him, making it impossible for him to see the puck through the gaggle of angels. And then the creepy one kept tripping him on purpose!

"Just doing my job," he would say. "What's life without a little challenge?"

His coach wondered why Bobby was so clumsy; his friends couldn't figure out why he kept looking off and mumbling to himself.

But if all that was bad, nothing could compare to what happened on Bobby's first date with Bonnie Hermosa.

It was eight o'clock at the movie theater, and the lights had barely gone down when the angels got to work.

"You really should put your arm around her," whispered the pretty angel in his ear—the first time she had offered advice on anything at all. So surprised was Bobby that he flinched, flinging popcorn all over Bonnie.

"Is something wrong?" Bonnie asked.

"No. No, nothing. I just slipped, that's all."

"So are you going to put your arm around her or not?" asked the pretty angel.

"He's too much of a wimp," said the creepy one.

"He's a good boy," said the plump one. "He won't do anything too forward."

"Enough!" Bobby grumbled.

Bonnie turned to him. "Enough of what?"

"Uh . . . enough coming attractions," he said. "When's the movie going to start?"

The bespectacled angel put a check on his clipboard and gave Bobby a thumbs-up. "Good recovery."

"Put your arm around her!" insisted the pretty angel. Finally Bobby complied, slipping his arm around her shoulder. Bonnie didn't seem to mind. The angels applauded, which made Bobby flinch.

"Can't you leave me alone!"

It had burst out of his mouth before the matronly angel could cup her hand over his lips. Bonnie turned to him, understandably annoyed. "What did you say?"

But now the angel of silence's hand was over his mouth, and he found himself tongue-tied. It took all his will to push her hand away. "I didn't mean you!" he finally said.

"Then who did you mean?"

And that was when the angels began a full-scale offensive on his brain.

"Just shut up and pretend it didn't happen," said one.

"Run to the bathroom quick!" said another.

"You're such a loser," said the creepy one.

"Let's all go get some ice cream," suggested the plump one.

So many voices and choices—all so confusing.

"Kiss her!" screeched the pretty angel, and Bobby found himself taking her advice. He leaned forward and planted a popcorn and soda-pop kiss on Bonnie Hermosa's lips.

For a moment at least seven different emotions played on Bonnie's face before she slapped him so hard across the face his retainer flew into the next row.

Bonnie got up and stormed out.

"Smooth move, moron," said the creepy one. "You don't kiss a girl without asking."

"At least your mother still loves you," said the plump one.

And then Bartholomew pushed his way to the front. Until now he had been content to just orchestrate the others, but now he stepped forward for some decisive action. "Sorry about this," he said, then he punched Bobby in the stomach. Bobby folded over, the wind knocked out of him. The feeling spread through his body, feeling more like a wave of embarrassment and humiliation than a punch to the gut. "Nothing personal," Bartholomew said. "It's just part of the job."

It was the same for weeks. Seven voices, seven courses of action. Words of comfort and praise, accusations and condemnations. Warm hugs and the occasional punch to the gut. Living with it didn't make it any easier—if anything, Bobby became more frazzled as time went on.

"I'm worried about you, Bobby," his mother said one afternoon. That was nothing new—she had worried about him even before he was blessed by a plague of angels that no one could see but him. But this time he knew she had reason to worry. These angels were driving him over the edge—in fact, the only thing that kept him sane was the knowledge that there was one thing they could not do. They could be in his face twenty-four seven, but they couldn't read his mind, and could never truly know what he was thinking.

When he searched online to find anything he could on the history of angels, he told them, "I'm just studying all about you—if I have to live with you, I might as well understand what angels are all about." Since the angels didn't believe it possible for Bobby to keep anything from them, they never suspected the true nature of his studies. Even when he began to research authors of dark, strange books. Even when he found one of those authors living in his town.

"The boy has a healthy interest," Bartholomew told his colleagues.

"I think it's sick," said the creepy one, who found most everything Bobby did to be sick.

From the things that author wrote, it was very clear to Bobby that he was different from the others. He knew too much—which meant that maybe he saw his own angels, too.

The book's author, Devin DeVries, lived in a mansion in the most exclusive part of town, with a gate so far from the main residence that the house couldn't even be seen from the street. Although the man had only one book to his credit, he appeared rich beyond reckoning.

"Does Mr. DeVries come from a rich family?" Bobby asked the butler who led him toward the morning room.

"No—Mr. DeVries came into his wealth rather recently," said the butler. "Good investments."

As they sat in the morning room, the angels flitted about in their standard orbits around Bobby, some flying, some pacing, some trying to distract him, console him, or challenge him, as they always did.

"I don't like this place," Bartholomew commented.

Then DeVries made his grand entrance. He was a man dressed in a thousand-dollar suit, with a gold watch and a glittering diamond earring. "You've come to speak to me about my book?"

"Yes," said Bobby, introducing himself. Mr. DeVries gestured for him to sit down, with a smooth wave of his hand that seemed more like a magician revealing a secret card. Bobby sat in a plush leather armchair and got right to the point, ignoring the whispers and comments of his angelic entourage. "You see your angels too, don't you, Mr. DeVries?"

The man didn't seem surprised at all by the question. "Yes, I did see my angels for a time. If we dream too vividly, they become visible to us—but you already know that from my book."

"You don't see them anymore?" Bobby asked.

"No, I don't."

Bartholomew perked up. "Splendid!" he cried. "Get him to tell us how we might become hidden from you again!"

Bobby shushed him, and DeVries smiled knowingly.

Then the butler entered with a pot of tea, poured two cups, and left.

"Please have some," DeVries offered. "I think you'll find the brew exceptional."

It was exceptional, all right; exceptionally disgusting. It tasted more like mud than tea, but Bobby just smiled, not wanting to be rude. Meanwhile, the angels chattered away, trying to tell him what to do.

"Run away."

"No—listen to what he has to say."

"Ask him if he has a daughter your age."

"See if there's anything good in his fridge."

Bobby put his hands over his ears. "Shut up!!"

DeVries grinned. "Are they giving you too much advice?"

"All day long," Bobby confessed, "and they're always there, watching me eat and sleep. They won't leave me alone!"

"They can't help it—it's their job, you know," said DeVries. "Now drink your tea—it will ease your mind."

The plump angel took offense at that. "Don't you believe him, Bobby. It's *my* job to ease your mind!"

DeVries slowly wove the fingers of his right hand into the fingers of his left. "As I said, I once saw my angels. And then I educated myself. You see, they do have one weakness. They can advise you, they can watch you, but they can't *make* you do anything—which means they can't stop you from doing anything either."

The angels began to grumble uncomfortably. Bartholomew leaned forward. "Let's leave," he said. "Let's leave right away."

"No," Bobby said, "I want to stay."

"Good for you!" said DeVries. "Exert your free will!"

Bobby smiled. Perhaps he had more power than he realized.

DeVries reached his slender fingers down to a small silver box that sat on an antique table beside him. "This snuffbox dates back six hundred years," he explained. "It's priceless, like most of the things in this house. But it's what's inside that makes it most valuable to you and me." DeVries opened the snuffbox to reveal that it was full of straight pins, each about two inches long.

"Select a pin," DeVries instructed.

"What for?"

"You'll see."

Bobby pulled out a pin. It was ordinary in every way.

"Now prick your right thumb with it."

All at once the angels erupted into a noisy argument, no longer advising him but fighting with each other as to what they should do. Bobby jabbed the pin into his thumb, and instantly the angels fell eerily silent, watching. Bobby withdrew the pin and handed it back to DeVries. A tiny bead of blood bubbled up on his thumb. Suddenly DeVries grabbed Bobby's hand and thrust his thumb into his cup of tea.

"Hey! That's hot!" But even as he said it, Bobby realized that the tea was chilling, as if his thumb were an ice cube cooling the water. In a moment the tea was freezing cold, and the liquid had changed from muddy brown to clear.

"Once you see your angels, they'll never be far from your sight," said DeVries. "Unless you remove them completely."

"Remove them?"

The angels suddenly cried out, demanding that Bobby leave, trying to turn his will—but he remained steadfast, and they could do nothing against his resolve.

"The removal of one's angels," continued DeVries, "requires a potion consisting of hummingbird wings and manatee tears, boiled in a purée of unicorn horn and the adrenal gland of a Himalayan yeti. That's what you've been drinking."

Bobby began to feel sick to his stomach, but he forced the feeling away.

"The final and most important ingredient was a drop of your blood," said DeVries. "Now only one part of the ritual remains. Do you truly wish to rid yourself of your angels, Bobby Jarvis?"

"Yes," said Bobby. "Yes, I do."

"Then repeat after me. . . ."

"Don't do it!" shouted the angels.

"We love you!"

"We hate you!"

"Who will comfort you?"

"Who will frighten you?"

"Who will give you passion?"

"Who will make you sleep?"

"Who will hold your tongue?"

"Who will push you to action?"

"Don't do it, Bobby!"

DeVries held Bobby's hand deep in the tea, which was quickly turning into ice. "With this brew," said DeVries.

And Bobby repeated, "With this brew."

"I thee absolve."

"I thee absolve!"

There came a flutter of wings and kicking up of dust, seven sudden gasps of air . . . and all the shouts were enveloped by sweet, sweet silence. The angels were gone.

"Where'd they go?" Bobby asked.

"Look at the pin." DeVries handed him back the pin and a huge magnifying glass. Bobby looked through the lens to see seven tiny angels stuck to the head of the pin.

"This is highly irregular," Bartholomew cried in a faint, high-pitched voice. "Highly irregular indeed!"

"And that's that," said DeVries. Then he took the pin from Bobby and stuck it into a little red pincushion that was already bristling with pins. "I've been collecting them," explained DeVries, "from other unfortunate souls like yourself." He slid the pincushion into a drawer in a rolltop desk.

Bobby didn't know how he could ever thank the man. "I should pay you something," he said. "I don't have much, but—"

DeVries just laughed. "Having your angels is payment enough," he said. "They're good luck, you know. Since I've started collecting them, I've won the lottery more than once. It is I who should pay you." Then he handed Bobby seven hundred-dollar bills—one bill for each angel.

Bobby took the money, wondering if perhaps angels might be worth something more—but in the end, it didn't matter, because they both got what they wanted. So Bobby couldn't complain.

That night, Bobby slept quietly and contentedly. In his dream he was alone at last on the ice—no one but him and the open goal ahead. There in the stands was Bonnie Hermosa, waving at him, forgiving him for being so strange on their one and only date. It was a dream for the record books, more vivid, more real than any dream he could remember. But then he was awakened by a nasty twist of his big toe.

"Ouch!"

He opened his eyes to a sea of faces around him. Not just seven, but many, many more.

"You nasty, nasty boy!" said the leader of this crowd of angels, all with silver wings and bodies glowing as bright as the sun.

"No!" shouted Bobby. "I just got rid of my angels. What's going on here? Who are you?"

The lead angel leaned forward menacingly. "Do you think that you humans are the only ones who have guardian angels? Ha! We are the seven squads of *archangels* who attend to the lives of your angels . . . but now that you've banished them to the head of a pin, there's not much for us to do, is there? So we've come to you."

"And since you, once again, dared to dream too vividly," said another, "we've been revealed to you."

Bobby swallowed hard. "You mean—"

"That's right, Bobby. We're *your* angels now . . . and we're not happy about it."

Bobby buried himself under his covers, but his blanket was quickly ripped away.

"Things are going to change around here," the lead archangel said. "There will be no more whining, no more nose-picking, no more nail-biting or any of the other unpleasant things you do. You will live by our standards now . . . because we'll always be watching you, Bobby Jarvis. All forty-nine of us."

Bobby looked at the crowd of disgruntled faces scowling at him, and suddenly felt his bladder loosen.

"I . . . I gotta use the bathroom," he told them.

The lead angel rolled his eyes. "Very well, if you must. Just give us a moment."

Bobby sighed with sad resignation. It was going to be one very crowded bathroom.

Special Deliverance

He walks toward the towering apartment building, his package clumsily balanced on his shoulder. It is dusk, and the sky burns a smoggy orange as he makes his way across the deserted square, where weeds squeeze between blocks of pavement, turning the concrete expanse into a giant checkerboard. Shredded newspapers, yellow with age, blow past and gather in the sieve of a chain-link fence. He zips his coat against the cold.

As he approaches the central apartment building, he spots a row of mailboxes, all pried open and rusted. But this doesn't deter him. The package he must deliver must be brought to the door.

As the twilight dies, losing itself to a starless night, he realizes that the desolation around him is worse than he imagined. This apartment building—the entire complex—has been abandoned by most of its residents. It's an oasis of sorrow in the midst of a thriving city. Just a few streets away, crowds of people go about their business, but here stand dozens of buildings filled with nothing but the hollow tones of the wind blowing across broken windows, like slow breath across the lip of an empty bottle.

The heavy glass door of the entryway creaks open as he leans on it, its hinges shrieking with bitter complaint. The glass door itself is clouded with layer upon layer of graffiti, etched into the glass with blade points. But it's more than mere graffiti; these scrawlings are runes. Perhaps not as ancient as some, but these runes are full of potent warnings.

Suffer eternity, reads one. *Don't be caught dead here,* reads another.

He takes a deep breath, shaking off the growing sense of dread, and heads for the elevators.

An elevator arrives in moments, its dented metal door struggling open with a scrape and a clatter to reveal the bleak gray box within. Like the glass doors of the apartment building, the elevator is covered in uniquely modern hieroglyphics. Some are rude, some are terrifying, but all are void of hope.

There is also a man in the elevator.

Shifting the awkward bundle in his arms, the delivery boy enters the elevator and turns to face the closing doors.

He looks at the order slip in the dim fluorescent light, and realizes the apartment number cannot be read. Too late. The elevator begins to move before he can push the button. It starts downward. The floor counter registers the basement and continues past it.

"Aren't we supposed to be going up?" asks the man who shares the elevator, wringing his hands, just the tiniest bit worried.

"Beats me. Which way were you going when I got in?"

"I can't remember."

The elevator continues down through three underground parking levels. The man looks at the padded package the boy carries, and wrinkles his nose. "Smells like dead fish."

The boy shrugs. "It's not for you."

The elevator reaches parking level three. The last floor. Yet instead of stopping, it continues its descent. The delivery boy begins to feel light on his feet, and senses the package lighten in his grip. *We're accelerating,* he thinks.

The man's eyes begin to dart around. He backs up into a corner. "Wait a second. Wait a second, this isn't right!"

It is then that the delivery boy notices that the man, pale and gaunt, is not entirely there. He seems only the shadow of a man. The boy gasps. He can see right through this man to the graffiti scratched into the wall behind him! It reads, *Abandon all hope.*

"This is all wrong!" wails the ghost, now huddled in the corner of the elevator. "I'm supposed to be going somewhere else! I'm not supposed to be here!"

Deeper and deeper. The elevator rattles back and forth in the seemingly bottomless shaft. Inside the elevator the boy notices the temperature rise. It's a dense, humid heat, a soggy heat that makes it hard to breathe. The delivery boy balances his package on one hand, being sure to keep it flat, and with his other hand hits the buttons that would send the elevator back up. But none of those buttons work. And suddenly it occurs to him that this elevator doesn't go to any upper floors. There's only one place it goes. Down.

"Stop the elevator! Do something!" yells his ghostly companion, but the boy can do nothing but feel his ears pop as the air pressure increases as they plummet through the earth.

Finally comes the telltale heaviness—sudden weight as the elevator slows. They have arrived.

The man flings himself against the doors. "No! No!" he cries as he tries to hold the doors together to keep them from parting. But his hands have no more substance than vapor. Gears grind, the doors labor open, and a ferocious blast of hot wind catches the delivery boy in the face. He has to turn away. When he dares to look again, the ghost-man is gone. But his wails can be heard echoing in the jagged stone corridor down which he has been dragged. A corridor that is angry red and lava-hot.

Someone is standing just outside the elevator door. A dark specter who seems coolly at home in this furnace of a place.

"I . . . am the Gatekeeper," the creature announces.

The delivery boy swallows his fear, takes a deep breath of the hot air, and holds up his package.

"Uh . . . yeah. You ordered a pizza?"

The Gatekeeper smiles, showing a set of sharpened teeth. "Yeah! And you're on time, too."

"We guarantee delivery in thirty minutes or less." The boy slips the box from its thermal hot pack, which suddenly strikes him as pointless in this place. As is his custom, the delivery boy opens the box for inspection. "Here you go—double onions and triple anchovies. Is that what you ordered?"

"Yes. Yes!"

"That'll be fifteen ninety-five."

The Gatekeeper pulls out a pen and a checkbook.

"I'm sorry, we don't accept checks," says the delivery boy.

The Gatekeeper is not pleased, but forces a pleasant smile. It comes out conniving and sinister. "I'm a little short today. Couldn't you make an exception?"

"Not a chance. But we do take all major credit cards," suggests the delivery boy.

This time the dark customer flashes his teeth in a threatening grimace. "They won't give me credit cards!" he bellows. "None of the banks trust me."

The delivery boy shrugs. "Not my problem." Then he pulls the pizza back from the Gatekeeper's long, bony fingers.

"I want that pizza!" growls the Gatekeeper, eyeing the delivery boy as if he might be dinner instead. But the delivery boy does not show fear. Instead he says, "Perhaps we could work something out."

The Gatekeeper folds his arms. "I'm listening."

"That man who was in the elevator with me . . ."

"Yes, that was Mr. Pratly. What about him?"

"Send him back with me, and you can have your pizza, anchovies and all."

The Gatekeeper's expression changes. He thrusts his chin forward, insulted and indignant. "Out of the question. But perhaps I can offer you something else you desire. Power? Fame?"

"Not interested." Quickly the delivery boy backsteps into the elevator. "No Pratly, no pizza," he says. "That's my final offer, take it or leave it."

The Gatekeeper folds his fingers into tight fists and raises them above his head in anguished fury. *"Blast!"* he screams to the steaming walls, and the stone itself recoils at the sound of his voice. There comes a rush of boiling wind, and suddenly there, beside the delivery boy, is Mr. Pratly once more, not a happy camper, but much happier now that he's back in the elevator.

The Gatekeeper snatches the pizza from the delivery boy. "Get out," he says with a wave of his hand. He begins devouring a slice of pizza.

But the delivery boy wedges his foot in the elevator door. "What? No tip?"

The Gatekeeper swallows hard, then leans into the elevator. "All right then," he whispers into the boy's ear with his onion-and-anchovy-tainted breath. "Here's your tip: stay off airplanes next Thursday."

Then the elevator door slides closed and the car begins its ascent to higher ground. Slowly the temperature begins to cool, and Mr. Pratly's relief is more powerful than the leftover aroma of the pizza. He takes a transparent handkerchief and blots it against his translucent forehead.

"I don't know how to thank you," he says.

"No worries," says the delivery boy. "Hey—if I were you, I think I'd get out of this neighborhood and take a train uptown. Way uptown."

"Yes," says Mr. Pratly. "Yes, that's exactly what I'll do."

As the elevator reaches the parking levels and continues up toward the lobby, the boy can't help but smile. There might be better jobs out there, but he can't complain. After all, who doesn't love a delivery boy?

Ralphy Sherman's Jacuzzi of Wonders

We were sitting in our hot tub, minding our own business, when *she* came out to join us. Vermelda.

Roxanne, my younger sister, let out a groan. "Ugh! Here it comes," she said. "Do you think it will want to sit in here with us?"

"Pretend we don't see her, maybe she'll go away," I said, but unfortunately, Vermelda did have a mind of her own—amazingly small though it was—and she was determined to warm up to us and force us to like her. She was my father's current girlfriend, but we knew she was after his money, just like all the others. Needless to say, we didn't like her very much.

"Hi, Ralphy. Hi, Roxanne," she said with a forced smile. "Can I join you?" Her skimpy polka-dot bikini made her look like she'd walked right out of a suntan lotion ad.

"I guess," I told her. "It's a free country."

She dipped a pink-painted toe into the water. "Ooh, it's hot," she said.

"The better to boil you with," responded Roxanne.

Vermelda chuckled uncomfortably, slipped her foot in inch by inch, and descended into the bubbling tub. She sat next to us and tried to make conversation.

"We were talking about different languages," I told her, "and how interesting some words are."

"Really," she said.

"Yes," I told her. "For instance, in Mexico, the most popular brand of bread is called Bimbo."

Roxanne nodded. "Bimbo bread," she said. "But in Mexico, they pronounce it like this: *Beeembo!*"

I looked at Vermelda and smiled widely. *"Beeeeeeembo,"* I said, very slowly.

Vermelda lowered her shoulders into the water. "So," she said, "your father's told me a lot about both of you."

I kicked my feet just enough to get her hair wet. "Really," I said. "He hasn't told us anything about you."

"But," added Roxanne, "I think we know everything we need to know."

Vermelda smiled uncertainly.

"Be careful where you sit," I told her. "People have been known to disappear in this Jacuzzi before."

"Disappear," repeated Vermelda. "What do you mean, 'disappear'?"

I raised my eyebrows. "Exactly what you think, Miss Hyde: they come, they have a soak, and they're never heard from again."

"Yes," chimed in Roxanne, "it's a mystery."

Vermelda wagged a fancy fingernail at us. "You two!" she said. "Your father told me about you and your stories." But the way we just smiled when she said that made her even more uncomfortable. So she changed the subject.

She looked up at the trees, then down the long expanse of our sizable backyard. "It must be nice," she said, "to live in such a big house. Your father must get lonely with no one to share it with. No one grown-up, I mean." And then she added, "I'm so sorry about your mother. It must have been terrible for you to have her taken from you so young."

"Oh," sighed Roxanne, "she'll be back."

Vermelda looked at us with the clueless eyes of a lab rat. "But . . . but I thought . . ."

"Yes, that's what everyone thinks," said Roxanne.

"But the truth is," I told her, "she was abducted by aliens."

"Oh really," said Vermelda, clearly not believing a word of our testimony.

"Mm-hmm," I said. "Right here in this very backyard. The ship came out of the trees and sucked her up through a straw."

"Pretty amazing," added Roxanne. "I saw it through my window. It's one of my earliest childhood memories."

"We get postcards from her occasionally," I said.

"But we can't read them," finished Roxanne. "On account of they're written in Alien."

A pulse of water surged in the Jacuzzi. A big bubble surfaced. It was getting dark, and the lights in the hot tub made it look like a bubbling vat of radioactive acid.

Suddenly Roxanne sat up straight.

"I think it's down there," she whispered. "I felt it brush past my toes."

"Felt what?" asked Vermelda, pulling in her knees.

"You know," I said with a friendly grin. "The Loch Ness Monster."

Vermelda sighed, relaxed, and crossed her arms. "Now come on, Ralphy," she scolded. "The Loch Ness Monster? In a Jacuzzi? How could that be possible?"

Roxanne looked at her with scientific seriousness. "We think there might be a space-time wormhole."

"This Jacuzzi's much deeper than it looks," I explained. "It's so murky—Dad never cleans it out. You can't even see the bottom, can you?"

"No," said Vermelda. "But . . ."

I lowered myself into the water until my lips were just above the surface. "I sent my toy submarine down there once, with a camera attached," I said. "It went down, but it never came back."

The water continued to churn. The pump sounded like the

engine of a great ship, a submerged groan, deep and hollow. I grinned.

"You know," announced Vermelda, her face getting more twisted and furious-looking by the minute, "a good boarding school would help the two of you learn the difference between fact and fiction. Someone ought to persuade your father to send you to one."

Roxanne folded her arms and stuck her nose in the air. "If you don't believe us, ask Dad."

"Of course, Dad probably won't tell you," I added. "He's trained to conceal the truth, no matter how much he's tortured."

Vermelda looked at us sideways. "Excuse me?"

"You know. They teach you that stuff when you're a spy," Roxanne whispered.

I rapped my sister on the arm. "Roxanne, we're not supposed to tell!"

"Oh yeah, I forgot."

"Your father's an accountant," insisted Vermelda. "I met him when he was doing my taxes."

"A *cover*," I explained. "I mean, do you really think an accountant could afford a house like this?"

Vermelda looked at us like a snooty poodle. "Maybe he got the money from the aliens," she said, painting on the sarcasm as thickly as she applied her mascara. "And they pay to keep him quiet about your mother's abduction."

My sister's lips quivered and I could see her pushing the tears out of her eyes. "You think that's funny?" shouted Roxanne, through the tears. "You think it's fun to tease kids who have lost their mother?"

Vermelda took on that laboratory rat look again. "But . . . but I was just playing the game—you know? Playing along with you two."

I took Roxanne under my arm and shot Vermelda an accusing glance. "You really don't have to be so cruel. Making fun of us. Calling our lives just a game."

"And I thought you were nice," pouted Roxanne.

I stared across the surface of the pool. The currents of the churning water seemed to change slightly.

"Ooh!" said Roxanne suddenly. 'There it goes again. Did you feel it?"

"That," proclaimed Vermelda, "was not the Loch Ness Monster. It was your foot."

I shrugged. "Maybe it was, and maybe it wasn't."

Vermelda shivered.

"Cold?" Roxanne asked.

Actually, the water around our toes *was* beginning to feel a bit chilly.

"Hmmm," I said. "It's as if water is being pumped in from a different source."

"There!" shouted Roxanne. "Don't you see it?" She was pointing to the center of the huge tub.

Vermelda jumped in spite of herself. Her knees were locked up tight against her chest, and she was staring wide-eyed at the bubbles. It's amazing the things you can see in the shifting shapes of hot-tub bubbles. I don't know what she saw, but she did start to look just a little bit anxious.

"Oh!" growled Vermelda, furious. "Now you listen here, you little brats! There's nothing in here but you and me. The bottom is only three feet deep, and I'll prove it!"

"I wouldn't do that if I were you," I warned.

She stood up. She went down.

I shrugged. "I tried to tell her," I said to Roxanne as we both gazed into the bubbling water. Then with a *blub-sputter-cough!* up came Vermelda, her perfectly coiffed hair now a wet mess hanging over her face.

"Help me!" she gurgled, reaching out her hand.

Roxanne and I just looked on with pity. "Can't you swim?" asked Roxanne.

And that was when *it* appeared.

Suddenly, from the center of the Jacuzzi, the creature's immense head rose up from the water and grabbed Vermelda in its wide, tooth-filled mouth.

Vermelda tried to scream, but the thing swallowed her in a single gulp. We watched a bulge slip down the creature's long neck, like a snake swallowing a mouse.

The monster roared, then pulled its head back down through the Jacuzzi, squeezing way, way down to the bottomless depths, where, in some way that we didn't quite understand, our Jacuzzi connected to that famous Scottish lake.

Of course the monster never came after us. After all, we fed it.

The tub returned to normal, except for the fact that it wasn't hot anymore. Now the only sound was the endless churning of the murky water. A single fancy fingernail came floating on the current of lukewarm bubbles and bumped against the side.

Roxanne shook her head. "Some people just don't listen," she said, and reached over to turn up the heat.

Dad came out into the backyard a few minutes later, wondering where Vermelda had gone.

"Nessie ate her," we told him.

He shook his head sadly. "Not again. Didn't you warn her?"

"Of course we did," I told him. "But she had a mind of her own."

"How awful," said Dad. "Who's going to eat that extra steak tonight?"

"You can take it with you," I suggested, "and eat it on your way to the Pentagon tomorrow."

Dad sighed in resignation and turned off the Jacuzzi. The light went out and the bubbles settled. "All right, come on inside, you two. There's a postcard from Mom in the kitchen."

"Really?" Roxanne raced off into the house, still dripping wet, and I followed.

Of course we couldn't read the card, but man, the picture on the front was great!

Terrible Tannenbaum

Endless rows of pine trees stretched as far as the eye could see, all pruned to a perfect peak. It was Christmas again, and Lani McDaniels trekked with her parents and brothers to select this year's tree.

"See all these trees?" said James, Lani's older brother. "In six weeks, they'll all be dead."

Eight-year-old Michael, Lani's younger brother, stared at James with wide-eyed shock. Apparently he had never thought of such a thing—that trees could live and die like people.

"That's right," continued James. "They'll all be axed so that we can have presents under a tree." James gave his little brother a nasty smile. "Merry Christmas."

"James, kindly keep your thoughts on the subject to yourself," said Dad.

Lani wasn't bothered anymore by the things James said. But it did bother her to see Michael tormented so.

"Will you look at this one," said Mom as she pushed through the pine branches of the lot. "This is a healthy one."

"Too small," said Dad.

"How about this one?" said Michael.

"Too thin."

"How about that one?" said Lani.

"Too fat."

"Why does it even matter?" said James. "Just kill one, and get it over with."

"James," said Mom, "why don't you go sit in the car?"

"Are you kidding?" mocked James. "I'm having too much fun."

It was easy for Lani to ignore James. She had grown used to him and his sense of humor. Besides, she had her own philosophy when it came to Christmas trees. To Lani, the trees on the lot were grown for one purpose only: to celebrate Christmas. Which meant that was literally what the trees lived for. If a Christmas tree did have a spirit, Lani reasoned it would want to be taken from the lot and brought into a warm home, where it could be adorned and surrounded by love. Each Christmas, Lani could feel the goodwill breathing from those happy trees.

James, however, never got into the Christmas spirit. When the family had purchased an aluminum tree one Christmas, he had complained that it was tacky—as unironically ridiculous as the pink plastic flamingo Mom maintained on the front lawn. Then, when the family decided to buy a live tree, James complained that it was a pointless, wasteful ritual. Each year on Christmas morning James would grumble that he never got what he wanted, even when he got exactly what he wanted.

"By the way," said James, "don't count on Santa coming this year. There's no such thing as Santa."

Michael's lower lip started to quiver. True, Michael was getting a little old to believe in Santa, thought Lani, but just because he did believe didn't mean that James had to tease him about it.

"You take that back!" screamed Michael.

"Take it back, James," warned Mom, "if you know what's good for you."

"Fine, fine," said James. "I take it back. There is a Santa Claus, okay? He comes down our chimney every single year with nice gifts for all the good little boys and girls, and he does lunch with the Easter Bunny in the off-seasons. Are you happy now?"

Michael stopped crying, and Mom sighed with relief.

"Santa knows you're a good boy, Michael," she said—but said no such thing to James.

They pushed their way through hundreds of trees until they lost all sense of direction. Lani played hide-and-seek with Michael, hidden in the dense forest of evenly spaced trees. Michael would occasionally get lost and cry until someone found him—but that was all part of the fun. Dad forged on, holding the heavy ax by its neck until they came to a little bald spot in the tree farm. In the center of that bald spot stood what looked like a single perfect tree. It wasn't until the family got closer that they realized several unusual things. First, the tree was surrounded by a thin layer of frost, even though the first snow of the season had not yet fallen. Second, all the other trees on the edge of the bald spot were leaning away from this tree in the center. It looked like they were actually growing away from it.

If trees had legs, thought Lani, *they might be running away.*

"Well, isn't that odd," said Mom, noticing the strange angles of all the other pines.

"Not at all," said Dad. "Trees don't always grow straight."

It was cold inside that clearing, colder than anywhere else on the tree farm. Mom zipped up her jacket and made sure Michael's was zipped as well.

"Cold front coming in," said Dad.

James stepped up to the tree and reached into it to see if there was any rot.

"Ouch," he said, and quickly withdrew his hand. He had pricked his finger on a pine needle.

"I don't like this tree," said James. "It has an attitude."

But if any of them had reservations about the tall, lonely pine, those reservations were wiped away when they saw the price tag on one of its lower limbs: eight dollars. The tree was eight feet tall, and any of the other eight-foot trees went for at least fifty bucks.

Dad was overjoyed. But Lani was feeling more and more unsettled by the tree. A tree shouldn't make a person feel that way, she thought.

"Maybe," said Lani, "the people who run the tree farm know something we don't. Maybe that's why it's priced so low."

"Nonsense," said Dad, hefting the heavy ax he used only once a year. "They must have mispriced it by mistake, and I'm not going to pass up a bargain like that." He swung the ax low.

THWACK. The heavy head of the ax buried itself deep in the tree's soft, wet wood. He pried it out and swung again.

THWACK. The tree groaned and creaked; the cold wind blew stronger. The surrounding trees seemed to take on a greater tilt away.

THWACK. At last the tree could hold on no longer. Severed from its roots, the tree collapsed down, its branches flopping to the side.

"We're going to have a fine Christmas," said Mom.

"The best ever," said Dad.

"Another one bites the dust," said James.

And the tree said absolutely nothing.

At home they sawed the base smooth and wrestled the tree onto the large stand, where an iron spike dug itself deep up into the tree's trunk.

Ten minutes later the tree had already started to tilt. No one seemed to notice, since they were busy decorating it. First, the lights. Then, the glass ornaments. Next, the special ornaments: baby's first Christmas, first Christmas together, and the like. They adorned the tree till its outer branches were shining and beautiful . . . while deep within, the twisted branches remained dark.

It was by far the tallest tree they'd ever had. Eight feet did not look that big on the lot, but here in the house, even with its vaulted ceilings, the tree seemed huge and imposing. When the family finished trimming the tree, Mom sat at the piano, and they gathered around it. As was family tradition, they sang "O Tannenbaum"—which none of the kids could sing with a straight face, as this was what they used to sing to tease Joey Tannenbaum, who lived across the street.

It wasn't until after they were done that they noticed how cold it was getting in the house, although the heater was turned on full blast. Even Moby, their goldfish, seemed to shiver in his bowl on the piano. They decided to have a fire, which warmed the fireplace, but little else.

"It's the humidity," said Dad.

"Bad insulation," said Mom.

But it was Michael who was first to suspect the truth.

"It's the tree," he said.

Lani and the others looked over to him, as he stood next to the tree. The tree seemed to be leaning toward Michael.

"It doesn't like us," said Michael.

The way Lani saw it, the tree wasn't just leaning—it was looming. Looming over Michael like a tidal wave waiting to crash.

Lani went over to the tree and put her hand near it. It did seem colder near the tree than anywhere else. She looked deep into the tree. There should be some light in there from all those lights strung around it, she thought. Why was the inside of the tree so dark?

Then she felt something soft and spiny like a caterpillar rub up against her arm. She gasped and slapped it away.

But it was only a sprig of pine needles.

She was about to laugh, until she realized that she was not the one who had moved closer to the tree. It was the tree that had brushed against her! A red ornament jangled ominously on the branch.

"Smile, sweetie!"

Her mom's phone flashed as she took a picture of Lani beside the tree. Did the tree flinch at the flash, or was it just Lani's imagination? She couldn't be sure—but there was one thing she was sure of: this tree, unlike any other tree she had known, had no feeling of Christmas goodwill.

That night, after the fire had burned out, the only glow came from the multicolored lights of the Christmas tree. They cast spiny shadows of red, blue, and green on the white walls.

James was in his room being antisocial, and before Lani went to sleep, she went in to give him a piece of her mind.

"What are you doing in here?" challenged James. "I thought you were downstairs sucking in some Christmas spirit."

"James, just because you don't like Christmas doesn't mean you have to ruin it for the rest of us . . . telling Michael there is no Santa, and all."

"Why should you care?" said James. "Maybe I'm trying to protect him—maybe I don't want him to be disappointed later."

"Maybe you just like to make people feel lousy." Lani turned to leave, but just as she reached the door, James said something that made her stop.

"There *is* a Santa Claus."

Lani turned back. "What?"

"I said, there really is a Santa Claus."

James was looking down at the video game he was playing. He paused the game for a moment and looked at Lani.

"He can fit down the chimney because he doesn't have any collarbones. His reindeer fly because nobody told them that they can't. He gets to every kid's house because he knows how to stop time and travel in between the seconds. And every once in a while, when he finds a bad kid, a really bad kid, he wakes him up in the middle of the night and tells him, 'Hey, son. I'm sorry, but you don't get a gift from me this year 'cause you've been way too naughty.' Just like he said to me when I was nine." James shrugged. "And I guess I've just been naughty ever since."

Lani stood there for a minute, almost taking it seriously. Then she shook it off.

"Ha-ha," she said. "Very funny."

"Laugh all you want," said James, "but that's why I don't like Christmas, and I hope someday Santa gets his."

Downstairs, their father unplugged the Christmas tree lights for the night, and the whole house was plunged into pine-scented darkness.

At three in the morning, everyone was awoken by a heavy *THUD* and the tinkling of breaking glass. It was the kind of dead-of-night sound that brought terror to any household.

"Mom! Dad!" Lani wailed. "Someone's breaking in!"

Lani came out of her room to see Dad racing downstairs with a baseball bat—all set to do battle with a burglar. He flipped on the light . . . but there were no burglars. In an instant it became clear what had intruded into their night: the tree had fallen onto the piano, leaving shattered glass ornaments all over the keys.

The fear that had woken Lani up still raged inside. She kept telling herself that it was just a fallen tree, but it didn't quiet the uneasy feeling that pounded through her. There was something about the sight that was terrible—like a car wreck.

Michael, who was peering down through the banister, began to cry.

"I don't like that tree, Daddy," he whimpered.

"It's okay, Michael," said Mom. "We'll fix it in the morning."

She and Dad lifted the tree off the piano. Pieces of broken Christmas ornaments rained to the ground. Baby's first Christmas, first Christmas together. All smashed to bits.

"We'll have to get a new base," said Dad. The steel legs were horribly twisted out of shape. "Funny," he added, "they said it could hold a tree up to fifteen feet. Metal fatigue, I guess."

Then Lani noticed that among the fine fragments of shattered ornaments were shards of glass much thicker than the rest. The fishbowl.

"Moby!" she gasped. From behind the banister, Michael began to whimper harder.

"It's okay," said Dad, trying to exercise a little damage control. "We'll get a new fish tomorrow. Maybe we'll get two. Maybe a whole family—how's that?"

Michael settled down and Lani helped her parents clean up the mess, and when they were done, Lani stared at the tree until Dad turned out the light. Lying on its side, the branches of the tree all swayed down toward the ground—but somehow those branches seemed to be moving, squirming, and it occurred to her that they never had found Moby.

Lani went to bed that night dreaming of a tree whose branches were octopus tentacles and whose trunk was the scaly body of a python.

By the time Christmas Eve arrived, the tree had fallen a total of five times. Dad had tethered it to the light hanging from the ceiling above it, and still it pulled loose from the cord. Now it was tied to three different spots in the room—the light above, the banister, and the upstairs railing. There was no way it was moving—it looked like King Kong in shackles. As for its trimming, they had given up on glass ornaments, since there were only two or three left. All that remained on the tree now were the unbreakable things—silver tinsel and popcorn chains. The walls in the corner of the living room were filled with gouges and green marks from where the tree had fallen, as if some battle had taken place there.

Michael wouldn't even go into the living room anymore, and Dad joked that they would probably have to put their presents under the tree—literally under the tree—to prop it up.

"When's the Christmas tree burn this year, Dad?" Michael asked. Everyone knew Michael hated to see the trees burn, but this was one year he was actually looking forward to it.

Although he wouldn't admit it, even James steered clear of the psychotic pine as best he could.

It was Lani who kept a close watch on the tree, puzzling over it. She imagined that if trees truly did have personalities, then a tree could be bad, the way some people might be bad.

She sat alone across from the tree as Christmas Eve faded into twilight. While everyone else watched *It's a Wonderful Life* in the family room, Lani peered into its darkness—watching it the way a guard might watch a prisoner. Its limbs blew with the breeze, even though there was no breeze, and when she looked into it long enough, she could swear she saw faces in there, staring out at her, but she was certain it was just her imagination. Why did they have to take this tree? Why couldn't they have chosen a tree that wanted to be a part of the celebration, as did all the trees they'd had in the past? Trees that weren't selfish. Or evil.

"I'll bet Santa will come and take it away," said Michael, peering in from the hallway. "Santa would never let a tree like that ruin Christmas."

It took a long time for Lani to fall asleep that Christmas Eve. She kept thinking about what gifts the morning would bring, but mostly she thought about the tree.

In her dreams, the tree, with its snake trunk and octopus arms, spoke to her in a slippery whisper of a voice.

"Have yourself a merry little Christmas," the dream-tree told her, then wrapped its tentacles around her and pulled her into its darkness.

Christmas dawn was frigid. Cold drafts had blown down the open flue of the chimney, filling the house with icy winter air and fireplace ash.

Lani awoke to the sound of bells jingling somewhere outside and met her brothers just coming out of their rooms farther down the hall. Not even the icy cold could blunt the joy of Christmas morning, thought Lani. Not even the tree. Lani smiled as she and her brothers reached the edge of the stairs.

"I know Santa brought me a new bike!" said Michael.

"I'll bet I got a whole mess of video games," said Lani.

"I'll probably get stupid clothes that don't fit," said James.

And with that, they clambered down the stairs.

James saw it before Lani did. He gasped, and his face became as green as the Christmas cookies they had eaten the night before.

Santa, it turned out, had indeed come.

Michael instantly began to cry and buried his face in James's chest. James, who normally would just push him away, held Michael tight. Lani could only gape. Holding on to the banister, she felt as if her legs would buckle beneath her.

The tree had fallen sometime in the dead of night. This time it didn't engulf the piano. Instead it pinned one brightly dressed, bearded old man to the hardwood floor.

Outside, sleigh bells impatiently jangled, and deer hooves restlessly scraped the roof.

Where are Mom and Dad? thought Lani. *Did they drink so much eggnog last night that they're sleeping through this?*

The man trapped beneath the tree turned his head weakly and spoke in a raspy, wheezy voice.

"Muh-muh-merry Chr-Chr-Chr—"

Lani looked to James. The corners of James's mouth had turned up in a sinister, Grinch-like grin. He raced off into the garage and returned moments later with their father's ax. Then he looked at the man beneath the tree.

"I've had about enough of you," he said, as he raised the ax high above his head.

"No!" screamed Lani. She grabbed Michael, turning his head so he wouldn't see.

The blade came down and sank deep into the dark trunk of the tree. From the tree came a hideous wailing cry.

"Watch out!" warned James. He swung again. Pine sap splattered in all directions, leaving thick, sticky clumps in Lani's hair. A third swing. *Thwok!* Then a fourth. *Thwok!* The tree shattered, its limbs tangled around the ax, but James pulled it free and raised the ax high above his head one last time.

"You're sawdust!" he said, and with that, he brought down the blade for a final blow that split the terrible tree in two, freeing the not-so-jolly man trapped beneath.

Michael and Lani helped him up. James, dropping the ax to the ground with a thud, stared the white-haired visitor in the face.

"Well," said James. "What am I now? Naughty or nice?"

"Please, I'm in no mood," said Santa. He turned to look up at the closed door of their parents' room. "Tell your parents to stay away from cheap trees. You get what you pay for." And with that he turned to go.

"Thankless old man," grumbled James beneath his breath—but apparently nothing escaped the man's large pink ears.

Santa turned back to James. "Very well," he said reluctantly, tossing James a small box. "I suppose you've earned it. It's in the driveway."

Inside the box James found a key.

"And James," said Santa Claus. "Do stop being such a royal pain, or I'll have to send the tooth fairy to punch out some of those pearly whites."

Once their guest had made his exit, they bundled up the remains of the tree and Lani set it on fire in the backyard. She watched as it burned with a furious flame, its darkness completely consumed and reduced to ashes in a matter of minutes. Then she set up the old aluminum tree.

In the end, Lani had to admit that Christmas morning turned out the same as always—for by the time Mom and Dad finally dragged themselves out of bed, the house was clean and there was nothing out of the ordinary to explain.

Nothing, that is, but the Porsche in the driveway.

THE WHEEL OF DESTINY

I turn away, but Mom gently touches my shoulder.

"No," she says. "Look at them. Study their faces. Memorize their faces."

I look at her, confused. "Why?"

"Because your memory of them is all they have left."

—from "Dawn Terminator"

Dawn Terminator

We lost contact with Denver at four a.m.

That's what the news anchor says. Her hair's a ragged mess, and her hands fidget in desperation—the kind of desperation news anchors aren't supposed to show.

I'm cold and frightened. Terrified of the night outside the huge airport windows and terrified of the noisy crowds moving in that darkness. I hate the dark—I hate the night. I've always been a day person—but that doesn't mean much anymore, according to the woman on the news.

In the crowded airport lounge, people stare blankly at the TV screen. A man curses beneath his breath, even as he rocks his baby in his arms. A woman gapes at the screen as she picks nervously at her peeling cuticles. None of these people can stretch their mind around what's happening. I can't either. It's too big—too awful.

So instead of thinking about it, I take a pencil and my sketch pad from my shoulder bag, figuring I'll find something to draw. The man with the baby. The woman tearing at her own fingertips. I always get an intense craving to draw when things around me get too rough to handle. Funny, the things you feel like doing when everything's coming down around you.

Mom reaches over and gently restrains my hand before I can lay pencil to paper.

"No, Lauren, not now."

Dad grabs my younger brother tightly. "We can't stay here, we have to move," Dad says. I watch the heavy current of panicked people flowing by, heading toward the gates. I try to see their faces, but they wash by too quickly for me to get an image I can hold. They won't slow down, because they know time is ticking away, and time has become everyone's worst enemy.

My family, like many other people, has stopped to rest and catch their breath, but wasting any more time here will be a mistake. There are thousands upon thousands of people crammed into the concourses and gates of San Francisco International Airport. We don't have any tickets, but then no one does. TSA didn't stand a chance of keeping everyone out. The officers have long since been overpowered, and the security checkpoints are gone.

"We'll get on a plane," Dad promises as we prepare to force our way into the moving crowd. "We'll make it." Dad's the kind of guy who always manages to get his way, but this is the only time it really matters.

"What will happen when the sun rises?" my brother, Kenny, asks.

"You don't have to worry about that," answers Mom. "We're never going to see the sun rise."

I check my phone. Forty-three minutes and twenty seconds until dawn. I guess we've all memorized the exact time morning will show its blinding face today. I start to imagine what will happen the moment the sun rises, but my mind shuts off like a circuit breaker—as if just imagining it will burn my mind to a cinder.

No one believed it could happen.

The scientists said it wouldn't—they swore that the warning signs were false and that only lunatics and crackpots would suggest such a thing. The truth is, they didn't want to believe that the sun could go nova.

But two minutes before midnight, it did.

At 11:58 p.m., Pacific Standard Time, the sun detonated with a force too immense to calculate—just like the crackpots said it would. Six minutes later, Europe, Asia, Africa—everything east of the Atlantic was gone. There was no one left to tell this half of the world what was waiting for us at dawn . . . but we knew.

We knew because of the way transatlantic phone calls suddenly went dead.

We knew because of how brightly the moon suddenly shone in the sky—so bright you couldn't even look at it.

But for our family, it was the honking of horns that woke us up to the truth. Thousands of blaring car horns, all blending together into a panicked siren, loud enough to wake the dead. Every road, every freeway was instantly jammed. We quickly joined in that honking madness, riding over sidewalks and yards, because the roads themselves were already clotted with abandoned cars. I made Dad drive with the dome light on, so Kenny and I wouldn't have to sit in that dark back seat—a dark that seemed worse than any I could remember.

In our race to the airport, we passed hordes of people looking heavenward, praying in the streets. I prayed too. Prayed that we would all be saved—that the earth would stop spinning and that the line of dawn would stop burning its way across the world.

The Terminator—that's what they call the line that divides the night from the day. It stretches from pole to pole, and never stops moving as the earth spins.

But it doesn't quite stretch from pole to pole. Far to the north there are places where the northern lights dance, and the night lasts for months on end. Places beyond the Arctic Circle. It's late November now—that means the sun won't rise there for at least three months. That's where we must go to escape the killing breath of the sun.

And we have forty-one minutes left to fly from the dawn.

As we try to force our way onto the concourse, more people press in. I see a kid I recognize, but he doesn't spare a thought for me—he's trying too hard to catch his breath. In front of us, the mob races past like a rain-swollen river. You can drown in a current like that. I imagine myself pulled down and suffocated beneath the feet of the moving mass. There are so many bodies that they block the fluorescent light from above—it must be pitch black down by the scuffling feet of the crowd. That's a darkness worth being afraid of.

Mom and Dad hold Kenny's and my hands tightly, and we leap into the dangerous crowd.

Instantly we are pulled into the current. I'm whipped in the face by the red-painted nails of a passing hand. A belt buckle scratches across my side. My bag slips from my shoulder, and although I reach back for it, Mom tugs me along.

"Forget it," she says. "It doesn't matter."

My bag is trampled, and swallowed, disappearing into the darkness. My sketch pad, with all my drawings, is lost—it was the only thing I wanted to take with me. The faces I had drawn.

Then my hand slips from my mother's.

"Lauren? Lauren!" I hear her call but can't see her.

"Lauren!" Her cries seem farther away, and all I can see are the dark textures of heavy clothes moving all around me. I'm surrounded by people, and yet alone in the crushing crowd. Although I want to scream, I know that giving in to panic will be even more dangerous than being separated from my family. So I bite my fear back and give my will over to the will of the moving mob. Pressed between the crying old woman to my right and the angry bearded man on my left, I let the mob carry me down the endless airport corridor, toward unseen gates of departure.

Gates 44, 45, 46. I see the signs pass by above me, but each gate is mobbed with people—I can't even see if there are planes at the ends of the Jetways. Suddenly there's a burst of cold air, as the human river bursts out through an emergency exit. My feet stumble down a set of metal steps, until I set foot on hard asphalt.

The airport tarmac is a huge expanse of concrete covered with airplanes all facing at strange angles. Not normal airport order. I wonder if anyone is even in the air-traffic tower.

There are people everywhere, racing in random directions. A woman with a raging knot of tangled hair uses her suitcase as a battering ram to get past, and she bounces me to the ground.

And there, through the forests of legs, I see a pair of cartoon-character Nikes I recognize—and they're moving away. But in the last few minutes I've learned some tricks of survival. I force myself forward, slamming my shoulders into legs around me, hitting people, tripping people—everything short of biting them to get them out of my way—until I finally reach out and grab that small foot with both hands.

Kenny screams and looks down.

"It's Lauren!" he cries. "I found Lauren!"

Dad pulls me into his arms. "Thank God! We thought we lost you!"

He and Mom hug me tightly, but only for an instant. There will be time for hugs later, if there's any time at all. I dare to look at my watch. Thirty-four minutes.

The crowds around us are thickest near the planes, where roll-away staircases are blocked by armed soldiers. I guess airport security has taken it upon themselves to pick and choose who gets to go on the planes, and it makes me angry—what gives them the right to make the choice?

Dad pulls us toward a plane where a soldier who couldn't be any older than eighteen bars the way, letting no one up to the hatch. He scans the crowd with wide, anxious eyes as if searching for someone.

We force our way forward until reaching the soldier.

"Back off!" yells the soldier. "This plane is full." He aims his weapon at my father's chest. Dad ignores the gun.

"I don't think you want to shoot me," Dad warns the soldier. "I'm a pilot."

The soldier's eyes light up with relief. "From the airline?" he asks.

"Does it matter?" my father answers.

The fact is, my father once flew fighter jets in the air force, and although he hasn't flown for ten years, he's the best hope for this plane. It's now I realize that there aren't enough pilots to fly all these planes.

"Only you can come," the soldier tells my father sternly. "No room for the others."

But Dad stands his ground. "Let my family on, or fly the plane yourself."

"There'll be other pilots," the soldier insists.

Dad glances at his watch. "Maybe, maybe not," he says. "All I know is that sunrise is less than half an hour away."

The soldier doesn't need any more coaxing. He nods, and we clatter up the stairs toward the plane. The soldier follows right behind us.

At the top of the stairs, I turn to see the mob forcing its way up the stairs. Their pleading cries rise above the rest of the crowd.

"Out of the way!" bellows the soldier. He pushes me into the 747 and swings the heavy door closed behind us.

Hands pound on the door outside, and through the tiny window in the door I see a man, his face pressed up against the glass by the mob pushing behind him.

I turn away, but Mom gently touches my shoulder.

"No," she says. "Look at them. Study their faces. Memorize their faces."

I look at her, confused. "Why?"

"Because your memory of them is all they have left."

And so I do as she says. I make my way through the crowded aisles, force my way to a window seat. Then I peer out the window, at the faces outside.

There are people on the wing now, and more climbing up the engine, to the wing. They pound on the hull until it sounds like a hailstorm. Men, women, children. They pull at the wing flaps in a mad frenzy. I study their faces. I give them names. Mr. Smith. Mrs. Josephs. Bobby, Angela, JJ.

I hear the engines start, and we begin to move forward.

The crowd moves away from the plane—even the maddened people on the wings jump down. Maybe they know that our hope is more important than their desperation.

Then, as we turn to get in line behind a dozen other jets waiting for takeoff, I see the first trace of the coming dawn.

The eastern edge of the sky doesn't shine a faint blue—instead it burns a searing, lethal white, fading into the darkness of the night cover still protecting us. It's just a hint of the dawn soon to come. A warning.

"We have to take off!" people around me shout. "We have to leave now."

I squirm out into the aisle and over a dozen people until reaching the cockpit where my father mans the controls. He has no copilot—only Kenny sits there, kicking his feet on Mom's lap.

I watch the planes before us, taking off one right behind another.

"C'mon, c'mon," my father says, gripping the controls with white knuckles as the eastern sky begins to burn a brighter white.

At last the plane before us accelerates down the runway, and Dad instantly powers our engines to full throttle, right on the other jet's tail—a dangerous but necessary move. I hold on tight as we pick up speed. I feel the front wheels leave the ground, and then the rear. We are airborne!

Dad instantly banks away from the plane just ahead of us, and soon we are heading northwest. I can feel our airspeed as it increases.

We're airborne, but I don't know how safe we are. The minutes fly by much too quickly, and twelve minutes after takeoff we punch through the highest layer of clouds. I dare to look out a side window as we take a sharp bank to avoid another plane.

That's when I see it happen.

The first true rays of sun assault the horizon . . . and the clouds boil away before it, until they are gone.

Far away, at the edge of the horizon, the towers of San Francisco burst into flames—and I swear I see the Golden Gate Bridge melt into the bay.

The tiny dots of planes just minutes behind us turn into fireballs, and Mom gently puts a hand to my face, guiding my eyes away from the window.

"Now's the time to stop looking," says Mom.

I wonder how long it will be until we become like those ill-fated people, disintegrating into the new day. Surely our plane was built to withstand extreme heat and cold. But I don't think its designers had this particular trip in mind.

Inside the cabin, the air temperature keeps rising, but Dad banks us due west and somehow finds even greater airspeed. I turn to him. "Can we make it?" I ask. "Can we outrun the dawn?"

"The 747 is the fastest passenger jet that has ever been made," he answers. "We'll see."

In less than a minute that glimmer of sun is gone as we surpass the speed of the spinning earth. The sun seems to set behind us while we keep our eyes locked forward into the trailing edge of night.

Twelve noon. At least that's what my phone says, but time doesn't mean much anymore. Neither does my phone, because it gets no signal, and will never get one again. It's still dark. We've been spiraling to the north for seven hours, and although the Dawn Terminator is still on the horizon behind us, just as white-hot as ever, it's slipping to the south, instead of east. We have already crossed into the Arctic Circle, and Dad banks the plane to the right. Soon we will cross directly over the North Pole ice pack, heading toward a place where the sun won't rise for months.

"What if we can't find a place to land?" Kenny asks, but no one answers him. There's no room anymore for what-ifs.

I leave Dad to worry about that and try to soothe myself by drawing on the back of American Airlines cocktail napkins. I've finished about five of them now and start on a new one.

"What are you drawing?" Mom asks. I show her the napkin I just finished. They say I have a talent for portraits, and now I have a real reason to draw them.

"Who is it?" Mom asks.

"A woman I saw in the crowd," I tell her. Then I hand her the stack of finished ones. "They're all people I saw in the crowd before we took off."

Mom looks at me with surprise and wonder, and hands me better paper.

"I think we've arrived," says Dad, almost an hour later.

We are over the northern tip of Greenland—Cape Morris Jesup, to be exact. It's one of the northernmost pieces of land on the globe. The glow from the fiery Terminator is far away now. That distant white glow will circle around the North Pole, threatening the horizon for months, until it finally engulfs the entire Arctic Circle. Then this icy land will pay dearly for its many months of darkness—for in the summer months, the midnight sun will burn, and this place will not see night until the fall.

"If the sun won't rise for three months," asks Kenny, "what happens after three months?"

Mom and Dad look at each other, unsure how to answer. But I know what the answer is. "We have three months to figure that out," I tell him.

He nods. "That's a long time," he says. I suppose to him it is.

"It'll be long enough," I answer.

My father seems to sit up straighter as he hears me say it. "Yes . . .

yes, I think it will be." I can almost see his faith in our survival growing with each second—my mother's, too, as if my hope was a seed for theirs to grow on.

The blue glow of a blinding bright moon paints a landscape of ice beneath us. I'd call it uninviting, but here and now, there's no place on earth I'd rather be. It's bright enough to land on—and bright enough to see a hundred other planes dotting the endless expanse of ice. We weren't the only ones who made it—although we are probably among the last.

Then I feel the plane begin its final descent. With that descent, I can hear voices in the cabin chiming forth offerings of hope.

"I'm a thermal engineer," calls out one man. "I can design heat shields, like the ones they use on spacecraft."

"Hey," shouts one woman, "what if we fly by night to the South Pole in the summer?"

"Hey," shouts another, "what if we find caverns to give us shelter in the spring and fall?"

"We can cultivate crops that grow in darkness. Mushrooms, maybe!"

On and on, until the world we've lost doesn't seem to matter anymore—all that matters is tomorrow, and the next day, and the next.

As I think of it, all at once I feel a rush of heated emotions rising in me with more power than the nova we once called the sun. I feel everything all at once. Anger, fear, sorrow, but also an incredible comfort, and intense joy. Now I realize that this great and awesome cosmic event is not an ending—but it's not really a beginning, either; it's a link between what was and what will be. We are that link. Mom, Dad, Kenny, and me, and everyone on every plane that made it this far. What a wonderful destiny to be a bridge to the future.

Tears cloud my eyes, and Mom puts an arm around me. "It'll be all right," she says. "You'll see." She thinks my tears are tears of sadness, but they're not—not anymore. Because now I know we'll survive, just as surely as I know the sun won't rise. With time finally on our side, we will find those safe caverns. We will build those heat shields. And when the angry sun does find us after the long night, it will find us ready.

We will adapt. I will adapt.

Our wheels touch the surface of the great expanse of ice, and as I look out the window, I have to smile through my tears. I've already learned to love the night.

The 💩 on Our Shoes

"Your hands are filthy, your hair is filthy—Lowell, you can't come to school like this, surely you must know that?"

Principal Karcher leaned back in his chair, perhaps hoping to distance himself from the unfortunate aroma of Lowell Burgess's clothes. Through the window behind him, Lowell could see the star field in constant motion; points of light swept past, like the heavens themselves were scrolling through his file, just as relentlessly as the principal did.

"Are you even listening to me, Mr. Burgess?"

Lowell sighed and forced himself to meet the man's eyes. "I could barely afford drinking water this month, Mr. Karcher. There was no way I could pay for water to bathe with."

The principal grimaced in something between disgust and pity—two emotions Lowell couldn't stand. "What about your neighbors? Surely they could lend you—"

"No one lends anymore. People are conserving for when we finally arrive on Primordius."

"Yes, I suppose they are." The principal looked down at Lowell's file. "But we're not here to talk about your hygiene, are we?"

Lowell couldn't help but grin. "I suppose not."

"Simulating a spin-quake and setting off the school's evacuation protocol is not a laughing matter."

"I didn't simulate anything, I just tricked the school's computer."

"Regardless, you disrupted the day's studies and caused unnecessary strife. If we were back on Earth, you would be expelled."

"Into space?"

"No, expelled from school." The principal sighed through gritted teeth. "But since there are no other schools for you to go to, that's not an option, is it?"

"Oh well."

Lowell had enjoyed watching the other kids race out of the school, in comical, ill-fitting radiation suits. All those clean-cuts with their sweet-smelling hair and superior attitudes climbing over one another to save their own lives. Kids like Ocean Klingsmith, who thought he was God's gift to the universe.

We're the ones bringing humanity to the stars, Ocean had once told Lowell. *But you? You're just the shit on our shoes.*

It was particularly entertaining to watch Ocean run.

Principal Karcher continued to flip through Lowell's file, going "Tsk" and "Pfft" with everything he read, like a tire losing air. Lowell looked past him, and out the window again. There weren't many windows in the hull of the Transstellar Biologic Insertion craft—or T-Bin for short. Glass was fragile and allowed too much energy to escape. A window on space was a perk reserved only for those in the highest positions. Principal Karcher, whose office was at the front end of the great rotating drum, was one of those people. No doubt the window was intended to give anyone sitting in the principal's office the illusion that the man in the chair, with the heavens spinning behind him, was an integral part of the awe-inspiring view. The irony was that it had the opposite effect. It made Karcher seem small and insignificant by comparison.

The principal closed Lowell's file. He suspected the man might have sent the file, and Lowell, out of an air lock, if one were readily available. "Your defiance of authority is bad enough, but I'm even more concerned about the habitual conflicts you have with your peers."

"They always start it."

"Of course they do."

Why wash with water? Lowell thought. He could bathe in the sarcasm dripping from the man. He decided it was time to keep his mouth shut and accept the lecture, or pep talk, or analysis—whatever Karcher wanted to call it. None of it changed a thing. The colonists on board were all supposed to be enlightened equals—but after sixty-seven years in space, the social structure had taken on a very particular pecking order. Kids like Lowell, for whom daily survival was a struggle, were treated like the dregs of humanity. Creating waves was the only thing that made it bearable. It wasn't just that he enjoyed the mayhem, though—he had enjoyed the challenge of hacking the school's computer. He was, by his very nature, a problem solver. Yet when others looked at him, all they saw was a problem.

"Listen to me, Lowell," Karcher said. "When we arrive on Primordius, survival will depend on us being a close-knit community. You can't afford to be an outsider. Do you understand?"

Lowell nodded but kept his true feelings on the matter to himself. For his entire life, he'd been an "insider," stuck within the steel walls of a rotating drum hurtling through space. His whole world, and the world of everyone he knew, was nothing more than a small farming town shoved into a cylinder less than a mile in diameter. Once they landed, he'd truly get to be an outsider. And it would be wonderful.

In Lowell's farmhouse, there was a sticky note on the refrigerator from his father that read *At the doctor's—home before dinner.* The note had been there for over a year. His father's chest pain that day was not gas, as he had thought. He was not home for dinner then, and would never be home for dinner again—but Lowell kept the note on the fridge, because it kept alive the notion that his father was still on his way back. Besides, if anyone could return from the dead, it would be Lowell's father. He was a problem solver too.

His father's death had left Lowell, who had lost his mother when he was a baby, on his own since just before his fifteenth birthday. Now he was sixteen, but sometimes felt much older. Perhaps back on Earth a kid would not be allowed to be on his own, but here on T-Bin, no one seemed to mind—or more accurately, no one cared. He'd plow his two-acre farm, plant it, and harvest it on his own. When he had water to irrigate, that is. Nowadays, between limited water and limited time, he could only work half an acre, leaving him with very little to sell or trade. Still, there were those who had less than he—which was why he always saved something to bring Maeve Beausoleil and her grandfather, whose farm had failed entirely. Today, Lowell chose some choice veggies to bring them—potatoes, onions, and broccoli, which made up the bulk of his crops—then headed out into the hollow cylindrical world he called home.

Lowell supposed that T-Bin might appear quite impressive to someone who hadn't spent a lifetime here. On the outside, it just looked like a giant revolving tin can, but once inside, an Earth dweller would be stunned by the surreal sight of ordinary farmland clinging to the inner shell, all held in place by centrifugal force. If you looked forward, the land curved upward in front of you, and if you followed it, you'd be looking at an upside-down farm above your head, nearly a mile away, before the land came back around to meet itself behind you. The very opposite of a globe. The very opposite of Earth.

The interior farming surface of T-Bin was half a mile wide, and 2.6 miles around.

"If you laid the land out flat," the older folks would say, "it would have the exact dimensions of Central Park," whatever that was. When Lowell was little, he used to think he could run fast enough to counteract the spin of centrifugal force and float up to the drum's center—but he learned that some forces are simply too strong to fight.

Dotting the curve of farmland at regular intervals were the homesteads. Cookie-cutter homes designed to look quaint, except for the fact that they were all stainless steel.

The main road serpentined all the way around the drum, in a single squiggly loop, like a snake devouring itself, and the Beausoleil homestead was a quarter turn from Lowell's, down that main road. To get there, however, he'd need to pass the recreation zone, where he would have to endure the snipes of other kids. Sure enough, as he passed the rec zone, the usual suspects were there, including Ocean Klingsmith and his entourage, all of whom left their basketball game to taunt Lowell.

Ocean was right at the top of T-Bin's pecking order. A sparkling specimen of humanity, whose entire future on the new colony was mapped out for him by his family's influence. With his mother on the city council, and his father in charge of water distribution, no matter what the new world was like, Ocean's life would be rosy.

When he saw the bag Lowell was carrying, Ocean said, "You're more of an idiot than I thought if you're actually bringing food to the Beausoleils. I'll bet Maeve's grandfather won't even survive the landing. Why waste good food on him?"

Ocean, like all the clean-cuts, had evolved a survival-of-the-fittest elitism. The way the clean-cuts saw it, whoever didn't rise to the top deserved to drown.

"Tell you what," Ocean said, tossing his ball to one of his friends. "Forget the Beausoleils—I'll trade you some water for those vegetables."

But Lowell knew Ocean all too well. He'd take the vegetables, then piss on Lowell's shoes and say, *There's your water.*

"Thanks, but no thanks." Lowell pushed past him, while Ocean's friends snickered.

"Hey, Burgess," one of them shouted. "If you won't bathe, at least go home, put on a radiation suit, and spare us your stink!"

Lowell picked up the pace, trying to tune out their laughter.

Lowell found the front door unlocked, and Mr. Beausoleil on the floor of his bedroom, moaning for help. He was dazed, but not hurt. Lowell got the old man into a chair.

"Fell on my way to the bathroom," he told Lowell. "What's the point of legs when you can't use 'em anymore?"

"Where's Maeve?"

"The marketplace," he said. "She found some things in the shed, thought she could sell them. I told her she wouldn't get anything for the stuff, but she won't listen to me. Good God, what is that stench? Is that you, boy?"

Lowell put down his arms, clamping his pits closed. "Sorry."

"Grab yourself a jug of water! Sponge yourself down, for goodness' sake!"

"You barely have enough to drink," Lowell reminded him. "I'll survive a little bit of BO."

"Yes, but I may not!"

And then from behind him, Lowell heard, "He doesn't smell that bad."

He turned to see Maeve. Like Lowell, she was sixteen. Like Lowell, she had lost her parents, and like Lowell, she was not a favorite of the clean-cuts.

"So did you sell anything?" the old man asked, and Maeve shook her head. "It's my generation's fault," Mr. Beausoleil said. "When your parents were all children, we spent so much time teaching them about survival, we forgot to teach them compassion."

"I think it sucks the way they treat you," Lowell said. "You're the last of the first-generation colonists—they ought to give you some respect."

Mr. Beausoleil considered it, looking down at his withered hands. "Things don't always turn out the way we expect," he said. "And I never expected to live this long."

"I'm glad you did, Grandpa." Maeve brought a blanket and wrapped it around him. "Thanks for the food, Lowell. I'll cook us up some dinner."

After dinner, when the solar lights dimmed, they sat on the

stainless-steel porch and tried to imagine the new world, which was now less than a month away. But how can you imagine a world that curves downward, when all you know is a world that curves up? How can you imagine sky when all you see when you look up is more ground? The teachers would show pictures of Earth in school, but only the most limited of images.

"You think they'd have given us more," Maeve said. "More pictures, more music, more art."

"Maybe they wanted us to make our own art," Lowell suggested.

"Or maybe," offered Mr. Beausoleil, "they didn't think any of it mattered." There was a sadness in his voice. Some sort of regret that Lowell couldn't decipher.

"Why wouldn't it matter?" Lowell asked.

"Why, indeed."

The old man was silent for a long time, but Lowell knew he wasn't finished. Finally he said what was on his mind.

"Very few of the original builders came with us. Did you know that?"

"No," said Maeve, moving a little closer. It also put her closer to Lowell. He thought he might put his arm around her, but decided he'd better not.

"And the ones who did join the mission were all older than me—old enough to know they'd be dead before we reached Primordius. While the rest of us had families within a few years, none of the builders ever had children. I always found that strange."

Lowell could tell he was getting at something—perhaps something that had been bouncing around his mind for years, but he'd never spoken of. Until now.

"You know what else is strange," Mr. Beausoleil said. "The water shortage. You see, T-Bin is a closed system. Just about everything is recycled. We're like a bottle. Water doesn't escape from a closed bottle."

"Maybe there's a leak," Maeve suggested.

"Yeah," agreed Lowell. "I know we've been hit by a few meteors over the years. . . ."

The old man shook his head. "Dents and dings, nothing more." And then he brought his voice down to a whisper. "Computers are of little interest to most of the colonists now, but in my day, people knew how to use them—and I was pretty darn good at it too. Still am. So a few weeks ago, I did some checking. According to T-Bin's computers, there has been no water loss . . . but when you compare the volume of water being used now to when we were launched, there seems to be one-fifth less. That's millions of gallons. So the question is, where is it hiding?"

Suddenly something occurred to Lowell. "The Klingsmiths! I'll bet they're hoarding it! They're in charge of water distribution!"

Mr. Beausoleil pursed his lips and considered the suggestion. "Maybe," he said. "Or maybe it goes beyond that. Maybe the builders had more important plans for that water."

"What could possibly be more important than water for drinking and crop irrigation?" Lowell tried to wrap his mind around it, but like T-Bin's main road, it just came back to itself. As for Mr. Beausoleil, he leaned back in his chair and said nothing more.

A week later the entire population gathered in the town square for the unfurling ceremony. In the entire sixty-seven-year journey, there had been only two such events. The first ceremony had been upon the launch from Earth's orbit—when the massive solar sail was extended from the forward end of T-Bin and filled with the solar wind, and the ship accelerated to nearly a quarter the speed of light. Today it would deploy again, this time expanding behind them, catching the photons from their new sun, and slowing them down like a solar parachute.

Lowell stood by Maeve and Mr. Beausoleil, who was wobbly on his cane but insisted on standing for the event.

Governor Bainbridge stood on a platform in front of the huge statue dedicated to the builders. Stalwart figures looking forever skyward.

"Today we mark the final leg of our journey!" proclaimed Governor Bainbridge to the four hundred gathered. "As our bodies are merely vessels of the soul, so our great home is a vessel, delivering us, body and soul, to a glorious tomorrow on our shining new world."

"I may vomit," grumbled Mr. Beausoleil.

"Please, Grandpa," said Maeve, "I'm trying to listen."

Lowell noted a few glowering glances from people around them. Some even moved away. It might have been Lowell's odor that did it. He couldn't be sure.

"We were charged with the mission of spreading life to the stars," bellowed the governor. "Today we rededicate ourselves to that mission." He held out his hands, as if he wanted to hug everyone in the crowd. "You fine people are the precious cargo of this perilous journey. May you all be delivered to our new home in peace and safety—and when you finally look upon the first Primordial sunrise, you will know that nothing we've done has been in vain."

"He should bottle that speech and sell it as fertilizer," Mr. Beausoleil said loudly enough for everyone around them to hear. "Better than the chemical crap we use now."

Then a woman with a pinched face and hair pulled into a perfectly tight bun turned and said, "If you don't want to come, you can stay right here. I'm sure no one would mind." And although she said it to Maeve's grandfather, Lowell couldn't help but notice that she made a point of glancing at all three of them.

The clock tower ticked down the seconds. Cheers erupted as the external cameras tracked the great sail deploying, and stretching taut, filled with the solar wind. Now a new countdown began. Three weeks until T-Bin achieved orbit around Primordius. Ahead of them in the crowd, Lowell could see Ocean and his family hugging one another, filled with über-joy for their über-future. Lowell wanted to feel his own joyful anticipation—after all, once they'd left this tin can, he'd finally have the space to put some distance between himself and these people. Yet Lowell found himself filled instead with a prescient dread as wide and swollen as the great solar sail.

"From now until the day we arrive on the new world, our studies will be about preparing us for the transition."

Mrs. March, Lowell's teacher, wrote the word "colonists" on the board.

"We have called ourselves colonists all these years, but we won't truly be colonists until we arrive—and our new home will require us to give the very best of ourselves."

Lowell noticed that she held eye contact with him as she said it—as if warning him he'd better get with the program. Lowell glanced away, and around the schoolroom. With fewer than a hundred school-age children, kids of various ages were grouped together into four classrooms. The younger kids in his class looked terrified, the older kids confident. The goof-offs cracked jokes under their breath, and the studious kids actually took notes as if there would be a test after they disembarked.

"The planet will have *weather*." Mrs. March wrote the word on the board. A lot of the kids looked confused, but no one admitted aloud that they had no idea what weather was. "Storms, and winds, and rain—which is beads of water falling from the sky. There may be extremes of heat and cold as well."

Something's wrong about this. The feeling pounded as powerfully as Lowell's heartbeat, but he couldn't figure out why he was so unsettled. It reminded him of when he used to play chess with his father. He would sense his loss three or four moves before it happened. He couldn't see all the moves that would lead him there—it was as if his brain saw something his conscious mind had yet to grasp. And everything about their arrival on Primordius screamed "checkmate."

"Fields will be rocky and hard to plant," continued Mrs. March, "and the only shelter will be shelter we find or build."

Then Ocean, slouching back in his chair, called out, "Will there be water enough for Lowell to take a bath?"

Snickers all around, and so Lowell said, "Will there be a cliff high enough for me to throw Ocean off?"

This time the only laugh came from Maeve.

"Gentlemen, please," said Mrs. March. "Disparagement is not our friend." Then she paused and said, "But yes, there will be mountains, and yes, there will be water. A full half of the planet is water—not quite as much as Earth, but more than enough for us."

A younger child asked if there would be "things" in the water, and Mrs. March quieted his fears. "Primordius is a lifeless world, but its air is oxygen-rich, and ready for life. We are bringing that life—which is why Governor Bainbridge called us 'precious cargo.'" Then she smiled. "And all of you are the most precious of all—for you will be the first generation to grow up as Primordians."

That was the moment when one small piece of the puzzle presented itself to Lowell. He raised his hand, and Mrs. March took a deep breath before she called on him. "Yes, Lowell?"

"Why no animals?" he asked.

The question threw her off-kilter. "Excuse me?"

"In Earth Studies, we were always learning about animals. Pets and things that we don't eat, as well as animals that we do—but we didn't bring any. Why?"

"Ooh—I can answer that!" said Mary Wilcox, hurling her hand into the air so fast Lowell imagined her fingers flying off and embedding themselves in the ceiling. "Animals eat too much, so if we brought them, we'd have to bring fewer people. So the builders decided we'd all eat a vegan diet, and there could be more of us on board."

"But if the mission is to spread life—" Lowell tried to point out, but Mrs. March cut him off.

"Mr. Burgess, I believe your question has been answered." Then she turned to the board and wrote the number *1.15*. "Gravity on Primordius will be 1.15 times stronger than the centrifugal gravity we experience here. That might not seem like much, but it will make the physical demands on all of us very difficult."

Lowell's hand flew up again, and he spoke without waiting to be called on. "Then why didn't the builders slowly increase the spin of T-Bin, so we'd be accustomed to the new gravity by the time we got there?"

"The builders couldn't think of everything, Mr. Burgess."

"But they did!" called out Maeve. "The builders planned out everything in T-Bin—it doesn't make sense they'd skip something so important."

"I'm sure they had their reasons," said Mrs. March. "Now please, we have a lot to cover in a limited amount of time. I will entertain no more questions today."

Day after day it was the same. Lowell would point out what appeared to be flaws in the builders' plans, only to be shut down by other students, or by Mrs. March.

"I think you're making some good points," Maeve told him, "but maybe Mrs. March is right. The builders had their reasons. I mean, they only had two jobs. Build this place, and get us down to the planet safely. You'd think they'd get it right."

"Yeah, you'd think," Lowell told her. "And you'd also think that water wouldn't vanish into thin air."

With one week to Primordius, the entire school was taken on a field trip to an area of T-Bin that had been off-limits for sixty-seven years: the "delivery ship" hangar. Within the massive hangar was a winged ship capable of carrying four hundred people.

"The builders anticipated everything," explained Principal Karcher, who had taken charge of the tour. "Population growth was regulated to make sure there were precisely the same number of colonists at the end of the journey as when the journey began. There's a seat for everyone."

"Where are the engines?" Lowell asked, and felt the communal groan of frustration from his classmates.

Principal Karcher, who was also seeing the delivery ship for the first time, looked it over, then said, "Well, clearly it's a glider."

"With no landing gear?" Maeve asked, throwing a wink at Lowell.

"Obviously," said Principal Karcher, with increasing exasperation. "This craft was designed to land on water, which the autopilot will find. Believe me—nothing here has been left to chance. Nothing."

Two days and counting. Classes had ended. Anything they needed to learn they either already knew or would learn once they reached Primordius.

The T-Bin Council was in session nonstop, and a slow leak of rumors had people on edge. Rumors that T-Bin was not heading into geosynchronous orbit, as expected. Rumors that the cargo bay of the delivery ship wasn't large enough to haul the farming equipment they would most certainly need. Rumors that the builders had not been quite as visionary as everyone believed.

"So what?" Ocean Klingsmith was heard to say. "So, we'll face a little hardship—it'll be good for us. And in the end, we'll conquer Primordius, and live like kings. Or at least some of us will."

It was officially announced that there had been a slight miscalculation, and T-Bin was not heading into any sort of orbit at all, but was going to crash on Primordius instead.

"Not a problem," Governor Bainbridge told everyone. "We'll have left in the delivery ship long before it happens, and our departure is still on schedule."

• • •

On the last night, Maeve showed up at Lowell's farm. Lowell had spent most of the day sorting and re-sorting the things he cared about into piles of things he *needed* to take with him, versus the things that he *wanted* to take. He kept trying to whittle down his piles so that it would all fit into his backpack, but he simply couldn't do it. In the end, he realized, if he wanted to survive, he could take nothing but food and water. When Maeve arrived it was a welcome relief, until he saw the tears in her eyes.

"You have to come!" Maeve told him. "It's my grandfather! I called the doctor, but he wouldn't come! He wouldn't! He doesn't even care."

They ran all the way to the Beausoleil homestead to find Mr. Beausoleil looking so cadaverous in his bed, Lowell thought he might already be dead. But then he slowly opened his eyes.

"Glad," he wheezed. "Glad not to see it. Glad to die before we get there. Before it happens."

"Don't say that, Grandpa!" Maeve took his hand. "You'll be on the ship with the rest of us. It's just one more day. You can hold on for one more day."

"Sorry . . . ," he said. "So sorry for you, Maeve. And for you, Lowell."

For a moment his rheumy eyes seemed to clear, and he held Lowell's gaze.

"You know something, don't you?" Lowell realized.

"Didn't know, but I suspected," the old man said. "So I did a little poking in the computer. There's a lot that's classified, but you can piece things together." He grimaced. Shifted. He took a deep breath to ward off the pain, then closed his eyes, too weak to keep them open. "The storage silos," he said. "They're all sealed behind the aft wall of the T-Bin drum. Off-limits. Computer-controlled."

Lowell knew about the storage silos. They contained grains,

chemical fertilizer, liquid oxygen—all the things that the colonists would need for a sixty-seven-year journey. No one had ever seen the storage area that held the silos, but everyone knew they were there. It was one more system that the builders had designed to work without any human interference.

"The silos should be empty. All used up," Mr. Beausoleil said. *"But every container is full."*

Maeve shook her head. "You must have misread it, Grandpa."

"But if it's true," Lowell said, "and we used up all the stuff in those silos . . . then what's in there now?"

Mr. Beausoleil's bony knuckles went white as he gripped Maeve's hand tighter. "So, so sorry, Maeve," he said, and then, before he released his final breath and let death take him, he hissed out one final prophecy.

"We are not the precious cargo. . . ."

Like the top and bottom of any tin can, there were two ends of the T-Bin drum. The colonists called the forward end "the lid," although it didn't open. Built into the steel face of the lid were the school, the medical center, the market, and various offices. At the other end of the drum was "the boot," and while the lid was designed to be aesthetically pleasing, with murals and mosaics layered into the steel, the boot was utilitarian and ugly. It held the physical plant that recycled water and reoxygenated the air when the plant life couldn't do it alone. It held the reactor that powered the lights, and kept T-Bin from freezing in the icy depths of space—but the largest part of the boot was dedicated to the storage silos. Pipes went in, pipes went out, and the automated system worked so efficiently, there was no need for anyone to bother themselves with what was behind the great steel wall.

There was a hatch on that wall, as intimidating as a vault door, which allowed entrance into the massive silo hold, but it had an angry red sign on it that read AUTHORIZED PERSONNEL ONLY. Apparently no one in T-Bin was authorized, for the door had never been opened.

On that last morning, with only a few hours left until the delivery ship launched, Maeve and Lowell buried Mr. Beausoleil right in the heart of his farm. There were regulations against such things, but like always, no one cared enough about their comings and goings to stop them. Folks were too busy preparing for their future to worry themselves over the last rites of the only original colonist, or the troubles of two unclean orphans.

As soon as Lowell and Maeve were done, and the requisite prayers had been said, they went straight to the silo hold.

The steel hatch had a security panel, and it required a password to be punched in. Lowell had never met a computer he couldn't hack—but this didn't even have an interface beyond the keypad. The only way to break in was to break the code.

While the rest of the colonists had a huge "Friendship Brunch," to gorge themselves on all the food they couldn't take with them, Lowell and Maeve stood at the silo hold hatch and tried dozens upon dozens of passwords that failed.

Lowell kicked the door, which succeeded in doing nothing but bruising his toes. "I refuse to be defeated by a lousy password!"

"There's less than six hours until the delivery craft leaves, Lowell. Maybe we should forget this, and start getting ready."

"No! Your grandfather was onto something." Lowell didn't care how limited the time was. That instinct that knew things three moves ahead was telling him that this was important. More than important, it was crucial.

"Look up there." He pointed to a brass plate above the door. It was a star chart that featured the area of space they were sailing into—or at least how that area of space appeared from Earth. Seven stars in a pattern that had become familiar to everyone on T-Bin. "Where have you seen that before?"

"Everywhere," Maeve said. "It's on the mural in our school. It's on the T-Bin flag—"

"No—I mean that exact brass plaque. I know I've seen it."

Maeve squinted as she looked at it and said, "Town square. There's one just like it on the builders' monument."

"Bingo! Let's go."

They hurried to the town square. In the center of the square was the statue, and at its base was a lofty dedication carved in stone. Beside the dedication was the brass plaque of seven stars.

"I think you're right," Maeve said. "There must be some connection."

Lowell stared at it, trying to put himself in the builders' places. Trying to think like them. Far away there was laughter from the Friendship Brunch, as if he was being mocked from a distance.

Maeve did not have his patience. "Staring at that thing until your eyes cross isn't going to solve anything."

And then she gasped. When Lowell looked to her, her eyes looked odd somehow.

"What is it?"

"Look at it again, Lowell—only this time cross your eyes!"

When he did, the stars were superimposed over the dedication, highlighting certain letters.

> THIS MONUMENT IS **D**EDICATED TO THE
> VISION**A**RY DESIGNERS AND THE DA**R**ING
> SOULS **W**HO JOINED IN THIS GLORIOUS
> PARTNERSHIP TO BR**I**NG LIFE TO THE
> STARS. THE I**N**TREPID AND THE BRAVE,
> WE **C**OMMEND YOU!

What the stars spelled out was unmistakable.

DARWIN C.

Could it be that simple? Lowell and Maeve rushed back to the silo hold door, and taking a deep breath, Lowell entered D-A-R-W-I-N-C.

Nothing at first. Then a clanging of bolts pulling back, and the huge door began to open. They were hit by a stink so overpowering it made them weak in the knees.

"Oh my God! What IS that?" Maeve covered her face and turned away.

The smell was so awful, it took all of Lowell's will to step over the threshold. Inside, he saw the silo hold—row after row of steel tanks a hundred feet high. They were swollen to bursting—and all of them were oozing foul-smelling gunk. They were no longer full of grain, or whatever else they had once been carrying. One look at what oozed out of them, and Lowell knew.

The silos were full of sewage.

A million flushes from sixty-seven years in space.

"I don't understand," said Maeve, still covering her nose and mouth. "Wastewater is recycled. And what can't be recycled is ejected into space."

"Apparently not."

This explained the missing water. Perhaps some of the water had been recycled, but the rest had been pumped right back into these vats of human waste.

"What were the builders *thinking*?" Maeve wailed.

Lowell couldn't stand the stench for a moment more. He stumbled out with Maeve, back into the fresh air of the T-Bin farmlands. As he caught his breath, it all fell into place, and he understood. He saw the minds of the builders, and he knew the truth. If your goal is to bring life to the stars, you don't start with the highest life-form. You start with the lowest.

"It was never the builders' plan to start a human colony!" Lowell told Maeve. "Our sole purpose on T-Bin was to create sixty-seven years of bacteria. We are not the precious cargo. Our crap is!"

But before they could even process this woeful epiphany, T-Bin's spin-quake sirens began to blare—and this time it wasn't Lowell's doing.

There had only been one spin-quake in T-Bin's history. A meteor had clipped it, and thrown the spinning drum several degrees off-kilter. The force of the meteor strike had killed anyone in the wrong place at the wrong time, including Maeve's parents. The hull wasn't breached, though, and ultimately the ball bearings that filled T-Bin's outer shell had done their job, flowing to where they needed to be, balancing the ship, and bringing its spin back under control.

However, this spin-quake was of a completely different nature. There was nothing in the ship's design to compensate for the gravitational pull of Primordius. T-Bin's smooth, constant spin became a wobble, growing more violent by the minute. It meant the timing of their departure was hours off—they were going to hit the planet much sooner than expected.

People left the Friendship Brunch in a panic, racing home to grab their belongings if they lived close enough, or racing straight to the delivery craft hangar. The ground shifted beneath everyone's feet like a fun-house floor, the artificial gravity no longer pulling in a consistent direction.

On the main road, Lowell and Maeve stopped people, trying to tell them what they knew—trying to warn them—but no one would listen. Finally they encountered Ocean Klingsmith.

"What the hell is wrong with the two of you?" he yelled. "Don't just stand there—get to the delivery ship."

For all their rivalry, Lowell wasn't going to let Ocean run off blind. "The delivery ship isn't what you think it is, Ocean," Lowell said. "I don't think it's meant to save you—but I have an idea that might!"

"You're out of your mind!" Ocean said, and then he looked at Lowell in a way he never had before. Lowell actually saw compassion in his eyes. A seedling of humanity pushing its way through his arrogance. "Listen, Burgess—we haven't always been friends, but that doesn't matter now. We're all colonists. Come with me, both of you. Get on the delivery ship, and if you want to argue, we can argue after we land."

Lowell shook his head. "I won't set foot on that ship, Ocean—and neither should you!"

Any compassion in Ocean's eyes vanished as quickly as it had come. "Fine—stay here and die here for all I care. It's what you deserve."

Then he ran off to join the others.

Maeve turned to Lowell. "If you really do have a plan, you had better tell me about it."

Lowell sighed. "I will. But you're not gonna like it."

The delivery ship launched from T-Bin. All colonists were accounted for except for two. With just a few minutes left until T-Bin entered the planet's atmosphere, Lowell and Maeve raced from Lowell's homestead toward the silo hold, both of them wearing radiation suits. Around them, entire orchards were uprooted by the spin-quake. Patches of earth flew past them as if they had been ripped up by a tornado. It was almost impossible to keep a sure footing as gravity kept shifting beneath them.

"This is pointless!" Maeve yelled as they ran. "Nothing can save us—T-Bin is going to crash and burn."

"It's going to crash," Lowell agreed. "But it's not going to burn. If it burns, then the mission fails."

"But the radioactive core—"

"If I'm right about this, it will be ejected into space. The builders wouldn't risk contaminating the planet with radiation."

And sure enough, as they approached the silo hold hatch, all of T-Bin was plunged into darkness. It could only mean that the core had just ejected.

They stumbled over tree roots and bits of the buckling road in the dark, until coming into the silo hold. Here, emergency lights every ten yards gave them enough light to see the curves of the silos, but nothing more. The stench was unbearable, and Lowell could hear the sloshing of the awful stuff within the silos. As bad as it smelled now, he knew it was going to get a whole lot worse. He sealed the soft helmet of his radiation suit, activated its oxygen supply, and found the ladder on Silo #106.

"Start climbing," he told Maeve.

She glared at him through the face mask of her radiation suit. "Do we really have to do this?"

"Do you have a better idea?"

She didn't answer him. Instead she started climbing. "I hate you for this."

But that was all right. She wouldn't hate him for long if they survived. And she wouldn't hate him for long if they died, either.

When they reached the top, Lowell opened the silo hatch and peered inside. Darkness—but he knew what was in there. Rather than thinking, he just jumped, submerging himself in the sickening stew. The sewage was thicker than mud. Maybe—just maybe—it was thick enough to absorb the force of a crash landing. In a moment he felt Maeve beside him, and he grabbed onto her. Now there was nothing to do but wait, and listen to the metallic groaning of the ship around them as it fell from space, and into the atmosphere of Primordius.

Ocean Klingsmith, like most of the T-Bin colonists, trusted the designers' master plan. Even after T-Bin failed to settle into geosynchronous orbit. Even after the spin-quake had forced everyone to evacuate earlier than planned, he still trusted the designers to deliver them to the new world safely.

As the delivery ship hit the atmosphere, it shuddered violently. Ocean could feel his teeth rattle, so he clenched his jaw. The air in the cabin grew warm, but the shields protecting the craft from the searing heat of reentry did their job. The ship held together. Finally, through the small oval windows of the craft, clouds came into view, white and puffy, just like images they had seen of Earth. The air became turbulent as they hit the clouds.

"Normal!" called out Governor Bainbridge, who sat in the front row. "Not to worry, turbulence is normal."

Even so, Ocean gripped onto the harness that held him in his seat. The computer flying their huge glider banked them to the left. *Toward water,* he thought, *maybe even the kind of water I'm named for.* He could imagine the craft landing smoothly on an ocean and coming to rest where the waters kissed the shore. They would step out and claim this world as their own.

But it didn't happen that way.

When the delivery ship punched through the clouds, the colonists weren't met with an ocean vista. Instead they were met with the prospect of a jagged mountain range. Those looking out of the windows gasped in fear.

"It's all right," Governor Bainbridge said. "The ship knows what it's doing. It can navigate us out of this."

They flew between the jagged peaks, banking left, and right—then suddenly the entire dome of the delivery ship ripped away, exposing them to the sky. They were pummeled by a violent force none of them had ever felt before.

Wind! thought Ocean, in a panic. *This is wind!* He could barely keep his eyes open against it, but he forced himself to look, and what he saw explained everything. Up ahead, the front row of seats were jettisoned skyward, sending Bainbridge, and a dozen others, up and out.

Of course! Ocean thought. *These are ejection seats!* It made perfect sense; the delivery ship was doing exactly what it was supposed to do! It couldn't find a safe place to land, so it was ejecting everyone to safety, sending them down by parachute. Ingenious! The designers had thought of everything!

The second row ejected. Then the third. Finally it was Ocean's turn. He gripped the harness, closed his eyes. And felt the sudden surge of force as he, and everyone beside him, were shot out into the open air of Primordius.

He opened his eyes, waiting for the parachute to open. He was still shooting forward at an incredible speed—he hadn't even begun to fall yet. Up ahead he saw the stone face of a cliff. *The parachute will open any second now . . . ,* Ocean thought. *Any second . . .*

But it didn't. And it finally dawned on him that maybe there were no parachutes. For anyone.

No! This can't be! Ocean's mind screamed as the face of the cliff swelled before him. *I'm a clean-cut! I'm the best and the brightest! I'm the future of humanity! I'm . . . I'm . . .*

Ocean Klingsmith hit the face of the cliff at two hundred miles per hour—so fast that his body liquefied like a bug on a windshield. The chair fell away, leaving a big red splat on the mountain—proof positive that the delivery ship had done exactly what it was designed to do: deliver its payload of warm, nutrient-rich biological material to Primordius.

The massive drum of the Transstellar Bacterial Injector—T-Bin for short—burst through the atmosphere, delivering a sonic boom to announce the arrival of life on Primordius. It plunged through the upper atmosphere, showing no sign of slowing down.

Within Silo #106, Lowell and Maeve clung to one another, afraid to be alone within the foulness around them. The fall through the atmosphere, the not knowing where or how this would end, was beyond terrifying. With their face masks pressed close, they couldn't see through the muck, but they could hear each other's muffled voices as they tried to comfort one another, until the roar of reentry drowned out everything.

Outside, the great drum, still smoking from reentry, plummeted in free fall, but the icy air of the upper atmosphere cooled it. Then, once it hit the dense, cloud-spotted air of the lower atmosphere, a multilayered array of massive parachutes deployed, slowing its descent.

Within Silo #106, the sudden pull of the opening parachutes sent Lowell and Maeve plunging deeper into the thick brown sludge, but not quite to the bottom. All was silent then.

"Are we dead?" Lowell heard Maeve say. "I think we're dead."

"Not yet," Lowell told her. But he knew that one way or another, it would all be over soon.

Even with a mile-wide array of parachutes to slow it down, T-Bin was far too heavy for a gentle landing. As it swooped into a valley where the mountainsides were curiously speckled with hundreds of red measles-like spots, it struck a jutting peak, then another, then another, until finally it began to rupture.

When T-Bin struck the first peak, Lowell and Maeve were hurled sideways within their silo of sewage, but Lowell had been right—the stuff was so thick that it absorbed the worst of it. It acted like a gelatinous shock absorber. They struck the side of the silo, but not hard enough to do anything more than shake them up.

The second and third strikes were worse. They bounced back and forth, and could hear the crunch of tearing metal. "This is it," Lowell shouted in the darkness, gripping Maeve tighter.

Then, five seconds later, their world ended.

When the great interstellar drum hit the valley floor, it tore completely apart, spreading its inner lining of farmland in a deluge of soil, shredded plants, and splintered trees that rained upon the valley.

The bacteria-rich storage silos broke free, the swollen canisters bursting as they hit the landscape, spewing fetid filth upon the jagged rocks from one end of the valley to the other.

Silo #106 tumbled end over end, until it finally split open, spilling forth its bubbling nastiness, along with two kids, who came to rest in a shallow pond of the viscous sludge.

The two had been pulled apart by the force of the deluge, and Lowell frantically searched for Maeve, trying to wipe the grunge from his face mask, but he only succeeded in spreading it like finger paint. For one panicked moment, he thought that she had been thrown out of range, or worse, impaled upon the jagged metal of the burst silo. He ripped off his helmet, ignoring the gut-wrenching smell around him, and he saw her struggling to stand on shaky legs. She fell over into the stuff, clearly too dizzy to stand, and just gave up. She sat in it waist-deep until Lowell arrived and helped her up, and they climbed onto the first boulder they could find that wasn't covered with yuck.

He helped her take off her radiation helmet and smiled at her. "Welcome to Primordius!" he said, and Maeve smiled back.

"Crash," she said, "but no burn."

"Told ya!"

Finally they took in their surroundings. They were in a great valley between towering peaks. There was a massive scar miles long where T-Bin had crashed. Now the great steel drum lay in two jagged halves, like a broken egg, and its innards lay strewn across the entire valley. They also saw the wreck of the delivery ship. There were no signs of survivors. Not even bodies. Lowell didn't want to consider why that might be. Then, as he looked out over the pungent valley of funk, something occurred to him.

"You know what this is? This is primordial soup! The bacteria will grow. It will get carried by the wind. It will evolve!"

"And what about us?"

Lowell considered the question. "The seeds from T-Bin are all over this valley. This stuff around us might be nasty, but it's fertilizer.

Plants will grow, and in a single season, there'll be stuff to eat—and in the meantime, there's plenty of food packed in the cargo hold of the delivery ship."

Maeve nodded. "It would never have been enough to feed an entire colony," she said, "but it'll be enough to feed the two of us."

"And," added Lowell, "we can use the parachutes to build ourselves shelter . . . to build us a home."

Lowell and Maeve took a long look at one another, both stunned by the implications of all this. The two of them. Alone. In the only life-filled valley on an otherwise lifeless planet. A valley that would soon be a garden.

"Let's move upwind before I hurl," Maeve finally said.

"Sounds like a plan."

About a mile upwind, where the stench of new life faded, they found a fresh spring forming a small lake. The water hadn't been fouled by the pungent stew of microorganisms that now flavored the rest of the valley.

By the side of the lake, they shed their dirty radiation suits. Lowell found that his own personal fragrance now smelled fresh and sweet compared to the malodor of the lower valley. The air around them was crisp—cooler than what they were used to in T-Bin, but not so cold as to be uncomfortable. It was refreshing—and the water of the spring was steaming, and warm to the touch.

"I've been thinking," Maeve said, as they gazed at the rising steam of the crystal clear water. "The builders never truly intended to start a colony, except for a bacterial colony, right?"

"Yeah . . ."

"And yet they provided that riddle—the star code that let us break into the silo hold. That means that they *wanted* someone to figure it all out, Lowell. Maybe not the whole colony, but someone smart enough—clever enough—to uncover the truth, and come up with a way to survive."

Lowell realized she was right. The clean-cuts were always talking about survival of the fittest, and how it was the builders' driving philosophy—but the builders had a very different idea of what that meant. It made him feel noble to know he was the kind of survivor they had in mind.

"I don't know about you," Lowell said, "but I could use a bath."

Maeve smiled. "You read my mind."

They stripped down, which might have felt awkward before today, but after what they had been through, nothing felt awkward anymore.

Together they dove into the warm spring water, and for the first time, in as long as he could remember, Lowell Burgess felt sparkling clean.

Number Two

A purpose, he thinks, a purpose in life. Everyone has a purpose in life. Yes, this is true—it has to be true—but what is his purpose? Will he have to search it out in a long quest, or will it come to him on wings, in a vision or a dream? Someone with great wisdom has brought him into this world—will that someone ever tell him why?

And how long will he have to wait for an answer?

Not long.

Not long at all.

Pulled out of darkness, and into a bright light he has never known before. Shapes swirl all around him, moving colors and lights, all out of focus. An eye, a face, a soft, warm hand lifting him up, making him feel wanted, needed. He wants to cry out with joy, if he only knew how to cry. Sounds of voices, talking, laughing.

And a grinding noise.

Moving now. Moving across the room, through the light, and toward the noise.

"Wait your turn," a voice says sternly.

In the center of the light is a round shape, and in the center of that round shape is a dark hole.

Moving out of the light and into darkness again, into the dark hole, filled with a strong, musty odor. His head is firmly caught in the darkness.

Tight.

Uncomfortable.

He begins to panic.

And the grinding noise starts once again. Loud, all around him—around his head, grinding and slicing.

Spinning blades.

Sharp gnashing gears, grinding against each other—they slice deep into him, cutting away. He screams, but no one can hear over the grinding. *Help me! Help me, please! Something's gone wrong!*

If someone listens, someone has to hear.

I'm alive!

If someone knows, someone has to care.

But the slicing, gnashing knives carve deep, taking pieces of him away forever. Cruel. Unfeeling. Until all that is left of his head is a dark pinpoint. His soft, sensitive core, once protected, is now exposed to the world.

Out of the darkness, into the light again, moving through the air, which painfully blows across the pale open wound.

The soft hand that gave him so much warmth before now holds him too tightly and flips him upside down. His aching face is pressed against a rough, flat surface and scraped against it until bits of him are left behind, silver-gray traces of his life draining away onto the clean coarse surface.

This can't be it! This can't be my purpose! he screams. *I am meant for more! Much, much more! Doesn't anyone hear me?*

But all that can be heard of his screaming is a gentle *hisssssss* as the little girl presses his face to the rough page and writes:

How I Spent My Summer Vacation

Fear-for-All

The headmistress had eyes that didn't quite focus on yours. That was the thing Seth first noticed. Dr. Stillwell was looking straight at him, but wasn't. It was as if her focus was off by just a few inches, like she was looking at a point somewhere in the middle of his brain.

"If you're trying to intimidate me, don't bother," Seth said. "I'm not afraid of you."

The tight-skinned, tight-lipped woman had a smile like a clean slice of a bloodless wound. "Then what are you afraid of?"

"Nothing," he answered, without hesitation. He'd had therapists asking him that question for years, and the answer never changed. Of course, no one believed him. Everyone was always so sure he was posturing, concealing some deep-seated fear he was afraid to utter. They could not accept the possibility of someone who was afraid of nothing. Not pain, not death, not retribution for his actions. Perhaps the very concept of *him* frightened them.

"What I want to know is why you accepted me into this school."

The bloodless grin never left Dr. Stillwell's face. "Why? Don't you feel you deserve to attend Oakheart Academy?"

"No, I don't. My grades are lousy, my attitude stinks, I've already been thrown out of two other schools—and yet you've given me a full scholarship. Why?"

"Let's have a look at your record, shall we?" She flipped open a fat folder on her desk. "Last year you took an acrophobic student to the roof of your school and forced him to look down from the edge."

"Yeah," Seth said, shifting in his seat. "I got expelled for that."

She flipped a page. "Six months ago you hit the stop button in an elevator when you found out the woman next to you was claustrophobic."

"Yeah. She wasn't happy."

"And we have a letter from one Krysta Coats claiming you terrorized her by taking her on a date to the circus."

"C'mon—it was just the circus."

"Did you know she was coulrophobic?"

"Afraid of clowns?" Seth shrugged. "Yeah, I knew."

The headmistress closed the folder gently. "People believe you did these things to be cruel. That you're a horrible, evil human being." She paused to let it sink in. "Are you?"

Seth looked away from her, hating her eyes. They were like laser beams converging on some spot in his brain, burning it away like you might burn away a tumor. Was he evil? Was he cruel? Certainly those things he had done were cruel—yet at the time, they didn't feel so.

"Why did you do those things?" the headmistress demanded.

"I don't know." he answered. But that wasn't entirely true. There was a part of him that did know, but only in the most glancing of ways. The way a ship's lookout knew the iceberg.

"I did it because I wanted to . . . understand." It was the only way he could put the feeling into words. That compulsion he felt to go to the roof, or to stop that elevator, or to coldly observe his screaming date there in the front row as the wire-haired, white-faced clown came right up to her, with that horrible painted smile. He had never jumped from an unexpected fright. He had never experienced terror. How could he help but find himself drawn to those who did? And in the end, his date stopped screaming, didn't she? So maybe he had actually done something good. Wasn't that possible?

When Seth met the headmistress's eyes again, she seemed very satisfied with herself. And with him as well.

"So, did you?"

"Did I what?"

"You said you wanted to understand. Did you?"

Seth thought back to the instances when he had sparked another's fear. Did he understand it? Perhaps for an instant, when their fear was so overpowering it surrounded them both. For just the tiniest instant in time he could wrap it around him like a cloak, almost feeling it—but it would only surround him, never penetrating. Then it would dissolve so quickly he could never be sure if he had felt anything at all.

"No," he told her. It was easier than trying to explain. Yet somehow he felt she needed no explanation.

"You never answered *my* question," Seth said, beginning to lose his limited patience. "If I'm such a bad seed, then why am I here?"

The headmistress slowly crossed her fingers before her. Her interlaced hands looked like a tarantula patiently awaiting its prey.

"You're here because you possess a quality that we here at Oakheart value above all else."

"What?"

And then she leaned forward and whispered so low it was just at the threshold of hearing, but with such intensity, it could have knocked Seth out of his chair.

"Fearlessness . . ."

His roommate was a football player. A big kid. The kind of guy who couldn't tolerate weird, weaselly kids like Seth.

"That's your side of the room," his roommate told him, on that first day, as if it wasn't obvious. "Hope you like country music, 'cause I play it all the time."

"Country's okay," Seth said. "if you can put up with some hip-hop."

"Not a problem."

Only after the music issue was settled did his roommate introduce himself. "I'm Wyatt," he said. "Wyatt Van der Meek."

"Van der Meek," Seth repeated. "Easy to remember. Just like that senator."

"Yeah," said Wyatt. "He's my dad."

Seth snapped his eyes up, to check if Wyatt was kidding, but he wasn't.

"A lot of bigwigs send their 'high-needs' kids to this school," said Wyatt.

"'High needs'? Like 'special needs'?"

"Nah, special needs is learning disabilities and stuff like that," said Wyatt. "High needs is . . . well . . . other stuff."

Seth would have asked what other stuff he meant, but he could tell Wyatt wasn't gonna go there.

He began to unpack his suitcase, and then he realized Wyatt was staring at him. It annoyed him, so he said, "You wanna help me unpack?"

"No, that's okay," said Wyatt. "So, you're the one they've been talking about? The one who's getting a free ride?"

"Yeah. So?"

"Nothing. It's just that Dr. Stillwell keeps telling us we gotta treat you good. She says you're very important to all of us."

Seth couldn't figure out why he'd be important to anyone, least of all to a senator's kid. He pulled back his linens to make his bed, and there between the sheets sat a cockroach. A big one, like the kind you get at the end of summer. Seth laughed. "Hey, Wyatt—you think this roach knows he's going to one of the most exclusive schools in the country?"

But Wyatt wasn't answering. Seth turned to see his roommate backed into the corner of his bed, hands spread out against the wall—his jaw locked and eyes peeled so far back it was as if he had no eyelids.

"S-st-step on it!" Wyatt hissed. "K-ki-kill it. Kill it now. *Now, now, now.*"

His breath came in such short, tight bursts, Seth could swear the kid was having a heart attack. He had seen this look before. He had seen it in an elevator. He had seen it on a rooftop. He had seen it at the Greatest Show on Earth.

"Ki-ki-kill it. Pleeeeeheeheese . . ."

Seth looked down at the roach. It wasn't moving very quickly to escape, probably because it was so fat.

"Kill it . . . Pleeeease . . . I'm entomophobic. I have a fear of bugs—you have to kill it!"

"What, this?" Seth picked up the roach and took a step toward Wyatt with the roach in his upturned palm. Wyatt gasped and pressed deeper into the corner. If he could, Seth knew he would disappear right into that corner.

"C'mon, it's just a cockroach." Seth took one step closer.

Wyatt was sweating. *"No. Don't!"*

Seth took another step, and Wyatt let loose a wail of hopelessness.

For the longest moment Seth just stood there. The urge to hold that stupid bug right up to Wyatt's face was overwhelming. The guy's terror was so intense, so out of control, and yet Seth couldn't feel it. He could see it. He could smell the fear, but not feel it. *If his fear becomes strong enough, I will,* said a little voice deep in Seth's mind. *Bring that bug to him, set it on the tip of his nose. Make his terror so powerful that some of it will sink into me, too. Then I'll feel it. Then I'll know.*

Seth closed his eyes. No. He wouldn't do it. If only because Wyatt was his roommate and he had to deal with him all year. Instead Seth fought down that irresistible urge to cultivate Wyatt's fear, and hurled the roach out of the window.

Wyatt relaxed immediately. A breeze blew through the window. It was as if the room itself was breathing a sigh of relief.

"Thanks, man," Wyatt said. "Thanks. Really. Thanks."

Then he reached out and grabbed Seth's arm. Seth didn't know what it was, but there was something weird about that moment. It made all the hairs on his arm stand on end.

He pulled away from Wyatt's grip. "No problem."

Seth very quickly came to understand exactly what Wyatt had meant by "high-needs."

At lunch, Wyatt introduced him to a table full of other students. Genevieve was the daughter of a software billionaire. Mauricio's mother was the lieutenant governor, and although no one knew what Kierth's parents did, the family was rumored to be "richer than God on Good Friday" as Wyatt put it. Everything seemed fine, until Seth got up to get a knife to cut his steak. Wyatt grabbed him by the wrist, pulled him back down, and quietly said, "Don't."

"Huh?"

"Just don't."

As Seth tried to process this strange request, he noticed that no one at the table had steak knives—or any knives, for that matter. There were no forks, either. Only spoons—and plastic ones at that. Then, when Seth looked around, he saw that every other table had kids eating with silverware, not cheap cafeteria stuff either, but real, polished silver—the kind his mother kept locked away in the china hutch. At his table, however, the kids were picking up the steak with their hands and biting into it.

Seth smirked. "What's the problem? You guys werewolves or something?"

They just looked at him blankly, as if maybe they really were.

"I mean—do you have a problem with silver? You know—silver bullets, silverware?"

They looked at each other, then looked away as if Seth had said something unspeakable. Finally Wyatt spoke up. "Genevieve has belonephobia."

"Fear of sharp objects," Genevieve explained. "Knives, forks, and scissors, mostly."

Seth let out a single guffaw of laughter. He hadn't meant to, it just came out.

Genevieve narrowed her eyes. "You think that's funny?"

Seth looked at those angry eyes and felt himself getting angry right back. "I don't know. Maybe. Don't *you* think it's funny?"

"Hey, he's new!" said Wyatt, jumping in. "Give him a break."

"The truth is," said Kierth, "we've all got some phobia."

"Everyone at the table?" said Seth.

"No," Kierth answered. "Everyone at the school. That's why we're here. That's Oakheart's specialty."

"You mean, you didn't know?" said Genevieve, as if she felt sorry for him now.

Seth looked around at the other tables. There were no signs of anything unusual, but then a phobia wasn't really something you wore on your sleeve. It was very personal. Very hidden. That is, until the moment the fear took over.

"I have catoptrophobia," whispered Mauricio. "That's a fear of mirrors."

Then Kierth pointed to himself almost as a matter of pride. "I'm afraid of numbers divisible by three," he said. "They don't even have a name for that!"

Seth just gaped at him.

"It's true. If there were six people at this table, I would have to leave."

Seth found himself stuttering, "B-but that's ridiculous! It doesn't even make sense."

Kierth shrugged. "Of course it doesn't make sense," he said. "It's irrational. A phobia is an irrational fear."

"If it made sense," said Genevieve, a little bit of anger still in her voice, "we'd be able to do something about it, wouldn't we?"

"So how about you?" Mauricio asked. "What are you afraid of?"

There it was. That question again. He was getting so tired of that question.

"Nothing."

"He's lying," snapped Genevieve. "Everyone's here for a reason."

Seth didn't answer her. Instead he looked down at his steak, then reached into his pocket and pulled out the Swiss Army knife he always carried. Usually he just used it to clip his nails. Today it would serve another function.

"Wh-what are you doing?" Genevieve asked, her voice already beginning to tremble.

"What does it look like? I'm cutting my meat." And then he pulled out the knife, plunging it into the meat.

The reaction was instantaneous. Genevieve stood up so quickly, her chair flew out behind her, her hands started to shake uncontrollably, and she let loose a banshee screech that brought silence to the rest of the dining room. She tried to look away, but her eyes were glued on that knife.

The others got up to help her. Wyatt reached over and took the knife away, and Genevieve just about collapsed in Kierth's and Mauricio's arms once it was out of sight.

"You're an asshole," Wyatt said, and slipped the knife into his own pocket, to make sure Seth didn't try it again. Silence still ruled the room, and Seth caught the eyes of the headmistress glaring down at him from the faculty table. No, not glaring . . . studying.

Then Genevieve strode over to him, pulled her hand way back, and slapped him so hard across the face, his head practically spun around. . . .

And in the instant that her palm touched his face, he felt something. More than just the sting of the slap, it was something intense and dark. It brought gooseflesh rising all over his body, just like Wyatt's touch had earlier. He couldn't explain it—but it was a feeling he remembered long after the sting of the slap was gone.

• • •

Seth sat alone at dinner, marveling at how quickly he'd been able to alienate himself from these kids. Why did he always do that? He chuckled bitterly to himself, wondering if perhaps he had a phobia after all. A fear of friendship. What would that be called? he wondered. Comradophobia? Amigophobia? Seth supposed there were as many phobias as there were things in the world to be afraid of. Still, he knew that a fear of friendship was not his problem.

It was embarrassing to have a table all to himself in the midst of a crowded dining hall, so he tried not to meet anyone's eyes. Still, there were some things he couldn't help but notice. Like the way Dr. Stillwell watched him from the faculty table. Or the way his roommate worked the room, whispering to other students and pointing at Seth. Or the way Genevieve was eating a thick lamb chop with a knife and fork.

Seth had chosen a hamburger tonight. He couldn't quite say why.

"I want out of here." Seth paced across the fancy Persian carpets of Dr. Stillwell's huge office. "I don't care if it's free. I don't even care if the next stop is juvie—I want out."

Dr. Stillwell sat calmly in her high-backed leather chair, studying him, always studying him. The headmistress seemed neither surprised nor bothered, which only enraged Seth more.

"Call my parents," Seth demanded. "I want you to call them now."

But she did not lift a finger to pick up her phone.

"Tell me, Seth," she said calmly, "in your opinion, what is the opposite of fear?"

"Why are you asking such a stupid question? I don't want to answer your questions."

"If you want to go home, you must answer my questions, stupid or not."

Seth pounded his fist on the desk. Dr. Stillwell didn't even flinch. "Fine. The opposite of fear is bravery. Are you happy?"

Dr. Stillwell shook her head. "That's a common misconception," she told him. "Bravery is a *reaction* to fear. Fight or flight. Those are the two reactions to a fearful situation. Those who fight are called brave," she said. "Or foolhardy, depending on the outcome."

"Why are you telling me this?" Seth asked. "Why does any of this matter?"

"Now, *there's* a question you'll soon be able to answer for yourself," she said, throwing him a flash of that terrible grin. "I see you've been spending some time with your roommate, Wyatt. Are you two getting along?"

"No," said Seth. "I don't like him. I don't like any of them. They're freaks."

This affected Dr. Stillwell more than anything else he'd said. She sat up slightly straighter in her chair. He could feel her bristling like a static charge.

"Tolerance is a virtue, Seth," she said, her voice just a tiny bit louder than before. "Heaven knows, many people have gone to great pains to tolerate *you*. A phobia does *not* make a person a 'freak.' I have more respect for the kids here than any others—and you should too."

"Do I get to go home, or not?"

"If that's what you want, then you shall go home," Dr. Stillwell said simply. "But first, there's something I wish to show you."

Then she reached into a lower drawer and pulled out a small cardboard box, just large enough to fit in the palm of her hand. "Our science lab has some very interesting specimens. Have you been down there yet?"

Seth shook his head. "What's in the box?" he asked.

"A gift," said Dr. Stillwell. "Something special, something just for you." She opened the lid of the box.

At first it appeared empty, and then two tiny antennas wiggled into view, followed by the body of a beetle, shiny and green—

—and Seth was struck by a sensation so foreign, so unexpected, it stole the very air from his lungs. He felt himself moving backward, and he hadn't told his feet to move. His eyes were locked on the bug, like somehow it controlled him. His chest tightened. His throat swelled so that he couldn't breathe, and he heard himself squeaking out rasping gasps as he tried to get air.

What was this? What was this feeling? His mind reeled, trying to comprehend its intensity. It was ruthless. It was vicious, like a thousand knives slicing through his brain, his heart, his guts. And still the beetle peered at him from the lip of the box, wiggling its horrible antennas.

Seth found himself in the very corner of the room, squeezing into that corner, trying to disappear. And Dr. Stillwell approached with the beetle in the palm of her hand. As she did, the feeling only grew worse.

"Make it stop," squealed Seth. *"Please, make it stop."*

"When you came to my office on your first day," she said in that calm, calm voice of hers, "you told me you wanted to understand. Now do you understand?"

It took all of Seth's will to make his head nod up and down. This was fear, he knew that now. This was what others felt. It was like a gash across his soul, making the very essence of his life vulnerable. How could anyone live with this?

"Please," he said, his voice just a whisper. *"Please, stop it."*

In one smooth motion Dr. Stillwell dropped the bug to the floor and crushed it beneath her shiny black shoe, grinding the beetle back and forth until there was nothing left of it. In a moment the fear was gone. The sensation that flowed through Seth now was as powerful and as unexpected as the first. He felt his throat opening, the pores of his body opening. Air flooded into his lungs. Satisfied relief numbed his brain like a drug.

"Thank you . . . ," was all he could say. "Thank you . . ."

He sat there in the corner, regaining his strength, relishing the depth of his own relief.

"Now then," said Dr. Stillwell, "tell me: What is the opposite of fear?"

And he gave her the answer that everyone else who attended Oakheart Academy already knew.

"Peace," he told her. "The opposite of fear is peace."

The headmistress offered him a satisfied grin. "Very, very good! Now it's time for you to go. There is a special assembly this evening, and you must get yourself ready."

Seth slowly lifted his head, as if it weighed more than his neck could sustain. "Assembly?"

"Yes. You mustn't miss it."

"I want to go home. You said I could go home."

"Of course," she said, with a calmness to her voice meant to soothe, but it only rinsed coldly over Seth like ice water, "but first the assembly. Your roommate is here to accompany you back to your room."

Seth turned to see Wyatt waiting at the door. He had no idea how long Wyatt had been there, or how much he had seen.

Wyatt looked at him oddly—Seth could not remember anyone ever looking at him in this particular way. Was it pity? No, that wasn't it.

"C'mon, Seth," Wyatt said.

Seth fought a battle to pull his emotions together and won, although when he stood, his legs felt weak, as if he were on the verge of fever. He could barely even feel his feet as he moved through the door and down the dark cherrywood hallways of the school. All the while Wyatt kept sneaking sideways glances at Seth, like one might do when escorting a celebrity—and it finally occurred to Seth exactly the way Wyatt had been looking at him back in Dr. Stillwell's office. It was awe. Wyatt had been awestruck.

"I . . . I don't know how to thank you," Wyatt said.

"For what?"

Wyatt didn't answer. Instead he said, "I went outside this afternoon. I took a walk through the rose garden."

"How nice for you," snapped Seth. "Did you pick a bouquet for your football coach?"

He expected some rude comment back from Wyatt, but Wyatt didn't take the bait.

"You don't understand," he said. "The rose garden is full of bees. There are spiderwebs stretched between the bushes. I don't go to the rose garden. But now I can." He hesitated for a moment. "I don't know how to thank you."

"Then don't," said Seth, trying his best to block the image of an insect-filled garden from his mind.

As they turned the corner toward the dormitories, several kids who had been chattering and laughing in the hall stopped and looked at him with that same strange gaze of awe. Then they began whispering to one another. *"That's him!" "He's the one." "Go shake his hand." "I won't do it—you do it!"*

Then a boy stepped forward. He wore a surgical mask—like people wore during the pandemic—and above the blue edge of the mask floated a pair of bulging eyes that pleaded with such intensity, Seth could swear those eyes were about ready to pop out of his face. The boy wore latex surgical gloves on his hands, too. With a deep breath the boy reached to his right wrist, peeled the glove off with a snap, and thrust his trembling fingers forward.

"I'm Theo. Pleased to meet you."

Seth had no intention of shaking his hand, but Wyatt grabbed Seth's wrist and guided his hand into Theo's until they met, clasping like train couplers. That strange flash of something not quite electrical shot from Theo to Seth, up his arm, to his spine. Synapses fired along his central nervous system, shooting up through the base of Seth's neck into the deepest, most primitive part of his brain. Seth gasped.

"Germs! You're afraid of germs!"

But Theo pulled off his surgical mask and dropped it, along with both gloves, to the floor. "Not anymore."

Seth could feel the walls of the hallway begin to squirm. Germs were everywhere. There in the corners. There on the hands and in the breath of all the kids around him. Everything, everyone was so unclean. He looked at his own hands. He would have to scrub and scrub and scrub them until every last germ was gone. How could anyone stand it?

Seth had to get away from there. Away from *them*. He bolted, and although Wyatt tried to stop him, Seth pushed past him, moving with the adrenaline speed of someone fighting for their life, not knowing where he could possibly go, but knowing that he had to leave. He found himself in a stairwell, and, hearing voices beneath him, he climbed up and up, until the stairs were gone, and a ladder went up through a small hole. He took the ladder and found himself in the school's bell tower. The school's massive bells hung above him; the immense bronze shells, blackened from age, held just a hint of their former metallic sheen.

As a fear of heights was not one of his newly adopted terrors, he had no problem going to the edge of the open-air belfry and collapsing on the ledge. He turned his face into the stone pillar beside him, refusing to look out over a world that suddenly seemed so choked with unknown terrors.

He felt sure someone would follow him, to drag him back down to the school, but no one came at first. Then finally he heard a voice. Ice water. But this time, with his thoughts so furiously aflame, that voice was soothing.

"I know what you feel," Dr. Stillwell said. "I understand, but I can never share it. There are many terrors that have passed through these halls, but they live within the students who come here. I can sympathize with their pain, but never share it. No one can. No one but you."

"Home," Seth hissed. "You promised."

And with that she dropped some pages before him. It was a legal document bearing his name and signed by several people. Two of the signatures he recognized as those of his parents.

"As you know, we offered you a full scholarship, worth more money than your parents could ever possibly afford . . . but the scholarship required that they surrender their legal rights."

Seth raised his eyes to look at her.

"You have been legally adopted by Oakheart Academy." She pulled back the document from him. "So you see . . . you *are* home."

"No . . ."

Then she did something Seth did not expect. She sat beside him on the ledge and took him in her arms. And he allowed it, for in this awful moment, even the embrace of a spider was better than no embrace at all.

"The bells have not rung here for more than ten years," she told him, her voice no longer ice to him, for he had grown accustomed to its chill. "Do you know why?"

Seth shook his head.

"They haven't rung, because we haven't had someone like you for ten years. There are few in the world like you, and we are honored to count you among our own."

Few like me, he thought. What did that mean? All his life he'd felt he was somehow different from others around him. The steeled fearlessness that dominated his life, the apparent cruelty with which he treated others. He had longed to be like others—to feel what they felt. Yet even now, as he was truly feeling their innermost pains, he was not becoming like them. He was becoming something else. "What's happening to me?"

Dr. Stillwell answered with ease, as if the answer was obvious. "You are becoming fear," she said. "*Their* fear. You have a solemn duty here. A holy duty. Your panophobia shall be a blessing."

"I don't understand."

"I think you do."

She was right. No matter how much he tried to deny it, he understood. He was a sponge for the terrors that filled every corner of Oakheart. A sponge begins hard and abrasive, as he had been all his life. Without even knowing it, he had been waiting his whole life for this dark purpose.

Tears now poured from his eyes with such intensity his head began to pound. "I can't do this. I can't *be* this. It's more than I can stand."

"Oh, you'll stand it," said Dr. Stillwell with complete confidence, "because you are strong. And soon you will come to know how much you truly want it."

"Want it?"

"We are never given a gift without the passion to use it."

Seth reached down into himself to see if this was true, but his thoughts and emotions were so shredded by the storm within him, he had no way of telling.

"I'm scared." It was the one emotion he was sure of. Until arriving here he hadn't known what that meant.

"I know," Dr. Stillwell said, still embracing him. "So many of us spend our lives trying to find our place in the world . . . but I envy you, Seth, because you know yours. There is nothing more fulfilling than knowing what you are."

"I . . . I am . . . I am fear," he said, trying it on like a strange set of clothes, only to find that it fit. Perfectly. "I am fear for all." His voice felt a bit stronger now. Sturdier. Hearing the strength come back to his own voice brought some strength to the rest of him as well. "They *need* me," he said, realizing that it was true. "More than anything else in the world, they need me."

"Yes!" Dr. Stillwell said, stroking his hair like a mother. "Thanks to you, they will overcome the fears that hold them back. They will make a difference in this troubled world, because of you."

"They will remember me."

"They will love you."

"Because I matter."

"More than you know."

Seth stood, looking out over the grounds, and the fields beyond the school. Insects, and germs, and sharp objects—all these things were out there, striking painfully against his soul, but Dr. Stillwell was right. No matter how awful the phobias felt, he was strong. He could bear it. Because it was his purpose.

The bells above slowly began to swing, until the clappers hit their mark. The powerful tolls, deafening and resonant, rattled him to the bone, and when they were done, he turned to Dr. Stillwell, his ears still ringing long after the bells had fallen silent. "The special assembly?"

"The bells have called the students to the great hall. You are the honored guest," she said. "Are you ready?"

I'll never be ready, thought Seth, but then, who is ever ready to accept their fate? "Yes," he said.

I have a purpose, he kept telling himself as he descended from the bell tower. *It is noble. It is good. Imagine me, chosen for something good!*

Two students, who barely had the courage to look upon him, swung open the doors of the great hall for Seth as he and Dr. Stillwell approached. The vaulted ceiling of the great hall towered before him, full of stained-glass windows and Gothic arches. The rows of seats were packed with students. A single aisle ran down the center of the hall, toward the stage. There was no podium on that stage, for what was to occur here would happen in the aisle. Even now the crowds of students were standing in the rows, pressing toward that center aisle, ready to reach out their hands toward him.

There was a sanctity to this mission. A holiness that would wash him clean, even in the face of his newfound terrors. Panophobia. The fear of all things. It would soon be his cross to bear, and the knowledge that somehow he would bear it gave him the strength he needed to take that first step toward his desperate schoolmates.

With his hands held out wide on either side of him, he began his journey down the aisle like a bridegroom toward the altar, embracing the knowledge that soon he would be very, very afraid.

Bad Fortune at Richard Yee's

The Greenblatts settled down for another dinner at Richard Yee's, perhaps the most famous Chinese restaurant in all of Brooklyn. They dined at Richard Yee's every Saturday night. It was a family tradition that everyone loved. Greenblatts loved their Chinese food with a passion.

Everyone, that is, except for Robin.

Her parents and brothers could have lived on lo mein, and don't even mention the kung pao situation. They could have had hot and sour soup pumped into their bloodstream intravenously, and they would have been as happy as sweet and pungent clams (Number 26 on the dinner menu). But Robin prayed that one day their tastes would change, and maybe she wouldn't be forced to suffer through yet another endless multicourse meal. It wasn't the food she objected to; actually, she enjoyed that part of it.

The problem was the cookies.

It started back when Robin was seven.

Aunt Sonia was visiting from Buffalo. She rarely came down to Brooklyn, but when she did, the traditional meal at Richard Yee's was always the first order of business. And so, the whole Greenblatt family had piled into the minivan and headed to Richard Yee's: Mom, Dad, Aunt Sonia, Michael, Seth, and Robin—who, even at the age of seven, knew her way around a pair of chopsticks.

The meal was delicious. Six courses spun around the lazy Susan in the center of the big round table until everyone was so stuffed they could hardly breathe. Next came the tiny scoops of green tea ice cream in the little silver cups.

And then the cookies.

Oh, how Robin used to love the cookies! Sweet vanilla and almond flavors carefully folded into that familiar crescent shape, with a surprise inside its shell. Never mind that they hadn't even been invented in China—they were still a part of the Greenblatts' dining experience. Since she had learned to read, fortune cookies were a special, delightful challenge, because they always contained big words. Everyone selected their cookie.

"Robin starts today," her mom said, which made Robin feel special. She cracked the cookie and read the little slip of paper.

"'You are generous of spirit and will move mountains.'"

"I believe it!" said her father. Then the reading went clockwise around the table.

"'Today is the tomorrow you worried about yesterday.'"

"'You haven't come this far to only come this far.'"

"'What good are wings without the courage to fly?'"

"'Showing up is the first and hardest step in anything worth doing.'"

Through the readings, Robin's brothers Seth and Michael were snickering and sharing glances. Robin could tell they were up to something but wasn't sure what.

Then came Aunt Sonia's turn. She broke the cookie in half with a loud snap and peeled out the tiny piece of paper, holding it at arm's length so that her farsighted eyes could read it. *"'You will be taken on Wednesday by freak accident.'"*

Mom gasped and Dad's spoon clattered to his silver ice-cream cup.

Seth and Michael, who had been ready to burst out laughing a moment ago, suddenly dropped their jaws and sank into their seats. If they could have disappeared into a hole in the floor, they would have.

"Let me see that." Dad snatched the little piece of paper from Aunt Sonia, then glared at Seth and Michael without saying a word. The twins cracked like an eggshell.

"It was Seth's idea," Michael blurted out.

"Yeah, but Michael bought the gag fortune cookies," shot back Seth.

"And anyway," said Michael, "it was supposed to be funny, not sick, y'know—they were supposed to say things like, *'Help, I'm being held prisoner in a fortune cookie factory,'* or something." They started elbowing and pushing each other. It was Aunt Sonia who saved the day. She began to laugh—and not just any laugh, but an Aunt Sonia laugh. Her laughter was always long and loud and contagious. In a few moments the whole family was laughing, and soon even the table next to them was in stitches as well, without even knowing why they were laughing.

Pretty soon they all forgot about the bad fortune. Then, the following Wednesday, they all said their goodbyes as Aunt Sonia boarded her bus back to Buffalo . . .

. . . and somewhere in the Catskill Mountains, the bus plunged off the road, down into the freezing cold of Kiamesha Lake. Everyone survived. Except for Aunt Sonia.

It was then that Robin stopped reading her fortunes.

It was a secret she kept for years. After every meal at Richard Yee's, Robin held the offensive little pastry in her hand, while the others read their little phrases of wisdom and fate. Finally it would be Robin's turn. She would hold that cookie in her lap, where no one could see, hating the awful cookie with every ounce of her being.

"Go on, Robin," her father would prompt. "Aren't you going to open it?"

No, she wanted to say. *I refuse to read it!* For deep in her heart, she felt certain that no one should know the future, no one should try to guess, and no one should serve up tiny shreds of destiny and pretend it was just in fun. There was nothing fun about it. Robin had already seen the results of a bad fortune.

She couldn't tell her parents; they wouldn't understand. So, week after week, she would take the little cookie, keep it hidden in her lap, unbroken, and, like a magician, she would pull out a blank strip of paper that she had cut from a notebook. Then she would hold up that blank paper and pretend to read, saying something like, *"Love will rain on you like stars rain from the heavens,"* or, *"For every smile you give, it will be returned one hundredfold,"* or something else that sounded both wise and vacant at the same time. Having heard the fortunes of her family a thousand times over, she knew how to fake it, and no one ever suspected that her fortune cookies went unopened. She would slip the unbroken cookies into her pocket, dispose of them in her own special way when no one was looking, and they would never be seen again.

Or so she thought.

It was the first day of the Year of the Dragon, Lunar New Year, when Robin's little cookie world began to unravel.

The Greenblatts were eating at Richard Yee's on that particular night, and the restaurant was packed and festooned with decorations for the Lunar New Year. At the end of the meal, it was business as usual for Robin: she pretended to crack her cookie beneath the table, then picked up a blank scrap of paper she had brought from home and pretended to read her fortune. All went according to plan. Then, just before she left, she went to the restroom, got rid of the cookie, and rejoined her family.

At home that night, however, she was disturbed to find something strange and mushy in the medicine chest, right beside the dental floss.

"Gross!" She flicked it out, and it landed on the bathroom counter, inert and lifeless. It was a wet fortune cookie. This was strange, because no one brought home unopened fortune cookies in their house—it was almost a sacrilegious thing to do. She was certain that she had flushed hers at Richard Yee's. But then where had this one come from?

"Michael! Seth!" she called, but there was no answer. She scraped up the soggy cookie and stormed downstairs to where her brothers were sitting in front of the TV.

The twins, now seventeen, never pulled tricks on Robin anymore, unless they were really good tricks—the kind she'd be mad about, but deep down appreciate on a conceptual level. This was not that.

"Who put this in the medicine cabinet?" she said, trying to sound as unbothered by it as possible.

They looked at the waterlogged pastry. Michael shrugged, and Seth said, "Not me."

"Well, someone had to put it there."

"Maybe we have mice," suggested Michael.

"Or squirrels," offered Seth. "They hoard nuts. Maybe they could go for fortune cookies too."

Robin decided not to press the issue. She took the cookie out to the back porch and smashed the thing beneath her heel. It made a sickening, squishy sound, like a snail crunched on pavement.

There, thought Robin. *That's the end of it.* She went to bed and slept soundly, putting thoughts of the rogue cookie out of her mind.

And in the morning she awoke to find another one on her pillow.

"Mom!"

Her mother came running. "Robin, honey, what is it? What's wrong?"

She was about to tell her mother about the mysterious reappearance of the cookie, but thought better of it. Instead she held the cookie behind her back and tried to make something up, but her mind drew a blank.

"Um . . . ummm."

Then her attention was drawn to something skittering across the carpet. She gasped. "A mouse!"

Her mother jumped. "Where?"

Robin pointed, but her mom turned too late, just missing the small blur that ducked under Robin's bureau.

"Uh . . . that's why I called you in," said Robin. "There's a mouse in my room." Once more she saw the light-colored blur dart off beneath her bed.

"Did you hear that?" Robin looked up.

Her mother looked up too, as if she could see through the ceiling. "I don't hear anything."

It sounded like a rodent crawling around in the attic. Then Robin heard skittering inside the wall. "There—do you hear it this time?"

Mrs. Greenblatt listened, then shook her head, but took her daughter's word for it and sighed. "Mice—just what we need."

But while Mrs. Greenblatt was disgusted, Robin left for school feeling oddly relieved. Mice must have been dragging all sorts of munchies around the house. The mystery was solved. The universe was back in order. Although there was one question she kept in the back of her mind all day. Where did the mice find fortune cookies?

A cloud of dust billowed downward as the exterminator climbed down his ladder from the attic. Mom and Dad waited in the hallway. Mom nervously scratched the dry skin of her elbows, and Dad looked gloomy, probably wondering what all this was going to cost. Robin sat in her room doing homework, but kept glancing at them through the open door of her room.

"Well," began the exterminator, "the good news is I can't find signs of any rodents anywhere in your house. But honestly, you *should* have mice, with all these things lying around."

Robin bolted upright in her chair. What was he talking about? She leaned back until she could see him through the open door. He was holding a handful of jagged little pastries in his hand. Fortune cookies.

"That's strange," said Mr. Greenblatt, examining the dusty relics the exterminator had given him.

The man shrugged, and wrote out a bill that made Dad grimace.

• • •

The family spent the following Saturday cleaning up the attic, where they were amazed to find dozens of fortune cookies scattered about the floorboards.

"Weird," Seth said. "Must be from the previous owners."

And since no one in the family had ever been up in the attic, no one contested the theory.

"Total slobs," Michael said, then made a move to crack open one of the stale cookies, but Robin slapped it out of his hand before he could.

"Hey, what was that for?"

"We just got this place cleaned up," Robin replied. "Do you want to get crumbs everywhere?" Maybe the others didn't know, but Robin had been in the attic before, and she knew the cookies hadn't been there when they moved in.

That night, at their weekly foray to Richard Yee's, Robin poked at her rice and toyed with her Mongolian beef, with absolutely no appetite, wishing she could be anywhere else in the world. The rest of the family shoveled down the food without speaking, and when the meal was over, the waiter approached with a plate of fortune cookies.

The Greenblatts looked at one another, and everyone but Robin burst out laughing. After the day's ordeal, the last thing anyone wanted was a fortune cookie. For a moment Robin felt relief wash over her, figuring that, for once, the ritual reading would be canceled tonight—and maybe every night thereafter. But her parents were creatures of habit, and couldn't let it go.

"Aw, what the heck," Dad said. "Let's see what they say."

"I'll go first," said Michael. He snapped the cookie open and pulled the paper out, studying it with a furrowed brow before reading it aloud. "Here's a weird one," he said. "*'Take care, for the fortune you shun today may consume you tomorrow.'*"

Dad went next. "Ooh," he said. "*'Someone you love is about to leave you.'*"

Mom chuckled. "Probably me," she said, then cracked her own cookie and peeled out the fortune. To Robin the paper seemed to squirm in her mother's hand like a tiny tapeworm. She couldn't stop staring at it as her mother read: "*'Set your dinner table for four. Begin tomorrow.'*"

Robin could feel the panic silently well up inside her. Didn't her family know? Couldn't they see what was happening? It was those vile cookies. They were plotting against her!

Crack! Seth ripped his cookie open and drew out the slithering piece of paper. "*'The Sister of False Fortune receives judgment at dawn.'*" Seth flipped the paper over to see if there was more. "What does that mean?"

Blank stares from Mom and Dad, a shrug from Michael, and nothing from Robin, who couldn't even look up from the table.

"Your turn, Robin," prompted Dad. Robin had to fight to keep herself from hyperventilating.

"C'mon, Robin," Seth said impatiently, "we don't have all night."

She had her slip of blank paper in her pocket, but her fingers trembled so much that she couldn't get it—and even if she did, she wouldn't be able to think of any false fortune to say. Still, they all stared at her, waiting for her to tell them what the Fates said.

"Robin?" Mom asked.

"Excuse me." Robin stood up, and her chair scraped itself back on the floor, a loud, jarring noise. In a moment she found herself in the bathroom, staring at her own wild eyes in the mirror.

Stop it, Robin, she told herself. *This is crazy—they're only cookies.*

But they were more than mere cookies—Robin had always suspected that. She thought back to poor Aunt Sonia—how she had laughed away her own bad fortune, only to be killed by it. Deep down Robin had always felt that the cookie hadn't merely predicted Aunt Sonia's fate. Somehow it had caused it!

Frantically, Robin reached into her purse, finding a felt-tipped pen. In the other hand she still held the offensive cookie, its secret message still trapped in the dark crevices of its twisted folds. If these hideous little pastries were the makers of fate, she would defy them to the end. With the pen she wrote on the surface of the cookie *NO FATE!* like a bright red tattoo, and she hurled the cookie into the toilet. She watched as the swirling waters spun it around and around the bowl, fighting to take it down into eternal sewer darkness.

When she finally stepped from the bathroom, hands cold and wet, her dad was signing the check, and her family was preparing to go. It was as if nothing had happened. But how could they not know? Didn't they understand what those fortunes had said? How could they not have seen the look on her face as she raced off into the bathroom?

Or maybe they did see, thought Robin, *and they're a part of it. . . .*

As soon as the thought dawned on her, it mushroomed and multiplied until it filled every corner of her mind. If this was a conspiracy, how deep did it go? Was it her brothers? Her parents, too? The exterminator—was he involved? How about the waiter, who so innocently handed out those malevolent cookies tonight? Suddenly something in Robin snapped like the crust of a fortune cookie, and she felt herself slip out of the arms of those she loved, and into a place where everyone was suspect.

"Get your coat on, Robin. It's cold tonight," said Mom.

"What's that supposed to mean?" snapped Robin, suddenly realizing that there might be hidden messages in everything the people around her said. Was it a warning that her life would be cold and empty? Did it mean her parents had decided to start giving her the cold shoulder? Then Mom threw Dad a glance. What did that glance mean? What were they planning to torment Robin with now?

"Robin," asked her father, "what's gotten into you?"

"As if you didn't know," was all she said.

She held her silence on the way home, and through the evening. While the others settled in for an evening of TV bingeing, Robin locked herself in her room, sitting knees to chest in the corner of her bed. When sleep came, it was cold and fraught with disjointed nightmares.

It was near dawn when the strange sound dragged her up from the depths of her troubled sleep.

Boink-boink-gurgle-boink.

It was a familiar enough night sound. Just like the creaking of their settling house, or the skittering of leaves across the roof, it was a sound she had grown used to, or at least learned to tolerate.

Blurble-boink-glubb-glubb.

It was, of course, the toilet—its porcelain intestines echoing a complaint as water slipped through an imperfect seal. Fixing the noise was simple—just a matter of jiggling the handle. But no one was getting up to do it. No one but Robin. Slowly she opened her door.

Gurgle-hiss-glubb-glubb.

It was louder than usual tonight. She turned on the bathroom light to see the clean waters of the bowl shimmering silently. Mom was insistent about clean bathrooms, and so the bowl was immaculate, full of Caribbean-blue water.

But tonight, something was causing a little tempest in that particular teapot. Robin narrowed her eyes as she noticed something in the very bottom of the bowl. It seemed to be moving, crawling its way up the drain. She slammed down the handle, but the water did not flush. Instead the water swirled and slowly began to rise, brimming, and delivering the crawling little mass to the surface; soggy and beige. She didn't need a closer inspection to know what it was, because on its waterlogged surface the words *NO FATE* were scrawled in her own handwriting, the deep red letters bleeding into one another.

Robin had to bite her lip to keep herself from screaming. With the water flooding the floor, she slammed the door and hurried back toward her room . . . but something stopped her. Another sound. This one outside.

She went to the hallway window, which was open just a crack, and looked out across the lawn.

Crunch-crunch, skitch-skitch. Something was moving beneath the piles of dead winter leaves. Something was burrowing beneath the ground. Many things. She could see the crisscrossing, slithering patterns they made in the ground, like a thousand moles burrowing closer and closer to—

She slammed the window to lock out the noise, but that wasn't enough. She had to seal them out any way she could. Tearing through the house as fast as her ice-cold feet could carry her, Robin went to every window and every door, bolting them and double-bolting them. She stuffed a pillow in the doggie door, she plugged up the garbage disposal, she closed the air-conditioning vents.

Her parents and brothers still hadn't woken up—and she wouldn't wake them either, for fear that somehow, in some way, they were allies of those evil little fortunes. Finally when she was certain the house was secure, she took a moment to sit down on the couch and catch her breath.

They would not catch her tonight. And tomorrow she would run. She would go far away where fortunes were not yet written. Surely there had to be a place like that—she just had to find it.

At first, the skittering she heard didn't register in her mind. It was just another one of those night noises she had grown accustomed to: ashes slipping down the chimney.

The chimney?

Instantly, Robin realized her fatal mistake. The flue was wide open, and she dared not go near it now, for they were already tumbling down.

She broke for her bedroom, letting lose a scream that might have woken the dead, and most certainly woke up everyone living in the house. Her parents and brothers came barreling out of their rooms as Robin crashed past, her arms flailing madly. She ducked into her room, slammed the door, locked it, put a chair in front of it, and sat down, her head in her hands, sobbing.

"Robin, what's wrong?" wailed her parents, pounding on the door. "What is it? What's happened?"

She wouldn't answer them. How did she know she could trust them? What if, when she opened the door, they weren't really her parents at all, but were beige shells of flesh, hollow except for a single message scrawled on a squirming white sheet? She couldn't open the door now. She didn't dare.

"Robin, please . . ."

She opened her eyes for an instant . . . and in that instant, she saw it. There, alone on the little round rug in front of her closet, right in the center of the rug's concentric rings . . . a single fortune cookie.

It didn't move. It didn't squirm. It merely waited. For her. As it had waited for her since that first day at Richard Yee's after Aunt Sonia's bus plunge.

As she stared at it, the truth came to her in bright clarity. A truth she had been hiding from everyone . . . including herself.

"What have I done?" She whispered.

She had never thrown all those fortunes away, had she? All these years, she had told herself that she had flushed them, or crumbled them, or shoved them into the trash. She had made herself believe her own lies. But the truth was, she had kept them—because as much as she despised them, deep down she was far too superstitious to throw away an unread fortune. Now a corner of her mind that she had always kept locked sprang open, and the truth spilled out. *She* was the one who had hurled the cookies into the attic. *She* was the one who had slipped a cookie into the medicine chest the other night. *She* was the one who had buried them in the yard the way a dog buries bones, knowing they were always there, waiting. And *she* was the one who had plunged her hand into the grungy toilet at Richard Yee's, desperate to get back her *NO FATE* fortune before it could be irretrievably lost in the sewers of Brooklyn.

Slowly, she made her way to the little cookie in the middle of the rug and picked it up. It was the perfect fortune cookie. Some cookies had their fortunes sticking slightly out of the end, like the flag on a Hershey's kiss. But not this one. Its message was well concealed within its snug but fragile folds.

With the thumbs of both hands, she pulled on the ends until the cookie wrenched in two, spilling forth its white paper soul. And for the first time in eight years, Robin cast her eyes upon her fortune.

Had she remembered the closet, she could have saved herself. Had she looked at it—seen the way the closet door bulged like a boiler ready to blow . . . but she was too focused on that one fortune, so she didn't stand a chance when the closet door exploded open, sending a suffocating slide of thousands upon thousands of fortune cookies on top of her, so much denser than they appeared, carrying so much more weight than anyone could have guessed.

The world went dark as the cookies began to cover her, spilling forth from the closet in an endless flood. It wasn't just all the fortunes she had hoarded over the years—it was all the fortunes in the world, it seemed. They spilled out upon Robin in a cascade of sweet-smelling destiny, impossible to ever deny. And as Robin felt the last remnants of her mind slip away, she began a chilling fit of maniacal laughter. Because the tiny slip of paper she still clutched in her hand read:

"You will be buried in good fortune."

Pea Soup

Death would have been better.

Nathan Everett was convinced of it. Death would have been easy compared to the torture of the drive to his grandparents' house. Eight unendurable hours cooped up in the back seat with a sister on each side. The three of them sat like caged animals as the dusk dissolved into night.

"I'm hungry," grumbled Nathan.

"You're always hungry," snapped Amelia, his older sister, the world's most unpleasant travel companion.

A billboard in the distance began to grow larger as they approached it, but Nathan didn't take much notice of it. Instead he tried to focus on his phone, which was at one percent.

For an instant the approaching billboard reflected their headlights, casting a pale olive light into the car, but the sign quickly passed, and the night dove back into the blackness that filled the awful crevices of the earth commonly called "the middle of nowhere."

Nathan wiggled his foot, which had fallen asleep—and even that slight motion was met by a violent shove from Amelia.

"Stop kicking me!" she complained.

"I wasn't kicking—my foot fell asleep, and I was—"

"Mom, will you tell him to stop kicking me?"

"But—"

"Ouch!" came a shout from his left. Nathan turned to see his younger sister, Katie, holding a hand over her eye. "Nathan hit me in the eye!"

"It was an accident," pleaded Nathan. "It was my elbow. . . ."

But Katie was already crying.

"You see how he's acting?" said Amelia.

It was no use. His mom flicked on the dome light and turned to him, extending her wagging finger. When she extended the wagging finger, it always meant that all hope was lost.

"Nathan, I swear to you, if you don't change your behavior . . . ," Mom growled, her finger still wagging hypnotically up and down. Nathan watched the bright red nail do its little dance beneath the dim glow of the dome light up above. "Just keep your hands to yourself."

"And his feet!" added Amelia—which, of course, was impossible, because Nathan sat squarely on the hump in the middle of the back seat, and the only other place to put his feet would have been his mouth.

"Why can't you all get along for once?" their father pleaded from the relative safety of the driver's seat. He reached over and turned up the radio, which dragged down a faint country station among violent bursts of static.

How much longer to Grandma and Grandpa's? wondered Nathan. *Five more hours? Six? And I'm expected to survive that long? Impossible!*

A rectangular shape appeared in the dark distance. With his phone now dead, Nathan let his eyes follow the approaching shape. Another roadside billboard. Nathan squinted until he could see it clearly. On it was a picture of a bowl, and in the bowl, something steamy and green: a swampy brew, thick and chunky. The words painted above the bowl read:

PEA SOUP—168 MILES!

Nathan grimaced. "Pea soup. Blech!"

Little Katie turned to him with her brown eyes wide in revulsion. "They make soup out of pee?"

Nathan sighed, not having the strength to respond. The sign loomed closer and brighter until their car passed into darkness once more.

Another hour of purgatory.

Dense white nebulas of fog brooded on the road, waiting to be pierced by a car on cruise control. Dad had shamelessly forced them to sing "A Hundred Bottles of Beer on the Wall." All hundred verses. Only they didn't sing about beer, since Mom felt it was an inappropriate beverage to dedicate so much quality singing time to, so they argued over what liquid to sing about. Nathan wanted root beer, Katie wanted apple juice, and Amelia wanted iced cappuccino. Dad abstained from voting, and as usual, Mom sided with Amelia. "A Hundred Bottles of Iced Cappuccino on the Wall" filled Nathan's aching ears for twice as long as beer would have.

When the song was over, Katie was asleep, stretching and poking her shoes all over Nathan's anatomy.

"Don't you dare wake her," said Mom, wagging her finger again.

Right about then, another rectangular shape appeared in the distance. The approaching road sign loomed closer until it seemed to be directly in their path—but that was just an optical illusion. In a moment it took its normal place on the right side of the road, growing brighter. The image was familiar: a large, steaming tureen of green. This time the sign read:

PEA SOUP—87 MILES!

As Nathan examined the image, he noticed that the soup wasn't chunky and gloppy at all. It seemed a smooth and shimmering bright green. For a moment, as the sign whooshed past, Nathan could swear he smelled the stuff. After three hours cooped up in a car with his family's various bodily odors, the smell of pea soup didn't seem that bad after all. Of course, it was just a trick of his mind, but he tried to hold on to that smell long after the sign had passed.

"You know, come to think of it, I'm getting a little hungry myself," said Dad.

The road did not turn. It did not vary a single degree to the left or right. Beyond the dark flatlands, a crescent moon rose, anemic and uninviting. With legs bruised from an hour of pummeling from Katie's feet, Nathan tried to see something—anything—of interest off the side of the road, beneath that sickle moon. Every once in a while, he thought he saw fields: rows of crops speckled with gray boulders. He tried to imagine those boulders as people hunched over the midnight crops—and when he stared out the window long enough, he could make himself believe that they actually moved. Nathan wondered if this place would look as bleak in the daytime . . . and wondered if those crops were of the edible variety. He was even more hungry now. There hadn't been a single place to stop for more than an hour on the desolate highway.

This time, when the road sign made its appearance, Nathan stared at its dark shape in anticipation as it approached.

"Turn on your high beams, Dad," he said.

The headlights flicked brighter, and the bowl of soup on the billboard seemed to practically leap out at them.

PEA SOUP   7 MILES!

This time the bowl was larger than before, and the soup within seemed to swirl and glimmer like liquid jade. Nathan had only tasted pea soup once before in his life. He had thought that once would be enough, but now the hunger in his belly was telling him differently. He could smell the soup now stronger than anything. He could feel it running down his throat, sweet and delicious. Suddenly there was nothing in the world he wanted more than pea soup.

"Hey, Dad! Maybe we should stop there and get something to eat."

"I was thinking exactly the same thing."

Those were the longest seven miles Nathan could ever remember.

A final billboard emblazoned with the words PEA SOUP—EXIT HERE! greeted them at the turnoff, and there, alone in the distance, stood the restaurant. It seemed tiny as they approached down a weatherworn two-lane road, but like everything else in this flat part of the world, looks were deceiving. By the time they reached it, Nathan could tell it wasn't just a little shack, but a full-fledged restaurant, two stories high, with rooms that seemed to stretch out in all directions. The entire structure was outlined with winking Christmas lights, even though it was March, and the parking lot was packed. It seemed to Nathan that every traveler for a hundred square miles must have stopped here.

"Must be a popular place," said Mom, the queen of understatement.

"Just park anywhere, Dad," said Amelia, rubbing her stomach, clearly as hungry as Nathan.

By now Katie had started stirring, and as she opened her weary eyes to the bright flashing lights, she quickly revived. "It looks like the North Pole!"

Katie was right. Nathan recalled a visit to a place called Santa's Workshop when he was little. It was full of animatronic elves, and featured electric bumper sleighs. This place reminded him of that—bright and inviting. In fact, a little too inviting.

"There!" shouted Amelia. "Park there!"

"That's a red zone, dear," said their mother.

"Who cares?" Amelia unlocked her door. "What are they going to do, tow us? There's probably not a tow truck for fifty miles!"

And since the huge lot didn't have a single parking place, Dad pulled right up to the red zone. Nathan, whose hunger was making him light-headed, didn't complain. The second the car was stopped, he pushed Katie out, took a deep breath of the brisk air, and made a beeline to the front entrance, where a crowd of people were heading in.

"That's odd," said their mother. "All these lights, and nowhere is the name of the restaurant."

"Who cares?" said Nathan. "As long as there's food."

"Yeah," echoed Katie, dragging her ragged doll behind her.

Inside, the crowd seemed to quickly disperse as an army of hosts and hostesses led hungry families into the cavernous depths of the restaurant. Finally the Everetts were alone, with a single young hostess. She seemed pleasant enough, although her platinum-blond hair was pulled into such a tight bun on top of her head that it seemed to stretch out her cheeks and eyes. Still, she had a heartwarming smile, and the softest of green eyes. She smiled at Nathan, and he found himself smiling back.

"My, my—you look like you've come a long way."

"And a lot farther to go," responded Dad.

"Well, I'm glad you found your way to our little corner of the world," said the hostess. "Party of five?" She reached down, finding five menus without even looking.

"Yes," said Mr. Everett. "How long's the wait?"

Her stretch-lipped smile widened to reveal a row of perfect teeth. "There's never a wait," she told them. "We pride ourselves on service."

She turned and led them past room after room of diners, all happily consuming their meals, and finally sat them down in a cozy oak room, with plaid carpeting and a crackling fireplace. The Everetts settled in and she handed them the menus. "I'll also be your server tonight," the tight-haired waitress said. "Today's special is pea soup."

"Big surprise," said Amelia.

"Soup's only two dollars a bowl," said the waitress.

"I'll have one!" Nathan blurted out.

His father threw him an I'm-wiser-than-you look. "Wouldn't you rather see what else is on the menu?"

"No," said Nathan, with conviction. "I want the soup."

"Me, too," said Katie, who now understood what pea soup was really made from.

"So do I," said Mom.

Dad sighed, putting all pretenses aside. "I guess I do too."

"I'll have the tuna salad," said Amelia.

The waitress/hostess took their menus and glided away.

"Two bucks!" mused Dad. "What a deal!"

His wife patted his hand. "Things are less expensive in this part of the world, dear."

With Nathan's hunger growing exponentially, he busied himself watching the other patrons. It seemed they weren't the only ones who were hungry. Across the room sat a policeman, digging his bread into a bowl of soup as if mining for gold, savoring every last bit of it. At another table an elderly couple lifted spoon to mouth over and over again, faster than they ought to be able to move. And at yet another table, a businessman gave up on his spoon and lifted the bowl to his lips, pouring its steaming contents into his mouth, chugging it down as fast as he could swallow. Little rivers of green coursed down his cheeks and onto his tie, and then he licked the soup off his tie.

A few minutes later the waitress reappeared and slid bowls before them. The edges were delicately carved and hand-painted in soft pastels, like the finest of china. Inside rested a perfect circle of pale green soup.

"I'm afraid we're having some trouble with the tuna salad," said the waitress to Amelia. "But here's some pea soup while you're waiting." She smiled at Dad reassuringly. "On the house." Nathan wondered what sort of trouble they could have with tuna salad.

Amelia took a deep whiff of the soup. "Well, I guess it couldn't hurt to try it."

Nathan's ravenous appetite was quickly taking control. He could feel the soup's rich aroma reaching up his nostrils, taunting and teasing. The smell was so overpowering, he felt he might black out. His peripheral vision went dim. His ears began to ring. He couldn't feel his fingers or his toes.

"Bon appétit," said the waitress.

It was as if Nathan were possessed. Suddenly he craved this soup with every ounce of his being. He craved it more than anything in the world. Nathan hungrily dipped his spoon into the bowl and brought the rich brew to his lips, letting its velvety creaminess spill over his taste buds.

Nathan couldn't remember how long it took him to finish off that bowl. It was as if he were lost in a trance. He might as well have been unconscious. The next thing he remembered was staring down at the empty bowl, and suddenly feeling very, very sad about its souplessness.

He looked up at his parents. Their bowls were empty as well. So was Amelia's. Katie was finishing off the last bit of her soup with the same enthusiasm she usually lavished on candy.

"More!" she demanded when she was done, completely dispensing with the magic word "please." No one corrected her because they all felt pretty much the same.

Their waitress glided up, just as pleasant as you please. "Our soup is something special, isn't it?"

Dad smiled at her dreamily. "I'll say. How about another round?"

"Certainly." The waitress gathered up their empty bowls. "Of course, only the first bowl is two bucks. Second helpings are twenty dollars apiece."

Nathan could see his dad's eyebrows furrow as he quickly calculated what the damage would be. But it was his mother who voiced dissent.

"That's robbery!" she said, extending her wagging finger. "You can't do that to people!"

"I'm sorry if our policy upsets you, ma'am," said the waitress, never losing the happy lilt in her voice. "If you'd like, I'll tally up the bill now, and you're free to go."

"But my daughter never got her tuna salad," Mom reminded her.

"I don't want it anymore," announced Amelia. "I'd rather have soup."

Dad gently grabbed Mom's wagging finger and lowered it to the table. "It's all right, miss. We do want seconds. All of us. And we'll pay."

Nathan had watched this interchange with a growing sense of helplessness and panic. But suddenly he felt all the tension release from his chest. He heard his sisters breathe sighs of relief as well. *I'm full,* thought Nathan. *But I'm even hungrier than I was before.* Deep down he knew that this should not be, but it was late, and he was tired, and he didn't want to start any battles within his own brain tonight. He just wanted to eat. Was that so wrong?

Meanwhile, across the room, a well-dressed woman plunged her face into a bowl of soup, sucking it up like a pig at a trough.

There was a motel behind the restaurant. They hadn't seen it because it wasn't very well lit. It seemed small from the outside, but once inside they realized the place was huge. It had many levels of tiny little rooms that resembled shelves in a filing cabinet. From the size of the place, Nathan figured it must have extended deep underground.

Nathan was relieved. It was good that they stay here overnight, he thought. It was the right thing to do. Especially because, after four bowls of soup, he could barely move, much less squeeze into the car.

A blond woman with a tight bun of hair stood behind the reception desk. Nathan thought she looked awfully familiar.

"Why—it's you!" exclaimed Mom, stopping short before reaching the desk.

Dad just smiled lazily at her. "You sure get around."

"Will you be staying with us tonight?" asked the hostess/waitress/hotel clerk.

"How come you're here?" asked Nathan. "I thought you were a waitress."

She shrugged. "I'm many things to many people." The woman held out a key ring on her finger, like the brass ring at a carnival carousel. Mom grabbed the key as quickly as she could.

"There's a free breakfast buffet in the morning," the woman advised them. "Muffins, scrambled eggs, that sort of thing."

But none of those things seemed very appealing at the moment. "What if we wanted something else?" Amelia asked. "What if we wanted . . . soup?"

The waitress lady smiled and winked. "Sure. But it'll cost a little extra."

The hotel room was not the kind of place the Everetts were used to staying in. No framed art prints. No minibar. Not even a TV. Just four painted cinder-block walls, and five small beds covered with drab green military blankets, tucked in so tightly it was hard to squeeze into them. The room was not meant for so many people, and the beds were pushed so close to one another there was no room in between.

"Just like five peas in a pod," Dad commented jokingly, but the thought made Nathan shiver.

That night Nathan dreamed he was drowning in an endless sea, but the ocean was thick, warm, and viscous. He tried to keep his head above the surface but couldn't. He went under, and when he opened his mouth to scream, it instantly filled with the familiar taste of pea soup. Suddenly, instead of wanting to escape, he wanted to swallow, and swallow again. He wanted to breathe the soup into his lungs and sink as deep as he could go, until he was lost forever in it. And that desire was so terrifying, Nathan woke up screaming.

When his eyes cleared, he could see it was already daylight. Bright daylight—not the slim rays of dawn. He was alone in the tiny motel room.

"Mom? Dad? Anyone?"

No one was there. He peered out through the small barred window, to see flat fields, then the highway, and more fields beyond. The farmland looked much more attractive in the daytime, but still, the desolation was unnerving.

More unnerving was the parking lot, for as Nathan left the room and crossed the immense lot between the motel and the restaurant in search of his parents, he realized that his sister had been dead wrong. There *were* tow trucks in this corner of nowhere. Dozens of them. The parking lot was now half-empty as tow trucks hauled away the cars. Nathan couldn't see their car in the lot anymore and wondered if it, too, had been towed away.

Nathan's walk became a run as he burst into the restaurant. He ran past the battalion of hostesses and through one dining room after another. But then he slowed, and stopped. He sniffed. The fragrant aroma of soup beckoned to him. It filled his mind now, slicing at his fear. *Slow down,* it seemed to tell him. *Take it easy. Things aren't as bad as they seem.* That pungent smell seemed to whisper to his brain all the things that would make him stop. And eat.

His parents were at the same table they had occupied the night before. They were wearing the same clothes they had worn last night, too, but now those clothes were barely recognizable. They were covered with layer upon layer of dense, green pea soup. It ran down their faces and speckled their hair. It puddled in their laps and dripped in thick pools on the floor. Nathan watched, speechless, as his mother lifted a bowl to her mouth and poured it down her gullet—most of it spilling down the front of what was once her favorite blouse.

Nathan screamed. It was the only thing that got their attention.

"It's about time you got up, sleepyhead," his dad gurgled. "Have some breakfast. It's already paid for."

"Dad—they're towing away the car! You have to stop them."

His father only laughed. "How do you think I paid for the soup?"

Nathan saw someone enter the room. No . . . he felt someone enter. He turned to see who it was.

"Is there a problem here?"

It was the waitress. The same one who had ushered them into the restaurant the night before. The same one who had given them their room. The same one who kept bringing them bowl after bowl after bowl of the terrible, wonderful soup.

"There's no problem," said Nathan's father. "My son's a little cranky because he hasn't had breakfast yet." Then he grabbed Nathan's arm with a slimy, soup-covered hand and pulled him toward an empty seat, where a fresh bowl of steaming soup was waiting for him. And yes, Nathan was hungry—hungrier than he could ever remember being—and he couldn't imagine eating anything else but that soup. It was as if his whole body had changed, and he could no longer digest anything else.

"Things will be much clearer to you, Nathan, once you've had something to eat," said Dad.

"Better sit down quick," said Amelia, "before I eat yours."

"Mmm," said Katie. "More!"

His mother wagged her finger at him. "Sit down, Nathan, and stop making a spectacle of yourself!" But her wagging fingernail was not red anymore. It was Granny Smith green. And so were her eyes. So were *all* of their eyes. Just as green as the waitress's.

Nathan turned and ran, but the waitress caught him. Her arms were much stronger than anyone's ought to be. Her smile remained, but her eyes showed a deep-seated anger. When he looked in those eyes, it seemed as though Nathan could see deep into some awful place. Those eyes had depth that went far beyond the back of her skull.

"Don't make this more difficult than it has to be," she threatened. Nathan could feel her fingers digging into him with bone-crushing strength as she tried to move him back to the table. Nathan struggled. He twisted and turned. Finally he freed one arm and reached up to grab any part of her that he could. He snagged his fingers around the bun of her hair and pulled, tearing free the barrette—an iron thing with teeth like a bear trap.

Shocked, she loosened her grip, and Nathan pulled himself free—in time to see her hair fall out of its bun. But it wasn't just her hair. With the iron barrette taken away, her pretty, tight skin began to sag and fold. Deep creases formed around her eyes. Her cheeks slid into jowls, and the skin of her neck buckled into flaps like the neck of a chicken. Only now did Nathan realize that her hair wasn't platinum blond, but stark white. She must have been hundreds of years old!

Nathan raced past her and burst out of the dining room, not knowing where he was headed. All around him he saw the other hosts and hostesses, each one the same: hair and skin pulled back to make them seem young, instead of ancient. They were all staring at him.

Nathan burst through a door onto a catwalk, and before him was perhaps the most horrible sight of all.

He had found the kitchen.

In the center was a pot—a cauldron—at least twenty feet wide and two stories deep. It was black and bulbous and filled with the bubbling soup. Mindless, green-eyed drones in drab gray rags stirred the mixture and added pound after pound of pureed peas, carrots, and spices, from a blender ten feet high. Nathan watched in mute horror as one of the workers lost his footing and slipped into the blender. No one cared.

Nathan turned and ran, even more desperate than before to escape. Finally at the end of his endurance, he burst into cold daylight.

He was in the parking lot, which was now completely empty except for a few buses—and beyond the parking lot were fields of crops. He could lose himself in those crops! He could disappear, and the old witch—or whatever she was—would never find him. He pushed himself across the empty parking lot, heading for the safety of the fields . . .

. . . until he saw the nature of the crop . . . and the hunched workers who pruned, weeded, and picked. Hundreds upon hundreds of workers in the fields around him, up and down every row, lovingly tending to their precious peas.

"Nathan," said a gentle voice behind him.

He turned. The witch's face was a wrinkled mask of age—but she held out her hand, and a worker gave her a new barrette. As she clipped it to her hair, the skin of her face began pulling back until the wrinkles were gone and she was once again the image of youthful beauty. Her eyes sparkled and no longer seemed angry. Now they seemed compassionate and full of pity.

"Why resist the one thing in the world you want more than anything else?" she appealed to him. "Why torture yourself, Nathan?" Several workers in tattered garments grabbed hold of him and pulled him closer to her. In one hand she held a thermos, and in the other, a fine china bowl.

"Nothing in the world is as satisfying," she said, with a musical, hypnotic cadence to her voice. "Nothing sticks to your ribs and fills you up like a nice bowl of soup."

She took a step closer, opened the thermos, and poured the silky liquid into the bowl. Nathan shook his head, trying to prevent the intoxicating fragrance from reaching his brain. "No!" he shouted through gritted teeth.

"It's all you'll ever want. It's all you'll ever need. Come, be with your family," she said. "Right now they're boarding a bus, bound for some new farmland we've just acquired. Two thousand acres. We need you to help plant the crop, Nathan. Don't you want to be with your family?"

She held the bowl out to him, and Nathan fought his hunger with every ounce of his spirit. *I can resist it. I can resist it,* he told himself, but as if reading his mind, she told him:

"No, Nathan. You can't."

At last the vapors rising from the soup reached up his nostrils like two fingers, pulling him toward the bowl. He felt his face lower, closer and closer, until the tip of his nose touched the surface of the soup, and the moment it did his will imploded and he gave himself over to the hunger. He pushed his face into the soup and began to drink.

"Very good, Nathan," he heard her say. "Soon you will join your family in the fields."

Yes. Yes, that's exactly what I'll do. He drew in another mouthful and swallowed.

"You'll labor day and night, planting and reaping, resting only to sleep. And at the end of each day you will be rewarded with a hot bowl of soup."

I'll work all day, every day. For the soup. For the soup. The smooth liquid filled his mouth and nose. He could feel it warming his stomach. He needed it more than he needed air to breathe, and so he kept his face deep in the bowl.

"And after a few years, if you're a very good boy, you'll get to work in the kitchen."

Yes! The kitchen! The shallow bowl had become bottomless. Nathan's face was pressed into it all the way up to his ears, and still he felt there was farther to go.

"And if you're very, very good, you'll get to hand-paint the china bowls."

Nathan finally drained the last of the soup, licking the bowl like a puppy, until not a drop remained.

"And if you give your life over to your work, someday, a very long time from now, you'll receive the highest honor of all. . . ." Then she wiped the soup from his forehead and cheeks, and whispered into his ear, "You'll get to be a waiter."

Sometime later, a bored boy stared out the window of his parents' car. It had been a long trip and there were many hours left to go. He watched the afternoon scenery pass by endlessly.

"Day laborers," explained his father as they drove past one patch of cropland after another. In each field workers swarmed over the crops like drones. "Hard work and low pay. A terrible way to treat people."

For a moment the boy thought he saw a kid in the crops looking at him. A boy about his age with a sad look on his face, and his lips smeared with something slimy green. But before he could get a good look, the car sped on and the laborers passed out of view.

"Hey, how about we stop and get something to eat?" suggested the boy's mother.

"Good idea, Mom." The boy glanced at a billboard looming up ahead. And he smiled. He knew just what he was in the mood for.

Majority Rules

*W**hat do you believe?"*

"What I believe is none of your business."

"Oh, but it is. It's more my business than you could possibly know."

"I'm not talking to you about anything. I know my rights. I'm a minor, you can't keep me here. . . . What are you laughing at?"

"You think this is a police station? You think you're here because you shoplifted some trinkets?"

"Who says I did? You have no proof."

"Your petty thievery means nothing to me. That's not why you're here."

"Then what's this all about?"

"As I said, it's about what you believe. Forget about trying to defend yourself against an insignificant crime. I don't care what you did or didn't steal. All I care about is the answer to my question. It's important that you tell me . . . what you believe."

"Why does it matter to you?"

"When you were little, did you used to go to the playground?"

"What kind of stupid question is that?"

"Just answer it. Eventually you'll understand."

"Yeah, I went to a playground when I was a kid. So what?"

"Did you ever go on a seesaw?"

"Of course. Does all this have a point?"

"Tell me what makes a seesaw work."

"You sit on one side, somebody sits on the other, you go up and down. Are we done yet?"

"Did you ever sit on the other side from one of your parents?"

"Yeah."

"What happened?"

"It doesn't work; they're too heavy. You stay up in the air."

"Ah, so the balance shifted entirely to the other side."

"I still don't get what this has to do with me."

2,400 years ago, a boy climbs a mountain. He knows he's not supposed to, he's been told never to climb the mountain. No one who has ever climbed the mountain has returned, and for good reason. These mountains, these jagged stone teeth thrust up through the earth, are a barrier. A barrier made by God to keep humble human beings from seeing what lies on the other side. All his life, the boy has wanted to climb the mountain, and now at fourteen he's finally grown the nerve. Only halfway up, his sandals are worn and his bones ache, but a driving will to know pushes him forward. If it is true that this is, indeed, the edge of the earth, it will be spectacular. Not just the view, but the knowledge of the truth will be spectacular, for then it will be more than just belief—more than mere tales told by grandparents. The power of knowing that this truly is the edge, and that nothing lies beyond it but the emptiness of space, will be the greatest power the boy could know. *I have been there,* he could tell his friends, and someday his children. Although they may not believe him, he will know the truth of it.

The old people all say that the earth is a flat disc. He wants to believe this, because there's comfort in knowing that the old ones are right. But not everyone thinks as the old ones do. There is talk of a mathematician whose work proved otherwise. More and more people are coming to believe this, accepting the mathematician's version of things as the truth.

The boy doesn't know what to believe, so he has to see for himself. He has to know.

His sandals are torn to shreds by the time he nears the peak of the mountain. Hand over hand he climbs, it seems only a few feet to the top, but every few feet yields more rock above him. His fingers are worn to the bone, but he will not stop. Then at last, after hours, after days, he finally crests the top and looks into the distance to see the most awe-inspiring sight of his life:

Nothing.

He sees nothing beyond the mountain.

The earth stops here. Above, the sky is still blue, but beyond the edge it fades into a darkness filled with stars that stretch to infinity. So it's true then! This is the edge, and the world is flat!

But then a wind blows up from the face of the mountain, kicking dust into his eyes. He turns away, he closes his eyes. All at once he feels a change—a change in balance, a change in equilibrium—as if someone far away has reached out and pulled a rug out from beneath him. He clings to the mountain to keep from falling, and he blinks to clear the dust from his eyes. When he looks out again over the edge, the sight is not quite so marvelous anymore. Suddenly, before him, where a moment ago there was star-filled space, are sunlit hills leading down into a green valley, and beyond the valley are more mountains. The earth doesn't stop here. It goes on, and on, and on, until it comes up behind him again, almost tapping him on the back.

He cannot explain it. He cannot understand what has happened between one moment and the next. Now his vision of the flat Earth is suddenly gone. *Perhaps,* he thinks, confused to the very core of his being, *perhaps it was just my imagination, and perhaps the world is round after all.*

"What if everything is like that seesaw? What if everything we know as reality is as unstable as the shifting on a balance?"

"I think you're crazy and I want to get out of here."

"In time, but first you must make a decision."

"If this isn't a police station, then what is it? If I haven't been arrested, then why am I here?"

"Fear won't help you now. You need a clear mind. Your decision must come from a clear mind."

"A decision about what?"

"About what you believe."

"I believe lots of things."

"Do you believe in God?"

"Yes."

"Do you believe that the universe is infinite?"

"Yes."

"Do you believe there is life on other worlds?"

"Uh, yeah, I guess."

"And do you believe that life on other worlds is friendly or hostile?"

"I don't know."

"Ah! Well, I think we've finally discovered why you're here."

The girl is tired of TV, and so she decides to go out in a boat. It's her favorite thing to do. She would usually take a boat out as far as she could on the cold, deep lake, then lean back with a book, and read until the sun sank low in the sky. But today there's something strange in the air—an eerie sense of foreboding she can feel even before she pushes the rowboat from shore. She's about three hundred yards out when she feels the boat rock.

A school of fish, she thinks, *perhaps a turtle.* Sure, that's all it is. The loch is full of many large creatures, and most are harmless.

Yes, many large creatures and one immense one, if you believe the legends.

The girl doesn't know whether she believes them, but she tells the stories to the tourists just as everyone does, because tourists are her family's bread and butter—because who would come to the loch at all, if it weren't for the legends of Nessie?

She's reaching down for her book, so she doesn't see it at first. All she sees is a shadow cast over the pages, and when she looks up, there it is, blocking out the sky: a massive head, gravestone-gray and dripping with slime. Its eyes are way too small and it bares a gaping maw of teeth. She draws in a breath, but so terrified is she that her throat closes, and she can't scream. All she can do is look at that awful tooth-filled mouth moving down toward her, ready to swallow her whole. And then suddenly, just before it reaches her, there comes a twinkling of light, and the entire thing dissolves into shimmering dust. Not just its head, but its body beneath the water vanishes so suddenly that the water rushes in to fill the empty space, almost sinking her boat.

And when the rushing water settles, there she is in a half-flooded boat, three hundred yards off the shore of Loch Ness. Trying not to think about what has just happened, she rows back to shore in a daze, her body numb from the icy water that has inundated her boat. She steps through the front door of her family's cottage, trying to figure out how to tell her parents what she has just seen, but finds that she can't tell them.

Her father turns to her. "You missed the show," he says. "There were these lousy scientists, said they proved beyond a shadow of a doubt that Nessie don't exist. They made a sonar sweep of the whole loch, they did. A sonar sweep!"

"Mmm," says her mother, shaking her head. "I daresay, millions of people must'a tuned in to watch."

"And all around the world, too," adds her father. "They've been showing the blasted thing for days."

Her mother sighs, "That's going to hurt the tourist trade. All those people no longer believing in Nessie . . ."

• • •

"The aliens—are they hostile or are they friendly? Quickly, there's not much time."

"I'm not telling you anything until you tell me who you are, and why it's so important."

"Very well then . . . I've been called many things throughout history . . . but based on current majority beliefs, I am what you would call . . . an angel."

"An angel . . ."

"Don't look so shocked. It's nothing too spectacular, really. I'm just a servant of the universe, same as you. A servant performing a function."

"I never really believed in angels. . . ."

"It doesn't matter if you *believe in angels; what matters is that enough people* do *believe in them to make me one."*

"I don't understand."

"Reality is a fluid thing, always changing. What was true thousands of years ago is not true now. For instance, thousands of years ago the majority of people believed the world was flat—and so it was. But there came a moment in time when there was a perfect balance. A moment in time when exactly half of humanity believed that it was flat . . . and half believed that it was round. It is my job to come to the world in these moments of balance."

"And do what?"

"And locate the person who will shift the balance to one side or the other. Like a seesaw. You see, when it comes to what is real and what is not, majority rules."

"And what does that have to do with me?"

"In just a few minutes your world is going to change forever, and you, my friend, are the fulcrum."

"Fulcrum?"

"The pivot point on which everything rests. Everyone else in the world has already confirmed their belief as to whether or not life in the greater universe is hostile or friendly. Even if they haven't voiced their opinion aloud, they've come to a decision in their own mind. But you are still uncertain. You stand right in the balance, halfway between two futures. What you believe will cause the seesaw of reality to shift to one side . . . or the other."

"What I believe?"

"Yes, exactly. What . . . you . . . believe . . ."

"It's not fair! How can everything rest on me?"

"You've spent your youth stealing trinkets without taking responsibility. Now responsibility has come calling upon you. I would say that's more than fair. It's justice."

"I know what I want *to believe."*

"What you want to believe and what you truly believe aren't always the same thing. Reach down. Discover where your belief lies. I know you enjoy playing games of world annihilation at the hands of ruthless, heartless beings. Now it's time to find out if you see those dark visions as true, or if they are, after all, just games."

"I need more time!"

"There is no time! By my calculations, you have less than one minute left. The decision must be made by then, and I cannot make it for you, so think! In your heart of hearts, are they hostile . . . or friendly?"

At the same moment, in another part of the world, a young boy stands in his family's rye field, while his father tries to make sense of what he sees. The whole family is there, father, mother, sister. Not necessarily because they *should* be there, but because in times of confusion and fear, it simply seems best for them to stay together. The crop circles have appeared overnight for three nights in a row. It is clear by their size and their symmetry that this is not a prank. There is no one in town smart enough to pull this off and get away with it. People scoffed—accused the family of doing it themselves. People looked suspiciously at the boy, and at his parents and sister. That is, until they came to their field and saw the formations themselves . . . and smelled the strange odor in the air. It isn't a stench, just an aroma; organic, yet completely unknown. It's the musk of some creature, which human senses instinctively know is not of this world.

"Look! Over there!" At the sound of his sister's voice, they all turn to the north and a vision assaults their eyes, filling them with absolute terror.

Impossible crafts of unimaginable size loom over the hills, getting closer. They have no wings, yet they hover in the air. Suddenly weapons fire, tearing holes into the hills themselves. Silos, barns and neighboring farmhouses explode in balls of flame.

The boy runs to his father, clinging to him. His mom screams and picks up his sister, who buries her face against her mom's blouse.

"Papa, do something!" the boy says, but even as he says it, he knows there is nothing his father can do. All he can do is hold his son with his strong hands, and watch. The boy will not watch this horror. Instead he closes his eyes, waiting for the end, but the end doesn't come . . .

. . . and as he waits, something changes . . .

He can sense the change around him, subtle and strange, like a static charge in the air. Instinctively he knows that something has shifted, like a seesaw tilting from left to right. He opens his eyes. The ships are still there, but there are no weapons firing, no hills on fire, and the barns, farmhouses, and silos are untouched. Not a single one has been damaged. *Was it my imagination?* he thinks. *It must have been.*

As he holds his father tight, the first ship in the armada lands right before them. A hatch opens, spilling forth light. The family cannot see through the stunning light of the doorway, but they can hear a voice, solemn and serene.

"We are here to welcome your world into the larger community," the voice says, with a deep sense of soothing assurance.

"We come as friends."

Opabinia

Myles wouldn't have believed it if he hadn't seen it with his own two eyes—a man, appearing out of nowhere in his room, in the dead of night, stuck halfway into the wall.

It was Myles Redhawke's first mysterious visitor, but not the last.

His father would have called it a dream, and his grandfather would have called it a vision, but Myles knew that it was real—he was awake, and completely alert.

This first night visitor was in a great deal of pain—so much pain that he couldn't even scream. The reason clearly had to do with the way he had materialized, halfway into the wall, his head and shoulders hanging out through the wallpaper like a weird trophy head.

Myles couldn't scream either—the shock of seeing a person, or at least half a person, appear in his room was too much for him. His throat closed up in terror, and he could only watch as the man struggled uselessly to pull himself free. Myles couldn't begin to imagine how incredible the pain must have been—to suddenly have the molecules of your body invaded by the plaster and wood of the wall, and the dense copper plumbing behind it. Even now, Myles could hear the pipes creaking and straining as they tried to share the same space as the man in the wall.

Myles wanted to turn away, but the desperation in the visitor's eyes was more powerful than his own fear. Myles felt drawn toward the dying man, and before he realized what he was doing, his feet were crossing the cold wooden floor toward the man.

"B-B-Bu . . ."

The visitor was trying to say something, but his lungs, invaded by the plasterboard wall, couldn't push out enough air for him to speak. Myles watched in the dim moonlight, close enough to hear, but not close enough to be grabbed by the desperate, struggling hands.

Then the visitor locked his eyes on Myles, forced his shallow breath a bit deeper, and hissed out a word.

"B-Bu-Burgess . . . ," he said. "Burgesssss . . ."

And with his last moment of life, the visitor tapped on his phone screen. Suddenly he vanished just as quickly as he had appeared . . . and every pipe in the wall burst.

When the Redhawkes purchased the home, they knew the plumbing was old, but they never suspected it would be explosive.

"Never seen anything like this," said the plumber, examining the hole. "What did you do, flush some dynamite?"

Of course Myles didn't tell anyone what had really happened. His father made it very clear that strange occurrences were not discussed in the Redhawke household. The last time Myles had tried to talk to them about strange happenings, it blew up in his face with more force than the exploding pipes.

It had to do with the voices.

Lately there had been people talking in Myles's head when he least expected it—but in a world where the only voices in one's head usually come from headphones, the announcement didn't go over very well.

"Voices? What do you mean, voices?" his father had said. "You don't hear voices!" It was as if proclaiming they didn't exist would make the voices go away. But they didn't. They only got louder, sometimes waking Myles out of a deep sleep. He never understood what they said, but he knew they were talking to him. Him and no one else. It made him feel important. It made him feel special.

It made everyone else think he was losing it.

"He's doing it for attention," his father had concluded.

"It's the stress of moving to the city," Mom had decided.

"The boy's a shaman," Grandfather announced, and that killed any hope of discussion—because Myles's father had spent his life distancing himself from the rich traditions that Grandfather held so dear.

So they did the acceptable modern thing and sent the boy to a psychologist, who did nothing but listen, which was useless, since Myles refused to talk to her.

And so Myles knew better than to tell his family about last night's visitor, and he didn't need a psychologist to tell him that seeing the visitor pushed things to a new level. Either he was very, very sick, or someone really was trying to communicate with him.

But the fact that there was an actual hole in the wall proved to Myles that he wasn't crazy after all. He just had to figure out who this "Burgess" was.

The second visitor suffered a fate even crueler than the first. Myles's walk to school through the city streets of Providence took him past a trendy block lined with coffeehouses, cafés, and a microbrewery and pub that manufactured its own brand of beer. Through the plate-glass window, you could see the vats of brewing hops and barley, and every afternoon the pub was packed with the unwinding business crowd.

At eight in the morning, however, the brewery was quiet as Myles passed by—until a sudden pounding came from inside one of the vats. The one closest to where Myles was passing.

"There's . . . there's someone in there!" shouted a worker, and a few minutes later they pulled a limp woman out of the brew. The vat had been sealed—there was no way she could have gotten in. Still, she was there.

Later that day, the news confirmed what Myles had already suspected. No one could identify the dead woman—and the only thing she had with her was a phone that had shorted out.

That night, after his parents had gone to sleep, Myles went into his grandfather's room and told him about the woman. The old man listened patiently as Myles recounted the story.

"I have the strongest feeling that she came from somewhere else," Myles told his grandfather. "That she came to speak to me—but she failed."

He thought his grandfather might come up with some powerful words of wisdom to explain the cruelness of this woman's fate, and her mystical appearance. But instead the old man just looked away wearily and said, "I think, maybe, your parents are right. And maybe it's best if you tell this to your psychologist friend."

After that, Myles decided he had to ignore the voices and the visitors if he was ever going to get past this. He would deny their existence; choose not to see or hear them.

But as it turned out, he had little choice in the matter.

"Don't be afraid."

The third visitor didn't appear in the wall, or in a vat of beer. Instead he appeared at the mall, sitting across from Myles in the food court.

A few feet away, a little girl in a ketchup-stained dress tugged at her mother's sleeve, pointing to the man who had just appeared out of midair, but other than that, no one noticed the sudden appearance—they were too involved in conversations and shoveling down lunch.

Myles wanted to scream long and loud until mall security arrived to take this invader away, but he didn't. Who would believe him? This visitor seemed just like anyone else in the mall, from his jeans to the backpack he carried. So instead of screaming, Myles filled his mouth with his frozen yogurt until the urge to scream had been numbed.

"I don't want to frighten you," the visitor began, "but we need your help."

Myles studied the man's face. He had features that seemed a mix of many ethnicities. Myles knew about that. Although his father was Manahonset Indian, his mother was mostly Irish—so Myles ended up looking like a redheaded, freckled Manahonset. But this man seemed even more a mix than himself. Even his eyes were a speckled hazel—not blue, green, or brown. Myles forced himself to look into the visitor's eyes, hoping to find something—proof of his intentions, maybe. Proof that he was honest, or proof that he was lying, but nothing about the visitor's eyes gave anything away. Myles didn't know whether he was safe or in grave, grave danger.

"My grandfather believes that ancient spirits can visit us . . . ," said Myles.

"Maybe," said the man. "But I'm not an ancient spirit." He brushed some crumbs off the table in front of him, as if the very presence of dirt offended him. "My name is Ryne," he said. "I come from the distant future—a time called the Age of Understanding. We've been trying to contact you for quite a while—you've heard us, no doubt."

Myles nodded. "Seen you too." He curled his toes in his shoes, determined not to show his fear. "So if you're from the Age of Understanding, how come the people you send appear in walls and get themselves drowned? Sounds like you don't understand much about time travel."

Ryne stiffened just a bit at the mention of it. "If you understood the nature of time as well as we do, then you'd know that time travel is imperfect," he answered. "Time is constantly moving—slithering, like a snake with its head and tail gripping the end of infinity. Time travel is not something to be taken lightly," he said. "In fact, we've come to understand that it should be avoided at all costs."

"Then why are you here?" Myles dared to ask. "And why are you bothering me?"

Ryne smiled, showing his perfect teeth, white as polished ivory. "Because, young man, we need you for a mission of great importance. You, and no one else."

Myles's heart, as fast as it pounded, picked up the pace. "You need me to come into the future?" he asked, not knowing whether he was more excited or frightened.

"No," answered Ryne. "Not quite." He leaned in closer and lowered his voice to a whisper. "Have you ever heard of the Burgess Shale?"

Myles shook his head. "No."

Then Ryne pulled out a small white stone from his pocket and dropped it into Myles's hand. As Myles examined it closely, he realized it wasn't a stone at all, but a tooth. A sharp, barbed tooth.

"The Burgess Shale," repeated Ryne. "I suggest you learn about it." Then he vanished as quickly as he had come, and at the next table, the ketchup-stained girl tugged on her mother's sleeve again.

Burgess Shale, the Wikipedia entry read. *Only ten feet high, and a city block long, the Burgess Shale is one of the most important discoveries of prehistoric fossils ever unearthed.*

Aside from his collection of plastic dinosaurs, Myles knew painfully little about the distant past. Until now, he had never realized it could be of any importance to him. Apparently, the Burgess Shale was discovered over a hundred years ago somewhere up in Canada. It held no dinosaur bones, however—these fossils came from a time millions of years before the dinosaurs, when life teemed in hot seas that covered most of the globe. Three hundred and fifty million years ago, to be exact.

Caught in a massive prehistoric mudslide, the fossils of the Burgess Shale are almost perfectly preserved, continued the encyclopedia, *and give us a clear view of the late Cambrian period.*

Myles scrolled down to see the bizarre collection of creatures unearthed in the shale. The *Anomalocaris*—a frightening beast with a round, tooth-filled mouth. The *Hallucigenia*—a tiny multilegged thing that seemed so strange to the man who discovered it that he was convinced he was hallucinating.

But nothing could have prepared him for the sight of the *Opabinia*!

It was spectacular, and like nothing Myles had ever imagined. Only three inches long, the unearthly creature had rows of gills running down the sides of its body, a single clawed arm growing from its head, and five eyes that gave it sight in every direction at once. It was weird, and wonderful.

No creature found in the Burgess Shale survives today. In fact, there is nothing even related to these creatures anywhere in the world. The end of the Cambrian period is marked by their mysterious extinction. These creatures were unique, and unlike anything else that ever lived.

Myles reached into his pocket and pulled out the strange hooked tooth Ryne had given him. Instinctively he knew that this was the tooth from the garbage-disposal mouth of an *Anomalocaris*!

The great extinction uncovered in the Burgess Shale forever changed the course of evolution, in ways impossible to comprehend.

Myles gripped the tooth tightly in his hand, wondering what all this had to do with him.

The time traveler next appeared in a phone booth as Myles walked to school the next day. They took the long way, speaking of things wonderfully complex and incomprehensible. Ryne bragged about his great knowledge and dazzled Myles with talk of temporal fractals, dimensional loops, and quantum-multiplistic theory.

"We have come to understand that there are eighteen distinct focal points in Earth's history," explained Ryne. "Some of them are prehistoric and others more recent—but put together, these eighteen events have determined the course of life, and of humankind."

"What are they?" asked Myles, hungry to know the great answers of the universe, uncovered in the Age of Understanding.

But Ryne shook his head. "Not for you to know . . . But I can tell you this—the event that created the Burgess Shale five hundred million years ago is one of the most important events of all. It's also different."

"What makes it so different?"

"Because unlike any other prehistoric event," explained Ryne, "our sub-molecular analysis of the Burgess Shale indicates that there was conspicuous human intervention."

Myles wrinkled his brow in confusion. "What do you mean?"

"I mean that at the time of the great Cambrian extinction . . . people were there. Two people, to be exact."

"People? But . . . but how?" asked Myles. "People wouldn't be around for millions of years. . . ."

Ryne produced a phone-like device from his backpack—just like the one the first unlucky time traveler had carried. "This is how."

Myles looked at it closely to see that the phone had a glowing green button, dead center.

"It has taken hundreds of years to generate enough energy to power a five-hundred-million-year time transport."

"To the Cambrian period!" Myles shouted. "To see what really happened!"

"You're catching on!" said Ryne, placing the time-phone-thingy in Myles's hands. "This is yours. I have my own."

"Wait—You mean—"

"I mean that you are to accompany me to the distant past. You will be witness to one of the most important events in prehistory."

Myles held the device as if it were a tiny nuclear bomb. "Why me?" he asked.

Ryne laughed as if the question was stupid and the answer obvious.

"Because in our infinite understanding," explained the arrogant time traveler, "we have concluded that of all the humans who have ever lived, you are the one who must go."

Myles let his words echo deep within his soul. He had always felt he was meant for something special in the grand scheme of things. Perhaps his destiny truly was a great one! But still, there was a part of him that wanted to know more—needed to know more. And he was afraid.

"Wh-what if I don't want to go?"

Ryne smiled in that superior way of his. "Oh, you'll go," he said. "History shows that you did go, and if there's one thing we know, it's that history doesn't change."

"But—"

Ryne dismissed Myles's questioning with a wave of his hand. It made Myles furious. Just because he was from the Age of Understanding didn't give Ryne the right to treat Myles this way.

"Whether it's today, or whether it's tomorrow, you're going to hit that button," Ryne proclaimed. "And when you do, I'll be waiting for you there, at the edge of the prehistoric sea."

Ryne did not come again. Not that night, nor the next day, nor the day after that. Myles wanted Ryne to return and plead with him to press the button. How could Ryne be so arrogant—so sure that Myles would go? But Myles knew the answer.

Because I've already gone.

Somehow, they knew the past. They understood the past, and if it already happened, Ryne was right—Myles would press that button someday and be transported to that impossibly distant point in history, when the *Opabinia*, the *Anomalocaris*, and many other strange creatures swam the seas.

What made it worse was that Myles really did want to go. It was a grand destiny indeed to be chosen to witness one of the most important events since the beginning of time—but what good was such a destiny if he had no choice in it? Being chosen can only be special when you have the choice to refuse. Without that choice, he was merely a tiny gear in the machinery of the universe. Machinery he could never change.

So he refused to push the button.

He refused for a whole month. He barely ate, he barely spoke. His parents, more worried than ever, sent him on extra visits to the psychologist.

Then came the dream. It came on a night when the wind howled and sounded alive with mournful wails. In his dream Myles was trapped in the Burgess Shale, buried beneath tons of mud that had hardened into rock over millions of years. And in the stone around him, a million creatures called out his name. "Myles . . . Myles," they cried. "Come to us . . . join us," they wailed. "You can't change what has already been. . . ."

A school of one-clawed *Opabinia* swarmed around him, moving through the stone, their five unblinking eyes staring at him. He tried to scream, but his mouth was filled with stone. He had no flesh—only bone. He was the fossil now. But he could still hear—and what he heard now was his own grandfather's voice resonating through the stone, telling the old stories that so few remembered.

Myles awoke in a cold sweat, gasping for breath, still feeling the heavy pressure of the shale all around him.

Finally the dream faded away, but the images remained in his mind. And that was when he knew he had to go.

He had to see the *Opabinia*—because he understood what it meant to be lost when the world changed. As he lay there in bed, Myles could hear his grandfather snoring weakly in the next room. Someday, Grandfather would leave this world, and he would take with him a history that rightfully should have been Myles's. That would be a cruel, unjust end as final as the *Opabinia*'s.

So he finally took the time-phone and punched the button. Not because Ryne said he would, but because the *Opabinia* deserved the dignity of a witness. Someone to affirm its life and tell its tale. Someone to make it matter.

The moment he pressed the button, an intense pain shot through him. It was like being turned inside out, while being fired from a cannon, while boiling in acid. He saw time peel away before him, the days spinning like a strobe light until the sun and moon were streaks in the sky. But he wasn't only moving through time, he was moving through space as well, rocketing through solid mountains, moving north, toward the Burgess Shale.

It seemed to last an eternity, and yet it was over before Myles drew a single breath—and when he did, the air was hot and thick with sulfur, like the smell of a million rotten eggs. The sky was red instead of blue and the air so humid he felt he could almost swim in it.

"There you are," he heard a familiar voice next to him say.

"Waiting long?" Myles sneered.

"Seven minutes," said Ryne. "Your machine was programmed to bring you here five minutes after I arrived—but, as I said, time travel is imperfect."

Myles looked out over the vista in front of him, and if there had been any anger, any frustration in him, it was washed away by the magnificent sight of Cambrian Earth.

Before him was a great inland sea, surrounded by cliffs hundreds of feet high. It was near sunset, and in the fading light, creatures left phosphorescent trails like underwater fireworks, stretching as far as the eye could see.

Myles could only stare in amazement.

"I know," said Ryne. "No one has ever seen such splendor, nor will anyone ever see it again."

"Can I get closer?"

Ryne nodded. "You can, and you must," was all he said.

Myles approached the water's edge, and there, wallowing in a tide pool, he saw them for the first time. *Opabinia.* They were only a few inches long, but breathtaking all the same.

Myles scooped one up, and it wriggled in his hand. Its exoskeleton was not a dull gray armor as the renderings had portrayed it, but a smooth multicolored shell, reflecting every color of the rainbow. Its five eyes were not empty and cold, but innocent and warm. The claw that grew from its head was not spiny and rough, but soft and velvety.

The creature was not a monster, but a wonder.

"Take a good look," said Ryne. "Your scientists don't know it, but this is the last place in Cambrian Earth that these creatures still exist." Then he pointed to the enormous cliff that overhung the great inland sea. "In half an hour, that mountainside will come crashing down, clogging this sea with poisonous mud. Everything in it will die."

Myles gaped at Ryne as he finally realized why this moment in time was so important. The mudslide that created the Burgess Shale didn't just capture a sample of these strange creatures—it snuffed out their very existence! In half an hour, the *Opabinia*, and countless other creatures, would become extinct!

Myles petted the back of the tiny *Opabinia*. How unfair, he thought, that something so wondrous had to die off.

He was still thinking of the doomed *Opabinia* when Ryne grabbed his hand. By the time Myles heard the clink of metal, it was too late. He looked down to see his arm handcuffed to a chain and the chain locked to a steel spike that was embedded in the stone beneath them.

"Wh-what's this?" Myles asked lamely.

"History in the making," answered Ryne, just as calmly as could be. "Do you remember that tooth I gave you? That tooth belonged to quite a large *Anomalocaris.* While your scientists were only able to take the fossil and reconstruct what the creature looked like, we, in the Age of Understanding, were able to uncover its entire genetic structure . . . and do you know what we found?"

Myles tugged at his chain. It clanked in the thick sulfuric air but held him tight.

"We found two very distinct chains of DNA," continued Ryne. "One belonged to the *Anomalocaris* itself, and the other belonged to the last thing the *Anomalocaris* ate."

Even in the hot air of the Cambrian dusk, Myles felt a chill rocket up his highly evolved spine. "Me?"

"You," answered Ryne. "No one else in the universe has your exact DNA. It took us many years to track you down, and many months trying to contact you, but ultimately we knew we would."

Myles screamed in furious terror, "You brought me here to be eaten?"

"Be proud," said Ryne calmly. "Very few people know their purpose in the universe."

There was a sound in the sea behind him, like a groan coming up from deep in the shimmering water. The clanking of his chain had drawn the attention of something beneath the waters.

"No!" screamed Myles. "I won't let it happen!"

"No sense fighting it," said Ryne. "It already did happen. It's just a matter of letting the event play through to its natural conclusion."

Still, Myles tugged on his chains. To die was bad enough; to be eaten was even worse. But to be eaten by something that would itself die in half an hour—Myles could not imagine a more meaningless end.

"So the only reason you came here was to feed me to this . . . to this thing?"

"No," said Ryne. "I also came to detonate this." He reached into his backpack and pulled out a bulky device with wires and a clock. Even in the Age of Understanding, a bomb looked like a bomb.

All at once Myles realized the full extent of Ryne's mission.

"You're going to start the mudslide that kills off all these creatures, aren't you!"

"That is my purpose," answered Ryne, "to prune the tree of evolution, and make sure that these creatures die, paving the way for life as we know it."

With his free hand, Myles reached for his time-travel device and punched the button. But nothing happened. In fact, the dim digital readout died completely.

"Your transporter only had enough power for a one-way trip."

And with that, Ryne turned and headed up toward the cliff with his bomb of extinction.

The water began to ripple around Myles's feet, and the school of *Opabinia* wallowing in the tide pool flung themselves back into the sea, in a race to escape the creature that was approaching.

A pearly white glow rose to the surface.

"No!" screamed Myles "No!"

The *Anomalocaris* launched itself out of the water and into the tide pool. It was only two feet long, but as deadly as something ten times its size, with sharp, gleaming pincers. It came at Myles, its circular, tooth-filled mouth ready to dine upon this newfound futuristic delight. Myles kicked it away with his foot, but it slithered back toward him again in the shallow water. Then a second one surfaced and launched toward him. And then a third.

"I will not die this way!" Myles insisted. He knew his will to live flew in the face of history, but still he fought his destiny with everything he had.

Over and over the prehistoric beasts attacked, but they had not evolved intelligence—they couldn't learn from their mistakes. Each time the beasts launched the exact same attack, and each time, Myles was able to kick them away with his foot . . . but one slip and Myles's foot would be caught in one of their deadly mouths, and that would be his end.

If he could break free from his chain, he could still run away. He could make it out of the ravine before Ryne detonated his bomb of extinction. Even if history said he didn't escape, he had to try.

When the next *Anomalocaris* attacked, Myles plunged his hand deep into its mouth, gagging it, and then pulled his hand out quickly. The dumb beast bit down, missing his hand, but caught the chain—

—and the force of its bite split the chain in two!

Myles kicked it away for the last time, scrambled out of the tide pool, and raced up the steep slope, following the footprints of Ryne . . . while behind him the three *Anomalocaris* slipped back into the sea, in search of other prey.

Ryne had been so sure of himself. They thought they had all the answers in the Age of Understanding—but they didn't, did they? For Myles had changed his own destiny. He had altered the course of history and would not end up in the bellies of the doomed beasts. His DNA would never end up on that tooth! Even as he climbed the mountain he could feel the change radiating forward from this moment, toward infinity—the great serpent of time writhing in agony as all of eternity adjusted itself. It was a feeling of enormous power.

At the top of the ridge Myles came across Ryne, kneeling over his bomb. He wasn't expecting to see Myles again, and when he did, the color drained from his face. It was wonderful to see the Man of Understanding at a loss for words.

"But . . . but you can't be here! It's impossible."

"Sorry," said Myles, "but we, in the Age of Silicon Valley, don't believe anything's impossible."

Myles ran forward and kicked the bomb away from Ryne.

"No!" Ryne screamed. "You don't know what you're doing. This bomb must go off! The mudslide won't happen without it!"

Now Myles was the one who could afford to be smug. "Maybe it's just me, but I don't believe in killing off endangered species—even ones that lived five hundred million years before I was born!"

Myles grinned and tore the wires from the bomb. It had no backup triggers because the Wise Ones hadn't expected that anyone would tamper with it. And so when Myles pulled its wires, its timer stopped dead.

Ryne, his eyes wide in disbelief, backed away from Myles in terror. "It will go off!" Ryne screamed. "It has to go off! You can't change what's already happened. You can't ch—"

And then the time traveler took one step too far, lost his balance, and tumbled off the prehistoric cliff.

Myles leapt forward, trying to catch him, but it was too late. He could only watch as the Man of Understanding tumbled a thousand feet into the great inland sea. There was a thrashing of white water, and his body was gone—devoured by a school of *Anomalocaris*—perhaps the same ones that were meant to eat Myles.

Feeling weak from the thinness of the oxygen and the terror of the moment, Myles fell to his knees and found himself staring at the defused bomb. But that didn't interest him. What interested him was the small phone-like device beside it. Ryne had dropped his time-transporter, and this one had the power for a return trip!

Myles took the defused bomb and hurled it off the cliff, so it could do no harm. Then he programmed a date and time into the device and punched the green button.

Intense pain turned him inside out as he shot forward to the distant future, and home.

His parents found him lying on the bathroom floor, his hand gripping his gut in pain. The trip home had been far worse than his trip to the Cambrian sea. It was as if his body had been shredded, re-formed, and shredded again. He could barely move. But at least he hadn't materialized in a solid wall.

"Myles! Myles, honey," wailed his mom. "Are you all right?"

Myles took a deep breath, and another, and another. The pain was quickly subsiding. "It was a dream," he told them. "Just a bad dream." Although he knew it was real.

His grandfather went to get him a drink, and his father helped him up. "C'mon, Myles, it's only a dream. Everyone has nightmares."

They helped him back to bed, and once everyone had left his room, Myles tried to replay what he had seen—what he had lived through—but the images were already getting lost in confusion. He couldn't even remember what Ryne looked like.

Ryne had been so afraid of Myles's changing a key event in history—but after all his worries, had anything really changed? For an instant Myles thought something might be different, but the feeling washed away with the memory of Ryne's face. No, the time traveler had been wrong. Nothing had changed. Everything seemed fine. Everything seemed normal. And that was good.

Myles fell asleep thinking of the great prehistoric sea. What an amazing sight it was!

He wouldn't have believed it if he hadn't seen it with his own five eyes.

Presumed Destroyed

By Neal and Brendan Shusterman

I am not defective.

I am not malformed.

My imperfections are entirely cosmetic. A discoloration in the steel along my handle. A vein slightly lighter, mildly less tempered than the rest of me. But my barrel, my chamber, my trigger and hammer are unmarred. My action is every bit as precise as any other.

And yet I was separated from my siblings, sorted into a pile of discards.

You cannot know the misery of being deemed unworthy of one's purpose, even before knowing what that purpose might be.

I was tossed into a holding crate, doomed to be melted down—re-smelted into that angry bright liquid from which I was forged. Destined to lose my identity in the fiery melting pot. This was to be my fate—but it didn't happen that way.

Instead I was saved.

It was not out of compassion. No, nothing so selfless. I was saved out of greed. A worker in the factory, whom I did not know, and did not care to know, stole away with my crate. All of us relegated for the furnace were instead offered for sale in a dark room to a shadowy man.

"See what I've brought you? There are more than two dozen here."

"Yes, two dozen substandard pistols."

"Minor flaws, that's all."

"I have a reputation."

"So only take the best of them."

"Fine. I'll give you forty apiece."

"Seventy-five."

"Fifty. My final offer."

"Take ten of them, and you have a deal."

"Agreed."

The shadowy man was the first to hold me in his poorly manicured hand, but he never pulled my trigger. I was nothing but a commodity to him, and he was merely a middleman to my destiny.

I was smuggled on a long journey in darkness, to a place far different from where I was forged. Plenty of time to wonder what I'd be used for. I knew the possibilities were endless. I come from a family of both fame and infamy. Distant cousins fought wars, bringing both devastation and freedom. Some kept the peace in the streets of cities, but were also abused by those sworn to protect. I tried to imagine the sort of hand I would fall into, and what purpose that hand would have for me.

In the end, I was sold in a filthy alley—a quick, quiet cash deal—but at least I now belonged to someone.

My first owner was a man of brutal camaraderie. I never knew the name of his gang, only that he belonged to one. From the moment he held me, I knew what I was to him. A symbol. An icon of his manhood, of his pride, of his ascension from impoverished mediocrity. To him I was a ticket to greatness. He would test the speed of his draw to an empty room. He would show me to his friends, bragging. And he would keep me loaded. There was always a bullet in the gullet of my chamber, lodged there, choking and heavy, in that penultimate position, awaiting the act. My act. My one true function.

I understood him all too well. He had passion, but it left me cold, for it was a careless passion. He believed my power to be his own and he took it for granted. On the rare times he fired me, it was a pointless act—such as the time he aimed me upward on New Year's Eve, in a vain attempt to pierce the sky. He pulled the trigger with such random, reckless abandon, I felt only shame.

Do not misunderstand, I didn't hate him. I pitied him, though. He thought my presence in his life would bring him respect, but how could it? Respect must first come from within, not from something held in your hand.

Then, in a moment of weakness, he resorted to crime. A store of convenience in the predawn hours of a violent summer storm.

The clerk seemed defiant, rather than compliant, when he saw me.

"Calm down, kid, put that gun away. No one's gotta get hurt."

"Shut the hell up, old man. Just gimme everything you got in there."

"You don't want to do this. Just—"

"I said shut it. Do I look like I'm playin' around? Give me all the money."

I felt hot in his hand. His sweat conducted his nervousness like electricity, and it empowered me. I felt alive, born anew, and yet disgusted by the feeling. Was this my purpose? Was this it? So compelling, yet so ignoble. I could feel his adrenaline as if it was my own. I could feel the fear on the other side of the barrel too, but I could feel something else. Something like experience. And it was not the experience of my owner.

"Hold on a moment . . . just let me open the register."

"What are you doing? Stand up straight, old man!"

And just like that, the tables turned. A standoff. I could see the gun the man was holding. A Desert Eagle .50 caliber. It was a beautiful weapon, which made me feel inadequate, inferior. It was as if that gun was mocking me, laughing at me. The shame of being used for a lowly heist was replaced by the embarrassment of being bested.

"Whoa, man . . . take it easy . . ."

I could feel my owner's cowardice. It had always been there. His bravado was just a thin veneer slathered across it like cheap paint on an old revolver. He was having second thoughts about this whole thing. Was I failing him, or was he failing me? I could not provide him what he wanted. I could not bring him true respect, and he could not give me a purpose. In a moment he faltered, lowering me just a bit, and my rival, the Desert Eagle, took its cue to shame me once more, for a weapon like that is all muscle, and no remorse.

The shot rang out like cannon fire and it burst into my owner's arm. He swore and cursed as he bled, but still he held me, cradled me. He ran, bursting through the door, setting off the convenience store's disturbingly cheery electronic doorbell. The clerk didn't even bother to yell at us.

We ran through the rainy streets. Cars whizzed by, people ignored the wounded man. I was shrouded in darkness, as he had stuffed me in his pocket, but I could feel his broken manhood, his lost dreams. When we got home, he closed me into a toolbox like a coffin, and I sat there for months. Time faded with no way to measure the days in the darkness.

Such was my existence. And in time, I came to believe I had no purpose. No reason to be. The prospect filled me with lethargic despair.

Then, after many months, perhaps years, he opened my steel sarcophagus, reached in, and pulled me out. His wound had healed, but I sensed in him a scar of firm resolve. He had a new intention for me, but it confused me, because I also sensed that he would never fire me again.

He slipped me into a pocket filled with crumpled dollars and stray coins. Small bills and spare change speak of such shallow, trivial things; what they have been spent on, or the wallets and purses they have known. Their chatter annoyed me, and it made me wish he would spend them frivolously, so I could be rid of them. As it turned out, he was far more interested in finding them companions than he was in me.

He took me out in an alley, perhaps the same one in which he had purchased me, and, as he held me up to show me off, I realized the truth. I was about to change hands! The bullet that pierced my first owner's arm, in a way, tore open a new future for me—for now I would pass into another's possession. Who would own me? I wondered. And for what purpose? Would I be used for a family's protection? Would I fire upon coyotes or other scavengers? Or would I be put on a pedestal in a collection, to be revered as a work of art?

"Okay. I got the money you asked for right here."

"Good. You came alone?"

"Yeah, of course. Just like you said."

"Good. Then take it, kid. I hope it brings you more luck than it did me."

And now, in the faint light of the familiar alley, I am thrust into the hands of my new owner, and I am reborn!

Into the life of an angry, frightened boy.

As the boy holds me in his cold, shaking hand, I know that he's different. I feel an unnamable pain in him—the kind that ricochets so quickly through one's soul, it cannot be caught, only pursued with increasing desperation. In him, I feel deeper emotions than I ever knew existed. A blinding spectrum of feelings my previous owner only scraped the surface of.

He stuffs me into his coat pocket. I couldn't be more snug if I were in a holster. The coat is snug on him as well, as if it's several years old and he has outgrown it, but no one has bothered to get him a new one. Or perhaps he's the one holding on to this thread of an earlier time—a time before he felt the need to have me in his pocket. I feel safe here, and yet not. I hear my first owner run off, and I never see him again. The boy runs in the opposite direction.

I long to comfort him—to soothe the rawness of his wounds. They are not like bullet wounds. Those are easy to see and define. Gun wounds are not subtle or deceptive, for more than anything, my kind is honest, even in dishonest hands. We speak in plain and simple terms. There is nothing ambiguous about a gun.

But the boy's wounds are of a different kind. Intangible. Hidden—even from himself. And they are deep. I'm not privy to the experiences of his life that brought him to this moment. We weapons are not blessed with a historical perspective on the lives we enter. We exist in the moment. We sense deeply the searing "now." And this boy's now is filled with mines and monsters.

I ride home in his car, nestled in the glove compartment. I come to know him even more as I lie among the detritus of his life. A forgotten theme park pass. A parking violation he's afraid to show to his parents. A cherry ChapStick that melts by day and solidifies by night. A folded envelope of school pictures that he doesn't want to keep, but can't bring himself to throw away. They all lie silently, for these things have nothing left to say to anyone. Here begins my deep desire to truly understand him, for only then can I hope to quell the demons that so torment him.

When the boy gets home, he takes me out again. He holds me tightly in those first few hours, extending me outward, his arm stiff, squinting one eye and pointing me at the wall. He says nothing. I hear nothing but a television from the other room. But the boy's hand feels so comforting, I relax and let him hold me. And I know in that moment that I will not be used today, but that I *will* be used.

He moves me from location to location, hiding place to hiding place, within his car. I am kept beneath the driver's seat. Then in a shoe box in the trunk. Then wedged in the gap beneath the spare tire.

When he does take me out, it's not to wave me in a show of bravado. It is merely to regard me. To take me in from every angle. To study me with eyes so intense, it would make me blush were I able. He shows me to no one. I am his secret.

Finally he brings me closer, deeper into his life. He moves me from the car into his sock drawer. A soft, warm place. It becomes my home. When he transfers me this time, there is something different about him. It excites me. I know that the day I will be used is near.

My days pass easily now, filled with muted anticipation. Surely I am more to him than an object in a drawer.

But weeks pass. Since the day he put me in the sock drawer, I have never been out of his house. I have become a domesticated thing. A pet waiting in silence for the return of my master. Some days he ignores me; others, he feeds me with his attention. I grow warm and grateful in his grasp. Once—only once—he sleeps with me beneath his pillow, and I am proud to be a protector of his dreams.

While my first owner once practiced the speed of his draw in the mirror, the boy draws me, but in a very different way. With pencil and paper. With his door locked, he leaves me perched on his desk, unloaded, always unloaded, and proceeds to sketch me. I am his model, and he captures me in that drawing—if not my weight and density, at least my personality. My striking profile. Then, to my absolute surprise, he hangs the picture on the refrigerator, like a child.

I want his mother to look deeper when she sees it—to question it. Instead she is just annoyed.

"I don't like it, Kirby."

"It's just a drawing."

"Why would you draw such a thing?"

"I don't know, I just felt like it."

She doesn't see me there, the edge of my grip sticking out of the pocket of his hoodie, like a dare. I'm still unloaded, but dangerous all the same.

"Could you maybe draw something a little less bleak?"

"How about a fighter jet?"

"Sure."

"Much more deadly than a pistol, but hey, if it makes you happy."

And if she were to see me in the moment, what then? Surely I'd be removed from the boy's presence. And although the thought brings me great sadness, and even greater anxiety, if my removal can ease his sorrow, perhaps it will be for the best. I grow guilty in these moments. I feed off his own guilt, and her worry. I feel worthless, unneeded, alone. I feel what Kirby feels.

But she doesn't see me. She doesn't even know to look. To her, a drawing is a drawing, and kids draw guns, and battles, and other violent things. They play games of graphic carnage and go on to lead productive, normal lives. She does not see that today a gun really is a gun.

He leaves the kitchen, returning to the disheveled sanctuary of his room, where he tears the picture to shreds and commences to draw a fighter jet blowing apart a defenseless town.

A day comes when I am once more freed from the sock drawer. Kirby handles me carefully and aims me like he did the first day he bought me. Then he stuffs me in his snug pocket, and before long we are running through the streets, just the two of us moving to the cadence of his drumming heart. I hear him racing up stairs. The cold wind brushes by, and I feel as if I am on top of a mountain. He pulls me out, and I see that in a way, it *is* a mountain. A corporate mountain. The mountain of the human machine. We stand on top of an office building, and he stands near the edge.

He holds me out in cold hands, just over the edge, but I know he will not drop me. There is a wild excitement in him, but behind that is that pain I feel every time he holds me. It's stronger here. Unbearable. I want to deny it, and exist in his excitement, but I know I can't. The two emotions go hand in hand.

Then he kneels down and looks over the edge of the building. A supermarket is across the way, where dozens of shoppers move to and from their cars, carts rattling.

He takes aim at an old man making his way across the street. He pulls the trigger.

Click.

"Take that!"

The man continues across the street, none the wiser.

Kirby aims again—this time at a teenage employee struggling to wrangle carts.

"You're toast, asshole!"

Click.

My clip is empty. All my bullets are back in the drawer. And I am glad. I am glad that this game can ease Kirby's pain.

Next, a middle-aged man fumbling with his keys:

Click!

Three teens sneaking beer out of the market:

Click! Click! Click!

"Serves you right, shitheads."

Yes, the game eases his pain, but not enough. It's like trying to bail water from a sinking, shotgun-blasted boat. With each pull of my trigger, there's even greater longing in him. Greater need to carve some sort of retribution out of the world.

"Hey! You can't be up here!"

A security guard has come onto the roof. He doesn't see me at this angle; he only sees Kirby standing there. I feel Kirby's sudden wish that the gun was loaded. I feel his intent. I feel him cursing that he did not bring bullets, and I feel myself being quickly stuffed back into his jacket as Kirby turns around in one fluid motion.

"What's the problem? I'm just taking in the view."

"You gotta get down from here, son. You're not allowed up here."

"Screw you. My uncle works for this company."

"I don't care if he's the president. Now get the hell off this roof before I call the cops."

I feel a knot of fear in Kirby's stomach. He takes off, and soon I am home, once more nestled among socks.

Alone again, I have time to ponder what Kirby has done with me today, what it all meant. I have been in human hands enough to glean more than just the powdery residual of right and wrong. I have grown to feel things beyond what was intended. A gun should feel a need to be fired, nothing more, and yet I find myself feeling a growing concern for the boy who wields me. If the gun was loaded, would he have shot the guard? Would he have shot the shoppers? Or is it truly just a game to him? A reality game. When does reality start for him? Is it when the bullets go into my chamber? Is that when it becomes real for him, or will it still just be a game? I see in my mind's eye the security guard lying dead in a pool of blood, and Kirby standing over him, holding me to the side. I see him dropping me and running off. I do not want to be abandoned. But I also don't want to abandon him. There must be another way this can end. There must be, but I'm not wise enough to see it.

For seven days he keeps me in the back of his sock drawer, ignoring me, perhaps denying my presence. I wonder if his own actions spooked him. If he has come to terms with what happened on the roof. I picture him growing older, keeping me as a trophy. Firing me at a shooting range. Years from now, teaching his children about me, how to use me, what I am. How dangerous I can be in the wrong hands. But even as I think about this, I know the wrong hands may be his. I bury my thoughts in a casing of denial, and when he takes me out again, I realize he's encased himself in denial as well. A denial of what happened on the roof, of his own self, his own future, and an inability to find a new one.

Today he does something he's never done before. He offers me to someone else. A girl. A friend. I didn't know he had any. I am relieved. I am jealous. I am ashamed of my jealousy. He would have her use me to defend herself, and I think for a moment that I will change hands once again. My destiny will rebound onto a different course. But no. She refuses. He puts me away. He takes me home.

But the following day he takes me out again, and this time he does something else he's never done before. He loads me . . .

. . . with a single bullet.

Something happened today. I don't know what it is. Something to his friend, perhaps? Whatever it is, it's tipped the boy off his delicate balance. I can almost feel him falling as he loads that bullet. I know what he plans to do. There's only one reason to load a single bullet into the chamber of a handgun.

And for all the power I have, I know I cannot stop him—and for once I wish I truly was defective. That my hammer would miss the mark, or shatter before striking the shell. I am powerless within my power.

His hand is colder than it was on the day he bought me. His hand shakes. His chest heaves with sobs. *Lay me down,* I plead. *Lay me down and walk away. Call your parents to the room. Let them see me. Let them know. There is nothing ambiguous about a gun! If they see me, they will finally tear through their own denial and pull you in from this icy edge.*

But he calls no one. He just closes his eyes. Then he presses the end of my barrel to his temple. I feel the pressure on my trigger, and I try to resist even though I know I can't.

We stay like this forever.

And then he jerks my barrel from his head, the bullet still in the chamber, unfired. His breathing heavy and uneven, as if he has just come up from deep underwater. He places me down on the table, staring at me, as if I've somehow betrayed him. Then quickly he puts me away. Not in the sock drawer, but in another shoe box, in the closet underneath a dozen other things. He hides me not just from others this time, but from himself.

And I am grateful.

I think it's over.

I think whatever crisis brought him to the brink has subsided, and his climb to a better place has begun. He may forget me, I think, or sell me, or save me for some nobler purpose, in a nobler time of his life. I can wait for that. Guns are notoriously patient.

But I am not forgotten.

The next day, he comes for me once more. To hold me. To ponder me, this time in an opaque sort of numbness. I cannot see through the veil of his thoughts today, but I do know that his intentions are no longer turned inward.

I sense such a weariness in his soul now when he holds me. I channel from him a hopelessness heavier than all the weapons in the world. I want to tell him that this pain will pass, as all pain does, but even if I could tell him, I know he would not believe me, and I think that perhaps I am damaged after all, for the pressure of his despair is breaking me. But I hold together for him, for if I can hold together, perhaps he can too.

Fire me, Kirby, I silently plead. *Take me to target practice. Expel that pain with my bullets, shredding a paper target. An effigy of the world you've come to despise.*

Or hurl me into the sea! Let that singular act of rejection free you. I can rest forever satisfied, even as I rust on the ocean floor, if I know you are saved. If my true purpose is to fly from your hands in an affirmation of your own life, so be it. I can accept the sacrifice.

But no. My purpose lies down a darker path, somewhere in the realm of the unthinkable. Now when he holds me I sense a decision has been made, for he grasps me with firm resolve. He loads my full clip. He slips me into his pocket. He says no goodbyes as he leaves the house this morning. He doesn't even turn back to look at it one last time.

He drives to school with the single-minded determination of a torpedo. Then, leaving his car idling in the red zone, he walks toward the building with ballistic focus, his footfalls steady, measured, and relentless.

And I know beyond the shadow of any doubt, that on this day, in this place, in these hands, I will meet my destiny.

And I am terrified.

ATTICS, BASEMENTS, WINDOWS, AND WALLS

I push myself away from the wall, stepping back until I am far enough away not to feel off-balance.

"What's behind there, Dad?"

He rubs his eyes and bites his lip.

"Your grandfather's behind that wall," he says.

—from "Retaining Walls"

Caleb's Colors

A tall figure in a dark coat stood in the doorway, silhouetted by the stark streetlight.

"My name is Rosetta Prax. I'm here about your son."

I didn't like her. Not at first. The way she spoke, it was so slow, so practiced and smooth. The way she said her name—hissing it like a snake. *Praxsssssss.*

"We've been expecting you," said my father.

The woman stepped into the light of the living room, where I could see that her dark coat was not black but brown. Not just brown, though—it was woven of many different colors, all intertwined until they blended perfectly into a rich mahogany. Her eyes locked on mine, and she smiled. I had to look away. Her smile was unnerving. It could not be read. Like her coat, it seemed to be woven of so many different thoughts and meanings that I didn't know what that smile was for.

"You must be the sister," she said to me through that smile.

I didn't like being called "the sister."

"My name's Shana," I told her.

She smiled again. "Shana. What a colorful name."

She strolled across our living room as if she were welcome, and my parents didn't do anything about it. Her presence was so powerful, my parents had no response.

Prax turned to Caleb, my little brother. Caleb sat at the kitchen table, the place he could most often be found, with a box of Crayolas. His left hand moved across a piece of paper, leaving lavender streaks.

When you first watch Caleb and his Crayolas, you might think his marks are random—just wild firings from a chaotic mind—but watch long enough, and you'll see shapes forming out of those wild lines, until you suddenly realize that you're looking at a sailing ship, or a mountain range, or a lion that seems so real you'd swear it might leap off the page at you.

And Caleb does all this barely even looking at the page. He'll just sit there, staring forward, rocking back and forth, in a way that could make you seasick just watching him.

"This must be Caleb," said Ms. Prax. "How are you, Caleb?"

"He won't answer you," I told the woman. "He's nonverbal."

But Ms. Prax only smiled that many-colored smile once more and said, "Oh, he speaks. He just doesn't care to use words."

I tried to stare this Ms. Prax down, but I couldn't. People who came to help Caleb promised us the moon, then they took our money and left Caleb no better than they found him. Caleb's condition gave my parents enough to fight about without having to argue over quack doctors—which was exactly what I assumed Prax was.

She smiled at me again, then she turned to my parents. "May we talk in private?"

"Shana," said my mother, "why don't you take Caleb upstairs and get him ready for bed?"

I was irritated that I couldn't be a part of whatever was going on, but also relieved that I could be out of Ms. Prax's sight. I didn't trust her. She seemed far too calculating and mysterious. I didn't like mysteries—especially when they were strutting around my house.

I took Caleb's hand and lifted him to his feet. He followed me upstairs quietly tonight. Sometimes it wasn't so easy. Sometimes he would whine and pull his hair. Sometimes he would scream like the end of the world had come. I had grown used to all of that—putting him to bed was a responsibility I had chosen to take on. But tonight he didn't kick and scream; he merely followed.

I took him to his room and dressed him for bed. All the time he stared forward with that blank look of his. He could stare for hours at the TV like that, and I always wondered what he saw there. Light and colors? Shapes moving back and forth? There were times when he would take a crayon to paper and recreate, line for line, the image of something he had seen on TV, as if his mind recorded everything he saw. Then there would be the times he would draw things too strange to have come from anywhere in this world. In one moment he would draw a place of terror so dark I couldn't bear to look at it, and then in the next instant turn the page over and draw a world of such intense beauty it would make me truly know that there was a God somewhere, because who else could put such a beautiful image into the head of a small autistic boy?

That was life with Caleb. A never-ending gallery of Crayola wonders that papered the walls of his room, floor to ceiling. Me—I could barely draw a stick figure . . . but it didn't make me jealous. How could I be jealous of a brother whose whole world had no room for anything but himself and his Crayolas?

I finished dressing Caleb for bed and left him. Sneaking out onto the stairs, I peeked down into the kitchen, where Ms. Prax sat with my parents.

"I've done much work with savants," said Ms. Prax. I bristled at the expression "savant." That was the label the world gave people like Caleb. People whose brains somehow got wired to do one thing better than anything else. There were people who could do instant math like a supercomputer but had to be taught to feed themselves. There were some who could memorize hundreds of books just by skimming through them but couldn't hold a conversation. I'd even heard of a little girl with level-three autism—completely nonverbal like Caleb—who designed aircraft for the military.

Dad sat with his arms crossed. Mom had called Rosetta Prax

on the advice of a friend, but it had been a long time since Dad had trusted therapists.

"Caleb's had every therapy in the book," said Dad. "I doubt yours will help any more than the others did."

"You don't understand," said Ms. Prax sharply. "I'm not here as a therapist, I'm here as an employer. I'm the owner of a small but prestigious art gallery specializing in unique works of art. Perhaps you've heard of it: the Galleria du Mondes."

My parents seemed as surprised as I was. If she wasn't a doctor, then what did she want with Caleb?

"We don't know of it," admitted my mother. "We're not really art patrons. . . ."

"My gallery seeks out special artists with unique talents," Prax told them. "A colleague of mine came across one of Caleb's sketches and sent it to me. I was quite impressed."

My mom stiffened in her chair. Until now she had watched Prax with wide and hopeful eyes. But now it seemed her hope was draining fast.

"Just what is it you want, Ms. Prax?" she asked coldly.

Prax grinned at her. "Simple," she said. "I would like to commission a large work from your son."

Mom laughed, and Dad, well, he just got angry.

"Listen," said my father. "We've got a little boy with a lot of problems. I don't like the idea of hiring him out as some sort of creative freak for the amusement of a bunch of snobs."

Ms. Prax looked down at her perfectly manicured fingernails, unconcerned with my father's anger. "You misunderstand," she said. "The sole purpose of my gallery is to give expression to creativity that would otherwise be lost. Your son has a gift, and I'd like to help him share it with the world." Ms. Prax paused for a moment, then took a deep breath and said, "I have a special interest, you see, because my own daughter was very much like your son."

"Was?" questioned Mom.

"She's no longer with us."

"I'm sorry," said Mom.

My father sighed, on the verge of giving in. "How much will this cost?" he asked.

Ms. Prax laughed heartily at that—loud enough that it made me jump. "It won't cost you, my friend, it will only cost me," she said. Then she pulled an envelope out of her pocket and handed it to my father, who opened it. There was a check in the envelope.

"Is this some sort of joke?" he said.

"No joke," said Prax, completely serious. "And that's only half. The other half is payable on completion of the work."

My mother was gasping as if she were hyperventilating.

"A million dollars? For a drawing by Caleb?"

"My gallery has some very wealthy patrons."

I could hardly believe it myself. I thought of the way Mom and Dad always bought those stupid lottery tickets, even though a person's more likely to get struck by lightning five times than to win once—and now the jackpot had come walking right into our living room.

"I'm sure Caleb's condition has left you with a great many expenses for his education and medical care," Prax reminded my parents. "This will pay those expenses with more than enough left over for you."

Well, Caleb might not talk, but money does, and Ms. Prax had herself a deal. As they came walking out of the kitchen, I tried to scoot up the stairs, into the shadows, where I couldn't be seen—but Prax saw me nonetheless. She stared at me with that strange smile again.

"Shana," said Mrs. Prax. "I would very much like you to come to my gallery and assist your brother in his creation."

I shook my head. "I don't do what he does," I told her.

"Of course not," said Prax. "But every artist needs an assistant."

"No," I told her. I wouldn't be bought, like my parents were.

My parents turned to me in shock, as if I had just thrown a stone through a window, then my mother turned back to Ms. Prax.

"Shana will be happy to go," declared my mother. Then she turned to me. "After all, it's summer vacation, so she has plenty of time, don't you, Shana?"

I didn't trust Ms. Rosetta Prax, no matter how much money she had. She wasn't just a rich woman who liked to help autistic kids—there was more to her than that. Still, this was a battle I knew I couldn't win. Three adults and a million dollars against little ol' me. No matter how far away from Ms. Prax I wanted to be, I knew I was destined to spend days, maybe weeks, with the eerie woman, watching Caleb paint.

"Fine," I said. "I'll go, but only because I want to make sure Caleb's treated right."

"Splendid," said Ms. Prax, handing my parents a card with an address. "I'd like Caleb and Shana at my gallery at nine o'clock sharp tomorrow morning."

After Ms. Prax had gone, I went back up to Caleb's room, where he sat on the edge of his bed, exactly where I'd left him.

I stretched him out and pulled the covers over him. He lay there looking up at the ceiling—a ceiling that was covered with his Crayola creations.

"Do you know you're worth a million dollars, Caleb?" I said to him. He blinked, but showed no signs of hearing me. "Do you even know what a million dollars is?" Still no response. I don't know why I always expected him to say something.

"Good night, Caleb. I love you." I turned off the light, went to my room, and slipped into a sleep filled with nightmares I couldn't remember.

• • •

Caleb and I took a bus to Ms. Prax's gallery, but instead of bringing us inside, she took us for a ride in her white Mercedes limousine. The limousine, she told us, was a gift from one of the clients of her gallery. I wondered how anyone—even a rich person—could give away a limousine.

We drove for an hour, into the heart of the city, until we stopped at an immense museum of art. All afternoon we wandered through the maze of exhibits.

"See how Monet uses light to capture the moment of sunset here," she said at one point. "See how Van Gogh's thick textures bring the sky to life," she said at another. "See how the tiny points of color in Seurat's work blend together the farther away you stand." Gallery after gallery, she had something to say about every artist, every painting, until my mind was so full of color and texture that all I could see was gray.

"Why are you doing this?" I finally asked her. "Caleb doesn't care. He's not listening to you. He doesn't know a Monet from a Manet from a Schmanet. He's severely autistic. Don't you understand that?"

Then she looked at me with that same cold stare she had given my father the night before. "I'm not talking to him. I'm talking to you."

"Me?"

I looked at Caleb, whose eyes wandered around, giving as much time to the thermostat on the wall as they did to the paintings.

"Caleb needs no words to tell him about these paintings," said Ms. Prax.

"So why are you telling me about it?" I asked.

"So that maybe you'll be able to understand some of the things he already knows," was her answer. Then she asked me something I'll never forget.

"Do you think that these artists were masters?"

"Sure," I said. "I guess."

Prax shook her head. "No. These artists could only bring a hint of greatness to their canvases. Shadows of possibilities, nothing more. They are failures." And then she leaned in close to me. "Would you like to see the work of real masters?"

And although I didn't want to go anywhere else with Ms. Prax today, curiosity had already begun to drill deep into my brain. I nodded my head and said, "Yes. Yes, I do."

She took us back to her gallery, where the walls were covered with canvases filled with dripping splotches of brown paint.

"You call these masterpieces?" I asked. "Looks like a lot of mud to me."

She shook her head. "This isn't the gallery. The real gallery is upstairs."

She opened a door and took us up a narrow staircase into a huge loft. It must have once been a factory or something, because it had brick walls, and lots of windows—but those windows were all painted over so no outside light could get in.

Surrounding us were dozens upon dozens of sheet-covered canvases, all five or six feet tall, and all resting upon heavy wooden easels. In the dim light of the huge loft, they looked like ghosts all facing in different directions.

"These are the works of the masters," she said, and began to pull away the sheets that covered them one by one.

Any doubts I had were gone the moment I laid eyes on that first canvas.

It was a landscape like nothing I had ever seen, and trying to explain it now is like trying to explain sight to a person who has never experienced vision. These were colors the human eye had never before seen. Colors that had no names, depicting a place too strange and surreal to be of this world.

The second masterpiece was in a different set of hues, but just as incredible: a scene of clouds billowing upward toward a sun that actually shone, lighting up the room. Deep within the painting, golden winged beings seemed caught in a glorious journey toward that sun.

The third was the most magnificent of all. A forest of impossibly exotic trees, swirling in a greenish mist. Hills rolled into the distance, and in the foreground the single limb of a tree curved downward, with a smattering of red leaves. It seemed so real I could almost smell the rich fragrances of the forest and feel the slow breeze that made the mist swim and shimmer. It was unearthly, and otherworldly, like the other paintings.

"You wish to touch the painting," said Ms. Prax. It wasn't so much a question as a statement of fact. "You may do so. These paintings are meant to be touched."

I reached out toward one of those redder-than-red leaves to feel its velvet texture . . .

. . . and when I drew my hand away, I was holding the leaf between my fingers!

I gasped, and let the leaf flutter to the ground.

Ms. Prax smiled. "The task of the artist," she said, "is the creation of worlds. Very few succeed. Many die trying."

In a small room behind the great gallery was a paint-splattered studio, and in that studio were a palette, brushes, and about a thousand brand-new tubes of paint, all set up in front of a canvas the same size as the others in the gallery. Only this canvas was empty.

Caleb stepped up to the canvas, standing just a few inches away from its surface, staring that blank stare of his, and Ms. Prax put a paintbrush in Caleb's hand.

"Do you believe in miracles, Shana?"

To be honest, I didn't know. But then my brother began to paint. Thick, heavy brushstrokes. In moments Caleb had begun creating a bright, wonderful work of art.

Then I saw something out of the corner of my eye. There was something shiny in Prax's hand. Shiny and sharp. I gasped and pulled Caleb away from the canvas as Prax brought the carving knife down . . . slashing through the center of the canvas. The fabric shredded from top to bottom.

"No!" she screamed furiously at Caleb. "Look at those brushstrokes! This is Van Gogh!"

I was so shocked, all I could do was push myself back against the wall in disbelief.

Caleb screamed as if he himself had been stabbed and didn't stop screaming until Prax brought another canvas. He quieted immediately and silently resumed painting. He dabbed his brush against the canvas lightly, creating tiny little points of light. Again, Prax's knife came down, shredding the emerging work.

"No!" Prax yelled. "This is Seurat."

Caleb wailed again and began to rock feverishly back and forth. Once more Prax brought a fresh canvas.

I wanted to grab Caleb and run, taking him away from this ranting, insane woman—and yet part of me must have understood what she was doing, and why she was doing it. Because I stayed. I stayed to witness Caleb's terrifying ordeal.

"We're not leaving here," shouted Prax, "until we're done."

On and on it went. I began crying, begging Prax to stop, but she wouldn't. She shredded canvas after canvas—one that looked like a Monet, and another like a Picasso. Caleb barely had a chance to get down a single brushstroke before that awful knife would come down again, sending him into a screaming fit, each one worse than the one before.

And then Caleb just shut down.

Prax put a new canvas in front of him, and Caleb didn't move. He stood there, red in the face, staring at the white fabric with an expression of emptiness worse than ever before—as if he were staring through the canvas with no emotion. No mind. He didn't even try to paint.

"Now you've done it!" I shouted at Prax through my tears. "Now he'll never paint or pick up a crayon ever again! You've ruined the one thing he can do, you monster."

Prax didn't answer me; she just looked at Caleb, waiting. Then I heard the faraway jingling of bells, and Prax left to greet a customer who had just arrived downstairs. She closed the door behind her, and Caleb and I were alone with the horribly empty canvas.

"Caleb," I whispered. "Caleb, you don't have to paint. You don't have to do anything. We'll get you home. I'll tuck you in bed. It'll be just like it always was. You'd like that, wouldn't you?"

Nothing. Caleb didn't even rock back and forth. Something was very, very wrong, and I cursed that horrible woman for doing this to him.

That was when I heard voices outside the door. I opened the door a crack and peered out to see Prax—her slick, smooth self, leading a couple through the great secret gallery. The man and woman hardly looked rich enough to invest in great works of art. In fact, they looked poor, worn, and tired, as if they'd seen more trouble and pain than most.

The man knelt down on the gallery floor, opened up a suitcase, and showed its contents to Prax.

"It's all there," said the man wearily. "Every penny we could find. Everything we own."

"I'm afraid it's not very much," the woman apologized.

Prax waved the remark away as if she didn't even how much or how little it was. "Have you chosen a work that suits you?" she asked.

The man and woman stepped toward the surreal landscape with the red leaves.

"Ah," said Prax, smiling her multicolored smile for them. "My daughter's. I hope you enjoy it."

And with that I could see the look of world-weariness leave the couple's faces. How would they carry it out? I wondered—it was such a huge canvas.

I leaned back to brush some hair from my face, and when I peeked through the hole again, the couple was gone . . .

. . . and a single leaf, redder than red, fluttered to the floor at Prax's feet. My heart missed a very long beat.

Prax immediately covered the painting with a sheet and turned.

"Come out, Shana," she said, having known I was there all along.

I stepped into the gallery and helped Ms. Prax adjust the sheet on the painting so it hung just right. She sighed in satisfaction, then closed the suitcase. I noticed it only seemed to have a few crumpled bills.

"This world we live in," said Ms. Prax, "is kind to some, but cruel to others. For those who would rather be elsewhere, I provide . . . alternatives." Then she smiled at me, and although her smile still seemed filled with many strange colors, I felt I could understand some of them now. "Perhaps there will come a time," she said, "when everyone will have to choose a masterpiece."

The smell of oil paint seemed to grow stronger around me, and I turned to see that Caleb had begun painting. He was working feverishly at the canvas—and this time it was different from before. As I stepped back into the studio, I could see the speed at which his hand was moving. His fingers were a blur. Even the colors he was putting on that canvas seemed far brighter, far more special than the colors that came from the tubes of paint.

All the time he stared through that white canvas as if the work was already there behind it and he wasn't so much brushing on paint as he was brushing away the emptiness. Soon he threw the paintbrush away and began to use his fingers, spreading and blending the colors from corner to corner. For half an hour we watched in awed silence, and half an hour was all it took.

"My God!" I said when it was done, but my words seemed far away, lost in the depth of the painting.

It was something entirely new, nothing like what any artist

anywhere had ever created. The world Caleb had made was both wilderness and city, both earth and sky. Wild winds swept through magnificent trees toward gleaming crystalline spires. Brilliant shafts of light spilled upon peaceful hills, and yet the light was balanced by deep shafts of darkness that swam with unknowable mysteries. Still, as new as all this was, it was somehow familiar. It was then that I realized that everything in this great work I'd seen before. A fragment on the refrigerator door. A sketch on Caleb's wall. Everything Caleb had ever drawn was just a shadow of this, his great work. His one work.

I reached toward it, wanting more than anything to reach into it—and instead I got my fingers covered with paint.

Caleb smoothed over the smudge I had made with my fingers.

"It's not finished," said Ms. Prax. "It needs a signature."

"But Caleb can't write his name."

Ms. Prax shook her head. "That's not the kind of signature I mean." Then she leaned over and whispered into Caleb's ear. "Go on, Caleb. Finish it."

And with that, Caleb reached forward and pressed his spread fingers against the center of his creation. He gritted his teeth. He squinted his eyes and pushed that hand against the canvas with all his soul, until finally his hand punched through the surface . . . into a world rich with colors. I could see the canvas changing, the flatness of it stretching out and back like a wave was rolling through it, until its depth reached the infinite horizon.

Caleb looked at his fingers there inside his painting, watching the light playing off them . . . then he lurched forward and leapt into it. Once inside, he threw his hands out. He spun around. He was dancing—Caleb was actually dancing! And then, for the first time in his life, he turned his head to look at me. And he smiled. It was a smile filled with more colors than Ms. Prax's. That was when I knew Caleb was finally where he belonged. Caleb didn't waste time saying good-bye. He turned and ran, hopped, and skipped deep into his world, until he disappeared into a place the canvas did not show.

My joy to have seen him so happy overwhelmed my grief at knowing he was gone. With my eyes full of tears, I reached my hand into that world too. I felt the warmth of that strange light. How I wanted to launch myself in there as well, but Ms. Prax had something else in mind.

"I need a gatekeeper," she told me. "Someone to decide whom Caleb would want in his world. Will you do that for me?"

I didn't answer her. Instead I went to a shelf, opened a sheet, and together we gently covered the canvas.

That night we brought Mom and Dad to the gallery, to show them Caleb's masterpiece—and although my parents can be dense sometimes, one look at the painting and they understood. My mother cried tears of both joy and loss, as I had. My father hid his feelings by comforting her.

Since then, I've been taking my own art lessons. I still don't know much about art, but I do know that there are places inside of us—palaces of glorious light and caverns of unknowable darkness. Magical places filled with brilliant, unimaginable colors that we suffer to bring forth.

I know I could never suffer the way Caleb did—to imagine a place so perfectly that it becomes real—but if someday I can paint just a shadow of the possibilities . . . perhaps that will be enough.

Retaining Walls

On a morning full of cold clouds, my father sweeps me out of bed and into his pickup truck—as if I have nothing better to do with my Sunday than to sit at his work site and watch grown men play with blocks.

"Have fun," says Mom, as if that were possible.

My dad smiles at her and waves as we drive off. It's the warmest gesture he can muster, now that they're divorced. Dad shoves a donut and a juice box into my hands as a makeshift breakfast, then he spirits me away to his work.

Big walls. That's my father's specialty. He built his first wall when he was nineteen, in the basement of an old house. From what I heard, a mudslide had caved in the weak basement wall, and Dad had gone in with Grandpa to build a strong retaining wall to hold the earth back where it should be. Thing is, Grandpa died halfway through the job, and Dad had to finish it alone. Since then, he hasn't stopped building walls.

As we drive, I can see my father's anticipation building. He likes his work—it invigorates him. You could say he lives for it, as if what he does has an importance beyond what I can measure. I always thought him small-minded to find such pleasure in the placement of stone. But then who am I to talk? I spend hours in front of a computer screen playing games. I guess the best I can say is that what he does is constructive, in the literal sense of the word.

My ears pop, and I realize we are heading out of town, up into the hills. Out of the window, through the early morning haze, I can see our town below us, a grid stretching toward the horizon.

"Nice view from here," he says. "Even better where we're going." He grins at me with a glimmer in his eye. "You'll like this one, Memo."

"I thought we were going to work on my pitching today."

"This is an important job," he reminds me. "I'm on a tight schedule. We'll do it next week."

Which is what he said last week, and the week before that. I only get to see him on Sundays—you'd think he'd be able to take that day off to spend with me, but instead of making time for me, he just squeezes me into what he's already doing, whether I fit or not.

We head up a dusty dirt path that seems to be made for things with feet rather than wheels. The cab of the pickup bounces, and I can feel the donut and juice sloshing around in my stomach like surf in a storm. Finally we pull off to the side of the dirt road, in the middle of nowhere, with a cliff to the right of us and a steep slope looming above us to the left. "We're here," he tells me.

"Here, where?"

"You'll see," he answers. Then he begins to climb up the side of the slope. I follow, feeling sleep still gnawing at my bones.

As we come over the top of the hill, I can see half a dozen workers—Dad's crew—busying themselves dusting and buffing the large boulders on a plateau. I see no house, no construction site. Nothing but a mountain.

"What's the deal here?" I ask him. "Where's the wall?"

"We're doing boulderscape today," he answers.

I know about boulderscape. No matter how much I've tried to ignore my father's work, some of it sneaks into my head. He's done whole patios and pools that look like natural rock formations, when in reality it's just mortar over chicken wire and rebar.

"Can you tell which is real and which I put in?" he asks me, proud of his accomplishment.

As I look around, I can't tell—but the thing is, what's the sense of putting fake rocks in the middle of real ones? I mean, usually it's rich people who put in boulderscape. They have my dad build pools, and waterfalls, and hot tubs in fake caves to impress their friends and neighbors. But out here, the only things to impress are coyotes and rattlesnakes.

He leads me to a sheer rock face looming above us, a dark granite mountainside that must have been here for eons.

"The real rock starts about ten feet up," Dad tells me.

I stare at him, dumbfounded. "You mean . . . ?"

"That's right," he says. "This stone face is a retaining wall. We built it!"

I shake my head, not getting it. "But . . . can't a mountain retain itself?"

Dad raises his eyebrows. "Apparently not," he says, then goes off to discuss the progress with his crew.

As I look around, I find a small spot that hasn't been finished: a patch of bare chicken wire in the midst of the boulders and evergreens, like a small hole in reality.

Humberto, Dad's best craftsman, spreads mortar across the chicken wire, hiding its fine metallic honeycomb.

Now I begin to notice the breeze. It's been chilly, and breezy, but up here, on this strange plateau, it feels different from the dry mountain cold elsewhere. It feels damp—and there's something about the smell. I take a deep breath and have a sudden flashback to a vacation we had years ago, in Florida. I don't understand why at first, but then the reason strikes me. It smells like beach. It smells like the ocean.

I hold out my hand to feel the breeze and notice that it's not blowing down the mountain, but blowing up—as if it's blowing out of the ground. I can feel it against my palm.

I turn to see that the workers all carry caulking guns and are going around the base of the boulders, filling in the cracks with thick cream, the kind of stuff you put around a bathtub to keep it from leaking.

I kneel down next to Humberto, and for an instant I think I see something through the wire framing of the boulder. I see a greenish-blue light. I see mist and clouds. I get dizzy, as if suddenly I'm looking down from a great height.

"Whoa!" I say, grabbing onto a boulder for balance.

"What's the matter?" asks my father, coming up behind me.

"I don't know . . . I think there's a cave down there . . . a pretty deep one."

"Really!" he says.

"Yeah! I tried to look into it but—"

"Did it look back?" my father asks.

"Huh?"

He grins. "Your grandfather used to say that when you look into an abyss, the abyss looks into you."

The thought gives me the shivers. I glance back down to peer in the hole, but Humberto has already smeared a thick patch of mortar over the chicken wire.

There are lots of reasons to build a wall, I suppose. To mark off territory; to hide things you don't want to deal with; to keep things in; to keep things out. To repair damage. There must be an awful lot of damage to repair, because my dad's always getting new jobs—sometimes halfway around the world. That's how good he is.

On Monday morning, I ask my mom about my father, and walls.

Mom doesn't answer right away. She slowly pours herself a cup of coffee, then she weighs her response very carefully.

"Your father's walls are special," she says. "Not just his walls, but his patios as well."

"And his boulderscapes?" I add.

She nods. "There are very few masons in the world who can do work like your father," she tells me. "He's a true artist. I love what he does."

"Then why did you guys split up?" I ask her, point-blank. It's a question I've never had the nerve to speak aloud before.

Mom takes a long sip of her steaming coffee. "I don't know if this will make sense to you, Memo, but when someone is as good as your father is . . . sometimes they become their work."

"You mean that talking to him is like talking to a wall?" I suggest.

She laughs out loud. "Something like that," she says, although I can tell there is much more to it.

I'm about to tell her about the mountain boulderscape and how strange it all seemed. I open my mouth to talk—but before I can, my hand saves me, by shoving a spoonful of cereal in my mouth and shutting me up.

Next Sunday I'm awake before dawn, waiting for my father to arrive. Until last week, I had never looked closely enough at my dad's work to notice or care about what he was doing—but last week's excursion has lingered with me. I can't wait to see what job we're working on today.

He picks me up at the usual time. Seven o'clock a.m.

"Are we headed to the mountains today?" I ask.

He shakes his head. "Nope, we're finishing up a wall downtown."

"What kind of wall?" I ask.

"The usual."

Half an hour later, we reach the deserted business district, where nobody comes on a Sunday. We enter a twenty-story building. The wall is on the fifteenth floor, in the offices of Moreland and Beck, Attorneys-at-Law.

The second the elevator doors open on fifteen, we are blasted by a breath of hot air from down the hall. And as we approach the offices of Moreland and Beck, the heat rises a degree with every footfall.

"Haven't they ever heard of an air conditioner?" I say, but even as I say it, I can feel the cooler air blowing from the vents above, fighting a losing battle to control the temperature.

In the law office, a spongy gray carpet has been rolled back, revealing the concrete beneath, and at the far end is a twenty-foot-wide stone-block wall where a window should be.

"That's a weird place for a wall," I tell my father.

"Walls go wherever you need them," says Dad.

As I get closer, the heat becomes more intense. My jacket, which was protecting me from the cold morning, suddenly seems ridiculous. I take it off and throw it over a chair. Humberto and the others are drilling holes in the existing cement floor and insert heavy three-quarter-inch rebar. Seems to me that they're spacing those bars closer than they usually do. I can see that they're building a second wall of cinder block, in front of the finished stone one.

"Two walls?" I ask my father. "Isn't that a waste?"

"Believe me, it's not," he says. He puts a trowel into my hand, then brings me a bucket of mortar. "It's about time you started to learn the trade," he tells me. "Our family has been masons for as long as anyone can remember. It would be a shame if that tradition ended with me."

I hold the tool in my hand, feeling clumsy, like I have no right to use it, as if it were a medical instrument and I were about to perform surgery.

"You spread," he tells me. "I'll lay the stone."

And so I join him and his workers building the second wall in the oppressive heat. The sweat beads on my face and rolls down my cheeks. I lick my lips and can taste its saltiness.

"Very good," he tells me as I spread the mortar as smooth as cake icing. "You're a natural. Someday you'll be building walls better than all of us."

The idea doesn't thrill me, but it doesn't sicken me either.

There are a lot of things I should be asking my father now. I should question him about why this wall is so hot, about the mountainside last week. But the thing is, communication has never been a family strong point. We've spent most of our lives holding things back and keeping problems out. It's hard to fight a lifetime of training, so I don't ask him the questions I want to. Instead I just spread the gritty gray cement and watch as Dad piles on the heavy blocks.

I keep my eyes focused on that first wall. I can feel the heat pulsing from it, like highway blacktop in summer. I want to know what's behind it. I reach forward to see just how hot it is, touching my fingertips against it.

"Memo! No!"

Too late. I touch it for an instant, and that instant is too long. I draw my hand back reflexively, feeling the shock of the burn even before the pain, and when the pain comes, it flows down from my fingertips in angry waves. I refuse to scream. I grit my teeth, and the scream comes out as a moaning hiss.

Dad grabs me and pulls me away.

"Humberto, the first aid!" he orders.

He leads me to an outer room, which is a bit cooler, but not by much.

As Dad tends to my throbbing fingertips, I can feel the pain turning into tears, which roll down my face, mixing with my sweat. Hanging on the wall around me, I can see the fire-suits they must have used to put up that first wall. *What's behind there?* I want to ask. *Why did you have to build this wall?* But I don't say a thing. I just look away as my father gently bandages my hand, and I watch as his crew rolls out thick insulation as pink as cotton candy to fill the space between the first and second wall.

Dad keeps me late tonight. Maybe he just doesn't want to face Mom's wrath when he brings me home with bandaged fingers. We grill burgers and I eat with my left hand instead of my right.

Away from his work there isn't much he knows how to say.

"How's school?" he asks. Fine, I tell him.

"How's baseball?" he asks. Fine, I tell him.

And in a few moments, there's nothing he can think of to ask me. But rather than letting the ball drop into an uncomfortable and distant place, I start to mention things I'm sure will keep him talking.

"What's the hardest part about building walls?" I ask.

His ears perk up with the question. "The hardest part is figuring out how to build them strong enough."

"Strong enough for what?"

"So that nothing can ever break through," he answers. "Strong enough so that the wall will last forever and ever."

I grin. "C'mon, Dad," I tell him. "Nothing lasts forever."

He thinks about that. "I guess you're right," he admits. "If things lasted forever, I wouldn't have a job."

He takes a bit of his burger and ponders me while he chews. "I want to show you something before I take you home," he announces, then he stands up, grabbing his jacket. "Let's go."

I have no idea what he has in mind, but I go along, not daring to ask what it is.

An abandoned house sits at the end of an abandoned road, at the edge of Dad's neighborhood. Broken windows stare at me like eyes, their tattered shades like drooping eyelids. They gaze out with the indifferent look of the dead.

Dad opens his car door and steps out. I follow. The sun is already gone from the horizon, and what little glow remains will fade in a few minutes, but we've brought flashlights.

There's a padlock on the termite-gnawed wood of the door, but it's easily kicked in with his strong foot.

Inside the empty dwelling we go, then down a rickety set of basement steps, to the only thing in the house that is sturdy. The wall.

It's a simple thing, made of red brick, completely out of place in this decaying home. About as out of place as the hot stone slab in the glass office building.

The ground beneath us is covered with two inches of water. A hundred rains from a dozen rainy seasons have taken their toll. Unused bricks and bags of old mortar are piled on a table, as if more work had been planned but got abandoned like the house.

"Every mason has his first wall," says Dad. "This was mine. I was nineteen," he reminds me. "I didn't know what I wanted to do with my life. And after seeing how hard my own father worked, I didn't think building walls would be for me—until this one." He touches his hand against a rough brick, feeling the troughs in the crusty mortar. "With each brick I laid in this wall, the clearer it became that this was my calling too. So I learned to love it."

I can't read the look on his face—which is no surprise. If I could read faces, I probably would have known my parents were getting divorced before they sprang it on me that day.

"It's just a wall," I remind my dad. "There's nothing special about it."

"Go up and touch it," he says to me, like a challenge. So I take a step closer, and as I do, I begin to feel dizzy. I suddenly reach forward, as if I'm falling down, but I don't hit the ground. Instead my hands slap against the wall, and I feel pain shoot through my burned fingertips. The hard, cold brick seems to have a gravity about it, pulling me closer—and there's a faint vibration in the icy brickwork.

I put my ear against it. They say you can hear the ocean when you put your ear to a seashell, but I've never heard of hearing something when you listen to brick—and yet I do. It's a hollow sound, cold and lonely, punctuated by an occasional rumble that sounds like a growl, and a *pfft-pfft-pfft*, like the flapping of wings.

I push myself away from the wall, stepping back until I am far enough away not to feel off-balance.

"What's behind there, Dad?"

He rubs his eyes and bites his lip.

"Your grandfather's behind that wall," he says.

When I get home that night, I don't tell my mother what happened to my hand. No matter how much she asks, I just tell her it's nothing and yell at her to leave me alone. Eventually she stops asking. I stay late at school through the week so I don't have to talk to her about it at all. Funny how when you don't talk about things, the easier they are not to deal with. I figure my head is about the best retaining wall there is, when it comes to holding things back . . .

. . . but by the end of the week, my little mental dike has sprung a leak.

Your grandfather's behind that wall.

It's a strange thing to say, even for my father. I half expected him to laugh after he said it, like it was a joke—but he didn't laugh. He just climbed silently up the steps and out of the old house.

The thing is, my dad's a very literal person—he doesn't think poetically. He thinks in solid chunks of reality. His mind works in brick and concrete—which means that when he says my grandfather is behind that wall, he means that my grandfather is behind that wall.

I'm terrified that I might actually ask him about it when I see him again. It will take all my strength to just go on like everything's normal. Whatever work site he brings me to, certainly there'll be more weirdnesses to occupy my imagination. Still, the wall in the abandoned house is like a brick in my head. What's behind that wall? What's behind all the walls my father builds? It occurs to me that he's never brought me to a wall when he first starts building it—only when the job is almost done. When it's too late to see the other side.

On Saturday night, I get a call from Dad. Apparently, he and Mom have been talking in secret—as usual—making decisions about my life without involving me.

"Memo, your mom and I have decided that it's best if we don't spend Sundays together anymore," he tells me over the phone. "My work sites are dangerous. More dangerous than you know. It's not a place for a kid."

All I can do is stutter and sputter like an idiot. "But . . . but I'm not a kid anymore! Please! I want to come. I want to know about the walls. . . ." And then, because I have nothing to lose, I say, "I want to know what you meant about Grandpa. . . ."

I hear him take a deep breath on the other end of the line. "I was wrong, Memo," he tells me. "You shouldn't be putting up walls all your life like me. You should find something you love!"

"But I want to be with you!" I scream at him, the tears exploding from my eyes like they did the day he moved out. "When will I get to see you now?"

"Vacations," he says. "Summer, maybe."

But the thing is, he doesn't take vacations—and if he won't take me to his sites anymore, then I'll never get to see him. That's what he means. We both know it.

"Memo, my work is getting harder. More repairs—more emergency work. You understand, don't you?"

I hang up on him before he can say anything else.

From behind me I can hear my mom trying to talk to me gently, like she can wrap her arms around me and make everything all better. She must be crazy to think I have anything to say to her now. I push my way past her, refusing to talk about it. If the only defense I have is closing myself off, I can do that just fine.

I go out to the garage, and there I find a pickax. It's heavy, but I'm strong. Stronger than my father thinks. I storm out of the house, ignoring my mother calling behind me. It's a long walk, but I know where I'm going.

I push open the ruined door of the abandoned house. The floorboards creak beneath me, and a stair cracks under my weight as I go down into the dank, waterlogged basement. A single clouded window sheds a feeble shaft of moonlight upon the brick wall. I waste no time in thinking. If I think, I may find a reason to stop myself.

I swing the pickax high and smash it against the wall. Chunks of brick fly in all directions. It might be solid, but nothing lasts forever. I swing the pickax again, and again, until I've made a crater in its red face.

I *will* know what's behind there. I will know what my father has spent his life doing; what he locks behind the walls he builds. I don't care if I have to shatter every single wall to know—and if I come face-to-face with the grandfather I never knew behind this one, then that will be just fine with me.

Another swing, and another. The hollow noises beyond the wall seem to grow louder, until finally the pickax crashes through to the other side. I pull it out and hear a whistling of wind, sucking out through a hole the size of my fist. I swing again, to widen the hole.

The flapping sounds and growls are louder. I hear screeches now, awful high-pitched screeches. Those sounds ought to make me stop, but my mind is like a car speeding off a cliff. I can't stop my hand from swinging the ax.

"Memo! Memo, don't!"

It's my father. Mom must have called him and told him I ran out with the ax. It didn't take a genius to figure out where I had gone. I can hear him leaping down the stairs behind me, and I know he'll stop me. He'll patch up the hole and never talk about it, like it never happened. But I can't let him do that!

I raise the ax and give one final, powerful swing.

And the solid brick wall shatters like glass.

I can see the fracture lines spreading through the brick in all directions. Then the whistling wind becomes a gale, and I feel myself being dragged toward a gaping hole six feet wide.

At the lip of the hole, I feel something sharp against my gut. I've been snagged by a piece of the reinforcing steel bar sticking out from the brickwork. I grab onto it to keep myself from falling into the hole.

"Memo, give me your hand."

My father reaches for me desperately, his sturdy hand stretching out for my madly wriggling fingers until he clasps them—but at that same moment I feel something at my feet, and I look into the pit.

In the cold, murky darkness, some creature is moving—a terrible living unknown, with beady, hungry eyes and reptilian wings. It opens a tooth-filled mouth and nips off the rubber tip of my running shoe, just missing my toes. Then it disappears with a flap of its veiny wings into the darkness, like a great white shark testing its prey before the kill. For an instant, as the mist is torn by its wake, I see a tortured landscape of nightmare trees and screaming skies of black ice. I feel my grip beginning to slip.

"Don't look, Memo!" warns my father. In an instant he is there with me, clinging on to the heavy steel bar, which suddenly seems as frail as wire—just as the unknown beast returns, its jaws spread wide.

My father swings his fist at it, but the thing clamps down on his wrist. I can feel his pain as he screams. Clinging to the rebar, I kick the creature over and over in its awful eye, jamming it with my heel, until it finally lets my father go and flaps away into deeper, colder regions of miscreation.

We pull ourselves out of the hole, tumbling onto the wet floor of the old basement.

Behind us is the wall—or what's left of it—and beyond the hole, the awful landscape swarms with things too strange and savage to be named.

I take off my jacket and wrap it tightly around my father's mangled hand.

"The hole . . . ," he hisses. "We can't leave the hole."

On the table rest the old forgotten bags of mortar. I hurry to them, tearing them open and letting the dusty mixture pour into the ankle-deep water at our feet. Then I grab the abandoned bricks one by one and move them toward the hole.

My father, unable to help, can only watch as I spread the mortar on thick with my hands and lay the bricks one by one.

There are no creatures near us now, but still, I won't look into the hole again.

When you stare into an abyss, the abyss stares into you.

"Your grandfather was working on this wall when he died," Dad says, as I lay brick after brick. "He had brought me here—to show me just what kind of work he did . . . but he looked too deeply into that place . . . and it swallowed him. I watched him fall, but there was nothing I could do. In the end, all I could do was finish the wall that he started."

I spread the mortar thick and slam down another brick. In spite of the terror I know I should feel, something about laying those bricks calms me.

"I'm not living with Mom anymore," I tell Dad as I close off one world from another with the last brick. "I'm living with you."

My father nods, realizing my decision is final. "If that's what you want," he says.

I smooth the mortar between the blocks. I know that I won't speak of this night again. Not to Mom, not to Dad, not to anyone. I will hold it back. I will keep it in the dark—as Dad has kept dark the many strange places he's seen through the holes of the world.

And I, too, will build walls.

After seeing that other side, there's an acceptance and understanding in me now. I know what my life has to be.

I suppose there are three kinds of people in this world. Some people live their lives around the holes—never finding them, never even worrying about them. Their lives are full and happy. Then there are others who keep falling through those hidden gaps, into nightmares they never knew existed. I wouldn't want to be one of them.

And then there are a few like my dad and me: restless people who spend our lives plugging holes in the unfinished corners of creation and building walls to hold back all the things that must never be seen.

Perhaps there are more holes than can be patched in a lifetime. But I've got to live on the hope that maybe, just maybe, we'll get them all . . . and the abyss will never look into us again.

Open House

Barbara sits at her kitchen table, staring at her cup of lukewarm tea. The windows tell of a gray day, and the gloom pours in, blanketing the room like a ground fog. The oven is always cold; nothing ever cooks there. A TV hangs on the wall; it never brings in a picture.

Barbara slowly sips her tea. It's sickly gray and tastes bland. She does not wish to know the nature of the brew—some things are better left unknown.

And she waits. And she waits.

He's been gone almost a day now, and Barbara's beginning to worry when he'll be back. But that decision is not hers to make. Nor is it Kenneth's.

She hears footsteps and then, all at once, the north wall of the kitchen—indeed, the north wall of the entire house—slowly swings open . . .

. . . to an unthinkable expanse of a bedroom, with a ceiling that touches the sky and a far wall that seems a mile distant. There, staring her in the face, is the monster-child.

"Good morning," she says. "Did you have sweet dreams?" She speaks with a pronounced lisp, and the word comes out "thweet." The monster-child is all of five years old, with brown hair in pigtails and bundles of energy in her massive muscles.

"What have you done with Kenneth?" Barbara asks, backing away from her rickety kitchen table.

The huge child then bounces on her bed, which is the size of a stadium. The heavy quilt that covers it is fringed in a hundred tassels the size of horse's tails. "I have him right here," she says. She pulls him out of a pocket in her pink overalls. Barbara can see the grimace of pain on his face and knows there's something different about him even before she realizes what it is.

"Kenneth, oh no!"

"The dog got him," says the girl. She jumps off her bed, carries Kenneth through the air, and sits him down on the chair opposite Barbara.

"He has a boo-boo, but I made it all better with a Band-Aid." The beige fabric bandage is glued across Kenneth's chest like a sash.

"Does it hurt?" Barbara asks.

Kenneth offers her a slight smile that doesn't compare to the bright-toothed smile he's always had. "I try not to think about it," he says. Barbara clasps his hand across the table to comfort him. "You look nice," says Kenneth, but then she always does.

The giant girl goes over to her desk and opens a tray that holds little cakes of watercolor paint. They watch as she busily dips a wet paintbrush into the paint, then into a plastic water cup, then into the paint, over and over again until the water takes on a cloudy, muddy tone. Then she brings the little plastic cup of water over and spills a drop of it into the small teacup sitting in front of Kenneth.

"I made you some more magic tea," she says. "Drink up, it's good for you."

Kenneth forces a "thank you" and sips the paint-water. Barbara can barely stomach it, but she tries not to let the girl know.

"How's yours?" she asks Barbara.

"It's fine," Barbara says, "just the way I like it." She fears saying anything else to the monster-child, who could snap their necks with a twist of her thumb.

"Let's go play outside!" The girl's voice booms with

high-pitched enthusiasm. "Let's play buried treasure in the yard!"

Barbara and Kenneth shudder in unison at the very thought.

"No thanks," says Kenneth, trying to sound as pleasant as possible. "I think we'll stay here today."

The monster-child frowns—and they both know that can't be a good thing.

"I liked you both better before my magic tea brought you to life." Then she slams the wall of their home so hard that the plastic bed bounces down the stairs.

"We've got to get out of here," Kenneth whispers.

It's night now. A pocked, mournful moon shines in from the little girl's window. The monster-child sleeps, her breath rising and falling in a rhythmic gale. Kenneth paces while Barbara brushes her hair with long, drawn-out strokes in front of a vanity with fake lightbulbs.

"It was better before," she says, thinking back to the days before the magic brew, when their thoughts had no more substance than the air between their plastic ears; those days when their limbs would not move unless the monster-child chose to move them. "Yes," repeats Barbara, "it was much better before we became aware."

Kenneth comes up behind her, gently touching her long hair. "Never say that," he says. "Don't even think it. We'll get through this."

But Kenneth's words have no comfort for her, and for the first time in her life, Barbara cries, shedding little cellophane tears that drift to the floor. "How much longer do we have to go on having tea parties and dressing up in hideous clothes?"

Kenneth takes a deep breath. "It ends here," he says finally, decisively.

Barbara stands up, looking deep into his opaque blue eyes. "You're not going out there," she says. "You can't go—it's not safe out there!"

Kenneth leans against the wall and the face of the house pushes open, leaving a space wide enough for him to slip out.

"Be careful," whispers Barbara, and he disappears.

• • •

He is gone for three days. Three days alone with the wrath of the monster-child. Barbara hides beneath the little plastic bed, she hides beneath the kitchen table, she even hides in the small trunk in the attic space, but still the child finds her.

"You've been bad!" the monster-child tells her. "Both of you! If you don't tell me where Ken has gone, I'll have to punish you."

"I don't know where he's gone," Barbara tells her truthfully. The child scowls at her, narrowing her massive eyes. Barbara can see into those dark pupils and finds nothing there. She wonders who is more empty inside: herself, or the girl? Barbara knows there is little more than air within the shell of her own plastic body, but what of the girl? Do flesh and blood necessarily mean the monster-child has a soul?

The girl's mother comes in now and again, a woman who stands so tall Barbara can't even get a good look at her face. The pleats of her skirt are like the ridges of a mountain, and her voice echoes from an unimaginable altitude, ordering the girl to clean her room or calling her down to dinner. Now, every time the mother comes in, the girl launches into a crying fit. "Ken ran away!" she cries. "You have to buy me a new one! You have to buy it now! Now! Now!" She kicks and screams—her pounding feet making all the furniture in Barbara's bright little house shake.

"He'll turn up," the mother says. "He always does."

And when the mother leaves, the girl is always angrier than before. This time she pulls open the wall of the little playhouse and drags Barbara out. "We'll have to force a confession out of you," she says with malevolent cheer, "just like I've seen on TV."

She then ties Barbara to the bedpost with some kite string, leaving her there for five agonizing minutes, before returning with leftovers from yesterday's dinner. The girl reaches onto her plate, grabs a hamburger patty, and rubs the greasy hamburger meat on Barbara. Then she opens the door.

"Snickers!" she calls. "Where are you, Snickers?"

"No!" cries Barbara. "Please! Please, not that!" But it is too late. Barbara hears the jangling of dog tags, and then the beast enters the room—a black-nosed, curly-haired monstrosity. A malicious poodle named Snickers.

Barbara screams as a tongue, foul-smelling and rough, rolls toward her like a tidal wave and envelops her. Fangs the size of stalactites gnaw at her, but she endures it, thinking only of the day when her purgatory will end.

"There are places you would not believe," Kenneth tells her. It is midnight. The girl sleeps, and the world is at blessed peace—but it will only last until morning. "There are great oval lakes with white walls, and bright plastic boats. There are building-block cities and fast wooden trains. There are cars that speed on a slim orange track. I have seen all these things!"

"I want to see them too!" says Barbara. "I can't stay here a moment longer!"

"Tomorrow," he tells her. "We'll wait until tomorrow. I have a plan."

"I don't know if I can wait," she tells him, then she shows him the jagged gnaw marks, a living memory of the fanged poodle-beast, etched into her arm.

Kenneth grimaces. "We could sand that down," he tells her.

She smiles. "You say the nicest things."

They endure the monster-child for one more day, all the while working on their plan.

"We're so sorry we were bad," they tell the girl, as they drink their watercolor tea. "We love you. We want to be with you always."

The girl grabs them and gives them sticky bubble-gum kisses. "You be good," she tells them, "and I'll never have to punish you again."

Then, as evening approaches, they set their plan in action.

"We want to watch TV," Barbara tells the girl. So she lifts them up and sits them in front of their little plastic television.

"No," says Kenneth. "Real TV. Downstairs."

"Yes, we want to watch with you!" Barbara adds.

"Oh, you sillies!" says the girl. "If I bring you downstairs to watch TV, Snickers will be after you."

"We don't mind," says Barbara, trying not to sound horrified at the thought. "We like Snickers."

The girl smiles, believing their every word, and after dinner, she takes the two of them downstairs and sits them on her lap.

Then, as the evening goes on, the girl's eyes begin to droop. Barbara feels the child's death grip on her begin to loosen.

"Now!" whispers Kenneth, and together they dive off her lap, scuttling across the plush fabric of the sofa, until finding the place where the cushion ends. Then they force themselves between the cushions into soft, dusty darkness. There, among popcorn fragments, coins, and gum wrappers, they listen to the muffled voices above.

"But I brought them down!" the monster-child complains to her father. "They were right here with me!"

"It's bedtime, honey," the father says. "We'll look for them tomorrow."

"I won't go upstairs without my dolls!" But her voice is weak and weighty with sleep. She doesn't have the strength to fight, and in the end, she gives up. Barbara peeks out to see the father carrying her up the stairs.

"Now?" asks Barbara.

"Not yet."

They wait until the mother puts Snickers on a leash and takes the beast out for a walk.

"Now!"

The moment the dog is gone, they burst out from beneath the

sofa cushions and race along the hardwood floor. "This way!" says Kenneth. "Follow me! I've been there! I'm sure I can find my way there again."

The wood gives way to the bright, flowery tiles of the kitchen, and before them is a door, open just a crack. It takes all their strength to push that door wide enough for them to squeeze through. Ahead of them now is a flight of steep gray wooden stairs, disappearing into darkness.

"Down there?"

"Yes! Trust me!"

Together they leap from one stair to another until finally they reach the dusty cement floor of the basement. Up above they hear the telltale jangling of Snickers's dog tags, and although he barks and scratches at the door, the mother pushes the door closed so the dog can't get down. They are safe at last!

But the space around them is anything but inviting. The basement is filled with sorrowful clutter. Disintegrating boxes, rusting paint cans, and the upturned bodies of dead insects stretch across an expanse of web-hung darkness.

"Oh, Kenneth." Barbara bites nervously on her knuckle. "Is this freedom? Is this bleak, awful place all there is? I thought you said there were wonders!"

He smiles at her. "Let me show you something." Then he leads her across the musty floor to a big black cavern: a heavy iron thing with a heavy iron grate. The bars of the grate are just wide enough for them to squeeze through.

What Barbara sees inside the gated cavern almost brings color to her face. Kenneth was right. "Oh! How wonderful!"

There in the center of the black, rugged earth of the cavern is a cabin! A beautiful log cabin, built of interlocking logs, with a green slat roof. Their dream house.

"I built it for you!" Kenneth tells her. "I knew you'd like it."

And although the walls of the cabin are bare, and the floor void of furniture, they know they will be happy here, far away, hidden from the monster-child dwelling above. For surely, the child will not think to look for them in the basement, and even if she did, she would never find their little home in the huge iron cavern.

It is as they sit there, inside their dream house, that a question occurs to Barbara.

"Kenneth," she asks, thinking of the small sign that was on the entrance to the iron cavern. "What does 'furnace' mean?"

Kenneth just shakes his head. "I don't know," he answers. "But there wasn't one in the plastic playhouse, so it must not be important."

He puts his arm around her, and she snuggles close to him. Barbara is confident that they will be safe here . . . and that even when the winds of winter blow in the world outside, their little dream house will stay very, very warm.

Mr. Vandermeer's Attic of Shame

I could tell you about time and space and fill your head with all that strange scientific stuff that scrambles your brain. I could try to tell you exactly how the attic came to be the strange and terrible place that it was. But to be honest, I don't understand that myself. All I know is that our neighbor, Mr. Vandermeer, built a place that was half magic and half science, and then filled it with the dark corners of his own soul.

My name is Lien. I'm fifteen and live in a small house on a small street in an old neighborhood that's changing. More and more stores are opening up in our neighborhood, where the Vietnamese lettering is just as prominent as the English. I suppose it makes my parents happy to see their native language—it must make them feel at home—but I was born here, and my English is far better than any Vietnamese I speak. But Mr. Vandermeer spoke fluent Vietnamese, and Korean, and Spanish, and just about every other language you could name. I always wondered why a man who never seemed to go anywhere would want to learn so many languages. Turns out, he had his reasons.

I don't know when it started—all I remember is the night I first noticed that something was strange. It was at three in the morning, on the night of a new moon. The sky was as nightmare dark as it could get, and somewhere beneath that cloak of darkness, I heard a far-off rumble. This sound was deep, resonating through the night, like a heavy, hungry beast. I wrapped my blanket around myself as I stepped out of bed, because my nightgown was too thin to keep me warm, then I peeled back the curtain and looked out the window to see the nature of this beast.

It was a truck. A big one. Eighteen-wheeler. It came down our block with its headlights off, barely able to squeeze beneath the heavy boughs of our tree-lined street. I kept my eyes on it as it slowly rolled down toward our house, its smokestack belching hot diesel fumes into the cold night. I heard the squeal and hiss of the air brakes, as it pulled to a stop right in front of Mr. Vandermeer's house, across the street from ours.

Mr. Vandermeer stood on his porch in a long overcoat, arms folded. "You're late," I heard him say to the driver as he got out of the truck. "Just like last month."

"Couldn't be avoided," answered the driver, then he went around to the back of the truck, and swung open the big double doors.

I brushed my long hair out of my eyes and squinted to get a better look. At first, I thought that perhaps this was a moving van, and Mr. Vandermeer was making a late-night departure. He was always a strange bird; very solitary, the type of guy who would grunt at you, or mumble something under his breath if you said hello, or throw you a rapid wave of his hand, and then run inside, as if he was too busy to engage a neighbor in conversation. I wouldn't put it past him to pack up and leave without saying goodbye to anyone. That was when I heard voices—a number of them, speaking in hushed whispers. I tried to pick out what they were saying, but it was in an Asian language—one I didn't understand. Perhaps Thai, or Indonesian. I heard footsteps on concrete, but the open rear door of the giant truck blocked my view.

I thought I might wake up my parents, and see if they could pick out some of the whispered words, but before I could wake them, the voices were gone. The truck was closed back up, and in a few moments it left, the throaty sound of its muffled engine trailing off as it turned the corner.

The lights stayed on in Mr. Vandermeer's house for about half an hour—but the curtains were pulled, and I couldn't see what went on inside. Finally his lights went off, and I drifted to sleep.

There's a trick your mind plays when you look at an empty room. When your brain just sees a floor, and a wall and four corners, it makes you see the place as something small and unpleasant; perhaps that's where claustrophobia starts. But add some furniture, and it all changes. The empty space becomes warm and homey; it becomes a room instead of a box. If you furnish it just right, you can even learn to feel comfortable living in a closet if you have to.

I know all about that, because, between my parents and my brothers, there're six of us living in a tiny two-bedroom house. I share a bedroom with my three brothers, which is kind of hard when you're the only daughter in the family. At night I have to close my eyes and imagine myself in my own room, where the posters on the wall are ones that I want, and there aren't always dirty socks and underwear strewn around the floor. My parents say that someday we'll have a bigger house, although they've been saying that for years.

But not all the homes in this neighborhood are like ours. Mr. Vandermeer's home, for instance. It's one of the larger ones, set on a double plot of land. An old two-story Victorian filled with rooms, and very well kept. Did I say well kept? I mean *perfectly* kept.

Mr. Vandermeer always had a pristine lawn, manicured as well as his fingernails and trimmed as closely as his short gray beard. His planters were kept full of winter-blooming plants in the chillier months, and replaced in the summer with more delicate warm-weather flowers. And in the fall, there was not a leaf to be found on the lawn.

"The leaves wouldn't dare to fall on his lawn," my mom would joke. "That man keeps everything in order. Everything in control."

I never thought much of it until I began to notice those late-night deliveries, and the strange voices. The fact was, now that I took the time to notice, there was always someone working on Mr. Vandermeer's house. When I went off to school, a gardener would be planting tulip bulbs, sweaty even in the chilly air. In the afternoon, someone else would be cleaning the drainpipes, or washing the windows, or painting the porch railing. And each day, I began to notice that it was someone different. It was the same inside. He had a housekeeper who would take out the trash and beat out the rugs every day . . . but the face I saw carrying those heavy, heavy trash bags to the curb was often different. One day it would be a Latina woman with eyes wizened from a life of labor. Then, a few days later, it would be a young Chinese girl.

"He goes through housekeepers like I go through stockings," my mother said when I mentioned it to her. "Some people are like that. Never satisfied with anyone's work."

And the fact that his workers were always of different ethnicities didn't seem odd to me, because I was used to living in this neighborhood. You see, our neighborhood is like a melting pot that never boiled, so nothing ever melted. Vietnamese families live among Latinos, among Koreans, among Armenians. While there are never any major battles between the groups here, there aren't many friendships either. We live side by side, but our circles never cross.

Still, as I watched those workers silently going about their business at Mr. Vandermeer's house, I knew there was something not quite right about it, but I couldn't say what it was.

There are times that a mystery begins to feel like a mosquito bite, irritating you in a place you can't scratch, until it seems there's nothing left of you but that nagging bite, screaming for relief. That's how it was with me and Mr. Vandermeer's house.

The next late-night delivery came in the rain. Again I heard the voices, and I snuck out to watch. Just as before, the voices disappeared into the house, the truck drove off, and the lights went out in half an hour. I just had to know what was going on in there. And so, the next Saturday morning, when Mr. Vandermeer went out for his morning walk—which he did like clockwork—I ventured across the street, where three gardeners pruned the bushes, and someone else detailed his spotless Mercedes on the driveway. So busy were they in their work that they didn't notice me stepping onto the property. I suppose they weren't used to visitors, because no one ever visited Mr. Vandermeer, except for the people who worked there.

Unobserved, I made my way down the side of his house to the backyard, where I found one more worker. It was a man. No, a boy. He couldn't have been any older that I was. He was thin, frail, dressed in fading, frayed clothes. There in the center of the backyard lawn, he labored over a brown patch in the lawn, carefully pulling up the dead grass and planting new seeds. Only, as I got closer, I could see he wasn't planting the seeds the way a regular person might plant them. He wasn't spreading them out to cover the dead spot. Instead he picked up each individual seed, and, with a pair of tweezers, placed it perfectly in the grass. Then he went back for another.

Mr. Vandermeer will see that, and fire him for sure, I thought.

"Hey," I called out, "that's not the way you plant grass."

He spun his head to me and locked eyes on mine. They were Asian eyes, like mine, but there was something different about them. Different from me, that is. The way he held himself, the expression on his face . . . even without hearing him speak, I knew that he hadn't been in this country long.

"Do you speak English?" I asked.

He bolted, heading straight for Mr. Vandermeer's back door.

"Hey, wait!"

I grabbed for him but he was too fast. Instead my hand fell on his back pocket, dislodging something there. It was a book.

"Hey, you dropped this!" I picked up the book and dared to do something that I never thought I actually would. I followed him right into Mr. Vandermeer's house.

The aroma hit me right away. The wonderful smell of Christmas and Thanksgiving all rolled into one. A turkey cooking in the oven; vegetables baking; sauce simmering. It almost whisked me off my feet.

The gardener boy spun around the banister post and sped up the stairs, turning back once to look at me. The expression on his face now was clear. It was fear. Terror. He was terrified of me, but why?

Then, as I looked around, I could see that he wasn't the only one. There was a housekeeper polishing the brass fixtures of an oversized fireplace. She had stopped in mid-stroke when she saw me barge into the house. Another maid was polishing the already spotless wood floor. She saw me, and her eyes registered even more fear than the boy's. She whispered an exclamation in some language I didn't know and hurried to leave the room, as if it was a crime to be seen by me. Through the swinging door of the kitchen, I saw a chef slink quickly out of view.

I tried to ignore their strange behavior and hurried up the wide staircase, to the second floor, holding the boy's worn book in my hand—but by the time I got there, he was gone.

It felt strange to be trespassing like this, but I did have an excuse. I had to return the book. I clutched the book tighter and slowly walked down the hall.

"Hello?" I peered into the open bedroom doors. No one there. Not in the master bedroom, or in the two other bedrooms. I even pushed open the door to the bathroom, but it was empty.

Only one door remained for me to check now. It was slightly ajar, and I couldn't see anything through the crack. At first, I thought it was a closet—that for some strange reason, this boy had decided I was such a threat, he had to hide in a closet—but when I opened the door, I saw steep stairs, leading up into darkness. It was an attic.

Suddenly I was startled by a stern voice behind me.

"Bạn đang lãng phí thời gian! Trở về với công việc!"

It was Mr. Vandermeer. He stared at me with cold gray eyes. From what Vietnamese I understood, I knew he was telling me to get back to work, thinking I worked for him.

"I'm Lien—from across the street," I said.

It took a moment to register, then his hard expression softened. "Of course you are. I'm sorry, I didn't recognize you. How can I help you?"

"There . . . there was this boy . . ."

Mr. Vandermeer smoothly pushed the attic door closed. "Yes?"

I still held the book, but suddenly I didn't want to give it to Mr. Vandermeer. I didn't want to give him anything. "Well . . . I—I just wanted to show him how to plant grass."

Mr. Vandermeer's smile left his face. He became just the slightest bit worried. I wished I hadn't said anything. "Was he doing a poor job?"

"No," I said, not wanting to get the boy in trouble. "I'm sure he was trying to do the right thing. It's just that he was using tweezers."

And then Mr. Vandermeer threw his head back and laughed. "Well, of course he was," Mr. Vandermeer said, putting a firm hand on my shoulder and guiding me back down to the first floor. "That's what I asked him to do."

"What?"

"How do you think I get my grass to grow so neatly? Every seed is hand-placed."

I thought about the size of his front and back yards. "But . . . how can that be . . . it must take months to hand-plant a lawn that way. . . ."

"And that's what his job is. Believe me, there are millions of people who would beg for a job like that."

I shrugged. I didn't know anyone who would. "I guess you must be rich to have all these people working for you."

"I'm an importer," he explained. "It affords me a nice income."

"What do you import?"

"Oh, this and that."

As we reached the first floor, the smell of dinner hit me again. "Big party tonight?"

"Yes," he said gently, as he led me to the front door. "Please stop by again. It's always good getting to know my neighbors."

Before I knew it, I was out on the porch, and the door had shut behind me. As I was crossing the street, I realized that Mr. Vandermeer's big turkey dinner couldn't be for many people. Because his dinner table was only set for one.

No sky today. We stay below deck. Rough sea makes my father sick. Captain says we will eat soon, but we still wait for the food. My mother says traveling to America is like being born. We must suffer the pains before we see the light of day.

"It's a diary," my brother Ran explained, as he read it and translated it from Vietnamese.

I closed the door to the bedroom, worried that our parents might discover we were snooping into someone else's business. With my two younger brothers off at soccer practice, it gave Ran and me some time to translate alone in our room. "I knew it," I said. "He's just gotten here." I felt a bit ashamed to be reading the entries in the gardener boy's diary, but my curiosity overwhelmed any shame I felt.

Ran flipped a few pages. "So Vandermeer's got all these undocumented people working for him?"

"We don't know they're undocumented," I countered.

"You're so naive," he said, finding another entry in the journal.

Sea is calm today. No storms. Too many people down here, though; many fights. People fight for space. People

> *fight for food. People fight for nothing. It's something to do to pass the time. My father says English is a hard language, but schools there will teach if I want to learn. And I do want to learn.*

Ran looked to me thoughtfully. "So you say there are always different people working at Vandermeer's house? And the old ones just seem to disappear?"

I nodded. "What do you think happens to them?"

Ran scratched his hair. "I think he eats them."

"Ran!"

"Sure. He gets people that no one will miss, has them do the yard, then cooks them up for dinner."

"Don't be gross."

"You said you smelled something cooking."

"It was TURKEY!"

"How do you know that human doesn't smell like turkey? Frog legs taste like chicken, don't they?"

I pushed him back onto his bed, and he laughed.

"That's not it," I told him. "There's something else going on there. I just can't figure it out yet."

I told him to turn to the last entry. He did. It was dated the day before yesterday.

> *Room enough for all of us here. I have my own bed. Hot water enough for whole family. Land to grow our own food. No time for school right now. Dad works the machine twelve hours a day. I work ten. Sisters work in factory. Mom farms. No frost here—food grows all year round. Tomorrow I work in Mr. Vandermeer's yard. A great honor. I hope I do not disappoint. Maybe then I won't have to go back to the machine.*

"Oh no! I ruined it for him!" I thought back to that fearful look in the boy's eyes when I chased him into the house. "I got him into trouble."

"What's this machine he keeps talking about?" asked Ran.

I just shrugged. "Keep reading."

Ran found his place and continued.

When I work at the machine, I turn my eyes to the sky, trying to remember that my time at the machine will pass. Windy today. Heavy clouds blow past and melt in the corners of the world. I look to the windblown clouds, and the great beams beyond.

"Kind of poetic," said Ran. He turned the page. "It ends there."

I took the diary back from Ran and looked at it thoughtfully. "I should get his book back to him. I wonder where he lives."

"I'm sure Vandermeer knows," said Ran.

There are some people who live in their own private world. They go about their business, away and apart from others, keeping guard over the things they do and the things they think, the same way they keep guard over the things they own. Their faces are NO TRESPASSING signs. Their words are wrapped in barbed wire. That was Mr. Vandermeer. But a NO TRESPASSING sign was also an invitation to explore and find out what was so special that it needed to be protected.

The next weekend, I stepped once more into Mr. Vandermeer's world, offering him no warning that I was coming. I didn't ring the bell—in fact, I waited on my own lawn, until I saw one of his housekeepers open the door to take out the trash. Then, as she went back in, I snuck up behind the bushes and kept the door from closing. I took a deep breath and quietly slipped inside.

Again, the overwhelming smell. Turkey once more, and the table set for one. Two men stood on ladders in Vandermeer's study, carving designs into the wood molding on the ceiling. Two women, with dark circles under their eyes, carried heavy cardboard boxes down from upstairs, then went back upstairs again and didn't come down. I could hear Mr. Vandermeer's voice—he was in the downstairs bathroom, instructing another worker. He spoke in a language that sounded European.

I slipped past the bathroom and into the kitchen. The chef was gone for the moment, and so I dared to open the oven and peer inside, unable to get Ran's cannibal suggestion out of my head.

There was a turkey in the oven. I sighed with relief.

"What were you expecting to find, Lien?"

I jumped and the oven door slammed with a jarring bang.

Mr. Vandermeer laughed, incredibly amused at my reaction. It irked me, and made me just a little bit bolder.

"So how come you're having turkey again?"

"It's Saturday," he answered. "I have it every Saturday. Like clockwork."

"And you're eating alone. Again."

His smile didn't falter. "A party of one."

"What a waste of food."

"If you'd like to join me, I could have a place set for you."

His offer actually sounded genuine, and although dining with Mr. Vandermeer was not something I really wanted to do, I accepted. "Yes," I told him. "I love turkey." It allowed me more time to figure out just what was going on in his house.

I called my parents and told them I was having dinner at a friend's house—I didn't dare tell them that it was Mr. Vandermeer, as they were convinced he was the lunatic of all lunatics, and they were probably right. We sat down in the living room to wait for dinner. He asked me questions about my family, about school, and what subjects I liked, and through it all, he kept a sense of patient control of the conversation that was as unnerving to me as the ticking of the grandfather clock in the corner.

Another woman came downstairs and put down a heavy box, then went back up.

"Would you like to see what I do?" he asked, and without waiting for an answer, he went over to the box and pulled out a blouse, handing it to me. The label said VANDERMEER FASHIONS. I looked in the box to find a whole collection of identical blouses. Nothing strange or awful was in those boxes at all.

"You import clothes?"

"In a manner of speaking, yes."

It was, in its own way, a letdown, and I began to wonder if Mr. Vandermeer was less mysterious than I had thought.

Another woman descended the stairs and deposited a box of Vandermeer Fashions at our feet. I noticed that this was a different woman than any of the others I had seen before, but her eyes were just as tired and worn. I felt a warm breeze caress my face, and searching for its source, my eyes were drawn up the stairs, to an open door. The attic door.

The woman went back up the stairs, began to climb up the steep attic steps, and disappeared into darkness. What was it about that attic?

And then it finally occurred to me what was wrong with all the workers at Mr. Vandermeer's house. There were never any cars out front, and none of the workers ever seemed to leave. They simply went into the house . . . and disappeared.

Mr. Vandermeer wasn't watching me—he was watching a butler exit the kitchen with several silver platters.

"Dinner is served," he said, and he went to the dining table, for the first time turning his back on me.

I knew this might be the only chance I had, and so I took it without thinking. Instead of following him into the dining room, I hurried up the polished mahogany stairs to the second floor and swung the attic door wide. If I hesitated, I knew I would lose my nerve, so I bounded up the attic steps into that warm current of air blowing down on me, until, in the darkness, I banged into a second door at the top of the steps. Air whistled beneath it. With my heart pounding in my ears, I turned the knob and pushed hard against the door. It flung open and I fell . . . onto dirt. Not the musty, dusty dirt that coats the floors of most attics, but hard-packed earth. I quickly got up to get my bearings, and what I saw around me, to this day I have no way to explain.

I was on an unpaved street. To the left and right of me, shoddy-looking concrete apartment buildings rose five stories into the air. Clotheslines crisscrossed like cobwebs between them, across a narrow dirt alley. People on bicycles bumped past me on the uneven alley, and I heard voices, dozens of voices, all babbling in too many different languages to distinguish one from the other.

Mr. Vandermeer's attic wasn't an attic at all. It was a ghetto.

Two strong hands gripped firmly onto my shoulders from behind. They carried with them a chill as potent as an electric shock. I froze in place.

"You are a meddlesome girl," said Mr. Vandermeer, with a furious, frustrated sigh.

I squirmed out of his grip and tried to get past him, down the attic steps. "I want to go now," was all I could say. "Please, can I go now?"

But Mr. Vandermeer stood in my way. "No. You wanted to see what was in my attic, and now you will see what's in my attic. You'll see all of it. And maybe then you'll understand."

He turned me around to face the street again. This time I dared to look up, and saw dense, billowing clouds blowing past. Above those clouds, through a mile-high haze, I could see the heavy slanted beams of the attic roof!

I look to the windblown clouds, and the great beams beyond . . .

That diary entry wasn't just being poetic—that boy was writing exactly what he saw!

The sun shone through a gap in the clouds, but I realized it wasn't the sun at all. It was a single massive lightbulb, dangling from a cord, a mile in the sky.

"You've shrunken us!" I shouted. "You've shrunken all these people!" But when I looked behind us, I could see that the attic door wasn't towering over our heads; it was exactly the same size as when I'd stumbled through it.

"I assure you that no one's been shrunken," explained Mr. Vandermeer. "I don't downsize people."

"Then how—"

"You will find, Lien, that space can be made in ways you've never even imagined."

And then he led me down the narrow street.

We strode through row after row of identical apartment buildings. As I looked into the windows, I could see whole families. Others lingered in entryways, as if they were overflowing from the crowded apartments—and as Mr. Vandermeer passed, they all lowered their heads in a show of respect. Or fear.

"Don't be fooled by appearances," Mr. Vandermeer said. "These people want to be here. They want to live this way. Some are refugees from warring nations. Others left their homelands to escape starvation and poverty. But here, everyone works, and no one starves."

We came out of the shadows of the tenement buildings to an open field, where dozens of workers planted and harvested crops. It was then that I began to hear the churning noise—a distant mechanical grinding that shook the ground.

"On the outside, my attic is only thirty-four feet across," explained Mr. Vandermeer, "but on the inside it extends for more than a mile in all directions. That's plenty of land for building, for planting, and for manufacturing."

He pointed across the field to the left. "My clothing factory," he said. "I have one hundred and fifty workers putting in an honest day's labor there."

I wondered how many hours made labor honest.

He turned and pointed to a complex to his right that spewed out white smoke from a high smokestack. "Concrete and steel factories, for building," he explained. "I employ three hundred and twenty-nine there."

I was still reeling from the sheer size of Mr. Vandermeer's attic space, but I tried not to show how disoriented and confused I was. "I guess you really are rich," I said. "To be able to pay so many people."

He turned to me as if I had said something in a language he didn't understand. "Pay?" he said. "There's no need for payment here. This is a perfect society, without money. If the people do their work properly, then I make sure they get what they need."

I felt that electric chill run through me again. "In other words . . . it's slave labor."

Mr. Vandermeer tossed back his head and gave his superior laugh again. "Lien, you are so naive."

Straight ahead of us, directly beneath the mile-high dangling incandescent sun, was another factory. It was from there that the deep mechanical grinding sound came. It must have been hot, for the air around it shimmered and rippled in heat waves, like a road in the desert.

"What's that place?" I asked.

Mr. Vandermeer hesitated, as if he really didn't want to tell me. But finally he said, "That is the space-maker."

As we drew closer, it became clear how very large this factory was, and then I realized it wasn't quite a factory. It was a single, open-air machine, full of gnashing gears and powerful pistons pumping up and down in an unrelenting rhythm. It was a beast of a machine that counted out time in perfectly metered beats.

On the fringe of this great machine, new gears, levers, and pistons were being installed, frantically welded together by workers, as if their lives depended on getting the job done.

"This is the most important part of our little village," said Mr. Vandermeer, as he led me deep into the superstructure of the clock-like mechanism. Around us, gears towered over our heads, and heavy springs coiled around themselves like pythons.

But by far the most amazing, and most disturbing, part of the machine was the human part, because everywhere you looked there were workers—hundreds of them, maybe thousands of them. They pushed and pulled on massive levers. They threw their bodies against giant flywheels, to get them to turn. They turned cranks, their bodies covered in sweat and their mouths contorted into strained grimaces. From each of their bodies, waves of heat radiated outward. Or, at least I thought it was heat.

"What does this machine do?" I asked. "What are they making?"

"They are making space," Mr. Vandermeer said, not at all bothered by the struggling workers around him.

"I don't understand."

And he proceeded to explain. "Surely you know that matter and energy are one and the same. $E=mc^2$? Matter can be converted into energy—it's the principle behind a nuclear bomb. Well, in the same way, space and time are interchangeable. That is, one can be converted into the other."

He led me up a narrow catwalk, where I could get a wider view of the immense machine. "These workers here . . . they are charged with the crucial task of converting time into space. Space enough to fit an entire village into my attic. Even now, they're building new wings to my machine, making it bigger as more and more people arrive. In six months it will double its power—and my attic will quadruple in size! In just a few short years the area inside this attic will be larger than most of the nations these people came from!"

I let his words hit me. I tried to absorb them, but it was simply coming too fast. A machine that converted time into space? How could that be?

"The time that you're converting . . . where does it come from?"

"From them, of course." Mr. Vandermeer gestured to the sweating laborers around us, too absorbed by their backbreaking work to even know we were there. "The time comes from their lives."

They were all of different nationalities, and yet, they were all the same, as if they had lost their individuality to the machine—just nameless cogs like the cranks and gears they turned. But one face in that crowd did look familiar. An Asian face, hair drenched in sweat.

"I know him. . . ."

It was the boy gardener, whose diary I had come to return. Only he didn't look like a boy anymore. He looked like a man—a tired, downtrodden man. The circles under his eyes were just as dark as those of the gray-haired laborers around him. It was then that I truly understood what Mr. Vandermeer meant.

"This machine," I said, "it ages them, doesn't it? It slowly pulls the life right out of them."

"And turns it into something far more useful!" insisted Mr. Vandermeer. "Room to live and breathe!"

"It's horrible."

"If it's so horrible, then why don't any of them leave? After all, my attic door is never locked."

I turned to look at the exhausted boy. He threw me the slightest glance but couldn't afford the energy to keep looking. He continued to pull and push on the crank that powered the engine that pulled the time from his life, radiating it outward from his body, in rippling waves of space. Waves that I had first taken for heat.

"These workers sacrifice their time for their families. They stay here because they know how much better it is than the outside world."

I shook my head, refusing to accept Vandermeer's twisted logic. "No. They stay here because they don't know how to leave. Sure, they can see the door, but they're afraid of what's outside it. They're afraid of you!" I pulled the journal out of my pocket and showed it angrily to Vandermeer. "This belongs to him! I found it when he was gardening in your yard. He has dreams. He wants to go to school and learn English."

Mr. Vandermeer just waved the thought away. "Why does he need to know English here? Why does he need further schooling at all? He knows all he needs to know."

I approached the boy as he labored at the machine. He didn't slow his pace, but I could tell that he knew what I was doing. Gently, I placed the diary at his feet. But he couldn't take his hands off the machine long enough to retrieve it, so it just sat there by the tip of his worn shoe.

"You don't own these people!" I screamed at Vandermeer, over the monotonous drone of the hellish space-maker.

The old man crossed his arms. "I own their time, I own their space, and I own every ounce of their labor," he said. "So I own all of them that is worth having."

My words began to fail me, and I found my emotions balling up in my fists. I pounded against Mr. Vandermeer's chest. I pushed him back against his own machine, but he kept his balance, and just smiled at me.

That was when I ran. I bolted through the maze of gears and workers, out into the great field, where more workers plowed at a panicked pace, as frantically as the machinists. Did they know they had no future except for whatever future Mr. Vandermeer chose to give them? Was this what they had hoped for when they left the shores of their distant lands?

I reached the overcrowded apartment buildings, winding through the maze, searching for the one door that would lead me out. I looked behind me many times but never saw Mr. Vandermeer following. And then I realized that he didn't have to follow me. I meant nothing to him. Once I found my way out, what could I do? I couldn't tell anyone—no one would believe me. All I could do would be to sit in my room, the horrible knowledge of this place stuck in my head, just as the people were stuck in this attic.

I finally found the door. Just as he'd said, it was not locked, it was wide open, as more women brought boxes of clothing from the factory down the stairs, then came back up again, to return to Mr. Vandermeer's little universe.

I pushed past them on the attic stairs, ran down the grand mahogany staircase, past the elaborate turkey dinner that was still set on the dining table, and out the front door.

All those workers tending to his home—Mr. Vandermeer could have a hundred people working on his yard and in his kitchen, and in the rooms of his house, and there'd still be hundreds more anxious to take their place the next day—anxious to be used by their landlord.

I raced into my own house, into my own cramped room, and cried for every soul trapped in Mr. Vandermeer's shameful attic.

My parents noticed that something was wrong with me, but they didn't know what it was. They figured I was overworked at school, or I was fighting the flu, or something like that. How could they know that my thoughts had been poisoned by what I had seen across the street?

"You should do something after school, Lien," my mother suggested. "A sport maybe, or computer club, or dance. Something that will cheer you up."

I thanked her for the suggestion but did nothing. I thought my depression was as deep as Mr. Vandermeer's attic was high. I lived like that for weeks. Until the truck came again. Its deep rumble pulled me out of my light sleep at four in the morning. This time when I heard it, I didn't waste time—I didn't convert it into space, either—I converted it into action. I wasn't sure what I was going to do, but I knew I had to do something. Quickly I dressed and ran across the street, as the driver opened the big double doors.

A wave of people poured out of the truck, as I knew they would. This batch of desperate newcomers were Eastern European—refugees of some bloody conflict. All their belongings were packed into tiny suitcases, and the driver shuffled them out like cattle, toward Mr. Vandermeer's front door.

I ran up to them.

"No!" I screamed, shattering the quiet of the night. "Don't go! He'll use you! You'll never get away!"

But the people pulled away from me, not understanding my words. Terrified that I meant them harm, they moved toward the warm, safe light of Mr. Vandermeer's door. But I knew that it was a false light.

Vandermeer heard me right away as he stood on his porch, shepherding in his huddled masses. He strode toward me with an anger in his eyes I hadn't seen before.

That was when I knew exactly what I had to do. I dodged him and pushed past the crowds of frightened people into his house. I wove around them on the grand staircase and pushed them out of the way as I climbed the steep stairs to the attic and pushed through the door at the top, into the narrow street.

It was dark and quiet up there. It was night, just like it was outside. Then I reached over and flicked on the attic light switch, and suddenly the entire world was lit by the dangling sun-bulb above. For Mr. Vandermeer, being God was as simple as turning on a light.

I heard heavy footsteps behind me. This time Vandermeer was chasing me, but I wouldn't let him catch me. I might not be the fastest runner in the world, but I'm not slow, either, and I ran with every ounce of my soul. Quickly I made it out into the field. Far ahead, the great space-maker churned away, boiling time into space. I headed straight for it, not sure what I would do when I got there, but knowing that if anything was to be done, it had to be done there. All the while Mr. Vandermeer was right behind, shouting at me, cursing at me, but his words only pushed me faster.

I burst onto the narrow catwalks between the gears and slaving workers of the space-maker, searching for a way to stop the machine. Surely there had to be a button or lever that would grind the thing to a screeching halt. But the longer I searched, the more I began to despair. Why would a machine that was never intended to stop moving have a cutoff switch?

I only slowed my pace for a moment, but that was all it took. Mr. Vandermeer grabbed me by the collar, pulled me off my feet, and lifted me out over the churning gears.

"I have no use for you," was all he said, and I felt his grip begin to loosen. He was going to drop me into the mechanism without a second thought!

Then, among the many movements of the intricate machine, I saw a new motion. An iron pole arced across the air and hit Mr. Vandermeer in the head. He let go of me, but as he did, someone else caught me. The one who had swung that pole. The boy with the diary. With his machine-strengthened arms he lifted me over the railing, to safety.

Vandermeer lay on the floor, dazed, but was quickly recovering. If I was to do something, I had to do it now . . . and suddenly I knew exactly what it was. This machine was like a clock—and like a clock, every gear was connected to something, which was connected to something else.

And clocks break down all the time.

I took the pole from the boy. It was heavier than anything that I had ever carried, but I wouldn't be holding it for long. With all my strength I rammed it into the teeth of the great gear in front of me.

Then I watched as the gear turned and tried to mesh with the cog beside it.

A screaming metal complaint resounded from the gears as their teeth tried to mesh, but the pole was firmly lodged in the way . . . and the machine just stopped.

Every gear, every piston, everything came to a screeching halt.

"No!!" Vandermeer got up and tried to dislodge the pole, but it was no use. The many workers ceased their labors, wondering what was going on, and the machine wailed as its last moving piece—the mainspring—continued to turn, building up incredible torque as it wound itself tighter and tighter.

All that energy had to go somewhere—and it did! The spring broke free, tearing out the gear that drove it, and that in turn tore out the gear beside that. In an instant, the entire machine was an exploding chaos of gears and springs. Massive chunks of metal tore free, gears rolled down catwalks, and everyone began to run for their lives.

Everyone except Mr. Vandermeer.

He alone stayed with the machine, mourning its destruction as it came down around him.

Together, the boy and I ran across the field, following the rest of the scattering workers. As we ran, I noticed our shadows begin to change, becoming longer. I looked up to see the great light in the sky shifting position, rapidly dropping, and saw the immense attic beams crushing the clouds into wisps of vapor as they came down. Now that the machine had stopped, the attic was losing space. The sky was falling!

By the time we reached the apartment buildings, crowds were pressing against the narrow attic doorway in panic, trying to escape the crushing roof as it came down. Somewhere along the way I lost sight of the boy, and I realized he must have gone to find his family.

How long would it take, I wondered, until the all the extra attic space was gone . . . and what would happen to everything trapped inside these walls?

As if to answer me, I heard a heavy crunch, and looked up to see the very tops of the apartment buildings crumble to dust as the roof beams squeezed down on them.

The crowd at the attic door was thinning now, as they gushed in a flood of humanity down the stairs. I was at the very back of the crowd. The farmland boiled and folded in upon itself, like a giant angry sea. I watched as the once-distant concrete-and-steel factory plowed into the empty apartment buildings like an ocean liner; and as the last gears of the space-time converter exploded heavenward, shattering the dangling light up above.

The ceiling continued to come down, crushing floor after floor of the tenements. The buildings pressed closer and closer, threatening to flatten me between them, as the alley disappeared. Then finally I was stumbling down the stairs, carried by the panicked current of immigrants through the Vandermeer house, and out the front door.

Only when I was standing on my own curb did I dare to look back. It seemed everyone had gotten out, except for Mr. Vandermeer. And as I looked at the house in the dim rays of dawn, I could see the walls begin to bow outward.

I knew what was about to happen.

Perhaps all the space had been taken out of the attic, but the mass remained. Thousands of tons of concrete and steel were compressed into that tiny attic space. I suppose the space-maker machine had kept the attic from feeling its true weight until now, but without that machine, the sheer mass of everything that had been inside was too much for the house to bear.

The entire attic fell through the house below it, and the walls exploded outward with a sickening crunch of splintering wood. The earth shook like the most violent of earthquakes, and when it was over, there was nothing left of Mr. Vandermeer's house but a hole fifty feet deep, punched into the ground by the superheavy attic.

Lights came on all around the neighborhood, and as people

began to come out onto their porches to see what had happened, the refugees from Mr. Vandermeer's attic began to disperse.

My family joined me on our lawn, thinking I had just come out of our house myself.

"An earthquake?" asked my father.

"No, a sinkhole," said Ran. "Look at that!"

But I was no longer interested in the hole across the street. Instead I turned my attention to the people who had escaped from the attic and were now homeless. They were all running, scurrying away, quickly disappearing into the morning in search of a new place—in search of some space of their own.

And for an instant I wasn't sure whether I had done something wonderful for them or something terrible.

I was so worried about the hurrying, disappearing faces that I didn't notice the one right in front of me. It was the boy with the diary. He stood there, with two girls behind him—the sisters he wrote about—and a man and woman who must have been his parents. They all looked troubled, even frightened, but it wasn't the same kind of hopeless terror that seemed to fill the corners of Mr. Vandermeer's attic. It was the fear of a challenge. The wariness of a new day.

The boy turned to look at me. He looked at me with a smile in his dark eyes and said something in Vietnamese. Like I said, I don't speak much of the language, but there are some words I do know.

"It's 'thank you,'" I translated back to him, knowing that they would be his first words in this language. "In English, we say 'thank you.'"

He reached out and heartily shook my hand. "Thank you," he repeated, in a heavy accent. "Thankyouthankyouthankyou!"

And then he left with his family, disappearing into the morning as all the others had.

"What was that all about?" asked my mother.

"I found something for him," I told her, "and I gave it back."

My younger brothers had already taken to dueling with wood fragments that had landed on our lawn, and the rest of us began the task of cleaning up the mess left in our yard, even before the police cruisers pulled onto our block to rope off the sinkhole across the street.

I don't know what happened to all the people who escaped from the attic. Perhaps some of them were sent back to where they came from, but I'm sure many more found the dream they left their homeland for. I know, because every once in a while, I'll see one of them walking in the street or shopping at the supermarket. Perhaps someday, I might even run into the boy with the diary again, and we'll talk about things and smile because we'll know that even without Mr. Vandermeer's infernal machine, there's time and space enough for everyone and everything in this world, if we only know how to make it.

Dark Alley

A rainy Friday afternoon. My bowling bag pulls down on my arm. If my arms were rubber, my knuckles would be dragging on the ground from all those Friday afternoons lugging my ball to Atomic Lanes. But it's something I have to do. Something I want to do.

"Do we have to bowl today, Marshall?" my sister Mia asks as we get off the bus. "My thumb hurts."

"Maybe it wouldn't hurt if you didn't suck it."

She pulls her thumb out of her mouth and hands me her bowling bag. "Then you carry my ball," she says. "It's too heavy." Mia's seven, although sometimes you'd think she was younger. Usually Mom's there when Mia comes home from school, but she works late on Fridays—the only weekday I get to go bowling after school.

The skies let loose as if the rain has waited for us to get off the bus. My waterproof jacket isn't all that waterproof. Mia's bright orange poncho makes her look like a walking traffic cone, but at least she's dry. Finally we reach the double glass doors of the bowling alley, and they slide open to admit us.

Instantly we are hit by the familiar smell of greasy pizza and floor wax. It's a madhouse. We wait in a slow-moving line in front of the counter until we reach the attendant—a heavy man with a stubbly beard and suspicious eyes.

"Size?" snaps the lane man.

"We have our own shoes," I tell him. "We just need a lane." I wonder how many years I have to keep coming here for him to know me by name. But then again, I don't know his name either. To me, he's just "the guy who gives out lanes."

"Sorry, all the lanes are full," says the lane guy. "I just gave out the last one."

I take a look down the alleys. Movie theaters and bowling alleys really clean up on days like this . . . a rainy afternoon can do that. But then I notice that there's a single dark alley, right next to lane twenty-four.

"What about lane twenty-five?" I ask.

"We ain't got no lane twenty-five," says the lane man. "It only goes up to twenty-four."

"But—"

"Look, kid, it's been a long day. All right? Why don't you give me a break? You want a lane, come back later."

Mia twirls her finger in her hair and grins at me. "Oh well, I guess we'll have to go home."

But then a jock in a letter jacket and his girlfriend—the ones who were in front of us and got the last lane—turn to us. "Why don't you bowl with us?" offers the girl.

The lane dude grabs my money, and we go off with them. They've been assigned to lane twenty-four.

While the couple bowls their first frame, my eyes wander to the lane beside us. It should be lane twenty-five, but unlike the other lanes, it has no number, and unlike the others, it doesn't share a ball return with another lane—it has its own ball return. The lane is unlit, and its pins are in shadows.

The couple have thrown their first frames, and since I'm not paying attention, Mia seizes the opportunity to pull her lightweight pink ball out of her bag and go ahead of me. She plods up to the foul line and drops the ball with a heavy thud, and it meanders its way down the alley, lazily taking down three pins.

"Yay!" she cries. On her second shot, she knocks down one more.

The pins are reset, and I step up to the lane carrying my personalized deep green ball. As soon as I'm in place, my mind begins to clear. It's always like that. I forget the rainy day. I forget school, I forget home; I just think of the pins and my ball. My dad was a great bowler. He tried to teach me, but I was too young, and then one night, after a long day at work, he fell asleep at the wheel of his car. I think about him a lot. I think about how I could have saved his life if I had been there, because I'm always alert in the car. But mostly I think good thoughts about him. Especially when I bowl. I imagine the way he bowled, how his ball never made a sound when it left his hand and touched the lane, gentle as a kiss. Each time I bowl, I try to do the same.

With the couple and Mia behind me, I focus all my attention to a pinpoint, lean forward, and begin my approach. At the perfect moment, I release the ball . . . and it clunks down hard on the wood, careens a crooked path toward the pins, and plops into the gutter before it can take down a single pin.

"Gutterrrr balllll," says Mia, like a baseball umpire would say. "Steeeerrrrike!"

"Tough break, dude," says the guy, his arm around his girlfriend.

I don't look at anyone. I put my hands over the little air blower to keep myself busy until the ball return spits my ball back to me. I take it and go for the second shot.

Again I prepare to imitate my dad's bowling form. I inherited my dad's big feet and long fingers—you'd figure I might have inherited his bowling skills too. Right? I throw the ball with all the heart and guts I can spare . . . and again it rolls diagonally down the alley, this time tapping the tenpin enough to make it wobble, but not fall down.

I stare at the pins grinning at me—like a full set of mockingly perfect teeth, before the bar comes down and sweeps them away.

The jock snickers, flipping back a lock of hair. "Not very good, are ya?"

His girlfriend raps him in the stomach.

But the fact is, he's right. I'm not very good. And how can I get any better if I can only afford to bowl once a week? I look around at the expert bowlers hurling strikes and spares in every frame. Then I turn to look at the dark lane beside us. I know why the attendant wouldn't give me the last lane: he didn't think I deserved it. He might be just "the guy who gives out lanes" to me, but to him, I'm probably just "that kid who can't bowl."

Suddenly the lights on the mysterious extra lane flicker on. I hear the ball return crank into action. I look back to see if the attendant switched it on from behind his counter, but he's not even at his station. And no one is coming this way to claim the lane.

"Thanks," I say to the jock. "But we'll bowl over here now. C'mon, Mia."

Mia dutifully grabs her ball and brings it over to the empty ball stand of the numberless lane. I figure someone will eventually kick us off, but until then, I'll bowl all I want to bowl!

As I put my ball down, I begin to feel uneasy, and I don't know why. It seems a degree or two warmer over here in this lane, and yet I feel a chill set in. There's a smell here too. An earthy, organic smell, like a wet pile of November leaves. And there's a sound—a whooshing, whispering sound. I turn my head from side to side, until I zero in on where the sound is coming from. It's the ball return.

"Can I go first?" asks Mia.

"Shhh!" I get down on my knees and lean closer to the dark opening of the ball return. Deep within, I can hear the groaning of belts, pulleys, and rollers, but beneath all that noise there's something else: a sound just at the edge of my hearing. I put my ear closer to it and feel against the side of my face a warm wind flowing out of the ball return. That wet-leaf smell is stronger here, and as I take a breath of it, that air feels strange. It feels thick and . . . well, unfulfilling—like the air you get when you keep your head under your covers too long.

Then the sound suddenly changes, and the air pressure flowing from the ball return seems to change too. There's a sudden mechanical rumble, and for an instant I see something large and white eclipsing the dark hole.

Instinctively I launch myself back, away from the ball return—and it's a good thing I have fast reflexes, because the second my head is out of the way, a bowling ball blasts out of the ball return, flies down the ball stand, and smashes into Mia's bowling ball with bone-crushing velocity.

"Close one, huh, kid?" says the jock with a smirk. I ignore him and look at the ball. It's shiny white—but not just shiny. It's wet, dripping with a clear, slippery slime that puddles on the floor beneath the ball stand.

"Gross!" says Mia. "A bowling-booger."

I approach it, not sure what to make of it . . . and that's when I notice that the force of its impact has cracked Mia's ball in half.

As soon as Mia notices, tears begin to pool in her eyes. She can't stand bowling, but that doesn't matter right now—all that matters is that something of hers has been broken. That always calls for tears.

"It's okay, Mia. It's all right, we'll get you a new one," I say, even though I'm sure a new bowling ball won't be in the family budget until her birthday, which is a long way off.

I turn to look down the silent, well-waxed lane, just waiting to be bowled on, then I look at the slimy white ball one more time. Suddenly I don't feel like bowling today.

"C'mon, Mia, let's go home."

"Can we play Barbies?" she asks.

"Yeah, sure, whatever, let's just go."

I put my own ball back into the bag and leave Mia's ruined one where it is. Then I take my sister's hand, and we head out into the rain.

When we get home, Phil is on the couch, watching ESPN.

"Hi, squirts," he says as we enter. Phil is Mom's current boyfriend.

Lately we find him over even when Mom isn't home. Phil eats our food, puffs cigarettes in our air space, and spends Mom's money whenever he can. I'd call him a sponge to his face, if I didn't think he'd hit me for it.

"You oughta get your TV fixed, everyone looks purple," he tells me, then blows a big cloud of Camel breath in my face. I cough from the stench of the smoke. He laughs.

"Your lungs are too sensitive, just like the rest of you," he says. "We gotta toughen you up, kiddo!"

"Yeah, sure, toughen me up."

Mia has already slipped off to her room to play, and since her ball broke, I make good on my promise to spend time playing with her. Anyway, it's better than being put down by Phil. Since he works a swing shift, he's always gone by five—just long enough to steal a kiss and twenty bucks from Mom before he saunters out the door.

That night, long after he's gone and Mia's gone off to bed, I sit with Mom over hot chocolate and ask her something I've been afraid to, because I've been afraid of the answer.

"What do you see in Phil, anyway?"

She chooses her words carefully, considering how she might respond. Finally she says, "He makes me laugh."

We're both quiet for a moment, and I can hear the rain lightly hitting the rain gutters. Gutters. It reminds me of my miserable performance today at the bowling alley. And it reminds me of the strange lane with no number, and its mean ball return. I'm about to tell Mom what happened, but think better of it. They grease those ball returns, don't they? Sure they do—that's why the ball was so slimy. That's why it shot out so fast. Suddenly I feel mad at myself for giving up a lane that I could have bowled on all afternoon.

Instead I say, "Mom, can I have some money to go bowling tomorrow?"

She sees how much I want it, and so she agrees. That night I go to sleep dreaming of perfect strikes down midnight alleys.

"I'll take lane twenty-five."

"We only got twenty-four lanes, kid," says the lane guy. Here, take number three."

It's Saturday morning at eight fifteen. The weekend leagues don't start for two hours, and only a few people are bowling this early. Lane three would be just fine, but instead I head in the other direction, all the way down to the end, to the numberless lane next to lane twenty-four.

Again it's dark, but then many lanes are dark, because no one is on them yet. As I sit down and put on my shoes, the lane comes on by itself. I can hear the rumbling whisper of the ball return again. Nothing wrong here.

I stand alone on the approach and hurl my ball down the alley, for once hitting the headpin exactly the way I meant to hit it. Six pins go down. Not a strike, but not a gutter ball either. Practice makes perfect. I anxiously wait for my ball to come back.

I throw one frame after another, some good, some bad, and even manage to get a spare in the ninth frame. The score for my first game: a 74, which is pretty good for me. I mark the final score down, then get ready to bowl a second game, hopefully even better than the first.

The pins reset and wait for me with a toothy grin. The ball return hums and groans, but my ball doesn't come back. I hit the pin-reset button again—sometimes the ball gets stuck back there, and it takes an avalanche of falling pins to jar it free. The bar comes down, sweeps away the pins, new pins descend from above, and as I expected, I hear my ball rolling back toward me underground. I wait for it to shoot out of the ball return. As it does, I reach for it . . . and my hand gets covered in warm slime. I look down to see a white slimy ball, just like the ball from yesterday. Quickly I pull my hand back and wipe it on my pants. The slimy white ball sits there, alone on the ball stand, and my ball never makes an appearance. Finally I hit the service button.

"What's the problem?" asks the lane guy, as he saunters over. "Aren't you supposed to be on lane three?"

"I liked this one better," I tell him, "but it ate my ball." I don't bother to mention that this is the very lane he insisted didn't exist.

"Lousy stupid machine." He glances back at the counter, where some customers just showed up. "Why don't you use one of our balls until someone can go back there and check it out?" He gestures to a rack against the wall full of balls, then leaves.

Usually the racks are filled with scarred, chipped black balls, but on the rack behind lane twenty-five, all the balls are white. I go over to examine them. They look exactly like the ball sitting in the ball stand—exactly like the one that shattered Mia's ball yesterday, only these are dry. I touch one. It's smooth, and its surface glistens like a pearl. I roll it over, then roll it over again, and realize something very peculiar about it, and the rest of the balls on the rack.

None of these balls have finger holes.

I go tell the lane guy, and he burns me a glare. "You're a real pain, you know that?" And since he has no more customers waiting for lanes or shoes, he begrudgingly goes around back to look for my ball. In a few moments, I can see glimpses of him through the pins of lane twenty-five, as he pokes around behind the pin-setting mechanism, trying to see where my ball got stuck.

I wait, and watch. Then suddenly the sweeper bar comes down, and the pins reset themselves.

"Hey, what the—" I hear the lane man grumble, then a jawful of fresh pins comes down. I hear a brief yelp from behind the machine. Then the pinsetter rises, leaving ten fresh pins, and I can't see the lane dude anymore.

I wait. I wait some more, but he doesn't come back. Soon there's a line of irritated people at his counter. Suddenly I get scared. I mean really scared—like maybe he's had a heart attack or something.

I run to tell the snack bar attendant, who gets the janitor to go look, but he finds nothing. Not a trace.

I don't tell them about my missing ball—suddenly it doesn't seem important. Instead I decide to take the lane guy up on his original offer. I go to the rack of hole-less white balls and shove one into my bowling bag. I can always get holes drilled into it. I leave, but as I stand near the exit, I steal a glance back at lane twenty-five. Its lights go out, leaving it dark again.

When I get home, Mom's out somewhere with Mia, but Phil is there, lounging on the couch and watching some cop show. Stale cigarette smoke hangs in the air like dirty layers of floating silk.

"How's life treatin' ya, Hank?" he asks.

"The name's Marshall," I remind him. "Like my father."

He takes a swig from his beer and glances at my bowling bag. "You know bowling's not a real sport," he says. "Throwing a ball down an alley—it's a no-brainer."

"Then you should be real good at it," I tell him.

He glares at me, but doesn't get off the couch. "Someday, kiddo, that wise mouth of yours'll shoot off one too many times, and someone'll clean your clock real good."

I grit my teeth every time he calls me "kiddo," but I let it slide like a bad gutter ball. He's not worth the effort, I tell myself. "Nice talking, Phil," I say, and go down into the basement.

Our basement is a cold, dim place where we put things we'll probably never see again. I find a clean corner for my bowling bag. After today, I don't know when I'll want to bowl again. And that pearly-white bowling ball is too heavy for me anyway—it practically ripped my arm off getting it home. I take a long, sorrowful look at my bowling bag before heading upstairs and turning off the light.

• • •

The lane guy never turns up. People figure he got bored of his job and moved on. I don't have my own theory, because if I tried to come up with one, I know I wouldn't like it. I just go about my business, go about my life, and pretend like it never happened.

The bowling urge doesn't return to me for more than a month, but when it comes back, it comes back in full force. Maybe it's that my arm muscles feel like they need to be used. Maybe it's that sound of tumbling pins I hear every time I walk past Atomic Lanes that makes me want to bowl again . . . or maybe, it's because one of my friends mentioned that there are twenty-seven lanes now and no one can remember the extra ones being built.

It's after school on Friday. Mia's at a friend's house, which means I can bowl by myself, and I can't wait! I race into the house—I've saved enough money to get the new ball drilled, and even if it's too heavy, I know I can get used to it. It's three thirty when I clatter down the rickety basement steps and turn on the light.

It takes me a few seconds to come to terms with what I see, and it comes to me in stages. First I notice that the floor beneath me isn't concrete, but wood. And the smell—it's not dry and musty, but wet and earthy. Suddenly another light comes on to my right, and I hear the soft groaning of some mechanism. I spin around to see . . .

. . . a bowling alley.

It extends through the edge of our basement, out past the foundation of our house. Past that foundation, I can see tree roots poking through dirt above the alley, and the red, exposed edges of sewer pipes. Someone's dug a tunnel under our street, just to fit a bowling alley in our basement. But who would have done this? And why?

Everything that had filled our basement is now pushed back into the far corner. Suddenly I feel light-headed and realize that I'm hyperventilating. I have to sit down, and like any bowling alley, there's a little row of plastic seats behind the scoring table. I sit down to catch my breath and stare toward the end of the alley, where ten pins wait in silence for a ball to take them down.

A ball!

I get up as quickly as I sat down, and search for the hole-less white ball. I leap over boxes and other junk in search of my bowling bag, but everything's piled so high now, I have to dig through everything just to find it. When I finally do find it, I realize that the bag's been torn open. I reach inside to get out the pearl bowling ball, but instead I find it cracked in half, its edges jagged and sharp. It's not at all like Mia's broken ball—this one is hollow, with a shell only a quarter-inch thick. I run my fingers along its curved surface inside, which is just as smooth and pearly white as the outside. It reminds me of something, but my mind doesn't make the connection. Not yet.

That's when I hear a voice. A deep, disdainful voice. "What the heck is this?!"

I peer out over the stacks of boxes to see Phil standing beside the ball return, gawking at the underground alley. Quickly I climb over the boxes, trying to keep calm and rational. Trying not to appear as frightened as I really am.

"Since when is there a bowling alley down here?" he asks.

I wrinkle my eyebrows and look at him as if there's something wrong with him. "Haven't you ever been in our basement before?"

"No . . ."

"It's always been here," I lie. "It came with the house."

"Humph," he says, all dismissive. "So if you have this thing in your basement, why do you waste your mother's money going out to bowl?"

Phil blows a cloud of smoke into my face, then turns to head back upstairs.

I don't know what comes over me then. Or maybe I do know.

"What's the matter, Phil? Afraid she won't leave enough money for *you* to waste? Because that's all you do, right? Spend what she makes, and whatever money my dad left us."

Phil hears me, stops dead in his tracks, and does a slow about-face. "What did you say?"

Standing on my new alley, I suddenly feel courage backing up my anger. "You heard what I said. You're a leech. And one of these days she's gonna wise up and just peel right off."

The fingers of his right hand curl into a fist, and his voice comes out low and guttural, like a growling pit bull. "You're in deep trouble, little man. You're gonna get yourself a lesson now."

"Go ahead, 'kiddo,' teach me a lesson," I say, figuring maybe after Mom sees the kind of lessons Phil teaches, she'll throw him out of her life for good.

He lunges at me, and I reflexively dodge out of his way. His momentum carries him onto the shiny waxed surface of the alley, and suddenly he loses his balance. His feet fly out from under him and he lands on his butt.

He tries to grab at me, but his momentum is too great, and the alley too slippery. He continues sliding toward the pins, almost seeming to accelerate on his way down the alley. I begin laughing.

Phil is frothing mad. "Why you . . . I'm gonna get you, you little—" but he never gets to finish. Instead he bowls right into the pins, taking them all down with a wooden crash. I laugh so hard my sides ache.

"A strike, Phil!"

I'd keep on laughing . . . I could laugh forever . . . but something happens. Something I could have predicted, if I had had the time to really think things through. If I'd had the time to figure out that the broken white bowling ball didn't look like a bowling ball at all.

It looked like an egg.

Suddenly the sweeper bar drops in front of Phil, blocking my view, and behind it, the heavy pinsetter comes smashing down on him like the jaws of a shark. Phil doesn't have a chance to say another word, and my own words become choked in my throat. I can't see everything, but I see enough to know what's going on. The silver pinsetter slams down again, and again, more powerfully each time. I can feel the ground shake with the force of it. Then finally the pinsetter rises up, and the sweeper bar brushes in, and brushes out, leaving a perfectly clean, pinless lane. Finally the pinsetter descends again, gently this time, depositing ten fresh pins, patiently waiting for a bowler. There's no sign of Phil anywhere.

"Phil?" I call, desperately hoping for an answer. "Phil?" But I hear no sound. Only the hollow breathing of the ball return.

I leave the basement in a daze, not ready to think about it, and not really knowing where I'm going until I get there. Finally I find myself in my mom's closet. Way in the corner there are a few sets of men's clothes—my dad's clothes, because, after all, there are just some things you can't bear to part with. I get on my knees, and beneath the dangling pairs of pants, I find what I'm looking for. A black leather bag, with my father's initials stamped on it in gold. They're my initials too. I reach inside and pull out a marbled red bowling ball, as shiny and smooth as the day it was made. It's heavy, and my fingers don't quite fit in the holes, but I could get used to it. I gently remove it from the bag and carry it down into the basement, where the living alley awaits, its pins grinning at me, the way my father grinned at me so many years ago, each time I threw a ball down a lane.

I stand far back, focus my attention on the pins, and with my father's ball I begin my approach. My arm swoops down, and the ball kisses the wood without a sound as I release it. I watch as the ball curves to the right, and then, just as it begins to curve back to the headpin, I turn my back and strut to the scoring console, just like my father used to do. I hear the smash of pins, and the heavy clatter as they fly in all directions. I don't even have to look to know that it's a strike.

• • •

Two months later. It's a cold, windy day, but that doesn't matter in my basement.

"One seventy-eight," says Mia, reading my final score. "Is that good?"

"Yeah," I tell her, "but it could still be better."

Mia picks up her new bowling ball from the ball stand. She's had it for several weeks now and likes it even better than her old one. "Can we play another game?"

"Tomorrow," I tell her. "Mom'll be home soon."

"No, she won't," says Mia coyly. "Robert's picking her up at work tonight. They're going to the theater."

As we head up the stairs, I have to smile. Mom missed Phil for about three minutes, and she didn't really question where he went. She figured he just moved on. Then she met Robert. I don't mind babysitting Mia when Mom's out with Robert.

Mia heads off into her room, and I take a few moments to relax in the living room, almost enjoying the ache in my shoulder I sometimes get after a good day of bowling. We haven't told Mom about the alley; we only bowl when she's not home, and we make sure to hide it behind a wall of boxes. Besides, she rarely even goes down there, so it could be many months until she finds it. And when she does? Well, we'll deal with it then.

As for the alley—it's behaved far better than that nasty one in Atomic Lanes. It always returns our balls and never sends them out of the ball return too fast. Like everything else, you get what you give, and we treat it very, very well. Just last week it started producing eggs, but we know what to do with those. After all, Christmas is coming, and we have lots of friends and relatives who bowl. The only problem is feeding it—but I've got that one solved too.

The doorbell rings, and I open the door to a grungy-looking, scowling slacker-dude. He's nineteen, maybe twenty. "Yeah, I'm looking for Marshall Stewart Jr.," he says, clutching a torn slip of paper in his hand.

"That's me," I say cheerfully.

"You?" he sneers. "You put up this ad?"

"That's right. Do you have the qualifications for the job?"

He looks down at his phone. "Let's see. 'Seeking lazy individual for the job of a lifetime. Must be difficult to work with, generally disagreeable, and have a bad attitude.' Funny ad. So, what kind of work is it?"

"We have a basement bowling alley," I explain. "We need someone to . . . uh . . . service it once a month."

"Sounds like a lot of work, man."

"Nah, it'll only take a few minutes."

"Cool. But why'd you have it listed under 'Food Service'?"

I offer him a shrug as I lead him inside, then I open the basement door. But just before we go down, he reaches into his pocket to pull something out.

"By the way, I smoke," he says. Then, without warning, he lights up, takes a drag, and blows the smoke in my face. "You got a problem with that . . . kiddo?"

I slowly lead him down the basement stairs. "You know what?" I tell him, and I can't help but smile. "I think this job is right up your alley."

THE LIVING, THE DEAD, AND THE UNDECIDED

"And now, ladies and gentlemen! The moment you've all been waiting for! We bring you something terrifying. Can you hear them? Scrape-scrape-scraping at your door? Can you smell them? Mouths dripping with the unthinkable? Behold! The most terrifying of all acts ever brought to you on any stage . . . the living dead!"

—from "Deadliner"

Dead Letter

Tomb it may concern, I have, for much too long, suffered from the insults, cruel attacks, and blatant discrimination in your newspaper. One might think that as the only newspaper in the town of Rancid Falls, you would learn to be fair and objective with the items you report. But in fact, in your paper, my kind have been treated with more disrespect than we can stand.

Haven't you ever heard the expression "show respect for the dead"? I suppose not! Let me tell you, it makes quite a few of us roll over in our graves—as you can probably tell from that rumbling sound you occasionally hear from the graveyard on the hill.

Oh sure, you write all these nice, flowery notes the day we go on to our final rest—but the second we try to return from the grave, we are no longer welcome. Suddenly those sweet, flowery things you've written become big banner headlines, turning our simple homecomings into horrible events, as if we were criminals.

For instance: your headline last week read CORPSE TERRORIZES FAMILY. I would hardly call climbing in through a window in the middle of the night and playing Beethoven on the family piano an act of terror. If the woman fainted and the children ran screaming down the street, that's their problem, don't you think?

A week before that, you ran a headline that read HEADLESS WOMAN CARJACKS CADILLAC. As if it had been her intent to steal that car! She was *headless*—the last thing she wanted was to be behind the wheel—

but when that inconsiderate driver ran away in terror, what was a poor headless woman to do? She had to drive the car if she was ever going to make it home.

What's so awful about it? Why would you deny a cold, lonely soul the right to slip into their home in the middle of the night and have a nice long talk with their family? Surely you would be thrilled to wake up one night to find your own dear sweet grandmother, whom you haven't seen for so many years, suddenly there beside your bed, smiling that wise grin of the dead. No doubt she's often thought of paying you a surprise visit (or at least that's what she told me).

The fact that more and more of the dead have been returning home should be a clear indication to you that your newspaper ought to be publishing more articles of interest to the dead. But all you seem to dwell on is how, after we've risen, we attack the living, turning them into one of us. Surely you can't see any harm in that—after all, we're just doing what creatures do naturally: increasing our numbers. Who are you to deny us that simple right?

And by the way, we resent the way your newspaper, and others, have referred to us in such insensitive and cold ways. We are not "zombies." That is a slur. The correct term for describing us is quite simply the "living dead"—and should you continue to refer to us in such unkind and bigoted ways, you will most certainly be hearing from the International Association of Living Dead Persons.

And now I would like to set the record straight on this business about us eating the brains of the living. Don't you see how ridiculous that sounds? Why on earth would a person who has risen from the grave want to eat a human brain (no matter how tasty and delectable it might be)? After spending all that time wasting away in the graveyard, don't you think we might have developed a craving for something better—like maybe a steak, or some Ben & Jerry's (ice cream—not their brains)? And anyway, I'm sure you'll agree there are quite a few people out there who could do with having their brains eaten. Oh, there are quite a few brains I personally can think of that would not be missed. And yours is high on my list. In fact, it's on all our lists. (That is . . . it *would* be if we actually did eat brains, and I'm not admitting that we do.)

But what galls me most, sir, are your laughable articles that announce the doom of mankind, and how you cheer the military's pathetic attempts to stop us from populating the finer neighborhoods of Rancid Falls. In fact, the only empty neighborhood in town is the graveyard. The dead have no use for it anymore, as we've decided that if we must return to ashes and dust, then we might as well live out our deaths in a comfortable home, spending eternity watching reruns of *Seinfeld* and *Friends* (which are certain to be on for all eternity).

In the end, sir, I'd like to remind you that in this world of eight billion living, breathing people, we are the majority. We've been here longer than you have, we will be here after you're gone—and believe me when I tell you that we have all decided it's time to come back.

So, when you hear that knock at your door this evening, and when you open it to reveal a hungry, grinning crowd, their heads tilted to one side in the dim streetlight, don't be afraid. It's only us.

Resurrection Bay

When a glacier calves, you can hear it for miles, the crashing ice echoing back and forth between the towering peaks on either side of the bay. Sometimes you feel it before you hear it—a vibration in your bones that makes your whole body resonate like a tuning fork.

Bones. They know the call of the ice. They sense the relentless push of the glacier. Not just the bones of the living, but the bones of the dead, too.

I'll tell you what I know—the strange things that happened one bleak and terrible September. I'll tell you once, but I'll deny I ever said it, and you'd be better off if you forget you ever heard it. But I'll tell you all the same.

People say it all started the day that newlywed couple died at the face of Exit Glacier, but they just say that because people like things to have a beginning and an end. It makes them comfortable. The truth is, it started before any of us were born. Maybe even before there were any people here at all.

"This world is older and stranger than any of us know," my dad says. "Never forget that, Anika." My dad's a helicopter pilot. In high season—that's summertime—he makes his living taking tourists up into Alaska's big sky to get a firsthand look at nature's majesty: the Harding Icefield, and the many glaciers that carve their way down the mountains feeding into Resurrection Bay. We live in Resurrection Bay, my dad, my brother, and me, in the port town of Seward. Seward, not Sewer. It was named after the guy who bought Alaska from Russia. Not our fault he had a lousy last name.

In Seward, it's all summer trade. A lot of businesses close up come fall and leave for the winter. But there are enough uses for a helicopter pilot in Alaska that my dad has plenty of work all year round, so we stay.

On the day those newlyweds died, Dad got quiet and paced around the house, doing things like looking in the refrigerator as if he might find something uncommon in there, then turning the TV on and off, like he forgot what show he wanted to watch.

"You think he saw it, Anika?" my little brother Sammy asked, as we watched our father bumble around the house that evening.

"He couldn't have seen it," I told him. "He was flying people up to the ice field when it happened."

"Yeah, but he coulda seen it from the sky while he was flyin'."

The truth was, Dad had given that very same couple a helicopter tour the day before, but the winds were too rough to land. Still, they wanted an up-close-and-personal experience with a glacier, so they took a self-guided walking tour, right up to the face of Exit Glacier. It's a glacier that hasn't reached the sea for maybe a thousand years. It just kind of stops a few miles inland at the silt-filled remains of its old track, which now looks more like a tornado path—a long stretch of earth cleared by nature's force, and filled with little hills that mark the glacier's advance in winter, and retreat in summer, when it melts faster than it flows—and glaciers do flow, just very, very slowly.

The newlywed couple ignored all the big red signs that said DANGER! STAY AWAY FROM FACE OF GLACIER!, and they went right up to it, touched it, and even got some old lady to take a picture of them while they stood right in front of it.

That was when a hunk of ice about the size of a truck calved off the glacier right over their heads, and in seconds, newlywed became newlydead.

"I think the glacier kilt 'em on purpose," Sammy said.

"Keep your opinions to yourself," I told him. "Especially the stupid ones."

So that night we had soup for dinner because Dad was too distracted to cook.

"I should have landed with them yesterday," he kept mumbling. "If I had, they wouldn't have gone out today, and they'd still be alive."

"It's not your fault, and you know it," I told him.

"I know, I know, I'm just saying."

My dad's life is a box of what-ifs neatly wrapped up in regret. Like the way he blames himself for Mom dying, even though he wasn't even in the room when Sammy was born. It's like he thinks if he feels bad enough about it, he'll wake up one day and it won't be true.

Me, I'm a realist. Things are the way they are. I move forward, kind of like a glacier—slowly and with no regrets, because I know what it takes to be happy.

The next morning the picture of the newlydeads that the old lady took was all over the papers—and not just the local ones, because it caught the smiling couple *and* the falling piece of ice, a few feet over their heads. It was just one more thing for Dad to make himself miserable about.

It was the third week of September. With fall setting in, more and more people were closing shop for the winter, escaping to wherever it was summer folk lived for the rest of the year. It wasn't exactly a ghost town here, but for the first few weeks it always felt like one until we got used to it again.

I decided to go up to Exit Glacier after school the next day—not just because of the tragedy, but because it had always been my favorite place. I could go there alone, and not feel alone. I could go there with friends, and somehow have a better time just because I was there. I had read my favorite books there in the glacier's shadow, and I had written my best poems—although I was never foolish enough to get too close to its face.

Going there on that day, though . . . it was more than just wanting to be in the company of the glacier. Maybe I was having some kind of intuition—or even a premonition—not the kind you see, but the kind you feel in your gut when you know something big is about to happen.

I went as far as last year's moraine—that's the mound of earth that marks how far the glacier pushed last winter before the summer sun melted it back. It was a good fifty yards back from the face of the glacier. There were other people around too—lookie-loos watching as the workmen hacked at the ice with jackhammers, and a bulldozer hauled ice away—all behind a police line that had gone up one day too late. They were trying to find the dead couple, but there was a lot of ice left to move.

I was content to keep my distance. I closed my eyes, held out my arms, and felt the glacier breathe.

Glaciers do breathe. It's a scientific fact. Cold air is heavier than hot air, and so, depending on where you're standing, you can feel the cold air breathing off the glacier, or the warm air rushing in. I always thought it was more than that, though. A glacier's breath is not a soulless thing. It's vital and fresh. It's the reason why tourists can't capture the truth of it on film—because it's not what you see, it's what you *feel* when you stand in front of a wall of ice.

As I stood there, feeling the breath of the glacier flow around my upturned palms, I finally realized the reason I had come. I had come to ask a question.

Why?

Why did you take those people?

What had they ever done to you?

And I didn't just mean this couple, but all the people who had lost their lives to Exit Glacier over the years. Ice climbers who tried to scale it and fell. People who slipped into a crevasse and were lost. And the many who, like this sad couple, became victims of falling ice.

Why?

And then I heard a voice behind me.

"You look like an idiot!"

I put my arms down and turned around. I knew that voice better than anyone's in town. It was Rav Carnegie, all spiky black hair and smirks. I hadn't spoken to him yet this school year, since we were giving one another a mutual cold shoulder.

"At least I have to work at it," I told him. "But *you* look like an idiot without even trying."

He laughed at that and then climbed to the top of the moraine with me. "Have they found the bodies?" Rav asked.

"They wouldn't still be digging if they'd found them."

Rav is what you might call my off-season boyfriend. During the summer, we hate each other, mostly because he's jealous of the summer boys I date, and I'm jealous of the summer girls that are always hanging around him. Then the summer people go, we make up, and it's back to old times.

Rav was short for Raven, which he hated, and Carnegie was a name his parents made up, because they were musicians and had once dreamed of playing in Carnegie Hall—and so when it didn't work out, they settled for stealing the name. People think he's part Tlingit, because of his dark hair, but he's not. I am, though, on my mother's side. Maybe that's why I've always felt a connection to the ice.

"They're never gonna find them," Rav said, as we watched the bulldozer haul away another heaping shovelful of ice. "The glacier moves forward faster than they can take the ice away."

"It's so sad," I said.

"They were stupid," said Rav. "Tempt fate, and guess what? Sometimes it gives in to temptation. Starburst?"

He handed me the piece of candy and I took it. This year a Starburst was the signal that we had made up.

We stood there for a while talking about the new school year, and how tenth grade wasn't much different from ninth grade, and then, as we turned to go, I felt a chill that penetrated deep. The breath of the glacier made my neck hairs stand on end, and there was a rumbling in the earth.

"Did you hear that?"

Rav shook his head, maybe because it wasn't a sound at all, it was a feeling—that vibration in my bones. I looked to the glacier just in time to see a fresh hunk of ice break free from the face and begin a long, slow plunge.

The workmen ran for cover, but the bulldozer driver was caught in his cab. He kicked at the door in a panic, until it finally it swung open, and he leapt out just in time. The massive chunk of blue ice hit the bulldozer, completely burying it.

"No way!" said Rav.

The workmen, now a safe distance away, peeled off their hard hats, scratched their heads, and counted their blessings.

Then I noticed something that no one else had seen yet. I had to focus all my attention to make sure it wasn't just my imagination.

Rav must have noticed the look on my face.

"What is it?"

"The glacier—it's moving."

"Glaciers are always moving," he pointed out.

"No," I said. "This glacier is *really* moving."

And then he saw it too. The glacier was pushing forward. Another chunk of ice fell, then another, then another. It was coming toward us—not at the speed of an avalanche, of course—maybe just an inch or two per second, but for a glacier that's lightning fast.

Now that bone-deep feeling was stronger than ever, and I knew that Rav was feeling it too.

Then something dawned on me, like a secret whispered in my ear—but it didn't come through words. It came in that bone-feeling shimmying up my arms and legs, vibrating in my joints.

The glacier wants something.

It wants something, and it's coming to get it. . . .

Glaciers are just like rivers. Watch a glacier in time-lapse, and you'll see it surging forward, digging into the earth, dragging hundred-ton boulders along with it. Glaciers are forces of nature as powerful as floods or hurricanes. They just do their devastating business much more slowly. Most of the time.

There was no scientific explanation as to why Exit Glacier decided to surge forward as suddenly and as powerfully as it did. That first day, they calculated that it was moving at a speed of fifteen inches per minute. That might not seem fast, but when a wall of ice a quarter mile wide decides to move like that, it takes out everything in its path—trees, buildings, bridges—everything. In a single day it had pushed forward nearly half a mile and had ripped out a major highway on its relentless push toward Resurrection Bay. And we all knew there was only one way it could get to the bay:

Straight through Seward.

If the glacier kept on moving, it would reach the city in three days and completely destroy it, pushing everything that couldn't move out of its way into the sea.

I made dinner that night, since Dad was off on an emergency run, flying geologists down from Anchorage.

"If I climb up on the roof, d'ya think I might be able to see the glacier from here?" Sammy asked me.

"No, but if you climb up on the roof, you'll fall off and break your neck, and I'll get to have your room."

He threw a pea from his dinner plate at me but said nothing more about the roof. I'm not sure whether he was more worried about breaking his neck, or me getting his room.

It was strange how the next day things went on as usual—at least at first. We had school that day, and although everyone talked about the glacier, we all went about our business, class to class. It was surreal—as if the glacier's approach was some alternate reality.

When I got home, though, reality hit. Dad had spent the day flying a team of experts over the glacier, so he knew more about this "phenomenon" than anyone else in town . . . and he was packing up all our belongings in his pickup truck.

You have to understand, this was more than just an evacuation for us, because to Dad, his home was very much his castle. See, after Mom died, Dad fixed up the house. He patched the roof, and painted the porch, and put up a white picket fence around the yard so that our house was the envy of Seward. It looked like the model of hometown America—but with one problem. Our household was one member short. Still, Dad kept up the house, the yard, and that perfect picket fence religiously, like they were the only things keeping us together. But the truth was, *he* was the only thing keeping us together.

So, you can imagine how seeing him packing things up in that pre-panic kind of way made me feel like the world was coming apart all over again.

"There's not much room," he told Sammy and me. "Just take the things you really care about."

He tried to comfort us by telling us that Seward wouldn't be hit for two more days, but debris was already being shaken loose from the mountains and landing on the road to Anchorage. If that road got taken out, the only way out of Seward would be by sea and sky—and there simply weren't enough boats or helicopters to do the job. After the initial numbness, people were beginning to leave town any way they could.

We couldn't leave yet, though; they needed Dad to fly the geologists around, so that night he took our over-packed pickup, and we all went to stay with Rav and his dad, since they lived on higher ground that was out of the glacier's path. Our fathers were good friends, because they had found a common misery: dead wives. My mom died giving birth to Sammy. She was Tlingit, and one of her brothers said it was punishment for marrying my dad, who's not. Because of that, Dad won't have anything to do with that side of the family anymore. Rav lost his mom just a couple of years ago. She was an ecologically conscious woman who became one with nature when she wrapped her Prius around a tree one rainy night.

"When I can drive," Rav once told me, "I'm gonna get a car with a huge Hemi engine and guzzle gas like there's no tomorrow, because nature deserves to suffer."

Rav's got issues.

Late that evening, while Sammy slept and Dad drank away his sorrows with Mr. Carnegie, Rav and I sat on his porch. Even from this far away you could feel the glacier churning up the earth, and hear the fracturing of ice and ominous falling of trees.

"Do you think you'll leave Seward for good?" Rav asked me. "It would suck if you left for good."

I was going to tell him that there'd be no Seward to come back to—that it was the end of life as we knew it. But instead I said, "We'll have to see how bad it is."

A breeze blew across the porch. Cold air out, warm air in. The glacier's breath. I shivered, and as I wrapped my arms around myself, I must have caught the clasp on my charm bracelet, because it fell and slipped between the wooden porch slats, disappearing into the darkness below.

"I'll go get a flashlight," said Rav. When he came back, we went under the porch, squeezing into the low, muddy crawl space draped with the abandoned webs of spiders long dead, and a few old cranky spiders that should have been dead, but for some reason weren't and were now really, really big.

But I wasn't going to think about that. The charm bracelet had been a gift from my mom, so I'd deal with the spiders—and Rav had a vested interest too, since he had bought me a few of the newer charms.

However, once we had made our way to the right spot under the porch, the bracelet was gone.

"Maybe it's still stuck in the slats," I said.

But when we looked up, it wasn't there.

That was when I felt something brush across my arm. Something cold. I gasped and dropped the flashlight, and it went out.

"Don't worry," said Rav, "I'll get fresh batteries."

"It's probably the bulb!" I called after him, but he was already gone.

I was alone now, and in the dark . . . but I had the eerie sense that I wasn't alone at all. There was some light coming down between the slits from the porch—not enough to really see by, but enough to catch faint glimpses of things. For a second I thought I heard breathing, and then something moved just a few feet away from me. Something big!

I panicked. I knew there were all kinds of wild animals in this area. Wolves and wild dogs. An angry raccoon could rip your eye out. A frightened bear cub could tear you to shreds.

I scurried away, painfully slamming my head against a crossbeam on the way—but in my panic, I had lost my sense of direction, and came up against the house instead of the yard. I turned again but banged up against a post—and now I could feel a presence very, very close to me.

Terrified now of the dark and of the nature of this thing I couldn't see, I desperately tapped my flashlight once, twice, and then on the third time, I must have hit it just right, because it came on—

—shining right into the face of the creature.

I yelped and leapt back, against the wall of the house, but held on tight to that flashlight, afraid to drop it again—afraid of being left alone in the darkness with the creature.

But then I realized this wasn't a creature at all. It was a person. A woman. Her clothes were tattered, her hair was matted, and her skin was so pale, it was almost blue. But that wasn't the worst of it. The worst was her eyes. They were a deep, deep blue. A shade of blue that somehow seemed even darker than black.

And she was wearing my charm bracelet.

I was so shocked, so freaked out, all I could say was "That's mine. . . ."

She slowly turned her head to look at her wrist, then took off the bracelet and dropped it in front of me.

"Wakeful," she said.

"What?"

"Awake. Can't sleep. Wakeful."

Then she tilted her head oddly, and her neck let out a sound like crackers crunching in your hand. "Don't I know you?" she asked.

I shook my head, even though I knew I had seen her somewhere before. I was sure of it.

"Yes," she said. "Yes, I *do* know you!"

Then one of those God-awful glandular should-be-dead-by-now spiders came webbing down from the crossbeam up above, landing right on her cheek . . .

. . . and the moment it touched her face, the spider frosted up and froze solid. It fell to the ground with a clink, like an eight-legged piece of glass.

I screamed and bolted as fast as I could, dropping the flashlight along the way, but I didn't care anymore. I stumbled in the darkness, until finally I came out from underneath the porch. I raced up the porch steps, just as my dad, Mr. Carnegie, and Rav burst out of the house, having heard my scream.

"What is it, honey? What's wrong?"

"You see an animal or something?" asked Rav.

I couldn't catch my breath. "No, not an animal." I let them help me inside. My head was spinning,

"I saw . . . I saw . . ."

I sat down—no—I collapsed in a kitchen chair.

"Anika, you're bleeding!" My father grabbed a towel and touched it to my bloody forehead.

"What did you see, Anika?" Rav asked.

So I grabbed the newspaper from the table and pointed to the picture on the front of it. The newlydead couple. The smiling woman in the picture. *"Her!"* I told them. *"I saw her."*

Stunned silence. No one knew what to say. Then a neighbor came bounding in.

"Did you hear? Did you hear?" he shouted, completely oblivious to what was going on around him. "The glacier's changed direction!"

"Glaciers don't change direction," said Rav's father.

"This one did. It's not heading toward the center of town anymore. It's just gonna catch the edge. Now they're saying it's just gonna take out Dunbar Street and everything west of it."

"That's . . . great," said Rav's dad, still a little bit rattled by what I had just told them. "There's nothing west of Dunbar Street but old warehouses."

But I shook my head.

"You're wrong," I told Mr. Carnegie. "There's something else west of Dunbar Street."

"What?" asked Rav.

I swallowed, feeling that chill of the glacier slide down my throat, making my stomach seize into a knot. "The cemetery."

On Thursday, at about two thirty in the morning, Exit Glacier, having plowed through the forest before it, took down the fence of Seward

Memorial Cemetery and gouged its way through. It took down headstone after headstone. It tore apart what few marble mausoleums stood there. They fell like houses of cards. The wall of ice churned up the hallowed ground, and then, when the entire cemetery was under the massive sheet of ice . . . the glacier stopped.

Just as quickly and mysteriously as it had begun its advance, the forward surge ended. Most people agreed that it was some kind of miracle. I wasn't so sure.

In the morning, Rav and I ditched school. I think half our school ditched, so they could join the crowds standing in front of what used to be the town graveyard, getting only as close as police would allow. Mostly our friends and neighbors were hoping for a moment of TV fame, and with all the reporters there, chances were good that some of them would be interviewed.

Rav and I didn't crowd the barricade like the others, because we were there for a different reason. Instead we climbed to the top of an abandoned work shed, where we could have a better view of the whole face of the glacier, and we waited.

Rav was not happy about being here, but he wasn't leaving either.

"What you're thinking is crazy," he said.

"I know."

"I should just walk away from you," Rav said.

"Then why don't you?"

"I guess I must be crazy too."

I smiled at him, and that made him look away. "You said you banged your head, right?"

"I didn't bang it that hard."

"It was hard enough to make you bleed," he pointed out. "You were in pain, and probably confused. How can you be sure what you saw that night?"

"Because I am."

We watched as the geologists took measurements, and the reporters reported. Not a single piece of ice had fallen from the glacier's face since we had arrived.

"I really don't want to spend a whole day watching a glacier not move," said Rav.

"I know what I saw the other night. It *was* that dead woman," I insisted, "and maybe it's not as impossible as you think. The Tlingit believe everything is interconnected. The earth and the sky, the ice and us."

"You're only half Tlingit," he pointed out.

I threw him a withering glare. "If what I saw was real—and it was—then there'll be proof."

"What do you expect to see? Dead people strolling out of the ice like zombies, looking for brains to eat?"

I turned back to the glacier. "No, not zombies. Not exactly . . ."

"Then what?"

"I don't know. There's not a word for what they are."

"And anyway," said Rav, "most of the people in that cemetery have been dead since, like, forever. There won't be anything left to come back."

"Permafrost," I told him.

"What?"

"There's permafrost six feet down. It's frozen all year round, which means that a lot of people will be perfectly preserved."

Rav got an ill look about him. He opened his mouth to say something, then closed it again when nothing came out.

We watched for a few more minutes in silence, then Rav asked me, "So, is your mom buried here?"

I shook my head. "No," I told him. "Her family took her to Anchorage."

"Oh." He was quiet for a good ten seconds before he said, "Mine is."

• • •

Nothing out of the ordinary happened at the glacier that day, or the next, so things began to settle back to normal. Many of the geologists, and all the reporters, left, because the glacier was now old news. Now it sat there more still than ever, its leading edge hunched on the cemetery.

It's funny how the rational world has a way of pummeling things that don't make sense into a neat little pile that it can push under a rug and dismiss. That whole business with the woman under the porch, for instance. See, the next day some homeless woman was found shoplifting in town. She was one of the summer people who didn't leave, because she apparently had nowhere to go back to. Even though this woman had blond hair, and the woman I saw didn't, it put enough doubt into my mind. Maybe that was who I saw. After all, it was just in the dim light of a dying flashlight, and as Rav was so happy to point out, I *had* bumped my head. My thoughts might have been addled. That made more sense than anything else, and with things getting back to normal, I'd rather believe I was temporarily confused than the alternative.

But there were things going on in the town in those few days after the glacier made its move. Had I been more observant, I might have noticed. I might have put two and two together.

. . . Like the way our English teacher, Mrs. Mason, suddenly seemed to have no interest in teaching at all. And when the bell rang, she left class even faster than us kids.

. . . Like the way that our mailman stopped delivering mail. He just stopped showing up. Word was that he didn't call in sick or anything—he just locked himself in his house and wouldn't come out.

. . . Or the way Betsy down at the nail salon kept redoing her own nails, happy as a clam, instead of doing her customers' nails.

But the only thing I noticed was the strange way Rav was acting—especially toward me. He was avoiding me—he wouldn't even look at me in class—and when I finally did corner him by his locker, he yelled at me.

"Just go away. I don't want to talk to you, okay?" And he stormed off.

He failed a math test that day, and I figured that maybe he was mad because I made him sit on that stupid roof watching for the undead, instead of letting him study. Rational. Simple. Easily explained away.

A week later, Dad went out on a date. Believe it or not, one of the female geologists he had been flying around had taken a liking to him. She was one of the few still in town to take readings, but I suspected that was just because she wanted to see more of Dad. I wasn't sure how I felt about it, but I wasn't going to ruin it for him.

It was a bright full moon that night, and Dad was going to take her on a moonlit flight over the ice field. Very romantic. I, of course, was left at home to babysit Sammy, but at around eight o'clock, Rav turned up on our doorstep, knocking so timidly, I was actually surprised it was him.

He stood there with his shoulders shrugged awkwardly up, like he was cold, even though he was wearing a heavy jacket. There was something on his mind. Something that was weighing on him so heavily, I could practically see his back curving from the weight of it.

"I just want to say I'm sorry," he said. "I shouldn't have acted the way I did to you."

Since Rav rarely apologized for anything, I decided to milk it. I folded my arms and leaned against the doorframe. "No, you shouldn't have," I said, pretending I wasn't ready to accept his apology, even though I was.

"Yeah, and I'm sorry."

That weight still lingered on him. As much as I wanted to make him suffer, I couldn't. "Apology accepted. So, what's wrong?"

"Nothing," he said a little too quickly. "Nothing's wrong at all. As a matter of fact, things are totally right." He gave off a weird little laugh, then he said, "There's something I want to show you. I know it's late, but do you think you can get out?"

"Sure," I told him. "My dad's not home anyway."

Then Sammy, who had snuck up right behind me, asked, "Can I come too?"

But the look on Rav's face said that Sammy wasn't invited. I figured this might be about his apology, and about us making up. The last thing I needed was Sammy along as a third wheel.

"No," I told Sammy. His face got all twisted, and his body got all limp-boned. "Anika . . . ," he whined.

I looked to Rav, but he shook his head. So I made a decision. "Sure," I told Sammy. "Of course, if you come, you'll miss Dad flying by."

"What?"

"Yeah—Dad's gonna do a low flyby and wave to us—maybe even set down and pick us up, to take us with him to the ice field."

"Really? D'ya think he'd land right on the roof?"

"Maybe," I said. "You know how Dad likes to surprise us."

Then I waited for a moment, before I shook my head and said, "Nah, forget it. He'll have to do it another time—you have to come with Rav and me."

"Why?" he said, getting all twisty and limp-boned again.

"You're too little to stay here by yourself."

He looked at me, deeply insulted. "Am not!"

And that was all it took.

Sammy promised to be good, and not to watch anything scary on TV, and I left holding hands with Rav, wondering what he had to show me, hoping it was something fun . . . and never even imagining the truth behind it.

There's a before and there's an after. There are those events that surgically slice your life in two, and once that happens, you know that you're on the other side of that painful incision. There's no going back to the way things were before. If you're lucky, the wound heals into a jagged scar. And if you're unlucky, it never heals at all, it just keeps bleeding.

The knife came down for me, on that bright, moon-pale night.

As Rav and I walked down the street, he said to me, "You know, I couldn't stop thinking about what you said the other day. You know—about that woman under the porch."

I shrugged. "I was just being stupid. It wasn't who I thought."

"I think maybe it was," Rav said.

That got me a little angry. Had I been so convincing that I had him believing it too? Or was he just making fun of me? Either way, I had spent so much brainpower trying to make the whole episode go away, I didn't want to bring it back up again.

Instead of going to his house, we turned left instead of right at the end of my street and walked toward Main Street.

"Where are we going?" I asked.

"You'll see."

He took me to his father's pub, which was closed. That was odd, because it was a favorite local hangout—especially this time of year, when most of the other bars were closed for the winter. Even worse, the windows were frosted in that white soapy stuff they use to mask windows when a place goes out of business.

"My dad's up north," Rav said.

"You mean Anchorage?"

"No, I mean *north*, north. But he'll be back soon."

Now, in most other places, when you say someone's "up north," it doesn't mean very much, but when you live in Seward, Alaska, all you've got up north are places so cold this time of year, you don't want to go there. They call winter the Hammer up here, because when it comes down, it hits hard, and all you can do is hunker down until the thaw. So the thought of Rav's dad going north for any reason didn't sit well with me.

"What's he doing?" I asked. "Hunting?"

"Yeah," said Rav. Then he thought about it. "Kind of," he said. Then finally, "No, not really."

"So where is he?"

"Prudhoe Bay," he told me. I got a shiver just thinking of it. Prudhoe Bay is so cold, it makes Resurrection Bay look like the Bahamas. It's where the Alaska pipeline starts, way on Alaska's northern shore, up above the Arctic Circle. One of the coldest places on earth.

"You guys aren't thinking of leaving here, are you?"

"No," said Rav, then he thought about it. "I don't know," he said. Then finally, "Yeah, maybe."

But before I could even consider the idea of life around here without Rav, he took his keys out and unlocked the door to the pub.

He opened the door a crack, then slowly peeked in. It was dark in there. Only faint diffused moonlight spilled through the clouded windows. I could hear music playing somewhere inside as we stepped in.

Rav closed the door behind us but didn't make a move to turn on a light yet. It was guitar music playing, an acoustic guitar by the sound of it—a gentle, mournful plucking.

"Don't be scared," Rav said. "It's important that you're not scared."

Then I began to get an awful feeling in my gut. The kind you get when the phone rings at two in the morning, and you know, in your heart of hearts, even before you pick it up, that it's really, really bad news.

I reached for the light switch, but Rav firmly grabbed my wrist before I could.

"You know all that stuff you were saying? About how the glacier dug its way through the cemetery on purpose, like it knew what it was doing?"

"I never said that!"

"But I know it's what you were thinking, wasn't it?" And then he said, in a terrible whisper, "Well, you were right."

Then he reached over and turned on the light.

There, in one of the farthest booths, sat a woman playing the guitar, but most of her face was in shadows. Rav, still holding my wrist, pulled me toward the woman. Something was telling me that I didn't want to see this—that I didn't want to be there at all, but my curiosity was more powerful than my instinct to run.

Her hair was dangling in front of her face and over the guitar strings as she played. The guitar was covered with frost, and icy condensation spilled from its open hole, like when you open a freezer door. Only then did I realize that the entire room was very, very cold.

And then Rav said, "I brought someone to see you, Mom."

She turned to me, her head moving in that same jarring, gritty way that the woman under the porch had moved. I instantly recoiled, backing right into Rav's chest, but he stood there like a boulder, not letting me get away.

"It's okay," Rav said. I don't know whether he was talking to me or to this . . . this *thing* in front of me.

"Don't be scared," Rav said, but how could I not be scared? I had been at this woman's funeral. She had been dead for two years. Even now her face bore the signs of death. Her lips were a little too thin, her eyes were set too deep in her face, her cheeks too sunken.

Rav must have known what I was thinking, because he whispered, "It was worse when she first came back, but each day, she's looking a little bit better. She's not as confused as she was either. Every day she remembers more and more. She's becoming like she used to be."

The dead woman held me in her gaze, eyes a deep blue, like the depths of a glacier crevasse. Then she forced her lips to form a smile. "Anika!" Her voice was both gentle and gruff. Inhuman. "How are you?"

Every ounce of me wanted to scream, but my throat felt frozen shut. I could only stare.

"Answer her," Rav prodded. "Don't be rude! She won't like it if you're rude."

I cleared my throat and swallowed "I . . . I'm fine . . ."

"Look how you've grown. Just like my Rav," said the woman who had once been Mrs. Carnegie. "Come closer, Anika."

Afraid to disobey, I swallowed my terror and took a step closer.

"It's so good to see you," she said. "I'm so happy to be back."

But the more I looked at her, the more I came to realize that this wasn't Rav's mother at all. The truth was in her voice, it was in her eyes, it was in her breath—that flow of warm air drawing toward her, cold air flowing away.

"You're not Mrs. Carnegie!"

Rav grabbed me, squeezing my arm to get me to shut up, but I just shook him off. "I don't know what you are, but you're NOT Rav's mother!"

She slowly breathed in . . . she slowly breathed out. "I don't know what you mean."

"Yes, you do!"

Then the smile left her face. She looked at me in cool calculation, and I thought at that moment, she could either grab me and hug me, or she could reach out and rip my heart right out of my chest. For her it would make no difference. But she did neither of those things. Instead she said, "I have her body, I have her memories, I feel everything she felt—her frustrations, her fears, her hope. And her love. I am her in every way that matters."

"Except for one," I told her.

"Stop it!" Rav shouted. I turned to him and shook him, trying to make him see.

"This is not your mother!"

"Don't you think I know that?" Rav snapped. He looked at the woman sitting in the booth, then looked back to me. "My mother's soul is gone. I get that, okay? But now she's got a new soul. It's not evil, it's just . . . different. It wants to be whatever we want it to be. *She* wants to be my mother." There were tears in his eyes now. "Who are you to tell me that it's wrong?"

When I looked back to Mrs. Carnegie, she was smiling at me, tilting her head. Then she said to me, just as that other woman beneath the porch had:

"I know you. . . ."

"Of course you do, Mom," said Rav. "It's Anika."

"No," Mrs. Carnegie said, still smiling. "That's not what I mean."

Then she reached toward me as if she wanted to touch me with those icy hands.

"No, Mom!" Rav said.

She stopped short. "I'm sorry," she said. "I forgot."

And when I looked at Rav's right hand, I understood why. He had touched her. How could he have kept himself from touching her? And now his fingertips, all the way down to the first knuckle, were white and dead. Frostbitten. The result of touching a spirit colder than a frigid arctic night.

I turned and ran.

"Anika, come back," Rav called, but I wasn't turning around. I burst out into the street, and as I ran, I could see the truth all around me now, everywhere I looked.

In one window I saw the mailman dancing in circles with his dead bride, his hands frozen to the wrist, and him not caring in the least.

In another window, Mrs. Mason, my English teacher, spoon-fed a baby in a high chair—a baby that had not survived to its first birthday.

And on a porch, a woman I didn't even know sat in a rocker, gently creaking—but it wasn't the wood creaking: it was her frozen bones. She waved to me, smiling that *I know you* kind of smile.

I just wanted to get home now, grab my brother, leave this place, and never come back.

I pushed through the gate and fumbled with my keys at the front door, only to find it unlocked.

"Sammy!" I called as I burst in. I could see Dad wasn't home yet.

He was still off soaring over the glaciers, with no idea what was going on in town. I didn't know where we could go that would be safe, but anywhere was safer than here. We could leave Dad a note and hide up in the woods, until he found us. "Sammy, wake up!" But when I went into his room, he wasn't there. Sammy loved to play hide-and-seek with me, but this was not the time.

"Samuel Randall Morgan!" I demanded. "You come out right now," because the one thing that always ended hide-and-seek was calling him by his full name. It was always my admission of defeat—proof that he had stumped me—and then he would bound out of his hiding place in victory. But not this time.

And then I began to think, *What if they got him? What if one of those things got him?* My head was spinning—I was hyperventilating, so I made myself sit at the kitchen table. *They're not zombies,* I told myself. *They're not zombies, you said it yourself, Anika. They're not monsters, they're just . . . other.* After all, Mrs. Carnegie hadn't hurt me . . . they wouldn't hurt Sammy. Still, I couldn't convince myself.

I splashed cold water on my face, trying to slow my racing thoughts. There had to be a logical explanation for Sammy's absence. He got scared. He watched something on TV that made him scared, and he went over to one of the neighbors. Of course! That's what happened! It was just a matter of finding out which neighbor's house he went to, that was all.

I stood up, steadied myself, and went out the front door.

As it turned out, I didn't have to look far for Sammy. Not far at all.

Dad's gonna do a low flyby and wave to us, I had told Sammy. *Maybe even take us with him to the ice field.*

And then I had left him alone. And what do little kids do when they're left alone? They come up with ideas, and not all of them are good. See, it would be hard to see a passing helicopter from a bedroom window—but other places might have a better view. A place like the roof, for instance.

Somehow Sammy had climbed onto the roof. I don't know if he ever saw Dad's helicopter go by. Maybe he did. Maybe Sammy got so excited, he jumped up and down, waving. Maybe that was what made him slip.

While I was off with Rav, Sammy had fallen off the roof—but he didn't break his neck like I was always warning him he would. He didn't break any bones at all.

I hadn't seen him when I first ran into the house, because I wasn't looking, but he had never left home. He had been here all along, speared on Dad's perfect picket fence. Now he lay there limp, over the fence, his arms and legs dangling, the tip of a single picket sticking through his torn Spider-Man pajamas. The cloth, the fence, everything was stained a horrible shiny red.

I ran to him screaming, praying that it wasn't what it looked like—that it was just a trick of the light, and it wasn't as bad as it looked. "No! No! No!" I wailed. "It's okay, Sammy, you're going to be okay." Even though I knew it just wasn't true.

I lifted him off the picket and laid him gently on the ground. "Sammy! Sammy!" I howled, as if screaming his name could change things. As if calling him could wake him up—but not even calling him by his full name would bring him out this time. I knew because his eyes were half-open, and there was nothing in them. I knew because his skin was as chill as the night. And I knew because when I tried to stanch the flow of blood, it did nothing—because there was no blood spilling from the wound. Because there was no beating heart to pump that blood out. Because my brother—my annoying, awful, sweet, wonderful little brother—was dead. Dead.

I knelt there and cried. This was my fault. Mine, mine, mine. What if I hadn't left him? What if I had taken him with me? I was my dad now, a ball of what-ifs wrapped in regret.

Dad!

How could I tell Dad? Once he found out, it would kill him. It would worse than kill him! My grief was unbearable, but mine would be nothing compared to his. This would destroy him.

It was thinking about my father that brought some clarity to my thoughts . . . and then something occurred to me. Something horrible, but at the same time wonderful. Sammy was dead. His spirit had left him. His *kaa yahaayí*, as the Tlingit say. And with all my heart I hoped that he was with our mother, and she was already holding him in her arms, comforting him, and bringing him into the next world.

Yes, Sammy's soul was gone . . . but his *body* was still here.

Somewhere far away I heard the beat of helicopter blades. The landing pad was a good mile from here. But once he landed, Dad would have to drive his date back to her hotel. Maybe I had some time.

I went inside, got a sponge and a towel, and washed down the pickets, until enough of the blood was gone that it couldn't be seen in the moonlight. When I was done, I looked to my brother, still there on the yellowing lawn, and took a deep breath, steeling myself for what I was about to do. I knelt down, grabbed him, and lifted him up in my arms. So many times I would carry him as he clung to me, but now he was a deadweight heavier than a boulder.

I carried him out of our yard and across town. My arms ached from it, but I withstood it, because it was nothing compared to the ache in my soul. I looked straight ahead as I made my way down the darkest streets of town, looking in no windows on the way, ignoring any cars that passed me until I was finally standing at the face of the glacier.

Then I laid my brother down on the jagged ice at its base. I took a few steps back and looked up at the frozen wall. It shone so brightly in the moonlight, it almost seemed to give off its own glow. The air around me was silent. *Too* silent. And that was when I realized the glacier wasn't breathing anymore.

No, I told myself. *No. It's just holding its breath. It's waiting. It's waiting for me.*

"You know me!" I called to the glacier—because it did. I had played in its shadow all my life. I had picnicked on the crest of its moraine, and read my favorite books feeling its breath numbing my neck. It watched as Rav gave me my first kiss, and I remember feeling the glacier smile as it breathed in, as it breathed out. We were connected. I had always felt peace in the glacier's presence, and although I felt anything but peaceful now, I knew I could recapture that feeling if I tried.

"I understand now," I told it. "All those lives you took. The jealousy you must have felt—to be near us, yet apart. *With* us, but not *among* us. But you're not taking lives anymore, are you? Because you found a way to see through our eyes. You found a way to be human."

Still nothing from the glacier. Nothing at all.

"You know me!" I screamed. "I've never asked anything from you all these years. But I'm asking now. Please . . . if there's any life left in you, set it free. Set it free, and give me back my brother. *Become* my brother."

But the ice was silent and still. How big was the spirit of the glacier? Into how many pieces could it divide itself? Even if it had brought back everyone in that graveyard, there still had to be a spark of life deep within its ancient heart. There had to be!

"Please . . . ," I begged.

And then I heard something—*felt* something resonating in my bones. An icy breeze flowed over me, smelling fresh and crisp . . . and the glacier began to move.

I felt the calving of ice and instinctively I jumped back. The glacier surged—a sudden lurch, rolling forward just a few feet. Ice plunged, and frost filled the air, settling on my hair like snow. And once it was done, and the wall of ice had fallen silent again, Sammy was gone. He had been taken under the ice.

The glacier then breathed one last time—a slow wheeze of icy air that faded into nothing. I knew it was truly dead now. Whatever life force had been inside it was gone.

Now Exit Glacier, like so many glaciers, would wither, melting back year after year, until it was gone completely. The glacier was dead. It had spilled the last of its spirit out.

And Sammy was beneath the ice.

I don't remember walking home that night, but when I got there, Dad was furious. "Where were you? Do you know how worried I was? Where's Sammy?"

"I was with Rav," I told him. "And Sammy . . . Sammy's with a friend."

And since it wasn't really a lie, he couldn't read any deception on my face. He told me we'd talk about my punishment in the morning. Then he told me to lock up.

But I didn't.

Instead I unlocked every door, every window in the house—and even though I went into my bedroom, I didn't go to sleep. I just sat on my bed, forcing my eyes to stay open, holding a vigil.

At three in morning, I heard the faint creak of door hinges, and I bolted upright in bed. Had I really heard it, or was it just my imagination? Slowly I went out of my room, down the hallway, and into the living room. The front door was open just a crack. There was a chill in the house now, and it wasn't hard to find the source. Frost spilled out like smoke from Sammy's open bedroom door.

Fighting the shivers that threatened to overtake me, I crept toward Sammy's room and peered in. Sammy was sitting on his bed, looking out the window at the setting moon.

"Sammy?"

He slowly turned to me. His skin was pale and blue and his eyes were as dark as a glacier crevasse.

"Can't sleep," he said in a voice both gruff yet gentle, childlike yet ancient. "Why can't I sleep?"

"It's all right, Sammy. Don't worry about that."

Then I went to the front closet to get my heaviest winter parka, and my best fur-lined gloves, and put them on. Back in Sammy's room, I sat down next to him and reached out to touch his frozen face with my gloved hand.

"I'm scared," he said, with ice crystal tears falling from his eyes.

"Don't be," I told him. "You're home now." Then I took him into my thickly padded arms to comfort him.

Dad will have to face this—he will somehow have to come to terms with it, making peace with this new reality. And once he does, the three of us will leave Resurrection Bay, because although winter is long here, it's not long enough. We'll have to go someplace that's always cold. I'll bet they could use a good helicopter pilot way up north, in Prudhoe Bay.

But for now, I hold Sammy, gently rocking him back and forth, feeling his breath numbing my neck. Warm air flowing in, cold air flowing out.

"I know you . . . ," Sammy says.

It only makes me hold him tighter, closer. "Yes, you do, Sammy," I whisper, ignoring the chill that pierces all my layers of protection. "And I know you."

Perpetual Pest

By Neal Shusterman and Terry Black

There's nothing to be scared of," Rudy said. "The dead can't hurt you."

Mark nodded—an unsuccessful attempt to hide how anxious he was. Sure, in the clear light of day that made logical sense, but now, with the moon casting shadows over the rusty wrought-iron gates of the Perpetual Rest cemetery . . . well, the whole thing seemed ill-advised.

"Maybe let's just go home," Mark said. "Save it for another day."

Rudy just laughed and scrambled up the fence, climbing hand over hand, then vaulting to the other side. He landed on his feet like a cat.

"Hand me the shovel."

Mark reluctantly slid the shovel through the fence bars into his older brother's eager grasp. Rudy was a senior at Piedmont High, when he wasn't in juvie, and had the bad habit of ignoring any and all consequences of his actions. Sometimes it was fun to get swept up in Rudy's exploits, but other times—like *now*—it reminded Mark why his brother spent so much time in orange overalls behind locked doors.

"This really isn't stealing," Rudy had said, "because you can't steal from the dead, right? Legally the dead don't own a damn thing."

There was one reason, and one reason only, that Mark was willing to sneak into the local cemetery and dig up rich people, and whatever valuables they had been buried with. He wanted a pair of SportQuest Trainers, the best athletic shoes on the market.

Endorsed by the NBA, worn by the best players, they had no equal. *With SportQuest Trainers,* the commercials said, *you can slam-dunk the moon.* Looking at the moon right now, full and bright, Mark could almost believe it.

Of course, Mark knew a pair of shoes couldn't turn him into a sports legend. But they had to be better than the dismal pair of no-name, shredded tennies he had now. Mom kept promising to replace them, but she meant another bargain-bin pair. He was tired of getting laughed off the court.

But Rudy had an idea. . . .

"Rich people are so greedy, they like to take everything with them to the grave," Rudy had proclaimed. "Earrings, bracelets, diamond necklaces, you name it. I even heard about a guy who was buried in his Ferrari."

It was a foolproof plan, Rudy insisted. Dig up jewelry that no one will miss, and sell it on eBay. All Mark had to do was hold a flashlight and watch for guards. Considering the fact that it would take six months of mowing lawns to afford the shoes otherwise, it seemed like a no-brainer. Until Mark was actually there, at the cemetery fence.

"C'mon, what are you waiting for?" Rudy asked from the other side of the fence.

Mark looked up at the iron sign above the padlocked gate. Rusty letters read PERPETUAL REST MEMORIAL PARK, but the *R* in "rest" had broken. Now it read PERPETUAL PEST.

Mark passed Rudy the flashlight through the bars. "You go on without me," Mark said. "I'll keep watch from out here."

"Screw that," Rudy said, loud enough to maybe wake the dead, or at least the neighbors. "Ya snooze, ya lose da shoes! You gotta be strong to make it in this world, bro. So climb the fence and let's do this. Show me how strong you are."

Rudy had a way of making everything look easy and seem reasonable. Mark wondered if his brother's influence would land him in juvie too, one day. Like maybe tomorrow.

Even so, against his better judgment, Mark climbed the fence, the iron crossbars hurting his feet because of his worn-out soles.

"Here, take the shovel. I'll find the grave," Rudy said.

"You mean you have one in mind?"

"I do my research." Which made it sound like this was nothing but a school project.

He started off into the graveyard under a twisted canopy of trees. Ground fog swirled around him in his wake, like a ghostly sea. Mark took a deep breath and hurried after him, not really wanting to venture any deeper into the graveyard, but not wanting to be alone, either.

Up ahead, Rudy's flashlight beam bounced over the grounds of the cemetery, picking out marble headstones and vases stuffed with wilting flowers. Shadows danced with every step, like dark, scurrying animals, and the whole place smelled of fresh-turned earth. Mark tried to catch up with his brother, the gloom pressing in around him like cold tentacles in the mist, but Rudy was moving too fast.

The graveyard was alive with unsettling sounds: the chirping of bugs, the hissing breath of the wind between headstones, the mysterious scratch, scratch, scratch, of something unseen, like undead fingers, scrabbling upward through raw dirt. . . . Mark shook his head, furious at his own imagination.

He finally caught up with Rudy, who had come to an abrupt stop.

"We're here," he said.

They stood before a grave marked by an imposing statue of a mean-looking woman on a pedestal. Maybe it was just the moonlight, but Mark could swear the statue's teeth were bared, and the woman's fingers were splayed like claws.

A plaque resting at the foot of the statue read:

MADAME VORACIA THORNHILL
1898–1962
"Mine is yesterday, I know tomorrow"
From the Egyptian Book of the Dead

"Creepy," said Mark.

"Creepy and *loaded*," Rudy said. "Mrs. Thornhill was married four times, and each of her husbands was filthy rich. They all died in suspicious ways. John Thornhill—the brother of her last husband—swore she was a murderess. He broke into Thornhill Manor one night and shot her dead." Then Rudy lowered his voice. "After the shooting, John Thornhill was locked away in an asylum until the day he died—all the while saying his brother's wife wasn't human, that she was some kind of monster."

"Do you think . . ." Mark's voice broke. "Do you think it was true?"

Rudy shrugged. "Only in the way people can be monsters." Then he grabbed the shovel and dug into the ground, pulling up a mound of moist earth. "Now hold that flashlight steady."

It took over two hours.

By that time, Rudy was exhausted. Mark tried to help a couple of times, but his older brother kept saying he was too slow and grabbed the shovel back. Soon sweat was dripping from Rudy's forehead in spite of the cold, and his breathing was ragged and hoarse.

"You'll get your shoes," Rudy said as he dug, "and I'll have enough money to get away from here forever."

"Away where?"

But Rudy didn't share the details of his final destination.

Then, just when it seemed Rudy was ready to give up, the shovel struck against something firm that resonated like the chamber of an instrument. Rudy scraped the dirt aside, revealing a smooth curve of dull, faded mahogany.

"Pay dirt," he said, which Mark noted was a weirdly appropriate expression.

From then on, it went quickly. Rudy dug furiously, and in less than ten minutes he'd cleared enough dirt to expose Madame Thornhill's coffin lid. It was scraped from Rudy's frantic digging, but still impressive: a large custom casket, as solid as the day it was laid to rest.

Rudy hunched down and gripped the lid with both hands. "Ready for the unveiling?"

"I don't know," said Mark, the flashlight unsteady in his hands. "Maybe this wasn't such a good idea—"

"Too late now." Rudy threw the coffin lid wide.

Mark gasped.

Madame Thornhill's body was shriveled like a mummy; the eyes had collapsed in their sockets. Even her fancy gown was decaying.

But that wasn't the worst of it. The worst was that Madame Thornhill did not seem entirely human.

For one thing, the dead woman's hands were wrong. They were bent back at the wrist, with stubby fingers and sharp, curving fingernails. Mark had heard that a dead person's fingernails kept growing sometimes—but not like these. These were the claws of an animal.

But stranger still was her face.

Madame Thornhill's nose—well, it wasn't really a nose, it was more like a *snout*, stretching her dry cheeks like taffy. Huge canine teeth poked between papery lips.

"Rudy, let's get out of here. Now!"

But Rudy hadn't seen the face and didn't notice the claws. His attention was on a necklace glimmering with jewels. "Those are diamonds!" he said. "I knew it!"

Mark didn't care about the diamonds, the SportQuest Trainers, or anything anymore. He just wanted to get as far from Perpetual Rest as he could.

"Rudy!"

"Quiet! I've almost got the clasp."

The clasp came undone, but the moment it did, the heavy necklace slid right into a hole in the center of Mrs. Thornhill's chest.

Mark could only shudder.

"Gross!" said Rudy. But it didn't stop him from reaching into her shattered rib cage to fish the thing out. He found it quickly and lifted it up. The diamonds glimmered in the moonlight.

"Okay, you got it," said Mark. "*Now* can we get the hell out of here?"

"Wait," said Rudy, frowning, "I think there's other stuff in there . . . whatever it is, it's shiny." Then he reached back into the dead woman's dry, dusty rib cage.

Mark realized what that shiny stuff must have been even before Rudy pulled it out.

Rudy looked at what he had in his hands and puzzled over it. "Freaky," he said. "These must be the bullets that killed her."

"Let me see them! Hurry!"

Rudy reached up and handed Mark the bullets. It was just as Mark suspected. It hadn't been ordinary bullets that had put this woman to rest.

"Rudy, these are *silver* bullets!"

"Really? Do you think they're worth something?"

Rudy still didn't get the big picture, but to Mark it was as crystal clear as the full moon above them. You don't waste silver bullets on human beings. Everyone knows they serve a very specific purpose.

Mark dropped the bullets into his jacket pocket and desperately reached out to grab his brother's hand.

"Come out of there, Rudy! Come out now!"

But Rudy took his time, admiring the diamond necklace in his hand. "Well," he said proudly, "our work here is done."

Mark tried to warn his brother, but he was suddenly unable to speak, dry-mouthed with fear.

Because Madame Thornhill was beginning to move.

Rudy realized it a moment too late. He looked down and saw life returning to the creature's sunken eyeballs, saw its upper lip twitch like a dog sniffing a steak. Rudy might have escaped if he'd scrambled away in the next instant, while Madame Thornhill's old dead limbs were swelling and flexing with recovered life. But he just stood there, frozen in disbelief—

And then the werewolf sprang at him with a snarl. Rudy went down under a flurry of teeth and claws, screaming. Mark saw nothing else, because he panicked and ran, dropping the flashlight. It bounced and fell into the open grave, throwing crazy shadows as Rudy fought for his life and lost, his screams quickly silenced.

Rudy was dead.

And the wolf was still hungry.

Mark looked back only once and saw something he'd never forget, not if he lived to be a hundred, which right now seemed unlikely. It was Madame Thornhill in stark silhouette, with her head thrown back and teeth bared, howling with such fury it seemed to echo for miles. As Mark watched, the werewolf leaped forward. With the silver bullets removed from its insides, the dry, ruined flesh was rapidly repairing itself. Still shrouded in her shredded gown, Mrs. Thornhill sniffed the air for game.

Her head swiveled toward him.

Mark ran.

There was nothing he could do for Rudy—he was dead. But maybe Mark could save himself. He knew he had only one chance to escape. Madame Thornhill might have been an ordinary woman without the light of a full moon, but now she was more animal than human—and there were things a human could do that a wolf couldn't.

Like climb a ten-foot fence.

If Mark could make it to the edge of the cemetery and clear the fence before the werewolf caught him, he might survive! He had a head start of about thirty feet. But wolves are fast—you'd have to be a track star to outrun them.

Or a basketball star.

Mark tried to pretend he was on the court, driving the ball through the opposing line, blitzing toward the hoop with only seconds left on the clock. He tried not to think about the savage predator pounding toward him, its barbed teeth and wet tongue ready to gobble him down like raw hamburger. He could almost feel its hot breath on his shoulder, the sting of its razor claws. He ran, harder and faster than he ever had before.

The fence was right in front of him now. Mark jumped and caught the iron bars, just as the back of his leg exploded in pain.

The werewolf had clamped its jaws down on his left calf, but he couldn't let the pain, or the sight of his own blood, weaken him. Mark kicked at the creature's face with his other foot. It let go just long enough for Mark to pull himself up toward the top of the fence, ignoring the pain in his leg. The thing leapt at him again but fell back down, unable to reach him. Mark felt dizzy and sick, but forced himself to keep climbing. He wedged a foot between the bars, shoved himself upward, and pulled with all his strength.

And then his foot got stuck.

He twisted and turned, trying to work it free. He couldn't. The bottom of his cheap, useless shoe had torn loose and was caught on a metal spur. In desperation Mark grabbed one of the iron prongs at the top of the fence and tried to hoist himself up with it.

It broke loose in his hand.

He fell.

And hit the ground at the werewolf's feet.

The creature looked down at him, drooling, its eyes gleaming with hunger. The werewolf looked ridiculous in Madame Thornhill's gown, but Mark wasn't laughing. He groped in his jacket pocket for the silver bullets but had no idea what to do with them.

Then the werewolf pounced.

Mark saw a quick flash of teeth like shredder blades. Because it didn't matter what he did now—no way would he live to see another sunrise—Mark did the only thing he could think of. He punched the werewolf.

His fist hit Mrs. Thornhill in the chest and went deeper than he expected. Much deeper—because although the wolf was alive again, its wounds had not yet healed entirely. Mark's fist went through the hole in the monster's chest, and the werewolf shrieked like a dog in pain.

Instead of devouring him, the werewolf froze like a statue and crashed to the ground.

Mark realized why. In his clenched fist, now buried in the monster's chest cavity, he was holding the silver bullets. He'd clutched the bullets instinctively, so hard that his knuckles hurt, as if a part of him knew they were his last hope.

Gingerly, Mark opened his hand and pulled it free, leaving the bullets inside. The werewolf didn't stir. It was dead. Again. Re-dead, instead of undead.

He climbed the fence once more, this time much more carefully, and left Perpetual Rest Memorial Park.

They never found out how Rudy died, and because no one knew that Mark had been there, he didn't have to explain.

The official story was that Rudy had joined a gang of vandals who had snuck into the cemetery. There was a fight, and Rudy was stabbed. Then coyotes must have gotten to him. Another body was found nearby, quickly identified as the remains of Madame Voracia Thornhill—fully human once the full moon had set. No one could venture a guess as to how or why the body had been left at the cemetery fence.

Their mom was heartbroken about Rudy's death. But she'd be

okay. She had always worried that Rudy would meet with an unhappy end. Rudy had always said he wanted out of here forever. Mark liked to think there was justice in the universe, because in a way, his brother got exactly what he had asked for.

"You gotta be strong to make it in this world," Rudy had told him. But you also had to be smart. Mark had made it out alive, and had even healed from a werewolf bite without anyone ever knowing.

Mark never got his SportQuest Trainers, but he found he didn't need them. That night in the cemetery had done wonders for his self-confidence. If Mark could outrun a charging werewolf, surely he could handle a basketball court.

Besides, he'd checked next year's calendar. Four of the games would be played during a full moon.

Just try to stop him *then*.

Yardwork

As I step outside, a strange feeling tugs at my spine. Perhaps that's what it feels like when you first step into a nightmare.

Don't be silly, Ariel, I tell myself. *There's nothing to be afraid of.*

Today the wind has brought an unpleasant smell sweeping across the neighborhood. It's tinged with a slight scent of fertilizer.

The smell's coming from Mr. Jackson's house. Mr. Jackson used to live here a long time ago. I can vaguely remember his beautiful garden—nicest in the neighborhood. He had a family, but no one knows what happened to them. They left, then soon after he left, and the garden just died.

For years that house has been an ugly blotch on our neighborhood. People would live there for only a few months before leaving, and then it became completely abandoned. Now it's covered with graffiti and filled with broken, boarded-up windows. It bothered me to have a place like that next door, but like anything, I got used to it.

Then last week, Mr. Jackson just came back, like he'd never left. Since then, I've been watching the house . . . and watching him. The house hasn't changed—he hasn't had anyone come to fix the windows or paint over the graffiti. All he does is work in his garden. The man sure does love that garden.

Now, as I step outside, I can hear him back there. I can hear the *skitch . . . brummp, skitch . . . brummp* of his little trowel digging up the dirt and throwing it aside. He's planting more flowers. Until Mr.

Jackson came back, there weren't any flowers in *that* garden. Nothing grew there but weeds that got filled with torn rags, Kleenex, and candy wrappers. Whatever the wind brought to our neighborhood got snagged in the thick growth of that abandoned backyard and stayed there.

Until last week, that is. That was when Mr. Jackson showed up and began hacking those weeds, putting them into trash bags, and hauling them out to the curb. The weeds are all gone now, and bit by bit that wasteland of a yard is filling with flowers.

"Don't go bothering the man," my mom had told me. But what she really means is, *Stay away from him, because he's not quite right. Leave him to his business, Ari. And maybe when his business is done, he'll leave forever and they'll tear that ugly house down.*

But Mom's asleep on the couch now, so she doesn't have to know, and I can't resist the curiosity itching at my brain. It's a few minutes after dark. A night chill has set in, and the sun is long gone, leaving a ribbon of blue on the horizon that's fading fast. I stand at the edge of our property, peering at the upstairs windows of the old house. Boards have covered most of those windows for years now, and thick spiderwebs fill the space between the boards.

Taking a deep breath, I cross over, through the gaping hole in the old wooden fence, into the world of Mr. Jackson. Here that dark and earthy fertilizer smell is stronger. There are no lights on in the house. I don't think Mr. Jackson has had the electricity turned back on.

He's back there all right, doing his yardwork—I can see his shadow now as I make my way down the side of the house toward the backyard. I can see that shadow on hands and knees in the dirt.

Skitch . . . brummp, skitch . . . brummp.

Holding on to a rusty old drainpipe snaking down the edge of the house, I round the corner to see him in the light of the half-moon. He's setting a fresh row of flowers in the growing garden. I can't tell what they are, because all I can see is black and white.

"Are those zinnias you're planting?" I ask, remembering that my mom liked to grow zinnias.

He doesn't look up at me. Maybe he didn't hear me—and good thing too. I've got no business here. I can just go back home, turn on the TV, and forget Mr. Jackson; no one would be the wiser. But then he speaks in a soft whisper of a voice that sounds filled with gravel and wrapped in cotton.

"Marigolds," he says. "Man-in-the-moon marigolds, they are."

Skitch . . . brummp. He plants one more, then finally turns to look at me. I don't see his eyes, just dark shadows where they should be.

"You're the Harrison kid?" he asks.

I nod, then say, "Yes," figuring he can't see my nod in the dark. "Ariel Harrison. But you can call me Ari."

"I see you lookin' out your window at me," he says. "Am I putting on a good show for you here?"

"It's not like that," I try to explain. "I've just been wondering why you're . . . I mean, look at the house. What's so important about the yard when the house looks like hell?"

"How would *you* know what hell looks like?" he asks me. *Skitch . . . brummp.* Dirt flies over his shoulder, and in goes another marigold.

By now I'm feeling all tongue-twisted and bone cold, and fear is clawing at my gut. I grip that cold drainpipe as if it can give me some comfort, and it comes loose in my hands.

Yelping, I lose my footing and fall to the ground, right into the bed of flowers.

"I'm s-sorry," I stammer, scrambling to my feet, wishing I was anywhere else in the world. When I look down, I shudder at the sight of the imprint I made in the flowers. The way the moon's casting shadows tonight, I can see the shape of my whole body, as if I'm still lying there.

I figure the old man is going to have a fit and start scooping out my brains with his planting trowel, or bury his little hand rake in the side of my neck, but he doesn't. Instead he just looks down at the crushed flowers.

"Those're no good anymore," he says calmly. "I gotta put in all new ones now."

He looks at me, and now I can see his eyes. They are ancient, the lids almost closing over them in tired sags of skin.

"I don't need you here," he tells me in that gravel-cotton voice. "I can do this myself. I don't need you."

Well, *I* don't need a second invitation to leave. I step back, stumbling over the broken drainpipe, and tear out of the yard, through the hole in the wooden fence, and back onto my own property, where the moon doesn't seem to shine quite as coldly.

I can't sleep that night, because I hear him through my closed window. Only now do I realize that he doesn't sleep—he works all through the night in that garden. *What is it about that garden?* I wonder as I lie awake. *Why is it so important to him?*

When the sun comes up in the morning, I drag myself out of bed and peer out the window. In the light of day, the garden doesn't look quite so creepy. In fact, it looks kind of pretty and peaceful. Rows of flowers of all different colors surround a single open patch of dirt. I wonder what he's going to put there.

Downstairs, I pour myself some coffee and drink it sweet and black, the way Mom does. "I think Mr. Jackson's going to put a fountain in the middle of his garden," I tell her as I sit across from her at the kitchen table.

"His business is his business," Mom says. But what she really means is, *I don't want you to go sticking your nose in that garden.* Mom's always been a mind-your-own kind of person.

She heads out for work. "Lock the door when you leave," she tells me, like she always does. Like if she didn't, I'd leave the door wide open.

As I eat, I can hear the rattle of a wheelbarrow next door. Mr. Jackson's busy with his endless yardwork. I'm about to head out for school, but before I do, I get an idea. See, I'm not quite as mind-your-own as Mom is.

In a couple of minutes, I leave the house, but instead of turning right and heading toward school, I turn left and slip through the hole in the wooden fence.

Mr. Jackson is where I knew I'd find him, in the corner of the yard, turning up the earth for a new batch of flowers and tossing the bigger stones into the wheelbarrow. He wears a long-sleeved shirt, buttoned all the way to the top, even though the day is hot. His hands are covered with dirt, and they're just as leathery and wrinkled as the skin on his face.

"I . . . I thought you might like some breakfast," I tell him. I hold the plate toward him. Just a couple of toaster waffles. No one's ever accused me of being a chef. "I put the syrup in a little cup on the side so they didn't get soggy. Oh, and a fork." I produce the fork from my pocket and place it on the plate.

He stands there looking at me like he's looking through a wall. Then he slowly makes his way toward me, careful not to trample his flowers with his heavy work boots. His feet drag as he moves, as if he's got no muscles in them—as if he's pulling his legs up from the seat of his pants like a marionette. He reaches out and takes the plate from me.

"Thank you," he says simply, then puts the waffles down on a cinder block and reaches into his pocket, handing me a wad of crumpled dollar bills.

I shake my head, not wanting to take the money, and, for that matter, not wanting to touch that dirty, puffy hand. "No, you don't have to pay me," I tell him. "The waffles are my treat—to make up for messing up your flowers last night." When I look down, I see that he's already replanted the area.

He shakes his head slowly. "I'm not paying you," he tells me. "I'm asking you to do something for me." He clears his throat. It crackles like eggshells breaking. "I was wrong," he says. "Last night I was wrong. I *do* need someone to help me. You understand?"

I shrug. "Sure. What do you want me to do?"

"Flowers from the nursery. Lots of flowers."

"What kind?"

He thinks about that for a moment, then smiles, revealing just a sparse scattering of rotten teeth. I have to cast my eyes down because I can't look at that awful mouth.

"Any kind you like," he tells me. "Pick your favorites . . . and buy a shovel," he says before I go, "a bigger shovel."

After school, I head right out to the nursery with the old wagon I used when I was a little kid. I don't know much about flowers, but I pick out a few trays of really colorful ones for Mr. Jackson's garden. Then I pull it all home in the rusty old wagon and present the flowers to Mr. Jackson.

"Help me plant them," he says.

I look at my watch. Mom won't be home for another hour. I've got minimal homework, so I figure, sure, why not. No good deed goes unrewarded, right? Anyway, I head for the patch of dirt in the middle of the yard, which definitely needs some color, when Mr. Jackson shouts, "No!"

It nearly makes me jump out of my skin. Then he quickly changes his tone. "No, not there."

"Oh, right," I say. "I forgot about the fountain. It *is* going to be a fountain, right?"

But he doesn't answer me. He just directs me to a far corner with my trays of plants.

For a few minutes we work quietly, but my mind gets to working overtime. I start wondering about that patch of dirt. Not what's going on top of it, but what's underneath. I start wondering how deep this garden is planted.

"Mr. Jackson, whatever happened to your family?"

He plants three geraniums before answering in his gravelly, toothless voice. "People break apart sometimes" is all he says.

I think of my own parents. Once my parents split up, I saw less and less of my father until I didn't see him at all. *People break apart.* I imagine my own dad fifty years from now, an old man in a garden. No way to find him; no way to talk to him even if I do find him. Just the thought of it makes me plant the flowers faster and faster, trying to drive the thought out of my mind.

"Your family didn't go with you when you left here?" I ask, unable to keep my mouth shut.

"Nope. There were just old folks where I went," says Mr. Jackson. "Old folks, nurses, and more old folks."

"Did they treat you okay?" I ask, realizing that he must have been in a retirement home.

Mr. Jackson thinks about it. "They cared for me, which is about the best I can say for them." Then he stops planting for a moment. "They cared for me," he says again, "but that wasn't home. *This* is. You understand?"

I glance over at the bald spot in the center of the yard again. "What's over there, Mr. Jackson? Is there something . . . under the dirt?"

"Nothing," he tells me. "Nothing but worms."

The light is growing dim now. I listen for the sound of my mother's car. Above us I can see large birds circling. Vultures. I can't remember seeing them in our neighborhood before.

Then I hear Mr. Jackson grunt, and when I look up, something awful has happened. He was digging with his little trowel and somehow slit his right arm, leaving a gash as wide as all outdoors—at least four or five inches.

"That's not good," says Mr. Jackson, in the same calm voice he used when I fell in his flowers last night.

"I'll go call a doctor!" I shout, but as I start to take off, he yells, "No! No doctors."

"But your arm."

"It's *my* arm and *I'll* deal with it."

He grabs a dirty rag from his back pocket, and I catch sight of the words stenciled on it. It reads DUVAL COUNTY CONVALESCENT HOSPITAL. He slaps the rag over the wound. I can't imagine a rag keeping back the flow of blood, but it does. Still, a dirty rag isn't something you use on an open wound.

"Mr. Jackson, maybe I should—"

"Get on home," he tells me. "Go on, your mother's home, I can hear her."

And he's right. My mother has just driven up.

"But . . ." I don't know what to tell him. He holds the rag over his wound, the expression on his face unchanging, as if a tear in his arm is no more dangerous to him than a tear in his shirt. It looks as though the flow of blood has stopped, but to be honest, I never really saw a flow of blood begin.

I leave, thinking all kinds of troubled thoughts. As I head out of the yard I see, sitting on a cinder block, the waffles I brought him that morning, uneaten.

It's later that night. Mom's asleep on the sofa again, her book open in her lap. I go to my room, pull out my phone, and dial a number that wasn't all that hard to find.

"Duval County Convalescent Hospital," answers a tired-sounding woman on the other end.

"I'm calling about a Mr. Isaac Jackson," I say.

A long pause on the other end, and then, "Are you a family member?"

"No. Listen, I think he's not quite right. I mean, he's here, and I think he's still supposed to be with you. I think he kind of . . . ran away."

"What do you mean, he's there?" the woman says, sounding alarmed. "Who is this? Are you from the medical school?"

"I'm just a neighbor, that's all."

"It says right here that Isaac Jackson was transferred to the medical school last week," which makes zero sense to me, but I take the number, and I call that one next. The guy who picks up the phone seems to talk to me between bites of whatever he's eating.

"Says here (chomp chomp) we were supposed to get him," he tells me. "But he never showed up (chomp chomp). Probably just a clerical error."

By now I'm beginning to get upset. "Well, somebody should come and get him," I say. "I mean, what if he's in trouble? Don't you even care?"

And on the other end I hear the creep laugh. "Ha! That's a good one! No, he's not getting into any trouble anymore (chomp chomp). Not unless those med students are playing practical jokes with their cadavers again."

My heart misses a hefty beat.

"Cadavers?"

"Yeah, you know, as in 'corpse.' As in 'stiff.'" He laughs again. "Yeah, med students are clowns. Those things end up in the wildest places sometimes!"

I end the call, and drop the phone like it suddenly got hot. As if getting the phone out of my hands can somehow change what I've just heard. I don't believe it. And yet somehow I do. And somehow I understand.

Outside, the clouds hide the moon, and it's as dark as if the moon weren't even there. As I leave my house, it takes a few moments for my night vision to kick in. When it does, I find the hole in the wooden fence and cross over into the cold loneliness of Mr. Jackson's world.

I can hear him back there—hear him moaning. I can hear him digging in the dirt. *Skitch . . . brummp. Skitch . . . brummp.* Slowly I round the corner where the drainpipe once stood, and there, in the center of the yard, is total darkness.

There isn't going to be a fountain there. That bald patch of dirt was not for a fountain at all. It was for a grave.

I peer in. I see, at the bottom of the ditch, Mr. Jackson covering himself with dirt. With one hand he weakly slices into the dirt wall and pulls it down around him.

"No time," he whispers to himself. "No time left. No time."

My eyes are full of tears, but I wipe them away.

"When did it happen, Mr. Jackson?" I ask him. And then I force out what I really mean to say. "When did you . . . die?"

He takes a deep breath, and it comes out like a raspy wheeze. "It'll be two weeks tomorrow," he says.

I swallow hard, choking down my own terror. "And you don't know where your family is, and no one would bury you?"

The only answer is that raspy wheeze.

I reach into the shallow hole and take the trowel away from Mr. Jackson. He begins to panic as I drag him out.

"No!" he says. "No time. No time. Getting too weak."

"Shhh!" I tell him gently. "Shhh. Someone will hear."

And then I look into those eyes that can barely stay open at all. I force myself to *keep* looking, this time refusing to look away from that awful face, trying to see the man he must have once been.

"What do you want me to do?" I ask.

In those ruined eyes I see tears beginning to form.

"Care for me," he says.

But I won't do that. Nurses and hospital workers care *for* him. But they can't care *about* him. Not the way I can.

I look at the grave. "It's not deep enough," I tell him. Then I grab the large shovel leaning up against the house, step into the hole, and begin digging, throwing dirt over my shoulder.

The old man tilts his head. I hear it creak and fracture on his slim neck. "You're one of the good ones, Ari," he says with a voice that keeps moving farther and farther back in his throat. "One of the good ones."

"Rest easy, Mr. Jackson. I'll give you a decent burial; you don't have to worry. I'll take care of everything, I promise. . . ."

Mr. Jackson smiles his awful smile, but somehow that smile doesn't seem awful at all. It seems wonderful and warm and filled with the kind of peace that comes from knowing things are all right. That things are in order.

I watch as Mr. Jackson lets his shoulders relax. Then his eyes close, his head sinks to the ground, and he finally gives his spirit over to the death that has been trying to claim his body. In a moment I know that he is gone—*truly* gone, the way he should have been two weeks ago.

Now I'm alone as I stand here in the darkness of his backyard garden, digging his grave.

I will bury you, Mr. Jackson. I will bury you in the place where you lived your good years. I will cover your grave with flowers, so it will be our secret, and you can rest, knowing that there was someone in this world willing to see you off into the next.

And I will not be afraid.

Skitch . . . brummp.

Skitch . . . brummp.

Deadliner

A *Night of the Living Dead* Story

By Neal and Brendan Shusterman

Some people called Owen a "profiteer." But there was a much better word for it. "Survivor."

This destabilization of society—this sudden outburst of wandering dead eating friends and neighbors—was an opportunity for a consummate survivor who could play his cards right.

He'd been a carnie for years before the outbreak. Aside from selling rubes on sucker games, society had no place for him: he wasn't wanted. He was expected to move on when the carnival did, and he obliged. He didn't like the rubes any more than they liked him. But when the hungry dead took to the streets, he knew this could be his chance to win the big prize. They called the summer of 1967 the summer of love. 1968 had brought the summer of death.

When it had first happened, he'd just finished setting up the circus tent in Savannah, Georgia. That was when they came wandering in. He'd watched men he'd worked with for five years getting eaten alive by the incoming assault—and the carnies with enough connective tissue intact after being bitten joined the forces of the dead with a passion. On that day he saved five people, and the legend about him began to grow.

He'd killed hundreds of them in the streets and neighborhoods of Savannah over the next few weeks. He went from dirty townie to town hero. A son of the Pacification. That was what they called it. "The Pacification." After six months, the living dead were under control, or so the official reports said. People were advised to travel in groups, always have a weapon, and stay away from dark deserted places. A commonsense practice when your rotting mother might just show up to eat you. Now we could go back to worrying about the Commies, who, people agreed, were far more of a threat than zombies.

And through it all, the big top still stood. Silent. Waiting. Owen knew it was waiting for him. There would be a new show now. And Owen would be the ringmaster.

"Careful with that truck! And keep your hands away from the windows!" Owen was amazed that he had to warn his workers to be careful with the cargo. He had thought all the people without common sense had been obliterated by this new form of natural selection. But idiots were as resilient as cockroaches.

"We got seventeen," Cristoph, his lead hunter, told him. "Five fit the profile you asked for. One of them you ain't gonna believe."

But after the things he'd seen, Owen could believe anything. The hunter told him who they had. Owen believed it—but only barely.

"A grand each for the normals, five grand for the specials, and twenty for your headliner." The hunter reminded him that there had been ten men on his team when they set out. Now there were seven. "The rest got bit and had to be put down. So you'll give me five grand each to give to their families."

Owen doubted the money would go to the families of the dead men, but that wasn't his business. He and his investors were willing to pay far more for this delivery than Cristoph was asking—so he only haggled him down a little before shaking hands.

"But you and your men will stay on," Owen insisted as part of the deal. "We'll need sharpshooters. Security. We'll work out a good wage."

Owen had a team of his roughies move the truck to the back of the circus camp. Everyone else gave it a wide berth. Owen looked to the rest of his employees. Their faces didn't look as excited as he'd imagined.

"Don't worry, y'all," he said loudly. "Hell, the lions are more dangerous than what we got in there."

"You're barbaric, Owen."

Owen turned to see Clara, the tightrope walker, watching the whole scene with a look of disgust that could have shriveled Owen in an earlier day. Clara was the best at what she did. Everyone in his show was. The Savannah Post-Apocalyptum was truly the greatest show on earth—so great that it didn't have to move. The world came to him—not just for the acts but to see Owen himself. Such was his legend. He was a zombie-killing Buffalo Bill. The new-world P. T. Barnum. People longed to rub elbows with the man who'd saved Savannah. He didn't rub elbows much, but he was happy to take their money.

"Clara, this is the business," he reminded her.

"It's barbaric is what it is. I've never seen anything so inhuman in my whole life."

"What about when they were banging at your door, threatening your life?" said Harry, one of the show clowns. He'd already gotten his makeup on for the evening, and it had already begun to melt off. Owen would have to make a point of scolding him for that. But for now, he was just glad the old rodeo clown had his back. He'd hired him from Texas, and he knew the man had lost a sister and an uncle to the beasts.

"You really want to treat them like us?" said Harry, with a laugh. "Lady, they *ain't us*."

"They were like us once," muttered Clara. "This is a circus, not a . . . not a . . ."

"Circus?" suggested one of the barkers, and everyone laughed.

"Hey, if people will pay to see it, it's fair game," said the show's juggler—a young man from Philadelphia named Ronnie, who had actually helped Owen take down more than a dozen dead in the first attack. He walked over, juggling half a dozen balls at an ever-increasing speed. Then he gave Clara a seductive grin. "You like my balls? People liked my balls. Said I had great balls. Then I switched to pins." He let the balls fall and pulled out a set of pins, producing them from behind him, like out of thin air. All part of his act. "Pins got me a bigger crowd on the midway. Flaming pins got me better tips. Then when the dead rose up, I switched to chain saws. This is the natural progression. Don't try to fight it." Although he didn't juggle chain saws to make his point. That was reserved for the show.

Owen could tell Clara understood but wasn't ready to accept. "It's the devil's money, then," she said.

"This is the circus," said Harry, with a laugh. "It's *all* the devil's money. Just look what you're wearing."

This got a laugh out of a few of the performers, and Owen took this opportunity to change the subject.

"We've got less than an hour till showtime. Business as usual tonight—but tomorrow we go dark for a month. We'll create a whole new show the likes of which has never been seen."

There were grumbles at the prospect of going dark, until everyone found out that they'd still get paid. The group split up—everyone went their separate ways except for Clara, who still looked at the truck. Even closed you could hear the ghastly groans from within. She turned to Owen, and rather than an insult or accusation, she softly said, "I don't think you'll be able to control them."

The simplicity of her statement, and her sincerity, gave Owen a moment's pause.

"Honey, I know them better than I know myself," he told her. "You leave it to me."

The two turned to see Cristoph and a few of his men—all with sidearms like gunslingers, rifles at the ready. They were already talking about taking shifts watching the truck of the living dead.

Clara took a deep breath. "All I know is that you don't take away the net until you're sure you're not going to fall."

Then she stormed off with the perfect gait of a tightrope walker.

Owen brought in professional makeup artists and costumers from Hollywood. "They're terrifying up close," Owen told them. "It's your job to make them look just as terrifying from a distance."

He paid the makeup artists the highest salary in the show. Although the dead were chained and shackled, when your hands are that close to such lethal mouths, it was worth quite a lot of combat pay. Owen wasn't going to begrudge them that.

One of the makeup artists—a young woman whose own perfectly designed face was testimony to her skill—burst out in tears when she saw their headliner. "I can't do this," she told Owen. "I just can't."

"She can't hurt you," Owen reminded the girl. "We have her secured so tightly, she can't even move her head."

But the girl quit anyway.

Owen brought in the best lighting and set designers. He hired special-effects coordinators.

"I want the audience to be three seconds from pissing their pants," he told them. "We want them to forget that there's a fence between them and the dead."

Within just a few short weeks, they had the ultimate act. Word got out and the Post-Apocalyptum, which was already wildly successful, became insanely so. Ticket sales were through the roof, even with prices jacked up beyond anything anyone ought to pay.

Owen's investors—dark-suited men who were either too fat or too gaunt, and looked a bit like the living dead themselves, were both optimistic and nervous. "This act of yours had better deliver," they told Owen.

He despised that he had to answer to them, but his confidence did not falter. "This is more than a gold mine," he told them. "It's a mint. After opening night, it'll be like printing our own money."

Cristoph, although a standoffish and unpleasant man, turned out to be quite a wrangler of the dead. Yes, he had hunted them up, but more than that, he took care of them. He got rancid meat from the market—because it was the only thing they'd eat other than human flesh. He made sure their chains were loose when they were in the truck, and broke the nose of one of the carnies who was getting his kicks tormenting them. Cristoph had worked as a zookeeper before the outbreak, specializing in venomous snakes, but he was well acquainted with the particular hazards of circus animals. What were the living dead but another deadly animal to control?

"I would like very much for you to be a part of the act," Owen told Cristoph.

"Me? What would I do? I'm not like you; I'm not a showman."

"You wrangle the dead better than anyone. Every animal act needs its tamer. Who better than you?"

Although Cristoph's agreement was reluctant, within days he was owning it like it had been his idea. The man actually cracked a smile as afternoon faded to twilight on opening night.

"You may actually pull this off," he told Owen.

Although Cristoph didn't know it, that vote of confidence changed everything. It gave Owen the nerve he needed to really take the show to the next level.

An hour before the audience was to be let in, he gathered everyone in the back room and informed his performers that he was having the safety fence between the audience and the ring taken down.

"Owen, are you sure?" asked Harry, his painted clown smile obscuring his true face, masking the depth of his concern. "I've seen those things . . . how they . . . *operate* . . . up close."

"The danger has to seem real," Owen said. "You've seen Cristoph working with them. He can handle them—and if it starts to go south in any way, he'll have six sharpshooters in plain view, with clear shots."

Owen looked to the back of the room and met Clara's eyes. The volcanic look on her face made him quickly look away.

"This is lunacy!" she shouted. "Doesn't anyone else here see how wrong this is? Hasn't anyone else lost someone to them? Or seen a relative become one?"

"I saw my sister get bitten, and my mother," said Horace, an old clown Owen had hired from a circus in Ohio. "Then they both came after me. It was my neighbor what put 'em down."

"I killed eighteen of 'em," said a young clown named Ralphy. "Used my dad's old truck. Ran 'em right over. These things ain't fast and they ain't smart. But still . . . one bite . . . For my dad it was barely a nick on his finger, but that's all it took. It wasn't long till he was one of them. In the end, I runt him over too."

The testimonies were sobering and left everyone in silence, suddenly transported back to their first encounters with the epidemic.

"Yeah, I lost people," said Gloria, an old showgirl who had become a sort of mentor to the newer girls. "I'll never forget that. But I'm not gonna let that cheat me out of good money. These things nearly ended us. I say we put 'em onstage and prove to the world that the show must go on."

A few "hear, hears" and claps were given, and Owen breathed a sigh of relief. No one seemed to agree with Clara, who threw her hands up, in far too much shock at her fellow performers to say anything.

"There are always frightful acts in a circus," said Ronnie, the juggler, as he tossed a few balls in one hand. "Always been that way. A circus is about the shock, and the awe. What's more shocking than the things we most fear, forced to perform for our amusement?"

• • •

Standing room only.

The audience couldn't get in fast enough when the doors were opened. They practically crawled over each other to get in, just like the dead. *People need this,* thought Owen. *This is a necessary public service.*

Each performer did their part to make it the best show they'd ever had. The clowns, led by Harry, made the audience laugh louder than Owen had ever heard them laugh. The trapeze acrobats were in perfect form, leaving the crowd with stars in their eyes. The only glitch was the tightrope act, which was a no-show. Clara had up and left without even as much as a note. Her loss. The girl had walked away from a million-dollar career.

It was all going wonderfully as the evening inched ever closer to Owen's big reveal. It was as though he could hear the electric buzz through the audience, the anticipation of what was to come. And he, being the ringmaster, kept everything in line.

When Ronnie's juggling act had finished, Owen raced out into the ring.

"And now, ladies and gentlemen! The moment you've all been waiting for! We bring you something terrifying. Can you hear them? Scrape-scrape-scraping at your door? Can you smell them? Mouths dripping with the unthinkable? Behold! The most terrifying of all acts ever brought to you on any stage . . . the living dead!"

The crowd gasped in shock as two great doors opened in the back of the tent. The dead shambled out of the darkness, with Larry and Carl, two of the troop's strongmen, holding them at bay with chains. A light came up on Cristoph, whip in one hand. Pistol in the other.

"Now, ladies and gentlemen, don't be alarmed," Owen bellowed to the gasping crowds. "Those chains are tempered steel. And as you can see, they are happy to make your acquaintance!"

The crowd's terror quickly turned into laughter, as they saw that the living dead had been done up to look like clowns; faces painted, costumed. As sinister as they were hysterical. Then the second wave was sent out, held by two more strongmen. These were not dressed as clowns. Their outfits were tattered, of course, but they wore replicas of what they had worn in life.

"In fact," continued Owen, "some of them you might already be acquainted with."

Now the spotlight began to single out five of the "special" subjects that Cristoph's team had been so lucky to catch. The first subject was hit by the spotlight. The audience began to murmur their both gleeful and horrified surprise even before Owen announced the name of the former senator from South Carolina.

The dead senator put up his limp hands to shield his glazed eyes from the bright light. Then he fixed his attention on a pretty young thing in the audience and stalked toward her, bent on feasting. The strongmen holding him pretended to drop the chains. The audience screamed. Cristoph snapped his whip and the dead senator fell back away, subdued. All part of the show.

"And to the left—you knew him as the king of late-night talk shows. But he's not doing much talking now!"

The dead talk show host wandered to the left and right. Uttered a moan that sounded eerily like the voice America knew all too well.

Then came the TV housewife who used to share her favorite recipes on the tube, but was no longer quite the picky eater she once was.

And the comedian famous for his goofy roles, but none goofier than his final one. They were subdued by Cristoph and forced to do tricks, to the delighted disbelief of the audience. The living dead might be mindless—but they were trainable!

Then the lights dimmed, and a hush fell over the big top.

"And now," Owen said, "I give you the star of our show. The headliner of headliners. A woman who needs no introduction . . ."

The spotlight came on, and there, in a pool of light, wearing a tattered replica of the gold gown she'd worn to last year's Oscars, was the movie star whose gorgeous face had once been the subject of countless billboards. Whose violet eyes had captivated millions. Who was Helen of Troy and Cleopatra combined. Now her jaw was slack, and her cheeks sunken. Her once-beautiful face now held the pallor of the grave without a grave to go with it. The audience gasped and groaned and wailed. What was it the juggler had said? Shock and awe? This crowd was certainly getting their money's worth.

This was Owen's shining moment. In his youth, he had always dreamed of meeting her. What he might say if he did. How he might win her heart. Now he had her. Not in a way he had ever expected, but she was here. It was true that all things come to those who wait.

For the other subjects, it was simple tricks, but not for the star of stars. She was better than that. She deserved something special. The men holding her let her chains go slack. Cristoph backed away, and Owen stepped forward.

"Dance for us, Miss Taylor," Owen said. "Dance for us!"

The dead movie star began to move her feet. She shuffled to the left. To the right. Her shoulders rolled. Her arms stayed limp. She was dancing the dance of the dead. And the audience slowly began to applaud, getting louder and louder until it rose into a fever pitch.

"Do you hear that, Miss Taylor? Do you hear it? You are still a star!"

Then she lurched forward with a throaty snarl, only to have one of the strongmen pull back on her chains.

As the cheers rose, Owen lifted his hands in triumph.

Then a sudden groan from behind him caught his attention. At first he thought it was one of the dead, but when he turned, he saw that it was Cristoph. He had dropped his whip, as well as his gun, and was down on one knee, holding his chest. He was pale. Very pale.

Owen hurried to him. "What are you doing? Get up! You have to get up, the act isn't over!"

"H-h-heart attack," Cristoph gasped.

"No! You can't! Not now!"

"All the . . . the . . . excitement. All the . . . all the . . ."

Cristoph's strength completely left him and he sprawled in the sawdust of the ring, gasping, grimacing, then was silent.

And the dead knew.

They saw that their wrangler—the only one who could truly keep them at bay—was down.

Owen knew what was going to happen a moment before it did, and he was powerless to stop it. Almost as if they had one thought—one mind—the dead pulled on their chains with strength that seemed beyond human. In all the rehearsals in all the weeks leading up to this, they had never shown such strength. They pulled the strongmen at the other ends of their chains to them. The men tried to get away, but there were just too many of the dead. No, they weren't smart. Yes, they moved slowly. But in numbers, the dead can do anything.

The strongmen didn't stand a chance.

When the audience saw the blood—saw the bits of flesh being ripped away—and realized this was not part of the show, they panicked. They began to mob the exits—but the exits were too small, and the crowd too dense.

And the dead, with no one to hold them back, began advancing on the crowd.

"Everyone, please! Please stay calm!"

But no one was listening to Owen anymore.

A rifle shot rang out. One of the dead—the senator—was taken down, but there were still sixteen already climbing over the first row of seats to get to the scrambling audience. A second shot rang out, missed the mark completely, and killed a man in the audience who was in the wrong place at the wrong time.

That was when Cristoph's sharpshooters abandoned their posts and ran, deciding it was every man for himself.

Maybe if he hadn't been so confident, Owen might have armed himself with a gun. But there was no time to think of that now. The shock was all he could focus on. The awe of seeing his life crash and burn.

The dead reached the audience. They feasted. They bit as many as they could. Owen fell to his knees. He watched as more and more people went down, and he knew that this would not end here. This tent would be the vector of a new epidemic. A new outbreak of living death.

Then he heard a groan that was far too close for comfort. He turned to see the movie star standing ten feet from him. Elizabeth Taylor, in the flesh—or what was left of it. She was still shuffling from one foot to the other, her tattered gold dress fluttering in the breeze coming in from the exits. The living were gone. The dead littered the stands . . . dozens upon dozens of those who had been killed by the zombies—too many to count . . . and now they were all beginning to rise.

The movie star gazed at him, her eyes cloudy, but still that shade of violet that made them so captivating. She began to shuffle forward, her head lolling to one side, her hands reaching toward him, her teeth snapping in anticipation.

She was not beautiful anymore, but then all beauty fades. Who was Owen to judge such things? There was the beauty of life, there was the peace of death, and now there was the terrible netherworld between.

Owen stood, dusted off his ringmaster's jacket, and held out his arms. "Shall we dance, Miss Taylor?"

And he let her take him into her cold embrace.

Loveless

The dead frames of ancient brick buildings loom all around you as you trek through the worst part of town, in the worst hour of night. You're cold, you're alone, and your body aches, but you must force yourself on. You have no choice. On every side of you, windows are boarded up, and walls are tagged with layer upon layer of graffiti.

No one lives here anymore—you're certain you won't find her, but you have to try.

Finally the number of the building matches the number scrawled on the slip of paper you carry. Upstairs, behind a broken window, is a hand-painted sign. You can barely read it in the moonlight. It says:

MADAME LOVELESS, PSYCHIC. PALMS READ. FUTURES REVEALED.

You've already been to three psychics, all phonies, but those psychics were visionary enough—and terrified enough—to see that you needed the real thing. That you needed the services of Madame Loveless. It took half the night following poor directions, but you've finally found her.

But if she's such a good psychic, then what's she doing living in an awful place like this?

Suddenly a voice behind you makes you jump. "If you're looking for Madame Loveless, you won't find her here," the voice says.

You spin to see an old man crouching in the shadows of a dim doorway. Beside him is a shopping cart filled to the brim with trash and trinkets.

"Building's been condemned for over a year," says the old man. "Rats are the only tenants now."

The old man steps into the pale streetlight. His skin is covered with layers of grime, and the grime covered by layers of clothes. He speaks in a high-pitched, raspy voice. "Just a second," he says, then rummages through his cart, coming up with a cracked, bulbless flashlight. He aims it at you, as if it works.

"Look at the likes of you! You certainly need a fortune-telling, don't you?"

"Do you know where Madame Loveless has moved?" you ask.

"I might and I might not," says the man with a smile. Knowing what he wants, you reach into your pocket and hand him five dollars.

He aims the dead flashlight at the bill, obviously hoping for more, but in the end he grunts and says, "Follow me."

He heaves his slight weight against the overstuffed cart, and it rattles across the broken concrete.

About five blocks away, you come to a wrought-iron fence around a park. The old man chains his cart to the fence, then squeezes through a gap. He leads you across a field of untended grass and ivy. As the street disappears behind you, you notice dim gray shapes all around.

"This park sure has a lot of benches," you mumble, but the old man offers you a dark chuckle. "Those aren't benches," he says. "And this isn't a park."

You look once more and finally realize that you are surrounded by tombstones.

"It's a shortcut," says the old man, waving his broken flashlight. "This way."

You stop dead in your tracks, not wanting to take a single step farther. The moon has slipped behind a dark cloud, and there is no light up ahead. If you turn and run, you can follow the glow of a distant streetlight back to the deserted street . . . but that would mean crossing back through the cemetery alone.

"A lot of people are scared of cemeteries," says the old man, "but there're no spirits here, only bodies. Spirits hate graveyards, because they don't like being reminded that they're dead." Then he pauses for a moment. "Of course, every now and then someone comes back to rest in their old body for a while, and they moan with whatever's left of their vocal cords."

You can almost feel the ground shake from the power of your own shiver.

"Oh, don't be so spooked," says the old man. "It's not like they can haul themselves out of their graves or anything. They barely got any muscles left, if they have any at all. Most they can do is scratch a little."

Somewhere far away you hear something scratching.

The old man makes his way up a hill toward a solitary family mausoleum. The name on the mausoleum is LOVELESS.

"I . . . uh . . . don't need a *dead* fortune-teller," you tell the old man.

"She's not so dead that she can't tell your fortune," he answers.

You have no intention of following him into a mausoleum, but then something occurs to you. This creepy person is wearing a heavy woolen hat, and in the dim light you can barely see beyond the wrinkles. That nasty, raspy voice doesn't necessarily belong to a man.

Only now does he take off his ski cap to reveal that he's not a man at all.

"Are you . . . Madame Loveless?"

The old woman smiles. "In the flesh."

The way you've figured it, Madame Loveless has little or nothing left of her sanity—which may or may not make her a good psychic. But she had better be good, because you must have your fortune now. You must know the truth.

"Please come in," says Madame Loveless.

You step into the dusty stone room. The small family mausoleum smells awful. It's cluttered with heaps of gnawed chicken bones and stinks of rotting food. A greasy crystal ball sits on an old wooden table in the center.

"This place is the only property my family owns," says Madame Loveless, as she pours herself some imaginary tea from a cracked, empty teapot.

"They kicked me out of my apartment, but I won't let them kick me off family property."

Another shiver echoes through your body as you wonder how desperate a person has to be to start rooming with the dead. Then you begin to wonder how desperate you must be to have come here at all.

Madame Loveless replaces the pot on the ledge above Claude Loveless, beloved father, who has been a resident of the wall for over thirty years. You shift uncomfortably in your seat as you watch the woman sip from her empty cup. Steam beads on her forehead as if the cup at her lips is filled with hot tea. She offers you some, but you don't want to share in her insanity.

"Are you real or another fake?" you ask. "I've seen plenty of fakes."

Madame Loveless puts down her teacup and looks you in the eye. She's the only one who has dared to do that for as long as you can remember.

"It's an honest question," she says, moving toward the iron door of the stone room. "The answer is yes and yes. I'm real and a fake at the same time. You see, most people who want their fortunes told are imbeciles who want someone to change their luck. Since I can't take away their troubles, I take away their money." And then she smiles. "But I can see you're different."

"Prove to me you're for real," you demand, and the old woman looks at you as if reading the truth right off your eyeballs.

"You come not only seeking to know your future," she tells you, "but to know your past. For many months you have wandered the nights alone, because the sight of you strikes fear into people's hearts. They don't understand what you are. But what's worse is that you don't understand either."

Somewhere far off in the forest of gravestones, you hear something moan. *This doesn't bother me,* you chant over and over in your mind. *This doesn't bother me at all.* But the truth is, with each passing moment, you are becoming more and more terrified, and you begin to feel that Madame Loveless isn't really insane at all . . . because the stone room around you has somehow changed. The dead flashlight is now shining a bright beam on the wall . . . and the old woman's teacup is full of steaming tea.

"Shall we begin?" says Madame Loveless.

There's no turning back now. You hold out your hand and brace yourself for whatever she has to tell you.

The old woman runs her fingers along the lines of your palm, her fingertips like old parchment.

"A well-crafted hand," she tells you. "Fine as any I've seen."

"What does it tell you?" you ask, trying not to sound as anxious as you really are.

Madame Loveless smiles. "What is it you want to know?"

You begin to anger. She knows what you need. She knows why you came here. She only has to look at you to see the awful state you're in.

"I'm not here to play games!" you tell her sternly.

She nods solemnly. "Few are," she answers, "but your questions must be specific, if you want the answers to mean anything."

You swallow hard and voice aloud the questions that have plagued you for as long as you can remember. "Why is my skin so pale and gray?" you hiss at her.

She flips over your hand, running her rough palm across the back of your fingers and up to your wrist. "Because your skin is as old as the mountains," she answers.

"Why am I always so cold at night?" you ask. "Why do I burn with fever in the day?"

She touches a hand to your icy forehead. "Because you rise and fall with the sun," she tells you.

"Why do my bones creak? Why does it hurt each time I move?"

The old woman grabs your arm and flexes it. You feel the grinding, and grit your teeth from the pain—the same pain you feel with each grasp, each footfall, each breath.

"Because the bones you speak of do not exist," she says. "And you feel the pain of a spirit not born to move."

And finally you ask the question you are afraid to have answered—the question that means everything, and may just destroy you if the answer is known.

"Who am I?" you ask.

The old fortune-teller leans in close and speaks in a whisper. "Not who you think you are."

You close your cold eyes and try to deny it. You have memories. You remember friends and a family. You remember a life.

"But that life is not yours," says the woman, reading your thoughts. "That life belonged to someone else."

You put your head down into your hands and weep, feeling stone-cold from the top of your head to the pale bottoms of your feet. There are no tears when you cry. And now you must admit to yourself that there never have been tears.

"It's not true!" you say.

The old woman reaches out her cup of hot tea and pours it across your arm. It should burn you, but it does not. Instead it just rolls off your pocked, hardened flesh.

"You see?" she says. "Your body tells the truth, even if your heart won't." Then she gently takes your hand. "Come, I'll take you home."

You stand, spirit broken, and she leads you out of the dark stone mausoleum, into the wind that slithers like a serpent through the endless hills of the graveyard. She leads you past tall stones, so old that the names cannot be read. At last you arrive at a dark pedestal. You can no longer deny the truth, for the memory comes back to you as you stare at it.

There used to be a statue on that pedestal. The perfect likeness of someone who died much too young. For a hundred years the statue stood over the grave as a monument for family to remember. Until family aged and were buried before the statue's unmoving eyes. Until the world moved on, and the rains and winds etched off the name carved in the gravestone beneath your feet.

And you forgot who you were.

So you stepped down from that place, forgetting that you were stone, searching for someone who could tell you your name.

"You place is here," Madame Loveless tells you, "on that pedestal, guarding the child beneath."

"But the child's forgotten," you tell her mournfully. "I'm forgotten."

The old woman considers this, and says, "I've given you the past. Now I'll give you the future." Then she looks into your eyes and tells you this: "Years from now, when I am nothing but dust, and time takes over this graveyard, you will be remembered. You will be taken from here and will stand in a warm place of honor. You will have value too great to measure. And people will visit. Thousands! They will not know who you are, but they will come just the same, and look upon you with admiration. It will come to pass . . . if only you can wait."

You know the old woman speaks the truth, because in this world of change and lost memories, time brings all things full circle. That which was discarded becomes priceless. Those who were abandoned will someday be loved—if you can hold on till that day.

And so you hope, because hope is all you have as you climb the granite pedestal and take the pose you know so well. Hope of a new life beyond the boundaries of time. Hope of a special place and purpose beyond this lonely grave.

Hope enough to give you the courage . . . to wait.

I'M NOT MYSELF TODAY

You are not in your right mind . . . and you're afraid to find out how wrong your mind truly is.

—from "The Body Electric"

The Body Electric

You are not in your right mind.

You knew it from the moment the lightning struck you, and as you stumble through the whipping, windswept branches of December-bare trees, you are certain your mind has gone terribly wrong. You know because the trees were green and alive in a summer squall only a moment before. Now they are as dormant as death, and the rain is now mixed with frigid, stinging sleet. You know because it was daylight when the lightning descended upon you, crashing from the heavens like the fist of God. It was only seconds earlier . . . but now it is night, not day, and the only thing lighting your path is the blinding flashes that the angry clouds discharge.

Stumbling over sharp rocks, you count the seconds between lightning and thunder. Five seconds. A mile away. The storm is moving off, beginning to ease, and although you feel relief, one question fills your thoughts. Why weren't you hurt when the lightning struck you? It had blinded you for an instant—you felt it coursing around you and through you, penetrating your mind, your spirit—and then it was gone, leaving summer turned to winter and day turned to night.

No, you are not in your right mind . . . and you're afraid to find out how wrong your mind truly is.

The rushing of water fills your ears, and you burst through the trees, almost falling into a river swollen by the icy rain. To your right is a small brick house, its windows lit by a gentle flickering light. You don't know this place, but it is far more inviting than the forest or the river. A woman stands on the porch; you can see her as you approach. She's wrapped in a heavy winter shawl.

"Al?" she cries. "Al, is that you? Get in here right away! You must be crazy to be gallivanting about in a storm like this!"

As you get closer, you figure the woman will see that she's mistaken. You are not Al, whoever Al might be. Stepping onto the covered porch, you shake the rain from yourself like a wet dog.

"Hi," you say. "Would it be all right if I came inside? I have to call home."

She looks at you with an odd expression. "Call home what?"

You're not sure what she means—but you're more troubled by your own voice than by anything she says. The timbre of your voice is completely wrong. You must be getting a cold.

"Maybe I should just text my father," you say, a bit put off by the woman at the door.

She shakes her head. "Your father has enough text with all those newspapers he reads. Come inside, dinner's ready."

Does she know my father? you wonder. Probably not—because your dad never reads newspapers; he gets all his news from his phone, but you realize that you couldn't text him if you wanted to. Your phone is dead, fried by the lightning. You'll need to call your parents from someone else's phone. Although by the look of things, these are landline kind of people.

Inside, the house is warmed by a fireplace and lit by flickering bulbs. No, not bulbs—gas lamps, like the kind they used long ago.

"That's weird," you say, clearing your throat to get rid of its strange sound.

In the kitchen, a man sits behind a newspaper. The table before him is set with a serving platter of chicken and dumplings, making you suddenly realize how hungry you are.

The woman hands you a towel and a beige button-down shirt. Its stitching feels funny; so does its collar. Just a little bit too small. "Better change into this before you catch your death of cold," she says.

"Hurry up, Al, so we can all eat," says the man.

"My name's not Al."

The man lowers his newspaper, not sure he has heard correctly, and looks you over. "One week working for the railroad, and the boy's already putting on airs!"

"Perhaps you'd prefer we call you Tom," says the woman, "or Tommy."

But that's not your name either. You are about to inform them of this, but then you catch a glimpse of yourself in a big hallway mirror, and the truth hits you like a second bolt of lightning.

You are in your right mind after all. Unfortunately, you're in the wrong body.

The kid in the mirror is not the one you saw in the mirror this morning. You look at your hands and your arms. You peel off your wet shirt and examine your birthmarks, freckles, and moles, which are as unknown to you as stars over an alien sky. You slip on the dry shirt and button it so you don't have to see that unfamiliar body.

"Well, what's it gonna be, boy?" says the man. "Do we call you by your first or middle name, now?"

Too dumbfounded to speak, you sit down in the hard wooden chair. Then, after several deep breaths, you say, "You can call me Al." Which, as you recall, is the title of a song—but you suspect these people will never have heard of it.

Satisfied, they continue to call you Al, and with nothing else to do, you begin to eat.

Later, the woman douses the light in a bedroom she claims is yours. "Good night, Al," she says. "Don't forget to say your prayers."

The woman's name, you've learned, is Nancy, but you've also learned that there's another term by which you should address her.

"Good night . . . Mother." You feel so strange calling her that; the words stick in your throat.

After she's gone, you study the room. There are several books on shelves, a handheld chalkboard with handwriting that's far neater than your own.

Everything you see makes you realize just how desperate your situation is—but nothing could have been worse than the glimpse you got of the man's newspaper. The date was December 3 . . . 1860.

Now you know why the lightning did not harm you—its powerful electrical surge was absorbed elsewhere, short-circuiting time and space, thrusting you into the body of an unremarkable boy named Al, in the unremarkable town of Port Huron, Michigan.

A void deepens within you as you try to fathom all the things lost. Your own parents are over a hundred years from being conceived. Your great-great-grandmother has not even been born, and your friends are lost in a future too distant for people here to imagine. There are no cars, no phones, no internet, no movie theaters. They haven't figured out how to record music yet.

Say your prayers, the woman told you, and so you kneel at the foot of your bed and pray, your eyes filling with tears, because if there ever was a time to pray, this is it.

You dream of fast cars and fighter jets, but you wake only to find that the world you now occupy considers such things to be wild flights of fancy. Absurd science fiction.

"Hurry, Al," you hear the woman you must call "Mother" shout to you from the kitchen. "Better get up or you'll be late for work."

Work, you think. Yes—that's right—last night your "father" said you worked for the railroad . . . but doing what? How could you show up there, not even knowing your job? So you head into the kitchen and strike up a conversation with your mother, who cooks up some dark pancakes she calls flapjacks, hoping to tease out some intel about your job.

"I'm tired of working for the railroad," you tell her. She takes it in stride, without even looking up at you.

"It's only been a week. Give it time."

"Yes," you say, "but it's the same old thing every day. . . ."

"No, it's not," she says as she serves you up some piping-hot flapjacks. "The newspaper is different every day. If you get there early enough, maybe you can read the paper before you start selling them to passengers."

You gloat happily. *So, I sell newspapers on the train.* "I guess you're right," you say. "But it's such a long walk to the train station."

She scoffs. "What a complainer you are! I would hardly call a half mile downriver a long walk!"

After scarfing down your flapjacks, you slip out the door, with all the information you need. "Later, Mom!"

"What's later?" she asks, not quite getting your futuristic lingo. You're out the door too quickly to explain yourself.

"Morning, Al," says the round, runny-nosed man who hands you a stack of papers. "Better run, the 8:40's about to pull out. Miss the train, miss a day's pay." The bundle of papers feels lead-heavy. Are you expected to carry these things?

You hear a train whistle, and the man glares at you. "Waiting for an invitation, son?"

Heaving the bundle of papers on a shoulder, you plod off toward the train. About halfway there, the steam engine begins to move—you can hear a series of clanks running down the spine of the train as each coupler tugs at the car behind it. The wheels grind into motion, and the whole train begins to move.

"Oh no!" You pick up the pace, but the train's already pulling out of the station. There's a baggage compartment, its door wide open. You cut a diagonal path, hoping to intercept the door before the train picks up too much speed.

Your legs pumping at full strength, you reach the open doorway and hurl the newspapers into the car. So far so good. You leap, figuring you just made it—but your legs are too tired to give you any momentum. You fall short and your fingernails scrape on the wooden floor of the baggage car. Halfway in and halfway out, your legs dangle beneath the spinning wheels of the accelerating train. You're slipping! If you fall, you'll be sliced in two! No surgeon in this time—or even your own—would be able to save you.

Your nails slip, and your body begins to fall beneath the train. You scream—

—and a pair of hands reaches out, grabbing you by the ears.

"I've got you, Al," the deep voice of the conductor says. He tugs you up by your ears so hard, you feel something snap inside your head. Your ears burn, they're ringing—but he doesn't release his grip. He lifts you by your agonized ears into the baggage car. The stinging pain in your ears brings a flood of tears to your eyes.

"Close call," says the conductor, not even noticing. You feel like screaming at him, but instead you try not to show the pain. After all, you should be grateful; the man saved your life.

Thanking him, you take your stack of newspapers and begin making your way through the stuffy, overheated train, selling your papers for two pennies apiece.

The passengers are all what you expect. Well-dressed businessmen, dainty women. The women are strongly perfumed, but it doesn't hide the stench of sweat already in the air. "Someone ought to invent deodorant," you mumble to yourself.

A man next to you chuckles and says, "Why don't *you*, Al? You've got enough chemicals in that cellar of yours to do the job!" The man must be a friend of your family. You return his smile as if you know him.

"Hey," he suggests, "maybe you can invent something that'll stop people from sweating!"

"An antiperspirant."

The man laughs, thinking it all very funny. However, there's someone else on the train who takes you seriously. He's a kid—same age as you—with reddish hair and a piercing gaze. He's staring at you from the far end of the car. It makes you uncomfortable.

"Paper?" you ask him, as you reach his end of the car.

The boy shrugs, and speaks in a heavy Scottish brogue. "No point in it. It's all old news."

"Suit yourself."

You're about to go on into the next car, when the kid says something that stops you in your tracks.

"What I wouldn't give for Wi-Fi right about now," he says.

You snap your head around so quickly, it makes your aching ears ring louder.

"What did you say?"

"I'm thinkin' that you heard me." The kid's smile is about as wide as the train. You look to the woman sitting next to him, who isn't fazed in the least. "That's me mum," he tells you. "She's deaf, you know—but even if she could hear, she'd be thinkin' it's gibberish we're talking."

You sit down in a seat facing his, dropping your pile of newspapers. "You're from the future!"

"Not anymore," he tells you. "I'm from the present now. And a fine place it is, too!"

"Fine?" you say, incredulous. "No cars, no electricity, no phones. What's fine about it?"

"The possibilities, Al! The possibilities."

"How come you know my name?"

He leans back, silent for a moment, grinning all the while, like he knows something you don't. Then he holds out his hand. "My name's Aleck," he says. "Got switched here in a thunderstorm, same as you, I'll fathom. I even had to learn me accent."

"No way!"

"I convinced my mother to make this trip to America. I told

her I wanted to see the world. But the truth is, I came to find you!"

"Me?"

Then he leans in and whispers. "We're going to be great adversaries, you and I. I thought we should begin with a friendship. Like two boxers shaking hands before the fight."

"I don't understand."

"Aye, but you will," he says, so sure of himself it makes you angry.

Then a man clears this throat behind you, and you turn to see the conductor standing in the aisle, hands on his hips, not too pleased with you.

You stand and pick up your bundle of newspapers.

"Sorry, sir," you say, not even knowing his name. "I'll get back to selling papers."

"You'd better do just that," he says in a voice suitably menacing, then he turns to Aleck.

"I'm sorry about that, young Master Bell."

"That's all right. I rather enjoy chatting."

It takes a moment, but you make the connection, like a circuit finally closing. "Aleck Bell? As in Alexander Graham Bell?"

He nods. "Remember the name," he says. "You'll be hearing no end of it soon."

The train vibrates and rolls beneath your feet, but it's more than just the train. You feel dizzy and dazzled by the presence of such greatness before you. Alexander Graham Bell! You even did a report on him, a couple of years back. It's hard to believe that this grinning kid sitting here is only a few short years away from inventing the telephone!

The conductor roughly nudges you away. "Move on! The next car needs papers too."

"Goodbye, Al," says young Master Bell. "Or should I call you Tom?"

And in a daze you say, "Call me Al. Everybody calls me Al."

• • •

With your feet still feeling as if they're on the train, you walk home. It was a long day, but that's okay. It's given you time to think; time to accept the end of your old life, and the beginning of a new one. You wonder how the real Al will do, over a century and a half from now, when he finds himself trapped in your old body, wearing Nikes, playing your Xbox, and trying to comprehend the mysteries of the web. You wish you could be there, but you know that you won't. You'll die somewhere around 1930, a very old man. That much you remember.

"Good evening, Mother," you say as you enter, giving her a peck on the cheek.

She laughs, looking up from the dinner she's preparing. "What's gotten into you?"

"Nothing," you tell her. "It's just a great time to be alive."

Then you open the door to the cellar. In the dim light spilling through the cellar window, you see a table down there, covered with jars full of chemicals and all kinds of little gadgets. You take a deep breath of joyful anticipation. The future rests down in that cellar—and someday there will be records, there will be movies, and there will be electric light.

"Thomas Alva Edison!" calls your mother. "Are you going to spend the whole evening tinkering around in that cellar again?"

You toss her a grin before you descend the stairs. "Remember the name," you tell her. "You'll be hearing no end of it soon."

Mail Merge

<***Welcome.You are in "Hyperwarp" chat room***>

Barbarella: So, like, what if there were an infinite number of parallel universes?

Wyrmhole: Yeah, but how could you get from one to another?

Morlock: If you could get to another universe, they wouldn't be parallel anymore.

StarWart: How do you parallel park in a parallel universe?

Barbarella: If you could move faster than the speed of light, you could punch a hole in this universe.

Morlock: Very carefully.

StarWart: :)

Spacecadet: My dad once got hit by a guy trying to parallel park.

Wyrmhole: Was he from a parallel universe?

Spacecadet: No, I think he was from Jersey.

Morlock: But you can't move faster than the speed of light.

MCsquared: Yeah—time dilation. Einstein predicted that.

StarWart: Jersey kind of is a parallel universe, know what I'm sayin?

Spacecadet: What's time dilation?

StarWart: It's what happens when your teacher is boring. A single period drags on for days.

Spacecadet: I had my eyes dilated once. Things were blurry for an hour.

Barbarella: It means that time slows down the closer you get to the speed of light.

MCsquared: At the speed of light time stops.

Wyrmhole: And you become heavier.

<***PIKA-CHELSEA has entered the room***>

Spacecadet: So if you go real slow, you lose weight?

PIKA-CHELSEA: HELLO. WHO'S IN HERE?

Barbarella: Mass, not weight.

Wyrmhole: Hi, Pika-Chelsea.

Spacecadet: I went to midnight Mass last Christmas.

StarWart: So how do you reach a parallel universe?

Spacecadet: My friends said the pope would show up, but he didn't.

Barbarella: You don't.

Morlock: Hi, Pika-che.

PIKA-CHELSEA: WHO ARE YOU PEOPLE?

Wyrmhole: Maybe time travel can send you to alternate dimensions.

Morlock: Maybe there's a different dimension for every moment in time.

MCsquared: Huh?

PIKA-CHELSEA: WHAT IS EVERYONE TALKING ABOUT?

StarWart: Stop shouting, Pika.

Morlock: Think about it. You go back in time, but you're really not going back in time, you're jumping to a parallel dimension where everything's exactly the same as this universe, just ten years back.

PIKA-CHELSEA: IS THIS THE POKÉMON CHAT ROOM?

MCsquared: Why ten years?

Spacecadet: I do NOT want to relive the last ten years!

PIKA-CHELSEA: I GOT SOME CLASSIC POKÉMON CARDS TO SELL.

Morlock: It doesn't have to be ten years.

PIKA-CHELSEA: I GOT CHARIZARD—HE'S REALLY RARE.

Barbarella: If you go back before you were born, you could become your own father.

Morlock: I'd rather die.

Spacecadet: I still don't understand.

PIKA-CHELSEA: I GOT A MISPRINTED BULBASAUR—WORTH A LOT!

Barbarella: Take a hike, Pika-Chelsea, you're in the wrong room.

StarWart: Wait, did she say Charizard??

Barbarella: Stay on topic, StarWart.

Wyrmhole: I understand your parallel temporal dimension theory, Morlock. In fact, I have a similar theory myself.

Morlock: I'm glad someone understands.

Wyrmhole: There's a different universe for every single quantum of time, right?

Morlock: Yeah, that's what I'm saying.

Wyrmhole: What about infinite universes that are identical, except for one small difference?

Morlock: I was just about to say that!

StarWart: Isn't Quantum an airline?

Morlock: I think that's Qantas.

Barbarella: They say time and space are interchangeable.

Spacecadet: I flew Qantas once. I had the chicken lasagna.

StarWart: My mom says I'm good at taking up time and space.

PIKA-CHELSEA: WHAT POKÉMON CARDS DO YOU HAVE?

Barbarella: Will somebody punt her out of this room?

MCsquared: Einstein predicted parallel universes.

StarWart: No he didn't.

MCsquared: Yes he did. It says so on Wikipedia.

StarWart: I rest my case.

<***PIKA-CHELSEA has left the room***>

Barbarella: Good riddance.

MCsquared: Interesting fact: Did you know Einstein was eaten alive by piranhas?

StarWart: No he wasn't!

Barbarella: And then there are black holes . . .

MCsquared: Well, he could have been, in a parallel universe. See what I did there?

StarWart: My parents say my bedroom is a black hole.

Spacecadet: I took a bus tour through a black hole once. It wasn't that bad.

Wyrmhole: You can't go in a black hole, bozo—you would be crushed to subatomic particles.

Morlock: You can't go into a black hole, dweeb—you would be crushed to subatomic particles.

Wyrmhole: Hey, we both said the same thing! How did you know I was going to say that?

Morlock: I'm spychic.

StarWart: Black holes are in space, Spacecadet.

Spacecadet: Can you see them with a telescope?

Morlock: I mean psychic.

StarWart: If you could, they wouldn't be black.

MCsquared: Stephen Hawking predicted black holes.

Barbarella: I like spy chic better.

StarWart: :)

Morlock: Stephen Hawking was cool.

Wyrmhole: Stephen Hawking was cool.

Morlock: There we go again. Spy chic!

Wyrmhole: Spy chic!

StarWart: My Mom was a spy chick.

Morlock: Hawking's amazing—the greatest mind in the world, in a damaged body.

Spacecadet: What about green holes and blue holes?

Barbarella: I think maybe Morlock and Wyrmhole are the same person.

Wyrmhole: As opposed to me, the greatest body in the world, with a damaged mind.

MCsquared: They should have frozen his head like they did with Disney.

StarWart: That's a myth. Disney wasn't frozen. But they did keep Einstein's brain in a jar without his permission.

Barbarella: Hey—maybe Morlock and Wyrmhole are the same person in parallel universes!

Morlock: Not very likely.

Wyrmhole: Not very likely.

Morlock: There it goes again.

Wyrmhole: There it goes again.

Spacecadet: Didn't Stephen Hawking write "The Shining"?

StarWart: No, that was Stephen King. Close but no Haw.

MCsquared: Haw Haw.

Barbarella: What do you think happens when two parallel universes collide?

StarWart: Traffic jam on the interstellar highway.

MCsquared: Big explosion.

Morlock: The end of life as we know it.

Barbarella: Maybe not. Maybe one just absorbs the other.

Wyrmhole: You mean kind of like two raindrops that get too close?

Morlock: Kind of like raindrops that get too close.

Barbarella: Wow—you guys really are kindred spirits.

StarWart: My mom says I'm in my own universe. A universal pain.

Spacecadet: I went to Universal Studios once. I threw up a little on the Harry Potter ride.

Wyrmhole: Hey, Morlock—are you really psychic, or are you just repeating me?

Morlock: Neither—I'm typing the same things you are, at the same time.

MCsquared: Stephen Hawking was my next-door neighbor.

StarWart: No he wasn't!

MCsquared: He was–in a parallel universe. Einstein was too. Before the piranhas, that is.

StarWart: And in a parallel universe, I come over to kick your ass. Oh wait—that's this universe.

Barbarella: What if you guys really are parallel beings?

Morlock: We couldn't be, we'd have to have more in common.

Wyrmhole: Nah, we'd have to have more things in common.

MCsquared: You'll have to find me first!

Morlock: Hey, Wyrmhole—what's your mother's name?

Wyrmhole: Angela

Morlock: That's my mother's name too!

Wyrmhole: You're lying!

Morlock: Am not!

MCsquared: Am not!

Wyrmhole: Oh, now MCsquared is repeating us too.

MCsquared: Am not!

StarWart: Guys, this is a sinking ship, and I'm bailing.

Barbarella: Bye, StarWart.

<★★★StarWart has left the room★★★>

Wyrmhole: Do you have a sister, Morlock?

Morlock: Yeah—her name's Taylor.

Wyrmhole: No way—that's my sister's name too!

Spacecadet: I saw Taylor Swift in concert once.

Barbarella: You guys are making this up, aren't you?

MCsquared: You're all a bunch of liars!

Wyrmhole: No, we're telling the truth.

Morlock: No, it's all true!

<***MCsquared has left the room***>

Barbarella: Two colliding universes . . . do you think they would just merge?

Morlock: I hope so, better than blowing up.

Wyrmhole: I hope so, it's better than blowing up.

Barbarella: You guys are really starting to freak me out.

Wyrmhole: Maybe great minds just think alike.

Morlock: Hey, great minds think alike.

Spacecadet: This is all too confusing and I've got homework. Bye.

Morlock: See ya.

Wyrmhole: See ya.

<***Spacecadet has left the room***>

Barbarella: So, now that it's just the three of us, what's really going on here?

Wyrmhole: Beats me.

Morlock: Beats me.

Barbarella: Are you guys friends, just sitting next to each other, laughing at the rest of us?

Wyrmhole: No, I'm in Idaho—I don't know where he's from.

Morlock: No, I'm from Odahi—I don't know where he's from.

Wyrmhole: Odahi?

Morlock: Idaho?

Barbarella: Parallel universes, with just a few small differences. Cool.

Wyrmhole: There's no such place as Odahi.

Morlock: There's no such place as Idaho.

Barbarella: This is wild—I'm gonna go post about this. TTYL.

Wyrmhole: No don't go!

Morlock: Don't leave us like this.

Wyrmhole: It's too scary.

Morlock: It's too scary.

<***Barbarella has left the room***>

Wyrmhole: Now what are we going to do?

Morlock: Now what are we going to do?

Wyrmhole: Stop that!

Morlock: Stop that!

Wyrmhole: No you stop it!

Morlock: No you stop it!

Wyrmhole: I feel kind of weird . . . do you feel weird?

Morlock: I feel kind of weird . . . do you feel weird?

Wyrmhole: Like the air is changing

Morlock: Like the air is changing

Wyrmhole: And I'm seeing double.

Morlock: And I'm seeing double.

Wyrmlock: Wait. Wait. I feel better now.

Wyrmlock: Hello?

Wyrmlock: Hey, is anyone else here?

Wyrmlock: Anybody?

Wyrmlock: Darn. I hate it when I'm the only one left in the room.

<***Wyrmlock has left the room***>

The Elsewhere Boutique

ONLY THIRTEEN SHOPPING DAYS UNTIL CHRISTMAS.

A giant sign at the entrance to North Bluff Plaza proclaims the words in big block letters. People rush across the slush-filled parking lot into the mall, as if their lives depend on getting inside. I guess my brother and I are no different; we're on a mission as well. We still have one Christmas gift left to buy.

"We'll be waiting in lines all day," whines my younger brother, Paul, who would much rather be watching football. "Can't we just do it some other time, Georgia?"

"There is no other time," I tell him, and drag his complaining ass across the melting snow, into the mall.

Once in the wide, warm corridor of the mall, we try to figure out which way to go. Should we go to the department store on the east end, where you need a gas mask to get through the perfume department, or should we go to the department store on the west end, where the clothes are so cheap, they tear when you try to take them off the hanger?

That's when we first notice a shop we haven't seen in all our previous shopping expeditions. It's just a tiny store, nestled between a card shop and an art gallery. A small sign over the entrance reads THE ELSEWHERE BOUTIQUE. Even though every other store is crawling with customers, no one ventures into the odd little place—perhaps because they're not advertising any Christmas sales.

"You want to check it out?" I ask Paul. He wrinkles his nose, clearly not wanting to set foot in anything called a boutique.

"I'd rather go to the arcade."

Still, I nudge him in, and we cross the threshold onto the clean tile floor of the empty shop. On the wall I can see row after row of little bottles—tiny things carved in crystal. They're shelved floor to ceiling, and the shelves stretch back as far as I can see. Apparently this store is much larger than it appears, recessing deep into undiscovered regions of the mall.

"It's perfume!" says Paul. "That's all, it's just a perfume store. Let's go."

But as I sniff the air, I don't smell the slightest hint of fragrance. If it isn't perfume, what *is* in those little vials?

"May I help you?" says the clerk—the only one in the store. He's a tall man, with a polished dome of a head so void of hair it actually shines, reflecting all the colors of the vials on the wall.

"We're looking for a Christmas present," I explain, "something for our father."

The shopkeeper smiles warmly. "How delightful! It's usually the parents, hurrying about to buy things for the children. Nice to see things reversed."

"Yeah," sighs Paul. "And we can't just go out and get any old thing—we have to get something 'meaningful.'"

The bald man nods knowingly. "I see. It certainly is hard to find meaningful presents nowadays."

"Yeah, tell me about it," I say, thinking back to Dad's birthday. We got him a birthday card that featured dead flowers, a pipe, and a wooden duck. None of the things on that card had anything to do with our dad. In fact, come to think of it, none of those things have to do with anyone's dad that I know. As for the present, we got him a socket wrench set—which was about as meaningful as the wooden-duck birthday card.

"Well, if *meaning* is what you're looking for," says the shopkeeper, "then you've come to the perfect place."

"So what *is* all this stuff?" Paul asks.

"It's everything!" the man says. "And nothing." Then he smiles with a grin of complete satisfaction. "It's elsewhere. Perfect and absolute."

He looks at us as if what he's said makes sense—as if it's all very obvious, and we'd have to be fools not to understand. I look at Paul, Paul looks at me, we both read the cluelessness in each other's eyes and then turn back to the shiny-headed man, and I say what is perhaps the only thing that can be said in this situation: "Can we have a free sample?"

"Well, I suppose," he says, "but it will have to be a very small sample." He turns to the wall behind him, moving his fingers in the air as if he's playing the piano. "What to choose, what to choose . . ." He scans the rows of tiny bottles and finally pulls one off an eye-level shelf. It's green crystal, but the sharp cuts in its pattern reflect a deep blue. He hands the bottle to me, Paul pulls it away, and I pull it back from Paul, giving him a dirty look. As the older sister, I do have some privileges, and one of them is inspecting fragile things first. I hold it up to my eye, watching how it reflects the light. I can't see anything through the refracting pattern of its design. There seems to be nothing inside—no liquid, no powder . . . nothing.

"Exactly what is it?" I ask. Paul pulls it from me again and examines it himself.

"Read the tag," says the man.

I look at the small tag tied around the bottle's neck. The tiny printing reads:

LOCALIZED BINARY RECONFIGURATION

Finally I dare to say the words that I know will make me feel like an idiot, but I have to say them anyway.

"I don't get it."

The man looks at us with mild pity in his eyes and proceeds to tell us something that I don't quite understand, and probably never will. "I deal in events that never occurred," says the shopkeeper. "Situations that might have happened but didn't, choices that were never made, moments that were lost. All the might-have-beens, large and small—those are the things I sell." Then he gently takes the bottle from us, holding it up to the light. "Here's a particularly small might-have-been: 'localized binary reconfiguration.' It sounds complicated, but it's really rather simple. It merely means that the 'elsewhere' contained in this bottle will only affect the two people who open it." He hands it to me. "Go ahead, it's your free sample."

I look at the bottle once more, trying to decide if this strange, looming man is trying to have some fun at our expense—yet he seems so sincere and so serious that it's hard not to believe him . . . and both Paul and I are desperately curious.

"Go on, Georgia." Paul's eyes dart nervously back and forth. "Go on, open it up."

I hand him the bottle. "You hold it, I'll pull the stopper."

Paul holds the bottle carefully, then I reach for the delicately carved crystalline stopper and pull it from the tiny bottle. It makes no sound. I look inside it . . . empty. Nothing inside. Nothing at all.

"There!" says the bald man, with excited satisfaction in his voice. "How do you like it?"

"How do I like what?"

"Why, your free 'elsewhere,' of course."

This guy's beginning to make me mad. I turn to my sister. "Paula, do you have any idea what he's talking about?"

Paula plays with her pigtails and shakes her head. "I don't see anything."

"Ha-ha, very funny," I tell the shopkeeper. "If you're trying to run a scam, it's not a very good one."

"You misunderstand, George," he says. "That is your name, George . . . isn't it?"

I try to stare him down. "Free sample, my ass! I guess you get what you pay for."

He laughs at that—a deep, hearty laugh that seems far too resonant for a man so painfully thin. Now I'm really getting mad. It's bad enough I have to miss football practice to go out shopping. I don't have to stand here being laughed at by a scrawny, funny-looking man.

I grab my sister's hand, fully prepared to walk right out of the shop, when the shopkeeper says, "Of course you won't be able to tell the difference. That's the whole point!"

I turn to him. "The point of what?"

"Don't you see? Once 'elsewhere' becomes 'here,' it's not elsewhere anymore."

"Just stop the double-talk," I demand, not wanting him to get the last word.

He holds the little bottle, plugging it up with the stopper once more. "Your old reality is now contained in this bottle. But since it's no longer real, you can't possibly remember it." Then he puts the bottle back on the shelf. I have to admit, as much as I want to shrug it off, I can't keep my eyes off that green bottle. I can't stop wondering what it contains. I want to leave, but I won't. Not yet.

"Okay," I say, "how about another free sample?"

"How can I do business if I give things away for free?" says ol' Chrome Dome, not as friendly as he was a moment ago.

I cross my arms stubbornly. "Do you want us to buy something from you or not?"

He sighs. "Very well." Then he turns to the wall behind him.

"No," I say. "I want to pick."

He tosses me an irritated gaze, then waves his hand, gesturing to the rest of the store. "Help yourself, George."

I begin to browse. Each delicate crystalline bottle has its own shape and texture—and each one has a small tag on it. While Paula keeps looking at the bright, shiny ones, my eyes are attracted to a row of jagged ones—shiny black obsidian bottles. I pick one up and hold it carefully in my fingers.

"You have expensive tastes," the shopkeeper says. "But a promise is a promise. You may sample this one if you like."

I look at the tag. It says, in that tiny, ballpoint-pen printing:

THERMONUCLEAR WAR—1998

"Hmm!" says the bald man, raising an eyebrow. "Nineteen ninety-eight, a very good year."

I take a firm grasp of the black stopper, pull it out, and glance inside. Nothing. Empty again. I blow into it and my own breath comes back to meet me.

"You know, someone really oughta put you out of business," I tell him.

They say there's a sucker born every minute, and I guess I'm one of them. I glance outside to the shredded remnants of the old mall. My parents say it once had a glass roof, but that shattered years ago. Now the cold snow of the nuclear winter just pours in night and day. I hear it was a real nice place once—but that was long before I was born, before the war in '98. I've seen pictures, though.

I take a glance at my radiation gauge and get mad at myself for wasting time in this store. I'm almost at my radiation limit, which means I won't have time to look for something for Dad today. I'll probably have to get him an apple again, like last year—and those things are so darned expensive. Christmas presents. That's one of the things I hate about being an only child, I don't have anyone to help me pick out gifts.

I prepare to zip my radiation suit closed and head out through the store's air lock, but the bald man grabs me by the scruff of my neck and pulls me back.

"Not so fast, George," he says. "I've given you two free samples. The least you could do is offer to purchase something."

Now I begin to get scared. Mom and Dad were right, I should

never have ventured to the surface. People are crazy up here, their minds rotted by fallout. Now I can think of nothing but getting to the safety of my home. I reach into my pocket and pull out a wad of bills and throw it at him.

"Here!" I say. "Here, take whatever you want, just let me out of here." Still, he holds me firmly and tallies the bills on the counter.

"Thirty-four dollars. Very well. You can choose anything from this shelf." And he points to a shelf on the wall filled with bright, colorful bottles. I grab the first one I see: a sky-blue one, with glimmering purple refractions. Anything to get out of his bony grasp.

"Good choice," he says, still holding on to me tightly. "Now there's only one bit of business left."

Then his hands seem to reach across the room. It has to be an optical illusion, but still, it seems as if they're stretching—as if they're rubber. He grabs the sample bottles I've opened, and since he doesn't have a free hand, he puts them into his mouth and pulls the stopper with his teeth, like a grenade—first from the black one, then from the green one. At last he lets me go. I lose my balance and slip to the floor. When I get up again, he has already stoppered the bottles and put them back into their places.

I shake my hair out of my eyes and grasp Paul's hand—there are very few times Paul will let me grab his hand, but he's just as shaken as I am by the strange man and the empty bottles. For once, Paul doesn't mind his big sister protecting him.

"Come on, Paul. Let's just go home. We'll find something for Dad some other day."

"But you've already got a gift for your father," says the shopkeeper. "A perfect one."

"Yeah, whatever!"

Then the shopkeeper smiles far too broadly, as if his mouth is made of rubber as well. It's as if everything about him is changeable and can stretch to any shape he likes.

I hurry with Paul out of the store and back into the busy shuffle of the stuffy, overheated mall, and then out into the cold, clean air of the parking lot.

Out on the street, we sit at the bus stop, lost in our own thoughts, watching the steam of our winter breath drift into the air and disappear.

I try to get the Elsewhere Boutique out of my mind, but the more I think about it, the more it troubles me. What if it were possible to bottle up all the things that might have happened but never did? And if those things were ever released into the world, how would we know that anything had changed?

"That guy was weird," Paul says, and shakes his head as if trying to shake all the weirdness out.

"He sure played a head game on us, didn't he?" I take a look at the little bottle I'm holding. Thirty-four dollars for a bottle of nothing. Well, at least it's pretty. Then I notice the little dangling tag, and curious, I turn it over to see what it says. The card reads:

BILLIONAIRE BUSINESSMAN

"Yeah, sure," I say aloud, barely able to believe that I wasted my money on this dumb little bottle. Well, maybe it won't be a total loss. I'm sure Dad will find some use for it.

Ralphy Sherman's Inside Story

Of course you don't have to believe it, but this is a true story. As true as my dad being a spy, and my mom being abducted by aliens. And if you don't believe me, you can ask my sister.

I suppose I should start before the frogs and the ants. I suppose I should start even before my cousins arrived.

As usual, Dad was away on top secret business when we got news that my cousins were coming, and Mom, well, we haven't seen her much since she was taken from our space-time continuum. So it was only me, my sister Roxanne, and our new nanny all alone in our immense house. (Actually, our nannies are always new, because none of them has ever lasted more than a couple of weeks, can't say why.) At any rate, we got an email from Aunt Millicent and Uncle Bernard that they were going on vacation, and since we had our big, empty house all to ourselves, could we watch our darling little cousins for them?

"Ugh," said Roxanne when she read the note. "I think I'm gonna hurl breakfast."

I knew how she felt, but Olga the nanny had no sense of the problem.

"They are your cousins," she said in a thick accent. She was from an Eastern European country where family was never turned away. "You should be happy to see your cousins."

To which I replied, "You don't know Candida and Bratt."

"Nonsense—I cannot wait to meet them," Olga chimed. "They cannot be worse than the two of you." Which in most cases, would probably be true—after all, most of our nannies leave with a scream, rather than a smile on their lips. But rumor had it that Bratt and Candida had populated entire mental institutions with the mentally—and sometimes physically—shattered remnants of their former nannies.

Roxanne and I counted the days until they arrived, like convicts numbering the days till execution. Two weeks . . . one week . . . and finally the dreaded day was here. Similar to the beginning of most natural disasters, I could hear the neighborhood dogs bark as their car pulled up in front of our house. The doorbell rang, and we found them there, deposited on our doorstep, with three massive suitcases. It looked as if they were prepared for a long siege.

Aunt Millicent was already running back to the car, which Uncle Bernard kept impatiently idling by the curb. "I'm sure you'll all have a wonderful time together," lied Aunt Millicent, trying to brush Bratt's sticky fingerprints off her mink as she ran. She leapt into the car, and Uncle Bernard burned rubber even before the door was closed, in no small hurry to escape. So here they were, standing in our foyer. Seven-year-old Candida was in her typical pink frilly dress. She had a smile from ear to ear and looked like an emoji. Beside her stood five-year-old Bratt. His hair was even messier and his face dirtier than I remembered, which was quite an accomplishment. His real name had once been Brett, but so many people called him Bratt that even his parents started calling him that. In fact, they might have had his name legally changed, although I'm not certain. In any case, there stood Bratt with his left index finger lodged so deeply into his nose that he was pulling boogers from the next county.

"Well, hello!" chimed Olga the nanny, throwing out her arms to greet my cousins as if they were normal children. Bratt gave her a grimace, revealing his missing front teeth.

"I'm bored," he said. "This place is boring. And you're ugly."

Olga was not thrilled by the observation.

Candida shook her head with a broad, knowing smile.

"Bratt," she said, "you're so incorrigible." Which was one of the tamer words people used to describe Bratt. Then Candida turned to my sister. She ratcheted her smile up a few notches.

"Hey, Roxanne," she said brightly. "I brought my Golly Miss Molly Happy Time Plastic Tea Set. Let's go have a tea party!"

Roxanne narrowed her eyes to slits. "I'd rather die," she said, but Candida just giggled happily.

"Oh, Roxanne, you're so funny!" she said. "Isn't she funny, Helga?"

"Olga," corrected our nanny.

"Whatever!" said Candida, and she dragged Roxanne into the den for tea torture. As for Bratt, he was already swinging from the chandelier.

The day quickly became a festival of shattered glass and splintered wood, compliments of Bratt. Five broken banister rails, four demolished vases, three shredded sofas, two dented appliances, and that weird-looking bird he nailed with a baseball in our pear tree. At first, poor Olga tried to clean up after him, but nothing could prepare her for this challenge. As for Candida, she was accustomed to making her way through Bratt's mounting debris, and she flitted around the house with a carefree smile so bright, you needed sunscreen. This was all to be expected—you have to understand, this was normal for our cousins. It was at dinner that things started to get weird.

Olga, rather than put up with Bratt's nagging, agreed to serve us all his favorite thing for dinner: Lamb-aroni. It was while we were picking through our Lamb-aroni that a frog fell out of nowhere into Bratt's bowl. Tomato sauce splattered onto everyone.

"What is this?" said Olga. "Who has dropped a frog into the Lamb-aroni?"

"Oops!" said Bratt. Then he grabbed the frog, tomato sauce and all, and put it in his shirt pocket. This wouldn't have bugged me in the least, because after all, Bratt has been known to bring worse things than frogs to the table with him. But you see, Bratt hadn't had a frog in his pocket when he sat down, and for the life of me, I had no idea where that frog had come from.

Then that night, while we were watching sing-along videos (at Candida's request, of course), another strange thing made an appearance in the room. I saw it out of the corner of my eye as it came hurtling across the room, bouncing with a clink off the glass of the TV. Olga picked it up and examined it. It was a tiny glass unicorn, perfectly molded, and just the size of your fingernail.

"How beautiful," she cooed. "Isn't that nice." But when she asked us whose it was, nobody claimed it.

It was as we were getting ready for bed that Roxanne pulled me aside and whispered to me.

"I don't know where that thing came from," she said, "but I do know one thing: Candida sneezed just before it hit the TV."

At around three in the morning, I was awakened by something cold and slimy hopping across my face. I brushed it away and sat up in bed. For a moment I thought it was a dream. But then I saw the covers undulating. I flung back the covers to find . . .

. . . frogs!

Not just one frog or two, but a dozen of them, hopping madly in every direction. It was almost biblical, if you know what I mean. A plague of frogs. I bailed out of bed.

"Oh, Olga!" I called. "Amphibian alert!"

Olga came running. When she saw the plague, she raced around trying to catch the frogs with a trash basket, but her efforts were wasted. There were simply too many of them . . .

. . . and that was when I noticed where they were coming from.

I was sharing my room with Bratt tonight. I had the lower bunk, he had the upper, and the frogs were all hopping down from his bed. The little snot-bucket had taken an entire collection of frogs to bed with him and didn't tell anyone!

Roxanne stood in the doorway, not wanting to join in our frogathon. And through all this, little Bratt slept, his mouth open and drooling.

Candida arrived, dragging her Raggedy Ann doll by its red-yarn head. "Oh, I'll take care of it," she said. We were all more than happy to let her deal with her brother's plague of frogs. "My poor brother," she said, "he really is a holy terror sometimes."

"There's nothing 'holy' about it," mumbled Roxanne.

Olga made Roxy and me some hot chocolate, and we left Candida alone to contend with the frogs. She got rid of them somehow, but I had no idea where she put them.

In the morning it was Roxanne's turn.

"Oh, yuck! No way!" Her yells woke me up at dawn, and I hurried into her room. There was a colony of ants running in black rivers up and down her walls and covers. But if Roxanne was tormented by ants, it was nothing compared to what they were doing to Candida, who had just awakened in the spare bed. You could barely see her beneath the moving army of insects.

"Oh! Oh! Dear me!" cried Candida, while Roxanne screeched out much more colorful words.

It took three cans of Raid and half the day to rid the house of the ants.

"Where did they come from?" Olga kept mumbling as she sponged ant guts off the wall, but I knew that wasn't the question we ought to be asking. The question was *why* had they come? This whole situation was a nuisance, and it was irritating to have nuisances that we didn't create. Roxanne took it upon herself to solve the mystery, while I spent the day chasing after Bratt.

I used to think that I had mastered being a royal pain, but I really had to hand it to Bratt: he was the true baron of butt pain.

"See, I can play golf," he said as he ran off swinging the club wildly. He proceeded to decapitate every plant in our garden.

"See, I can drive!" he said as he backed Dad's precious sports car out of the garage . . . and right into the fountain.

"See, I can swim good," he said, and dove headfirst into a scummy, stagnant pond in the woods behind our property. I think it was the pond that finally slowed him down, because just before dinner, he claimed to feel sick.

"Feel my throat," he ordered me. "Do I got swollen glands?" He showed his neck to reveal so many dirt rings that you could probably tell his age by counting them, like a tree. I reached out to feel his glands.

They were swollen all right, but there was something else about them that wasn't right, because as I held them beneath my thumb and forefinger . . . I could swear they were moving.

There was something strangely familiar about the feel of Bratt's swollen glands. They reminded me of something that I couldn't quite place. . . .

Shortly before dinner, Roxanne came out of hiding to report her findings to me. You see, she had been avoiding Candida all day because Candida wanted Roxanne to play with her Dental Hygienist Barbie. Roxanne would rather have swallowed hot coals.

Roxanne called me into the den and shoved a little glass vial under my nose.

"Sniff this," she said, "and tell me what it smells like."

I took a deep whiff and cringed. It was an aroma all too familiar. "Candida!" I said. "It smells like Candida. What is it?" Roxanne leaned closer to me and whispered, "Equal amounts of cinnamon, ginger, and nutmeg. Plus a pinch of ground clove."

I wrinkled my forehead, not getting it. "That's weird."

"But that's not all. Take a look at this!" She revealed a small cup, inside of which were tiny, white, crystalline granules.

"What is it?" I asked.

"Taste it."

Reluctantly, I dipped my finger into the cup and lifted it to my mouth. The taste was unmistakable.

"Sugar!"

"It was all over Candida's sheets," Roxanne told me. "That's why the ants came."

"She went to bed with candy?" I suggested.

Roxanne shook her head. "Are you kidding me? Little Miss Perfect doesn't even eat candy."

I thought it all through. There had to be a good explanation for this. "Sugar and spice . . . ," I mumbled.

". . . and everything nice," added Roxanne. She opened her palm to reveal a whole menagerie of tiny glass figurines—the kind that seemed to fly across the room every time Candida sneezed. "That's what little girls are made of."

My jaw dropped as it all began to come together, and I realized what Roxanne was trying to tell me. It made sense in its own strange and unusual way. I tried to recall what the matching nursery rhyme for boys was, and although I couldn't recall the whole thing, I remembered enough of it, and now it finally dawned on me exactly what Bratt's moving, swollen glands felt like.

They felt like snails.

Suddenly a cry rang out from the backyard, and Candida ran inside in a panic. For the first time in her life, the smile had left her face. I hardly recognized her.

"You have to help! Hurry! Bratt's hurt himself really bad. Inga!" she called "Inga!"

"Olga," I corrected, and calmed her down long enough to find out what had happened. Apparently her little brother had been out back chasing squirrels with a pitchfork when he tripped and had the kind of accident that only happens in a mother's nightmares.

We all ran out back to help our poor little cousin. Bratt was lying in the grass, crying his eyes out. He had a big hole in his side where the pitchfork had speared him, but he wasn't bleeding. Not a drop. Instead he was wallowing in a pool of frogs and snails and furry, squirming things that I could not identify.

"What are those?" I asked, pointing.

Bratt snuffled, then shouted at me, "They're puppy-dog tails, butthead!"

Well, Olga took one good look at those tails and she was a nanny no more. She turned and ran off into the sunset, and we haven't seen her since.

Meanwhile, Bratt's condition had gotten serious. His three primary ingredients were hopping, slithering, and squirming away faster than any one of us could catch them.

"We have to get him to the hospital!" screamed Candida. "He'll need a transfusion."

And although I shuddered to think where they would get enough puppy-dog tails for a transfusion, I did as I was told. I called 911 and put it in the hands of professionals.

Modern medicine is an amazing thing. I don't know how the doctors did it, but they had Bratt stitched up and shipped back to us in less than a week.

His parents, having heard about the accident, reluctantly cut their round-the-world vacation short.

A week after the accident, we all sat at the breakfast table together. Candida sat primly, eating Shredded Wheat like a good little girl, and Bratt scarfed down Sugar-Frosted Cookie Dough cereal. Everything was back to normal.

"Well," said Uncle Bernard, ruffling Bratt's tangled hair, "sounds like you had quite an adventure!"

"It stunk," grumbled Bratt. "The hospital was even more boring than here." He hiccupped, and a small tree frog hopped from his mouth into the cereal.

"Don't open your mouth so wide, dear," said his mother. She scooped up the frog and popped it back into her son's mouth. "It's rude."

Uncle Bernard sipped his coffee, then frowned. "A little sweeter," he said. Then he tipped Candida's head, and a stream of sugar ran from her left ear into his coffee. "I think you've learned your lesson, Bratt," he said. "No playing with pitchforks unless it's under adult supervision."

Bratt only grunted and continued to gum his soggy cereal.

It was as they were leaving that I asked the final question that would solve the last remaining riddle about my cousins' unique family.

"Candida?" I asked as they were heading out the door. "How is it that your parents can afford a round-the-world vacation?"

"That's simple," she said. "My parents are made of money."

Which explains why they jingle when they walk.

The Soul Exchange

Down the long, empty corridor, in the chrome-and-tile bathroom of Bloomingdale's, Kiara closely examines a pimple in the mirror.

Her face, in every other way, is perfect, but that's not what Kiara sees. She sees the ugly whitehead on her cheek; Vesuvius about to erupt and wipe out Pompeii. She imagines half of Manhattan must know about the zit by now. Her stunning eyes, her perfect hair, her media-worthy smile mean nothing to her as long as that thing sits on her cheek.

"It's so ugly," she mumbles. "I hate my face!"

The lonely restroom is not so lonely. An old woman has entered. She comes to the mirror beside Kiara and tries, with bony, shaking hands, to put lipstick on her thin lips. Kiara notices how the crone's rouge sits on her wrinkled cheekbones; splotches too round and too red. She looks like a clown. Kiara has no love, nor patience, for the elderly. To her, a woman like this has no business wearing makeup. What good is it going to do? You'd need a cement mixer to hold the makeup it would take to spackle in those wrinkles. You'd need a machete to cut through the hairy mole on her chin.

The old woman steals a sideways glance at Kiara in the mirror. Her eyes are veiny and the pupils cloudy.

"Can I help you?" snaps Kiara, her voice booming far too loudly around the gray-tiled room. "You know it's not polite to stare."

"You have a pimple," says the woman, her voice as rough as sandpaper. Probably from smoking, thinks Kiara. Stupid woman. It's a miracle she's even lived this long.

"I know about the pimple," says Kiara, striking an irritated pose. "So why don't you mind your own business?"

Kiara dots the solitary spot with foundation that perfectly matches her skin tone, but it's still not enough to hide the miserable eruption. Still the old woman looks at her. The woman, Kiara notes, wears an ill-fitting coat that must have been very expensive once. Some sort of fur. But now it's moth-eaten and mangy. She wears jewelry also—not the cheap imitation stuff, but the real thing. A diamond as big as an almond. What a waste for something so precious to be on someone so wretched.

"I couldn't help but hear you, dear," says the old woman. "You sound very, very unhappy with yourself. You poor thing."

Kiara looks in the mirror again and grimaces at her own reflection. She wants to rip her awful face off and flush it. Her best friend and occasional enemy, Veronyka Knibbs, is prettier. She hates, hates, hates Veronyka Knibbs, but most of all she hates her own face, and the zit it gave birth to.

The old woman smiles, and her thin lips disappear, revealing two rows of yellow teeth. "I understand what you're going through," the old woman says.

"How can you understand anything?" snaps Kiara.

"My bones may be old," says the woman, "but my mind is still keen. I remember my youth." Then she reaches into her pocket and pulls out a business card, holding it out to Kiara with a quivering hand.

"Give him a call," she says. "He's sure to help. He knows what you need."

Then the old woman turns and limps toward the door. Kiara follows her out and watches as, cane in hand, the woman makes the long trek down the empty hallway to the department store.

Kiara looks at the card. Burgundy lettering on a shiny gray background.

Dr. Morgan Taylor Voyd
Discorporeal Physician
Extractions and implants while-u-wait

Kiara has no clue what any of it means, but the chicken salad in her stomach doesn't feel too happy about it. Suddenly she doesn't feel like shopping today.

Tonight is pizza night for the popular crowd at East End Academy. On pizza night, they go out to Little Guido's and eat pepperoni pies with extra cheese, then talk about all the people they hate, such as teachers, parents, and anyone who's not at the table with them.

Veronyka Knibbs is there, and as she arrives, Kiara says a silent die-slowly-and-painfully prayer to herself about Veronyka before they sit to eat. Kiara sits next to Tristan, her boyfriend of the month. But she'd much rather be sitting next to Veronyka's boyfriend. He's the goalie of the varsity soccer team. Tristan, on the other hand, is a junior like the rest of them. He's captain of the JV wrestling team. Big deal.

Tristan sits there, with his arm clamped around Kiara's shoulder, like they were Siamese twins connected at the wrist and neck.

"I'll just have a salad," says Veronyka. "I don't need all that grease." And then she looks at Kiara and adds, "It could give me zits."

Kiara smiles, pretending that it doesn't bother her. She can feel the zit on her face, like a slice of pepperoni on an otherwise pristine pie. She turns her face away so that the others can't see it, but they do. Her friends have radar when it comes to details of personal appearance. They can spot an out-of-place hair from a hundred yards. They can smell a dying fashion trend like body odor.

Tristan looks at Kiara's face and zeroes in on the zit. He takes his hand from her shoulder. "You know," he says, "there are soaps you could use for that."

"Ha-ha," says Kiara, covering it with her hand and intensifying her silent death-prayer toward Veronyka. When the pizza comes, Kiara refuses to eat. Instead she pulls out the card the old woman gave her and considers it. Dr. Morgan Taylor Voyd.

"Who's that?" asks Tristan, not minding his own business.

"Some doctor," says Kiara. She tries to hide the card, but Tristan grabs it.

"What is he, a zit doctor?" asks Tristan.

"No, he's a discorporeal physician," she says, trying to sound wise, as if she knows what it means.

Tristan passes the card around the table, to Kiara's humiliation.

"Must be a shrink," says Veronyka. "A good therapist can really help with emotional issues."

"He's not that kind of doctor!" insists Kiara. "And anyway, I'm not going to see him." She grabs the card back, crumples it up, and hurls it across the room. It lands right in the trash.

"Two points!" announces Tristan, and slips her into his boy-friendly headlock again, in spite of the zit.

Tristan talks about himself as he walks Kiara home. He's in the middle of professing his undying belief that there's nothing fake about professional wrestling when Kiara interrupts him.

"Tristan, do you think I'm pretty?" she asks.

Tristan shrugs. "Yeah, sure, why not?" he says—which doesn't mean much, because Tristan would say anything as long as he got to show her off to his friends in public places.

"Am I prettier than Veronyka?" Kiara dares to ask.

Tristan hesitates. "Well . . . ," he says, "you're both pretty. You're just pretty in different ways."

The answer infuriates Kiara. She takes his hand and pulls it behind his back in a move that rivals the best of wrestlers.

"Ow!" yells Tristan. "Lemme go!"

"You were supposed to say yes," she tells him. She pushes him away and heads off in the other direction. Tristan, still dumbfounded, doesn't follow.

She retraces her steps down First Avenue and ducks back into Little Guido's. Then she digs through the trash, past greasy half-eaten slices of pizza and sticky soft-drink residue, until she finds the crumpled business card.

Deep in the unknowable parts of Brooklyn, overgrown sycamores line the streets of the old neighborhood where the doctor lives. Tree roots buckle the sidewalk into concrete accordion folds. The homes are brown brick, and although it's a bright day, the trees block out every trace of the sun.

Halfway down the street, a shingle hangs outside the doctor's home office. M. T. VOYD reads the shingle. APPOINTMENTS REQUIRED. Kiara has already made her appointment.

She rings the bell, and a moment later the doctor answers the door.

"Come in, Kiara, I've been waiting for you!" He's a tall man, as gaunt as a skeleton, with teeth that are a little too white. His head is clean-shaven and buffed to a shine. There seem to be none of the usual markers to measure his age.

"Did you have a hard time finding the place?" he asks. His voice is soothing, yet at the same time cold and slippery, like wet ice on a glass table.

"No," answers Kiara. The truth is, she barely had to look for it at all. It was as if she was drawn right to it.

The doctor has a huge cherrywood desk, spotlessly clean. His walls are covered with diplomas and certificates from the best universities and finest medical associations. He folds his long fingers together and sits at his giant desk across from Kiara, smiling.

"Just what kind of doctor are you?" asks Kiara.

"I began as a surgeon," Dr. Voyd tells her. "A brilliant one, oh, yes. Surgical techniques have been named after me. I am in textbooks."

"But you're not a surgeon anymore?"

"I got bored with that kind of medicine," he tells her. "Too easy. No challenge. But in my extensive travels, I have seen many things that science cannot explain." He smiles, revealing those spotless teeth. "That is the kind of medicine I practice now. The kind of medicine you need."

Kiara can feel her knees shaking. "How do you know what kind of medicine I need?"

Dr. Voyd laughs deep and heartily. "Isn't it obvious?" he says. Then he gets deadly serious. "You are unhappy with yourself. You think there must be a way to change those features of yours. Those eyes that are just a tad too small. Those ears that are a little too prominent. And then there's that unsightly blemish on your cheek. Am I right?"

Kiara nods, entranced by the way this man has examined her need the way another doctor might examine her throat.

"Well, I am in the business of makeovers."

Kiara's heart pounds with anticipation. "You can fix my face?"

"Not just your face, but everything. I can give you a new look—a new feel. I can give you a new body." And with that he stands and ushers Kiara to a door that opens up into his spacious house. Only it is not a house. It looks more like a hospital from the Dark Ages. Or a morgue.

The walls are painted black and covered with strange symbols. Hanging from the ceiling are dolls, each with a single pin piercing them through the heart . . . and beneath each doll is a body lying on a narrow steel table. At least a dozen of them. Their slow breathing is the only sign that they are alive.

"Welcome," says Dr. Voyd, "to the Soul Exchange."

Kiara, her curiosity overcoming her terror, steps into the room to get a good look at the people on the tables. They are not the most beautiful specimens of humanity. Very unattractive, by Kiara's exacting standards.

"It's a simple procedure," explains Dr. Voyd. "I extract their souls and implant them into new, more desirable bodies."

"How come they're all so ugly?"

Dr. Voyd sighs. "Once my clients trade up, I sometimes get left with bodies no one wants."

Kiara can understand that. It's just like at last month's cheerleader bake sale. The lousy cookies never sold, leaving a roomful of baked goods nobody wanted.

"But . . . I don't want any of these bodies."

Dr. Voyd smiles his toothy grin. "I have one coming in tomorrow that is perfect for you." Then he reaches into a folder, pulls out a wallet-sized photo, and presents it to Kiara.

The moment Kiara sees the face in the picture, she knows it's right! The girl in the picture is about sixteen, like Kiara, and perfect! Thick locks of wavy hair. Smooth skin, a wonderful smile. She is far more beautiful than Kiara—or even Veronyka. Yes, this will be the perfect exchange!

"It is my policy," explains Dr. Voyd, "that if you agree to the exchange, you may take nothing with you. Your personal belongings, your money—all must go to whoever inherits your old body. And whatever she has becomes yours. You understand?"

Kiara nods. It will be worth it. Now only one question remains.

"How much?" she asks.

"For you," says Dr. Voyd, "three hundred dollars."

Which is precisely the amount Kiara can withdraw from an ATM. She thinks about it and nods. "It's a deal."

During school the next day, the anticipation hangs heavy over Kiara. She withdrew the three hundred dollars first thing that morning. She can practically feel the weight of it in her purse, which she constantly clutches to make sure the money's still with her, not trusting it in her locker or her backpack. The exchange is to take place at four o'clock in the afternoon, sharp.

Throughout the day, she keeps glancing at Veronyka and can barely contain her mocking laughter. *Ha!* she thinks. *Tomorrow I'll walk into school—everyone's eyes will turn away from Veronyka and turn to me!*

By the end of the day, she can't keep it to herself anymore. She has to tell someone. On the way out of school, she pulls Tristan aside.

"I want to show you something," she tells him. Then she ever so carefully pulls the picture of her new self out of her purse. "What do you think of her?" she asks him. "Don't you think she's beautiful?"

Tristan's eyes go wide as he stares at the picture, then he looks at her worriedly. "Is this a trick question?" he asks.

"Just answer me: Do you think she's beautiful?"

"Well . . . yeah," he says. "But . . ."

"But what?"

Tristan holds the picture closer. "Her hair's kind of goofy-looking. . . ."

Kiara lets out an irritated puff of air. "Well, she can change her hair. That's easy."

Tristan hands her back the tiny picture. "So, what's the point?" he asks.

Kiara smiles slyly. "You'll see."

Four o'clock sharp. The wind blows through the thick sycamores, and the rustling leaves are so loud Kiara can't hear herself think as she races down the street.

"Everything is prepared," says Dr. Voyd as Kiara steps in, handing him the cash. "Follow me."

They pass through the room full of unwanted bodies to a smaller back room, lined with a dark and gritty metal Kiara guesses must be lead. A body lies on a stone slab, covered with a sheet from head to toe, and above it dangles a doll, pinned like the others through the heart. A second stone slab waits for Kiara. Dr. Voyd closes the heavy leaden door, and it seals the room like a bank vault.

"Lie down, Kiara," says the good doctor. "This will take only a little while."

Kiara lies down and watches as the doctor takes another doll from a shelf, then comes toward her with scissors. She tenses, terrified of what he might do. He brings the scissors to her face, then moves them off to the side, snipping a lock of her hair. Then he takes that hair and carefully sews it into the seam of the doll's cloth head. "I have long studied effigies and surrogate mysticism," he said. "You might call this a 'voodoo doll,' but there are dozens of cultures around the world that use object substitution in ways that defy conventional science."

"Is this going to hurt?" Kiara asks.

"Not in the slightest."

Kiara tries to fill her mind with thoughts of the perfect face she will have. At last Dr. Voyd takes a long hatpin with a round pearl-colored head and holds it in one hand, the doll in the other.

"Take a deep breath and hold it," he instructs. She does, then watches as he jams the pin through the doll's heart.

Sudden blackness colder than the dark side of the moon, and emptier than death.

Kiara feels herself moving through the darkness. It could be a million miles, it could be a million years; time and space have no meaning now. The cold is unbearable, but she has no mouth to scream, until—

She gasps, a deep breath of air that rattles in her lungs, then opens her eyes to see the cloudy cloth that covers her face. She pulls it back, revealing a bright light above. Out of focus. Then the light is eclipsed by Dr. Voyd's shiny round head.

"You can get up now. The exchange is complete."

Kiara sits up, feeling achy and weary. She looks to the other stone slab, but her old body is not there.

"You were in transition for an hour," explains the doctor. "During that time, the other client took possession of your old body and left."

Kiara reaches up to her face. It doesn't feel right. Something is wrong. Her face feels cracked and rough like elephant skin. There is something round and fuzzy on her chin. A hairy mole!

She looks at her hands and screams. But no one can hear her in the leaden room except for the doctor.

Her hands are old. More than old—they are ancient: wrinkled and weak, covered with the age spots of thirty thousand sunrises.

Dr. Voyd smiles coldly. Mockingly. "Another satisfied customer," he says, and hands her a mirror.

Kiara is now the old woman—the same old woman who gave her the card. This was the body she has exchanged for her own!

"No!" shouts Kiara, but her voice sounds frail and thin. "This can't be me."

"What's the matter?" says Dr. Voyd. "Mrs. Wentworth is a beautiful woman! Of course, not as young as she was in that picture. But beauty is ageless."

Now Kiara understands why the hairstyle in the picture didn't seem right.

"You can't do this to me!" she screams. "I'm only sixteen!"

"Correction," says the doctor calmly. "You *were* only sixteen."

She cries through her blurry, aged eyes.

"Of course," says the doctor, "if you're not happy with Mrs. Wentworth, I could give you one of the people in the other room."

"I don't want any of them!" wails Kiara. "I want someone young! Someone beautiful."

Dr. Voyd crosses his arms. "Well," he says, "I can make such an exchange for you, if you bring in a young subject to exchange with."

At last some hope! "Yes!" she cries. "I'll bring you someone as soon as I can!"

"And then of course there's my fee," explains Dr. Voyd. "To put you in a young body . . . that will cost you an even million dollars."

She gasps for air, her breath taken away by the mere thought.

"But I don't have a million dollars!"

Dr. Voyd puts a large, firm hand on her shoulder. "Come now, Mrs. Wentworth. Of course you do! Have you checked your bank account lately?"

An early fall day, several weeks later. The old woman feeds pigeons in the park, all the while looking sideways at a group of loud high schoolers. Faces she recognizes. She wears jewelry so heavy she can barely lift her hands. But she does. She lifts one to her cane and painfully forces herself to her feet, making her way down the cobblestones to the group of kids.

Her former body is there, with someone new inside it. Tristan and Veronyka are there as well. They laugh and make fun of anyone who walks by. The kids see her coming and start to laugh hysterically.

"Here comes your last girlfriend," says the Kiara-body to Tristan. Tristan thinks it's just a joke.

The old woman hobbles forward, her weary eyes fixed on Veronyka. She takes a card out of her pocket and holds it out to the gorgeous young girl with her trembling old hand.

"I've been watching you," says the old woman desperately to Ver onyka. "I know a doctor who can help you. He can make you look even better than you do now. He knows what you need."

The Kiara-body laughs cruelly as if it is one big joke. She can afford to laugh; she is no longer trapped in Mrs. Wentworth's body.

Veronyka looks at the card with disgust and hands it back to the old woman. "Thanks, but no thanks." Then she smiles. "I've already been to Dr. Voyd. In fact, I was there before you were."

The Kiara-body laughs again. In fact, both girls laugh, evil and cold, like two members of a dark and secret club.

The old woman feels dizzy. She begins to fall backward, and Tristan catches her. "Hey, are you okay?"

He helps her up, and she shrugs him off. "I'll be fine," she says, and limps away, not daring to look back.

So Veronyka had been a client. Of course! She should have known! The fact was, Kiara had come to realize that there had been many, many others who had been through Mrs. Wentworth's body. She was certainly a rich old woman. When the whole thing began, a year ago, she had fifteen million dollars, according to her bank statement. Then, about once a month, she wrote a check for a million dollars—always to Dr. Voyd, as different people were tricked into her body and bought their way out. It's like a game of musical chairs, and every turn costs a cool million—until someday soon the money will run out, and someone will get trapped in poor Mrs. Wentworth's chair for good.

Voyd is a genius. And now he is very, very rich. She admires him almost as much as she hates him.

As she makes her way toward her decaying mansion across Central Park, someone comes running up behind her.

"Yo, old lady, wait up!"

It's Tristan.

"What can I do for you, young man?"

"That doctor you're talking about," he says. "Is he a doctor for guys, too? I mean, can he make a guy better-looking too?"

The old woman looks him over slowly. This is something she has not considered. "Perhaps," she says, then reaches into her pocket and pulls out the card, handing it to him.

"I think he'll know what you need too," she says. "Call him for an appointment right away."

"Thanks," says Tristan with a big smile. Then he turns and runs off.

The old woman grins at the new prospect. It's not what she

expected—and of course there will be many, many adjustments . . . like getting used to the wrestling team, for one—and then there's the problem of dating her old self.

But she'll learn to adapt, because, in spite of everything, his youth is certainly worth a million dollars. And beggars can't be choosers.

Clothes Make the Man

An alarm blasts.

Then the carousel jerk-starts, slowly turning around and around. It's not the kind of carousel you find at the amusement park, but the kind you find in airports—that stainless-steel mechanical thingamabob that sends the luggage on a slow ride around the baggage claim area.

"Why does it always take so long?" barks my father impatiently as other people's suitcases come flying out of the dark chute. "Is there only one person working back there?" My father is an annoyed traveler. I don't know if he's like that when it comes to business travel, but whenever we come along, everything annoys him. There's a food cart in the aisle when he wants to go to the bathroom, or the seat won't recline, or our luggage takes too long to arrive.

"Luka, you and Luisa go to the other side of the carousel, and if our bag comes out that side, let me know."

My sister, Luisa, rolls her eyes at me as we trudge off to the other side. With my father, it's like a competition—an Olympic sport. We have to get our luggage and escape from the airport before all the other travelers, or we lose.

"He's just upset that our vacation's over," I tell Luisa. To be honest, so am I. Maui was like another world compared to Cleveland. And tomorrow we're supposed to go back to school with jet lag. What fun.

Dozens of people, wearing heavy winter coats over their flowery

Hawaiian shirts, fight for space at the far end of the carousel. Luisa and I weave our way in between them and get to the front, where we have a clear view of the baggage slide. Mom and Dad's bag is the first of our luggage out—a big monster of a suitcase that barely fits through the hole. Luisa's is next—a little flowery thing Grandma got her last year.

I wait . . . and wait . . . and wait.

Across the carousel I can see Dad tapping his foot.

"Next time, we're packing everything in two big bags," he proclaims as he comes around to wait with me. "No more waiting around for little cases." He shakes his head disgustedly. I guess it's my fault the luggage handlers haven't gotten to my bag yet.

The crowd thins out as we wait. Outside, twilight quickly becomes night, and still my bag hasn't arrived.

"It figures," fumes Dad. He glances at his watch for the billionth time, and I grin. "Don't worry, Dad, it's only two in the afternoon . . . Hawaii time." Pretty funny. Until I notice that my dad isn't laughing. He quickly adjusts his watch to Ohio time.

Finally, after every other bag has been pulled off the carousel and the rest of our flight has left the baggage claim area, my bag is spit out of the hole and slides down toward us.

"Hallelujah!" My dad throws up his hands and says, "Grab it, and let's go."

I pick up the bag. Although I crammed it full of souvenirs and a hundred other things, it feels light—but Dad is already storming his way out of the terminal with Mom and Luisa, so I don't have time to think about it. I just hurry along after him, pulling my suitcase behind me.

"You mean, you got the wrong suitcase?"

Luisa and I are still up that night around two in the morning. Mom and Dad are zonked out and are snoring away, but Luisa and I aren't so lucky. Since I can't sleep, I figure I'll unpack—but when I zip open the case, nothing inside looks familiar.

Luisa reaches in and pulls out a leather glove. "Aren't these your gloves?"

"No. Why would I take gloves to Maui?"

I pull out layer after layer of clothes. They're kid's clothes, all right, but not this kid's. I search for the address label attached to the handle, but there isn't one.

"You're gonna have to tell Dad," Luisa says.

The idea doesn't thrill me. Telling Dad will open up a nasty can of worms that I'd rather not deal with. I can just imagine him pacing around the kitchen at dawn, going on and on about how I should look before I leap. Then he'd drag us back to the airport and complain to the flunkies at the airline, making a federal case out of it and embarrassing all of us in the process.

I try to remember what I had in the suitcase. Summer clothes that I'll outgrow by June. A bunch of shells that I wouldn't know what to do with anyway.

"Maybe I don't have to tell him," I suggest. "I mean . . . maybe these clothes will fit."

"Are you serious? You're gonna wear someone else's clothes? What if they're diseased?"

I pull out a T-shirt. I don't recognize the design on the front. It's not a sports team or rock group or anything—just a weird swirl of colors. I sniff it to see if it's clean, and Luisa practically gags. "Oh how gross!" she says. They're clean . . . but there's something about them that smells kind of strange. It's like the way everyone's house has its own unique smell. I suppose clothes must be that way too . . . but the scent on these clothes seems totally unfamiliar. I kind of like it, though.

I slip on the T-shirt. It fits perfectly, and the fabric feels softer than any other T-shirt I've worn.

"Problem solved," I announce. "I'll try on the rest of the clothes in the morning, and we don't have to tell anyone."

I can tell that Luisa's not too happy about the idea of taking someone else's bag. "When you think about it," I explain, "it's a fair exchange. Mine for theirs." I figure if they want theirs back, they can find us, but until then, I have a new set of clothes.

I turn, heading toward my bed, but Luisa stops me.

"Luka," she says, "don't move!"

I freeze. The last time she said that, there was this big Hawaiian spider crawling on my beach blanket. Luisa moves toward me from behind, and I feel something on my back. I go stiff, until I realize it's only Luisa's fingers, tickling my back.

"Ha-ha, very funny," I say. But then I realize that although I have a shirt on, there's no fabric between her fingers and my back. She's tickling me through a hole in the shirt. A pretty big one, by my guess.

"Great," I say. "I get a cool shirt from someone else's suitcase and it has holes in it."

"It's not a hole, Luka," says Luisa. "I think you should look in the mirror."

I step into the bathroom, my back to the mirror, and crane my head as far as it will go, to get a glimpse of my back.

"Hmm . . . that's weird," I say. It's another sleeve. I try twisting my neck further, to get a better look at it. Finally I take the shirt off. There's no denying that my new shirt has a third sleeve.

"Maybe it's an irregular," suggests Luisa. "Mom always buys irregular T-shirts. They're cheaper."

Maybe. But somehow I find it hard to imagine a T-shirt company making that sort of mistake and still selling it to people. Then again, I've heard of big corporations trying to sell people toxic waste, so you never know.

"Yeah, maybe," I say. Then I put the shirt back on. Extra sleeve or not, it feels comfortable enough to sleep in. More than comfortable—it feels . . . right. And somehow I feel more content. So content that I slip right off to sleep.

Mom, in her maternal wisdom, lets us miss a day of school, so we can sleep in and catch up with Ohio time. I don't wake up until noon, and the first thing I do is head for the suitcase.

I pull out the shirts on top and hang them up. Problem is, the shirts don't fit properly on the hangers. Could be because they all have three sleeves.

I search for tags, and any other kinds of labels or logos that might tell me what the deal is, but all the tags have been cut out—just like my own clothes. Whoever owns these clothes doesn't like the tags scratching their neck either.

Beneath the shirts are the pants. My heart speeds up a bit as I pull a pair out, worried that I might find three legs. But no—the pants look normal. I try a pair on. They look like jeans, but the weave seems much finer. They don't fit as well as the shirt. Kind of baggy.

I reach down to zip up the fly and realize that there's no zipper. No button, either. Sure, the fly's there, but there's nothing to hold it closed. Great. Here's one pair of pants I won't be wearing in public.

"How come you're wearing those backward?" Luisa says from the doorway. I turn to see her standing there, still half-asleep.

"They're not backward," I inform her. "They just don't fit."

"Oh," she answers, and yawns as she shuffles off to the bathroom. I hitch up the pants on my hips, then remember what Luisa said. I take off the pants and put them on the other way.

They fit perfectly.

In fact, they fit more comfortably than any other pants I own. See, Mom says I'm always in between sizes; my pants are always either too tight or falling off my hips. But these feel like they were made for me.

Only one problem: Why is there a zipperless fly in the back? Not even in the seat of my pants, but higher—more like in the small of my back? But even with that weirdness, the pants *feel* right, like the shirts. So rather than worry about it, I make sure my three-sleeved shirt is out over the pants instead of tucked in. That way it covers the little hole, and no one has to know it's there. No one has to know about my shirts, either, if I wear a jacket over them.

As Luisa passes by, on her way back from the bathroom, I call her into my room.

"So, what do you think of my outfit?" I ask her.

"Great, if you like wearing stolen clothes."

"They're not stolen," I remind her, "just accidentally borrowed." And then I turn my back to her. "Will you scratch my back?" I ask.

Luisa reaches in through the third sleeve and scratches me between the shoulder blades—where it's been itching all night.

"Hey," she suggests, "maybe that's what the hole in the shirt is for—back-scratch access."

Which is as good an explanation as any. I don't tell her about the hole in the pants.

"Looks like you're getting a rash," says Luisa. "Your back's getting all lumpy."

"Must be something I caught in Hawaii," I tell her.

There's a fresh layer of snow on the ground, so I put on my coat and head out, taking two of the three gloves in the suitcase. It isn't until I try to make snowballs that I notice there's a space for a sixth finger.

An hour later, I'm back in my room with the suitcase. I just can't seem to get it out of my mind—but I don't talk to anyone about it, not even Luisa. I'm usually bad at keeping secrets—when strange things happen, I'm the first one to announce it to the world. But somehow this little piece of baggage has become a very personal and private thing. I guess everyone has things they don't want to share with their family. Sometimes it's just dumb things, and other times it's earth-shattering stuff. I try not to think about which category the suitcase falls into.

There are other things in the case too. Silver coins that float up off your palm, as if they're filled with helium. A pen that writes with light instead of ink. In a side pocket, I find two small devices that look like earbuds, but they don't quite fit in my ears. I don't know what device they're connected to, but they're playing. I wouldn't call the sounds that it plays music—it's more like clicks and screeches—but the more I listen to it, the more soothing it feels. It does have an interesting rhythm, in a way.

And then there's the can.

It's small and looks just like any other can of food, although there's no label. In a way it's the most disturbing thing of all, simply because it's normal. What would normal canned goods be doing mixed in with this stuff?

I can't sleep that night, mainly because of the way my hands and back itch, as if I'd fallen in a potent patch of poison ivy. But deep down I know it's not poison ivy at all. Instead of sleeping, I turn on my flashlight and take a long look at a picture I found in the suitcase's side pocket. There are people in the picture, and although it's a bit blurry, I can make out their faces. I suppose it's a family. Two parents, two kids. I don't know them, and yet I feel something for them, as if I did. I want to know them, but I can't say why.

Mom slips into my room, and I quickly hide the picture.

"I brought you a snack," she says, offering me a plate. "You barely touched your dinner. I thought you might be hungry."

"No thanks," I tell her. Truth is, I haven't had much of an appetite since we've gotten home from Maui.

Mom sees me rubbing my itching back against the wall, and she offers to scratch it for me, but I don't let her, because I know she'll see how the rash is swelling.

She looks at me strangely for a moment and asks, "Where'd you get those pajamas?"

"Hawaii," I tell her, which isn't a total lie. They are more comfortable than any pajamas I've ever worn—especially now, because I don't quite fit into my regular clothes anymore. They've gotten tight in strange and unexpected places. I guess I'm having a growth spurt.

After Mom leaves, I finally fall asleep thinking of the people in the picture, and the little canister of food, which seems creepier the more I think about it.

The world changes forever the next day. Not the whole world, but the small part of it that I occupy. It starts with a fight—the kind of fight you have when you've packed day-old snow a little too tightly, so your snowball leaves a major raspberry on your friend's cheek when you throw it.

I hurl the ice-ball at Leo Shea, because he threw one first. Problem is my throw is a lot stronger than Leo Shea's. The ice-ball impacts on the side of his face, and he turns to me with eyes that scream schoolyard massacre. There are a dozen kids around us as Leo rushes me. He rams into me, and his momentum takes me down.

Leo's on the wrestling team, so it doesn't take long for him to pin me in the snow. As I look into his eyes, I can tell he's not about to use a wrestling move on me. Not unless loogie-hurl is an accepted wrestling maneuver. I struggle uselessly as he summons up a major midwinter-flu-season mass of phlegm, and then, before he can fire it at me, someone swings at him, punching him across the face with enough force to send him sprawling in the snow five feet away.

I look around to see who saved me, but there's no one else close enough to have taken the shot.

Then I see my friends' eyes bug out. I see them back away. I see the hand that punched Leo Shea. It's above my head, reaching down to flick some snow from my eyebrow. The hand—the arm, I realize—is mine.

Screaming, I tear off my coat. Although I can't see my back, I know what it looks like. There's an arm—looking just like my others—growing through the third sleeve in the middle of my back.

My friends all back away from me, then run.

"Wait!" I call after them. "Wait, I can explain." But I can't. Not really.

I feel something in the small of my back too. Something growing out of that little backward fly. It's a tail, thin and curly, like the tail of a pig, and as I look at my gloves, I suddenly realize that the sixth finger-hole doesn't flop around limply anymore . . . because now there's something to fill it.

I race home screaming, trying to outrun my fear, but it follows behind me just as closely as my third arm.

It's dark. I've locked myself in my bathroom. Luisa keeps pounding, demanding to be let in, but I'm not opening the door for anyone. My parents don't know yet, but they will soon enough.

I tell myself that I didn't know what was happening, but that's a lie. Deep down, I knew. Maybe not at first, but somewhere along the way, I knew. And I guess I knew there was no way to stop it once it started. No matter how many two-sleeved shirts I put on, no matter how many five-fingered gloves, I would never be the way I was. Because the new clothes felt right.

On the counter in front of me is the can. Although it looks like any old can of tuna, I know there's no tuna inside. I know it without having to look. I hook on an old can opener and turn the crank. It turns in a slow circle, and I laugh, because it reminds me of the airport carousel that began this new chapter of my life.

I don't know why the suitcase chose me, but it did. Or maybe it was just dumb luck. Anyway, it doesn't matter now. As I turn the can opener with my other two arms, I bend my third elbow and press my new arm firmly against my back. I suppose we could move someplace where no one knows about it. I could hide it in normal shirts, covered by bulky sweaters. Or maybe I could lock myself away in a basement somewhere, where no one can see. Maybe. But right now, I can't even think beyond tonight, and telling my parents. How do you tell your parents something like this—something that will change the way they see you forever?

The can opener makes a full circle, and I pull open the lid. I knew it. I knew it because I heard them. In the dead of the night I heard them moving inside the can.

Blue, wormlike things—hundreds of them sliding over one another, trying to hide from the light. I know I should be disgusted, but "knowing" and "being" are two different things. And the fact is, I haven't lost my appetite. I simply haven't been hungry for the food in the kitchen. I didn't know what I was hungry for until just now . . . although I did have a sneaking suspicion. That's why I brought a spoon.

They arrive the next day. Something told me that they would. So I pack a suitcase. I watch with Luisa and my parents as they land on our lawn in a ship that seems to me what a minivan might look like, if Ford built them for interstellar travel instead of rush-hour gridlock. Luisa cries silently, and my parents, well, they're still locked in the same shock they've been in since last night. Either they've accepted it or they're denying any of this is happening; I can't say which.

As I stride forward, suitcase in my third hand, the boy rolling my old suitcase steps forward as well, and we meet in the middle of the lawn. He's wearing my old Cleveland Guardians shirt and my favorite jeans. He only has two hands with five fingers on each, but I know that's not the way he started. I'm sure he began looking much like his family standing by the van.

"Hi," he says.

"Hi," I say back, and turn to take a look at my old family. "They're okay," I tell him. "You'll learn to love them."

But he just grins at me. I realize then that his English stops at the word "hi." I suppose both of us will be learning new languages.

We look at each other for a moment more. He seems pleasant enough. We probably could have been friends, if circumstances were different. But now all we can do is pass each other as I move into the arms of his family, and he moves into the arms of mine.

My new father smiles at me, speaking strangely. He greets me by clasping my third hand above our heads, in a sort of bizarre high five. My new mother smiles, and my new kid brother offers me a fresh can of food.

As I look at the worms squirming in the can, something suddenly strikes me as very funny. "Wow, what a nasty can of worms this is, huh?" I say, and laugh long and loud. My new family laughs as well, but they have no idea what they're laughing about. That's okay.

As I get into the "van" and strap myself in, my new brother hands me a book. On the first page is a picture of an odd-looking fruit.

§ is for §«¶«∞

Okay. I'll deal with this. Somehow I'll find a way to deal with this, I know I will.

My dad always said that life is like a game of poker. I suppose you learn to live with the hand you're dealt. Even when it's three of a kind.

YOU REAP WHAT YOU SOW (THE WORLD OF *SCYTHE*)

Rasmus spotted the scythes first. Four of them. That's how he knew. Scythes of the purge always traveled in groups of four. Like the Four Horsemen of the biblical Apocalypse. It was designed to instill fear, as were the skull patterns on their robes. It worked.

—from "None More Beautiful Than I"

None More Beautiful Than I

A *Scythe* Story

Rasmus was not expecting to travel—he was fine staying put for the foreseeable future. But life—and death—had other plans for him.

The hypertrain ticket had appeared on Rasmus's phone as he rode his bike home from school. It arrived with an unusual chime to alert him of something out of the ordinary. *Amsterdam to Frankfurt; Frankfurt to Rothenburg ob der Tauber, a small town in the Bavarian Region.* At first, he thought the ticket was an error. But how could it be? The sentient cloud—which most people were now calling "the Thunderhead"—never made mistakes. Was this trip a surprise from his grandmother? An unscheduled vacation for them? He tried to paint it positive—but a part of him already knew the ticket was the portent of something darker.

"No, Rasmus, this is not my doing," his grandmother confirmed when he arrived home. She looked pale. Distracted. And although she wouldn't say it aloud, he knew what she was thinking. *The purge has come to Amsterdam.*

If that were so, then the ticket was a lifeline. And it could be their only one. Rasmus asked the Thunderhead about it.

The tickets were not, in any way, arranged by me, the Thunderhead told him, then gave an odd, roundabout explanation. *It is my understanding that the tickets were purchased for you by the acquaintance of a friend of one of my Nimbus agents. Beyond that, I do not have the authority to discuss it.*

The truth was not in what the Thunderhead said, but in what it *didn't* say. Because the only thing it had no authority to discuss was scythe business. It couldn't interfere in the purge of mortal-borns. However, an acquaintance of a friend of a Nimbus agent was far enough removed from the Thunderhead that it didn't violate the separation of scythe and state. Rasmus could just imagine how the Thunderhead had handled it:

"I am thinking that a holiday for Elke Vanderlip and her grandson would be prudent for their states of mind," it would have casually said to one of its agents—and if that agent concluded that maybe this had to do with the mortal purge, well, that was the agent's business.

Rasmus was not born mortal. He was sixteen, which meant that humanity had officially achieved immortality over thirty years before his birth. But his grandmother, who had raised him for most of his life, had been a teenager herself when natural death was extinguished. The purge hated nothing more than those who came of age right at the cusp of eternal life. As if they were somehow less deserving of it.

"I will leave and take refuge," she told him, as she packed a small suitcase. "You don't have to join me."

But Rasmus knew otherwise. If a scythe of the purge were to show up to glean his grandmother, and she wasn't there to be gleaned, they would take Rasmus's life instead—if only out of spite. Scythes of the purge were known to be ruthless, and their dark ideology left no room for mercy or nuance in their gleaning choices. If you were born mortal, and you were caught in their sights, you were dead. If you assisted someone who was born mortal, you were dead as well. So, with the purge gaining momentum around the world, perhaps this journey should have been expected, because it was inevitable.

"We'll go together," Rasmus said. "It will be an adventure."

His grandmother nodded, and they spoke no more of it as they packed.

• • •

The Amsterdam train station was the largest maglev hub in the EuroScandian Region. Dozens of hypertrains going to hundreds of destinations. And although many things had changed in the years since humanity gained immortality, travel had not—it was still a complicated affair, with irritated crowds, whining children, and luggage getting in everyone's way. Of course, the Thunderhead had done away with delays, and there was no more lost luggage, but people still found plenty to complain about. Even so, the Thunderhead encouraged travel.

In a perfect world, humans should be free to explore, expand their experience, satisfy their curiosity—and what are we seeking if not a perfect world?

Unfortunately, many of the world's Scythedoms had a very different definition of perfection.

Rasmus spotted the scythes first. Four of them. That was how he knew. Scythes of the purge always traveled in groups of four. Like the Four Horsemen of the biblical Apocalypse. It was designed to instill fear, as were the skull patterns on their robes. It worked.

"Do you think they're looking for us?" Rasmus asked.

"Let's not find out," his grandmother said, keeping her face down—because although a kerchief could cover her telltale gray hair, nothing could hide the age in her eyes, and the wrinkles on her face.

The trick was avoiding the scythes without appearing to. And while everyone might try to avoid normal scythes, no one but mortal-borns steered clear of scythes of the purge. Running, or even turning in a sharp direction, became a red flag to them, and they would pursue.

His grandmother suddenly became flustered, grabbing his phone as the scythes strode closer. "What do you mean you can't find the ticket? It's right on your phone!" she said, as if they had been in the middle of some conversation. All right, so this was a ruse—something to give reason for any anxiety the scythes might read in them. Rasmus could play along.

"I don't know," said Rasmus, grabbing his device back. "It was right there a second ago."

And she snapped it from him again. "You always have too many apps open—that's the problem!"

And then a deep voice rang out beside them. "You there! Stand where you are!"

Rasmus and Elke froze.

And the four scythes strode past them, zeroing in on a man who did not seem old at all.

"You think you can fool us by turning a corner, Mr. Konik," said the lead scythe, "but no matter how many years you turn the clock back on your age, your birthdate remains the same."

The resonance of the scythe's voice had grabbed the attention of everyone nearby—just in time to see the flash of a blade, and hear a yelp cut short. Mr. Konik fell to the ground. His eyes gazed upon his killer, holding eye contact in defiance, until it was clear there was no one behind those eyes anymore.

And then one of the other scythes—a woman as stone-faced as the one who had killed Mr. Konik—came toward Rasmus, looking at him with her piercing eyes.

"An unfortunate consequence," she said, and raised a finger, pointing at Rasmus, who felt his knees becoming weak.

Then he followed her finger to a spot of blood that had splattered on his shirt. "Our apologies," she said. "But it will come out in the wash."

Then the four of them breezed off, leaving the dead man for a cleanup crew that was certainly on its way.

"Angelika! Günter!" called a woman coming toward them as they stepped off the train in Rothenburg. She approached with warm eyes and outstretched arms. Rasmus looked behind him, thinking she must be greeting someone else. Only when she folded her arms around him did he realize that the greeting was for him and Elke. Rasmus quickly surmised that this was yet another ruse and he needed to play along. So for the moment he was Günter.

"How was your trip?" the woman said. "Easy, I hope."

"There was . . . an incident," Elke said, without getting into details. "But all ended well."

Not for Mr. Konik, thought Rasmus. *And it's not over for us, either. There's no telling when it will be over.*

"We're glad you're here," the woman said, leaving Rasmus to wonder who "we" was. Then she lowered her voice to a whisper. "Follow my lead. The purge has eyes and ears everywhere."

"Even here?" asked Rasmus. "But I thought the Germanic regions were anti-purge."

"We are," the woman told him. "But we can't keep out scythes from other regions. All scythes have free rein to go wherever they please—which means the purge knows no borders."

Then, as if to chase away the dark specter of the purge, the woman brightened and said, "Oh, but you must try some of our Bavarian pastries! Straight from my favorite *Konditorei*!" She reached into a canvas bag and handed each of them a crusty, chocolate-drizzled ball that couldn't possibly taste as delicious as it looked. But it did. A dozen different flavors and textures, each dissolving into the next; chocolate to coconut to marzipan. Having barely eaten a thing since escaping Amsterdam, Rasmus groaned as he devoured the rich, sugary cake.

"Schneeballen," the woman said. "A specialty of Rothenburg. There are also some Krapfen in there for you. In the north, you might call them Berliners. But don't call them that here, or you might get into a fight."

She glanced around, confirming that no one was paying them conspicuous attention, then gently moved them off the platform and toward the street. "Come, Uncle Rudolf is waiting for you."

She led them down a rustic cobblestone street to a quaint

restaurant with cheerful green shutters, then took them through the restaurant and up a well-worn staircase to a room with modest furniture.

There was a scythe behind a desk.

The sight of him made both Rasmus and Elke freeze in their tracks. Rasmus's heart missed more than one beat. Was this a trick? Had they been caught?

"Don't worry," said the woman, urging them forward. "Scythe Mössbauer is one of our Bavarian scythes. As anti-purge as they come."

The scythe's robe was a deep maroon and covered with an atomic pattern. The hood covered his face, leaving his eyes in darkness.

"Please sit," Scythe Mössbauer said. "I kill, but I don't bite." Rasmus could see the smirk on the visible half of his face.

"And who do you kill?" Elke dared to ask.

"No one who comes here seeking asylum, I assure you," he answered. Then he folded his arms and recited from memory. "Elke Vanderlip, born when years were still numbered. 2023, I believe, which would make you seventy-two years of age. You haven't turned the corner yet, I see. Why not?"

"I suppose I wanted to experience a natural life for as long as I could. To honor those who came before me."

"And has the experience of age served you?" Scythe Mössbauer asked, seeming to be genuinely curious.

"It has," Elke answered. "But it has also slowed me down. I was planning to set back to thirty upon reaching a natural seventy-five."

Scythe Mössbauer waved a hand. "You'll do it sooner. Advanced age telegraphs your mortal-born status."

"Perhaps I'm proud of it."

"The dead cannot be proud," he snapped. "They cannot be anything but dead. If you want to honor those who came before, then live in defiance of the mortal purge."

Elke sighed but did not argue. Because he was right.

"And young Rasmus! How noble of you to join your grandmother in this dangerous endeavor. If you wish, we could give you shelter and schooling here in Rothenburg. You do not have to join your grandmother in hiding."

"I'll go where she goes," Rasmus said.

"Will you grant us immunity from gleaning?" Elke asked, already tired of this dance of words.

The scythe shook his head. "Unfortunately, no. Granting you immunity will alert the purge. They will track you, and then glean you the instant your immunity expires a year from now. Which means immunity for the mortal-born is little more than a delayed death sentence."

Rasmus then recounted to him the story of what happened at the Amsterdam station. The four purge scythes, and their unlucky victim.

Mössbauer sighed and shook his head. "So Amsterdam has been infiltrated by the purge. How sad. Once upon a time, Amsterdam was a haven against persecution by a cruel regime. Did you know that?"

"During the Second World War," Rasmus said.

The scythe smiled. "Good for you—you know your mortal studies."

"We live one canal over from the Anne Frank house," Rasmus said. Then had to correct himself. *"Lived."* Because now everything before this moment was past tense.

Scythe Mössbauer folded his hands on the table before him. "We here in the Germanic regions have not forgotten the deeds of our ancestors. They weigh on us, and remind us to be vigilant. Perhaps that is why the Germanic regions stand so strongly against the mortal purge."

"And yet you can't stop it."

"Only the Grandslayers can stop the purge," Mössbauer said, with a hint of disgust. "But so enamored are they of that floating city they've built that they never leave it. And they're too busy arguing with one another to see what's going on in the rest of the world." He shook his head sadly. "The so-called Island of the Enduring Heart looks inward, when it should be looking outward. However, I do have faith that, in time, the Grandslayers will see the damage being done and stop the purge. But until then, all we can do is resist. Resist, and provide refuge."

Then he rose and went to a window, peering out at the quaint, colorful street. "My town is a wonder, is it not?"

"It certainly is beautiful," said Elke.

"So beautiful that it was spared in that same war you spoke of. By a Merican commander who chose not to bomb Rothenburg, because his mother had spoken so fondly of it in his youth. Amazing how such a small ray of light can cast such a broad glow. I like to believe that my small acts of kindness might do the same."

"Were you born mortal, Your Honor?" Rasmus dared to ask.

"No, I was not. Yet in spite of the purge, there are times I envy those who were. I can only imagine what it must it be like to have begun your life knowing without question that you will die . . . and then to have that death sentence commuted." Then he smiled at Elke. "The once-mortal see life differently from we post-mortals. Scythes of the purge despise that difference. Why does humankind still cling to the need to hate?"

"Perhaps we won't always," Rasmus offered. "Perhaps we can learn from the Thunderhead."

"Optimism is the folly of the young. And yet we should all be so foolish."

"So we are to make our home here in Rothenburg?" Elke asked.

Scythe Mössbauer shook his head. "This is but a stop on your journey. You are headed to a place of greater safety."

"What is our destination, then?"

"To the south," responded the scythe, "near the border of the Alpine Region, there is a scythe in a castle. He keeps the castle entirely off-grid—so no one within its walls can be detected. He hails from the Florentine Region, although he shifts Scythedom allegiances as the whim suits him, and is now our neighbor. He has taken it upon himself to save mortal-borns—and as long as you do not displease him, you will be safe from the purge."

"What do you mean 'displease him'?" Rasmus asked, but it was not a question Mössbauer was keen to answer.

"Safe travels to you," he said. "From this moment on you are off-grid." Then he lifted his head just enough to reveal the kind, but grim expression on his face. "Take heart in knowing that the mortal purge is the last plague of humankind. Someday it will end. And the world will regret what it has done."

When one speaks of fairy-tale castles—the sparkling magic, charming royals and princesses, both beautiful and unreachable—it is Neuschwanstein Castle that they imagine.

To say it was impressive would be an understatement. Rumor had it that Neuschwanstein was the inspiration for the various Disney JoyZone castles that still speckled the globe—although now they were under the benevolent administration of the Thunderhead, rather than the white-gloved hand of a corporate mouse.

The Neuschwanstein Scythedom was a Scythedom of one. It was the isolated, solitary domain of His Honor, Scythe Dante Alighieri.

The Florentine Scythedom, where Alighieri was first ordained, had not agreed with him. It was tiresome and lacked any sense of style or humor. They were dour and as sour as limoncello that has turned to vinegar. In the end, they banished him, but he much preferred to think he banished himself.

Being mortal-born, he could not support the purge, for fear that they might someday force him to self-glean. Instead he saw the purge as an opportunity. He had the power and position to save people, which would make him a savior. And how could he not love that?

• • •

The self-driving publicar that carried Elke and Rasmus Vanderlip up the winding road toward the isolated castle was a "publicar" in name only. It was not on any public network. Instead it was under the jurisdiction of Alighieri's off-grid Scythedom—which meant their journey could not be tracked.

Even from a distance, the very presence of the castle on a mountain overlooking placid Lake Alpsee dominated the landscape.

"For a scythe trying to hide people, he isn't keeping a low profile, is he?" Rasmus commented.

"Maybe hiding in plain sight gives him an advantage," suggested his grandmother.

"Or maybe he's not hiding at all."

His grandmother shrugged. "He's really not the one who has to hide," she pointed out. "And if he's larger than life, then it's easier to take refuge in his shadow."

A pair of scytheguards greeted them as their car pulled into the castle courtyard. The guards weren't dressed in the standard uniform. Instead they were all white pants, brass buttons, and frilly sashes. They were like palace guards from many hundreds of years ago.

"That looks really uncomfortable," Rasmus said to one of the guards, and his grandmother shushed him.

"You get used to it," the guard said, without as much as a grin. Then he turned, pushing open a huge wooden door. "His Honor is waiting for you."

They entered the castle, while behind them, the publicar sped away, winding back down the mountain and leaving them firmly planted in a strange, anachronistic realm.

Rasmus and Elke were led up a winding stone staircase to a massive throne room. Red marble columns on the ground floor, blue columns in the gallery above. And gold. So much gold. The furniture was ancient and smelled of the ages—that aroma beyond the end product of decay: no longer rancid, but vaguely organic and tinged with a faint dusty funk. Yet in spite of that, everything in the castle looked new—as if it had all come from a museum.

At the far end sat Scythe Alighieri on his throne. His robe was pearl-white silk, like the fabric of a million-dollar wedding dress. His throne, on the other hand, was the darkest stone Rasmus had ever seen. Clearly it was designed to contrast with the white of the robe, making Scythe Alighieri appear to glow.

The man was handsome. Even beautiful—but not quite in a human way. He was beautiful in the way an elf of Middle-earth was beautiful. Unblemished, peach velvet skin, a perfect flow of hair. An ease about him, as if the air itself bended to his will.

There was an entourage of nearly a dozen people around Scythe Alighieri. Courtiers and sycophants to attend him and amuse him. Some lounged at his feet, others held trays of food and drink. And one woman seemed to have no function other than brushing the scythe's long, flowing hair. There were others who seemed to be there to simply fill out the scene, like a baroque painting. It was a tableau of extravagance and excess, with Scythe Alighieri at the center.

"Stand tall, Rasmus," said Elke. "First impressions are important."

"Elke and Rasmus Vanderlip," announced a girl standing by Alighieri's side. A girl who seemed to be sixteen or seventeen—no older than Rasmus.

The scythe raised a hand and gave them a little cupped royal wave.

"You may approach," Scythe Alighieri said. "I wish to inspect you."

They crossed the throne room toward him.

"Welcome to my humble home," he said.

"Not so humble, dare I mumble," said an oddly dressed man to his left, who was clearly the official court jester, although Rasmus could tell he wasn't very funny.

"Thanks to my benevolence, this castle is now your home for

the foreseeable future," said the scythe. "You shall be given food and shelter, and in return you shall provide service according to your talents and abilities. We are a communal society here; everyone contributes." Then he leaned back into the throne, signaling the designated brusher to brush his hair again.

Although it was not in her nature to do so, Elke bowed her head to him. "Thank you for providing us with sanctuary, Your Honor."

Then the girl who had announced their arrival—the proud-looking one at the scythe's right hand—spoke up again.

"His Honor does not provide sanctuary!" she said. "He provides opportunity. And if that opportunity hides you from the purge, that's your business, not his."

The girl had a presence about her, despite her youth. Rasmus wondered what her story was.

"Catrina is correct," Scythe Alighieri said. "These are days of subtlety and nuance, and we must be careful with the words we use. Keeping an extensive staff to service this glorious, venerable castle must not be confused with blatantly challenging the mortal purge. Instead we are at a tangent to it, avoiding the slightest interaction. In this way, it doesn't notice us."

Catrina then made eye contact with Rasmus and gave him the tiniest hint of a grin. Rasmus did not return it, because he wasn't sure what that grin meant. Was it one of mockery, or of approval? Did she like his first impression, or did she find him laughable? And why should he even care?

"Well," said Elke, "thank you for taking us into your service."

"Yes, thank you, Your Honor," echoed Rasmus—the first time he'd spoken since entering the throne room.

The scythe ignored him and turned his full attention to Elke.

"It is my understanding that you are quite the musician."

Elke began to stammer. "I—well—it was many years ago."

"Time matters little these days," said Alighieri, then motioned to a guard in the corner, who pulled off a sheet from a large object, revealing the harp beneath.

Elke drew a deep breath at the sight of it.

Rasmus knew his grandmother had once played the harp. He had a single memory of it from his early childhood—but Elke hadn't played since the day Rasmus's grandfather was gleaned. Her harp had since been sealed in a leather case and relegated to his grandfather's study, which was now just a storage room for all the things that Elke wished to forget. When he was little, Rasmus had been afraid of it. To him, the thing resembled a misshapen tombstone.

"Play for me, Elke," said the scythe.

"I'm out of practice," she told him. "And my fingers aren't what they used to be."

"I will not allow you to hide behind age, Elke. Play."

It wasn't a request, it was an order, and she had no choice but to obey. So she went over to the harp, sat on the stool beside it, and gently tilted it down to her shoulder. A hush came over the throne room. Then she began.

Rasmus expected it to be beautiful. Because in his heart, he believed his grandmother capable of anything, but she was right; her fingers were weak and out of practice. Rasmus didn't know the piece she played, but he recognized every missed note, every chord plucked that didn't ring true. She went on for a painful minute, then stopped.

"I am sorry, Your Honor."

Scythe Alighieri sighed. "I am disappointed, but you have plenty of time to prove yourself." Then he turned his attention to Rasmus.

"And what shall we do with the boy?"

"I'm sure I'll be able to contribute, Your Honor," said Rasmus, taking a step forward. "I happen to be skilled at woodworking, and can build things for you. It has been a family business for generations, and although it's been just a hobby for me, well, my pieces have won awards. I think you'll be pleased."

The scythe didn't even nod. He just let Rasmus's offer drift past like a fly headed toward a window.

"We are in need of a lamplighter," the scythe said. "You will be our new lamplighter."

Perhaps Rasmus took a moment too long to process that, because Catrina chimed in from her position at Alighieri's side.

"Thank His Honor for giving you such an important position!"

"Uh . . . right. Thank you, Your Honor. I'm sure I can be a good . . . lamplighter."

Rasmus stepped back, trying to ignore the sting of having his skills dismissed as inconsequential. But Scythe Alighieri wasn't done with him yet. He rose from his throne and came closer, continuing to look Rasmus over as one might study a horse.

"You are quite a handsome young man," said Alighieri.

Rasmus couldn't meet his eye. "Some have said so, Your Honor."

Then Alighieri grinned, amused by Rasmus's unspoken concern. "Don't worry, boy—I have no intentions toward you; it's merely an observation," he said.

"But if he *had* intentions," added Catrina, "you would be thankful for them as well."

He looked Rasmus over a moment more, then sighed. "You have such beautiful hair. Too bad you'll have to lose it. Catrina! Take him down to the barber."

"Lose my hair, sir?"

"Yes—a lamplighter with hair such as yours is a fire hazard," said Alighieri. "It must be cut off."

Catrina led him down a narrow spiral staircase to an expansive kitchen, where a dozen cooks labored over countless copper pots, preparing dinner.

"Are all of them mortal-borns under Scythe Alighieri's protection?" asked Rasmus.

"Every last one of them."

"But you're not mortal-born."

"And neither are you."

In the hallway beyond the kitchen, she stopped and turned to him, looking him over in the way Alighieri himself had, but with a different intention. Less "observation," and maybe some of the interest that Alighieri didn't have.

"You do know why he's sending you to the barber, don't you?"

"So that my hair doesn't catch on fire," Rasmus responded.

That made Catrina laugh. "You're not a bright boy, are you, Rasmus Vanderlip?"

"I'm smart enough."

She leaned in closer to him, as if what she was about to say could not be said too loudly. "Your looks are a threat to him," Catrina explained. "No one in the castle can be more beautiful than he." Then she chuckled. "You're lucky it's just your hair. He's been known to order collagen injections to make an attractive face look swollen and lopsided."

Rasmus had always known he was easy on the eye, but he wasn't the kind of person who exploited his good looks like some others might. At least not consciously. But here, they couldn't be exploited. Here, his looks were a liability.

As for the barber, he clearly had specific instructions, because he didn't give Rasmus's head a clean shave. Instead Rasmus was shorn, like a sheep at the hands of a blind shepherd. His hair was uneven and clumpy and ugly.

"Be grateful," Catrina told him once the butchery was done, although Rasmus wasn't sure what he was supposed to be grateful for.

Rasmus's room was functional, and comfortable enough. There was a wardrobe with clothes harkening to ages past; uniforms that a royal lamplighter might have worn in the nineteenth century. The clothes were stiff and rough and weighty, but as the guard had said, you got used to it.

While the castle had all the wiring necessary for electrical lighting, Scythe Alighieri insisted that all fixtures be returned to their original state: as vessels for actual candles.

To be lamplighter meant that Rasmus was responsible for replacing each and every candle in the castle's many public rooms. Between the hanging chandeliers, and the standing candelabras, there were hundreds upon hundreds of candles to replace every day and to light every evening at sundown. Mercifully, there was someone else whose job it was to clean the melted wax each morning. The woman who did it was stoic and spoke little to Rasmus.

"Make sure the candles are straight, or they'll melt more than burn, creating extra work for me." That was pretty much all she said to him.

At first Rasmus thought that, like Scythe Mössbauer, Scythe Alighieri saved mortal-borns from the purge because it was the right thing to do. But it didn't take long for Rasmus to realize that Alighieri was not motivated by conscience. He was a man of self-interest, and nothing more.

Alighieri would not disagree with that assessment. He was very clear in his belief that self-interest was the only interest worth having. In Alighieri's mind, self-love was the greatest love of all. And he couldn't love himself enough—which was why he needed others to love him as well.

Catrina was right—Alighieri did see an attractive young man such as Rasmus as a threat. Not just as a challenge to Alighieri's supreme handsomeness, but a threat to his power. Dante knew that good-looking men commanded attention and gained followers they didn't necessarily deserve. He knew, because he had been one of those young men gifted with looks, and knew how to wrap the world around his finger. He determined early on that there must not be anyone more beautiful than he in his orbit.

He assumed Rasmus, once his hair was mangled, would find his will mangled as well, and would disappear into servitude like so many others in the castle.

Alighieri assumed wrong.

When Rasmus next saw his grandmother, he walked past her and didn't even recognize her until she called out his name. On Scythe Alighieri's orders, she had turned the corner, resetting back to twenty-five. Seeing her like this was disturbing, but Rasmus knew he'd have to get used to it.

"My fingers are much more nimble now," she told him. "Youth can do that."

"You don't seem like yourself, Grandmother," Rasmus told her. "And I don't just mean your age."

Elke sighed, and considered how she might respond. "Did you know that this castle was not designed by an architect?" she said. "King Ludwig II hired a theatrical set designer."

To look around, it made perfect sense. It all seemed ripped from a Wagner opera.

"We must think of this as a great pantomime," Elke said. "A long-running performance. That's the only way we'll get through it."

Elke's rejuvenated fingers were quick to recover their skill at the harp. Her music was there at every meal and gathering. Elke's fingers were overworked, and so became sore with blisters struggling to become calluses. Her nanites would dose her with painkillers that made her vague and dreamy.

"Oh, Rasmus," she would lament. "I am dosed one degree short of addiction but two degrees short of relief. My fingers will adapt in time, but for now it's agony."

Rasmus had little to offer her but sympathy and hope. "I hear the

Thunderhead is developing better pain nanites. More powerful, and nonaddictive."

To that Elke gave a weak smile. "Soon the very idea of pain will be unfamiliar to us. I wonder who we will be then?"

Rasmus did not feel pain, only increasing numbness. Day after day, he endured the monotony of replacing and lighting candles. He longed to talk to his old friends, or at least the Thunderhead, because it always had words of wisdom to temper him. But the Thunderhead could not intrude into a scythe's domain—and a domain was exactly what it was. It was as if the outside world didn't exist, and Alighieri, like the Little Prince of lore, existed on his own planet.

It didn't take long for Rasmus to come to understand the true nature of servitude at the castle. Scythe Alighieri did not give sanctuary to just anyone; mortal-borns weren't just vetted but *scouted*. Alighieri would put in his request for one type of person or another; an artist, a mason, a chef; and the agents in his employ would seek out a mortal-born who filled the need. It was, in fact, Elke's history as a harpist that had earned a place for her and Rasmus at Neuschwanstein Castle. And although the man had saved Rasmus and Elke from the purge, Rasmus grew to despise him more and more.

There were plenty of things Alighieri did that infuriated Rasmus—because it made the man's nature so very clear.

Like the time he ordered his subjects to dance through the night and into the following day to see who would be the last to drop.

Like the time he said so many horrible things to the unfunny jester that the man broke down in tears.

Like the many times he would randomly demand people to express their undying love for him. Sometimes in words, but other times in deeds.

"Cut off your small finger to show your devotion to me," he told one woman. "Don't worry, your nanites will grow it back."

And then there was the seemingly random way he would choose evening companions.

Does he desire them, Rasmus wondered, *or is it just that he desires to control them?* There was no way to know. The man reveled in keeping people guessing.

"I want to remain an eternal mystery to myself, and others," he was known to say. They weren't his words, but stolen from his "Patron Historic," the original Dante Alighieri—who, if he knew the man who had taken his name, would be rolling in his grave.

Occasionally there were new arrivals to the castle. Mortal-born refugees that Alighieri deigned to allow in his presence. They were so thankful for sanctuary that they didn't think twice about giving him the veneration he required.

Among the next batch of arrivals were a cellist and a flautist.

"I will, in time, have a full orchestra," Alighieri mused. But for now it was just a trio. The music of harp, flute, and cello was an odd but beautiful ensemble—both wistful and mournful at once. They sounded a bit like a music box. Automaton players wound up to play at their sovereign's whim.

"He's turned us all into slaves," Rasmus said to Catrina one day, when she came to inspect the quality of his lamplighting work—which she did often.

"I could tell him you said that. I could make him aware of your lack of gratitude."

Rasmus fitted another candle into place. "But I don't think you will."

"It should terrify you that I'm even considering it."

Rasmus climbed down the ladder to face her. "I don't terrify easily."

"Careful what you say, candle-boy. Scythe Alighieri's beneficence only shields you as long as he wills it."

Which made Rasmus wonder. "Has he ever cast people out?"

"From time to time. He has no problem ejecting people who don't show him the proper respect."

"You mean people who don't worship him as a savior."

"He *is* your savior," Catrina said. "If worship is what he requires, then why not give him what he wants? It's a small thing to ask in exchange for your very existence."

Then she strode off, leaving Rasmus to smile—knowing she enjoyed the banter between them as much as he did.

Rasmus couldn't stop thinking about Catrina. There was something about her. Something secret. Something mischievous. Not like the twisted whimsy that saturated the rest of Scythe Alighieri's fiefdom, but something that almost defied it. As if there was a joke behind the joke, and Catrina was the only one who knew it.

She continued to check on him more often than necessary. It was obvious: she clearly enjoyed watching him—and Rasmus had to admit that knowing she'd be there made his monotonous work bearable.

"Your hair is a marvel," she teased, as she leaned against a marble column, watching him set candles in one of ten candelabras in the ballroom. "It looks even worse than the first day. Truly hideous." It was just the two of them. She only came to watch him when no one else was around.

"You just want to run your fingers through it."

Catrina grinned. "Maybe I do, and maybe I don't."

He set a final candle into place. This was the last room of the day. All that was left was to light all the candles he had placed in the ballroom. The day was beginning to dim into dusk, but he didn't light the candles just yet.

"Why are you here, Catrina? Here at the castle, I mean. You know I'm here because of Elke, but what keeps you in Alighieri's service?"

Catrina shrugged. "Maybe I like being here."

"So you'd rather be here in Dante's personal inferno than be out there in the world?"

Catrina pulled a candle from its place and studied it. Scythe Alighieri didn't use manufactured candles. There was someone in the castle who made them by hand. Another full-time task that was entirely unnecessary.

"I was already in the castle when Dante arrived," Catrina confessed. "Neuschwanstein had been abandoned for many years. I was squatting here with some other unsavories."

"You were unsavory?"

"For a time. We liked the idea of living off-grid, and in an old castle. Then Alighieri arrived and told us leave. He gleaned our leader when she refused, and that was enough to make all the others run like rabbits."

"But not you."

"I knew I could be of use to Alighieri. I know all the secrets of the castle. Hidden passageways and forgotten stories. The skeletons in its history. There are a lot."

The ballroom was getting dimmer. Rasmus knew he should continue his work, but in the moment, that didn't seem to matter.

"Anyway, he kept me around because I knew stuff," said Catrina. "Like the quirks of the old heating system. The rooms that stay warm in winter, and cool in summer. And since he came alone, banished from Florence with no entourage, I was the first of his entourage here. He needed me to be his mirror, telling him how beautiful he was, since there was no one else here to do it."

Then Catrina looked down—perhaps considering whether she should confide in him further than she already had.

"He's going to make me his apprentice," she finally said. "He's going to make me a scythe."

"He told you that?"

"No, but he's clearly training me for it. He has me travel and bring him people to glean."

"You're not traveling now. . . ."

"He only gleans when it suits him. When it serves some larger purpose. But as long as he's content, he has no need to glean—and since he's a Scythedom of one, he doesn't have a quota."

By now the room had gotten dim, and with the dimming light, they found their voices growing quieter.

"Shouldn't you begin lighting the candles?" Catrina said.

"I should," he said, taking a step closer, "but there's plenty of time for that."

Because they were both more than ready to linger in shadows together.

Rasmus's time with Catrina was the one thing that kept him going through the months at the castle, trying to survive and outlast the purge. The intrigue and danger of a secret romance added spice to the blandness of being the castle's "candle-boy."

"If he finds out about us, he'll eject you," Catrina teased. "He'll throw you to the wolves—maybe even literally. I wouldn't doubt it."

"Just me?" asked Rasmus. "Not you, too?"

She shrugged. "He sees me as his protégée. He'd probably just wag a finger at me and punish me by driving you out."

It was fear of being driven out that kept everyone in line. And just when Rasmus thought he might be able to let his guard down, someone suffered the consequences of rubbing Scythe Alighieri the wrong way.

Like the woman who cleaned the wax.

She had grown less enthusiastic about her endlessly monotonous work, and thus had skipped a few spots. Scythe Alighieri slipped on one of those spots and fell. Nothing was bruised beyond his ego, but when one's ego is the size of the moon, it can be a crisis. Alighieri cast her off without a second thought.

"You are no longer of use to me," he told her, and within the hour she was put outside the castle gate to fend for herself in an afternoon dusted with snow that was growing deeper by the minute. Whether she was found by the purge, no one knew, because once she was outside the gate, she was no longer a part of Alighieri's world.

The purge did find Alighieri's world, however. And that day was the beginning of the end of many things.

There was a bell in the castle's highest tower. But it never rang. There were clocks of all shapes and sizes throughout Neuschwanstein's many grand rooms—but none of them were wound. All were frozen at the aesthetically pleasing position of midnight. Or noon, depending on whether one was an optimist or pessimist. Alighieri detested the ticking of clocks, but even more so the tolling of bells. In olden days such giant iron bells were relentless in their slow, ominous rhythm. They rang out their solemn moan at funerals, calling the living to mourn the dead. They marked the inexorable, indifferent passage of time, and Alighieri hated the very concept of time.

"I am as timeless as the world," he proclaimed. "In fact, it was I who came up with the idea of naming the years rather than numbering them once we achieved immortality." This was, of course, a lie. He had had nothing to do with it, but with no one to contradict him, he could claim whatever he pleased.

Yet in spite of his hatred of tolling bells, he ordered that the ancient, dusty rope that ran up into the bell tower be pulled, making Neuschwanstein's bell ring long and loud early one February morning.

"There will be a conclave at noon," he announced. "Not of scythes, but of mortal-borns. The reason for this gathering will be abundantly clear once we convene."

As Scythe Alighieri loved all sorts of drama, his many "subjects" were both excited by the prospect of a show and fearful that they might be the unwilling victims of a circus.

• • •

Rasmus heard the tolling, as everyone did—and rumors were already circulating as to what this might be about. Some said there was a traitor among them and that Alighieri would publicly accuse the culprit, then glean them. Others felt sure that the scythe had grown tired of providing refuge and was going to cast them all out of the castle. Anything was possible—but Rasmus had a sense that the rumors were wrong, because Catrina was more excited than worried. She knew something but wasn't going to tell. All she said to him before she took Alighieri's side in the throne room that day was "This should be interesting!"

The throne room was packed with all of Alighieri's "children," as he called those to whom he gave refuge—but a wide aisle was maintained from the entrance to the throne. The bell tolled again, twelve times for the noon hour, and as the last reverberation faded, the door opened and someone was escorted down the aisle, with guards on either side and a third behind.

It was a scythe.

His robe was of magenta satin—the color of bougainvillea—but it was anything but pleasant, because there on his chest was a skull, stitched into the fabric. This was a scythe of the purge! The sight of him caused many to gasp, and the rest to whisper in nervous, hushed tones. It could have caused a panic, but by the way the guards held him so disrespectfully as they forced him forward, it was clear this scythe was not a friend of the court. He was a prisoner.

The man's expression was as arrogant as could be, and he did not look to the mob on either side of him, only toward Alighieri and his baroque tableau of courtiers. Then, once the crowd had recovered from their initial shock, people began to hiss at the magenta scythe in disdain—Rasmus included—but Alighieri raised his hand to quiet them.

Catrina stepped forward. "This is Scythe Draco of Mediterranea, Your Honor," she announced.

"Such an ugly man for a robe so attractive," said Alighieri, lounging casually on his throne. "But I suppose everything in life is a balance."

"Kneel before the presence of His Honor Scythe Dante Alighieri, Sole Sovereign of the Neuschwanstein Scythedom!" Catrina demanded.

Draco scowled. "I will not. No scythe kneels before another—least of all before a mortal-born scythe."

Now the room was silent as everyone waited to see what would happen. What show would Scythe Alighieri put on for their (but mostly his own) amusement?

"You scythes of the purge are so byzantine," he quipped. "Even more so than I!"

"Your menagerie of mortal-borns will not survive," Draco said. "They will all be gleaned, I assure you."

Alighieri laughed. "By whom? By you?"

"There are plenty of others to do the job," snapped Draco.

"Oh—do you mean your three friends? The other scythes you arrived with?"

Murmurs from the crowd again. Of course there were others! Purge scythes always traveled in groups of four!

The armor of Draco's defiant visage weakened. "Where are they?" he asked.

"I'm not sure," said Alighieri, although he clearly was. "Guards, does anyone have any news to report of this man's conspirators?"

A scytheguard stepped forward from the crowd. "The three other scythes felt sudden remorse over their part in the purge," the guard announced. "They were so ashamed that they drowned themselves in Lake Alpsee."

And with that, Draco's iron facade fell. It was, Rasmus had to admit, glorious to see the man so demoralized.

"Well, there you have it," said Alighieri. "Your friends self-gleaned. Can't say I blame them."

Draco's face turned nearly the color of his robe. "What have you done! This is unthinkable! Unforgivable! They did not self-glean! Clearly they were murdered!"

"Are you accusing my guards of lying, Scythe Draco?"

"They would not end their own lives!"

"The only witnesses claim otherwise—and there is no one to refute it, so it will stand as a triple self-gleaning."

"*I* refute it!" bellowed Draco.

"Noted," said Alighieri with calculated calm. Then he rose from his throne and stepped down closer to Draco. "I give you two options, Dishonorable Scythe Draco. You can abandon Mediterranea and pledge your fealty to me as your High Blade . . . or you can leave."

"I will never serve you!"

"All right, then, you have chosen to self-glean."

"What?"

"Wasn't I clear?" said Alighieri. "Either you serve me, or you leave this life. You chose the latter." He turned to Catrina. "Bring the instrument," he said quietly.

"Bring the instrument!" Catrina shouted.

Out from behind the throne, three guards wheeled a platform that contained a sword with a hilt studded in diamonds. It was dramatically lodged in a stone base. It was every bit as impressive as Excalibur, but unlike the infamous sword in the stone, its hilt was embedded in the stone, not its tip. Instead the tip pointed skyward, like a silver stalagmite.

"You shall self-glean by thrusting yourself upon the sword," Alighieri instructed, while around him people craned their necks to watch. Rasmus, on the other hand, took a step back. The last time he had been this close to a blade this sharp, he had been splattered with blood.

"I will do no such thing," said Draco.

"I understand," said Alighieri. "It's such a difficult thing to accomplish alone." Then he pulled the sword from its base and held it, swishing it through the air. It was so sharp it seemed to cut space itself. "Who shall assist Scythe Draco in his self-gleaning?" Alighieri asked—and although everyone was more than happy to see an end come to a scythe of the purge, no one volunteered.

Then Alighieri's gaze settled on Rasmus. Looking back, Rasmus would realize that this was not in any way random. Like everything Alighieri did, it was calculated.

"My lamplighter has brought forth much illumination to this court. It is only fitting that he assist in the dousing of your miserable light."

Then he put the sword into Rasmus's hand.

"You shall assist Scythe Draco in his self-gleaning."

The sword was lighter than Rasmus expected—but its weight was in its purpose. He cast a quick glance at Catrina, who looked both troubled and flustered.

"Your Honor," Catrina called out. "The lamplighter isn't skilled with a blade. . . ."

"Oh really," said Alighieri with a slimy little grin. "From what I hear, Catrina, he's quite good with the thrust."

Rasmus swallowed hard. So much for their secret—but that was the least of his troubles now.

"Go on, lamplighter," coaxed Scythe Alighieri. "Help Scythe Draco end his unhappy life."

"Don't you dare, boy!" said Draco.

"Do it!" ordered Alighieri. "Through the heart, with a final twist at the end."

Rasmus knew he had to follow the order, but such a thing was not easily accomplished. He sought out his grandmother in the crowd, and even she nodded to him. But try as he might, he couldn't do it. He just did not have it in him to end a life—even the life of one so odious as a scythe of the purge.

Then, as he faltered, Catrina came forward. In one smooth move, she wrested the sword from Rasmus, approached Draco, and ran him through without the slightest hesitation. Then she pulled the blade out, letting the scythe's body crumble to the floor.

"There. It's done, Your Honor," she said.

But Alighieri was far from pleased.

"Who gave you permission to do that?"

"Scythe Draco needed assistance in self-gleaning, so I provided it."

"You were not asked!" screamed Alighieri.

"But Rasmus couldn't do it. . . ."

"It's not for you to decide what he can and can't do!"

Now Catrina began to stammer. It was the first time Rasmus ever heard her unsure of herself. "But—but—I thought—since I'm the one you're training to be your apprentice . . ."

"Apprentice?" said Alighieri, as if he had never heard the word. "Is that what you think? That your service here is leading to *apprenticeship*?"

"I—I stand by your side, Your Honor! I hunt for you, and bring you people to glean. I—I—"

"You are a *servant*," Alighieri told her with a disdainful, dismissive sneer. "You are an accessory, like this ring on my finger. How dare you assume you are anything more!"

Alighieri could have stopped there. For his own sake, he should have. But he didn't.

"I have no intention of taking on an apprentice. And if I did, it certainly wouldn't be a scrawny, mewling girl!"

Rasmus could see the moment Catrina snapped. He could see it in her eyes. But she was wise enough—or shocked enough—to hold herself together.

"Your Honor," Rasmus said, gently taking the sword from Catrina and setting it back down on the stone. "She made a mistake. But she's loyal to you—you know that. . . ." But rather than helping, it only poured salt in the wound. Catrina practically burned him with the fury in her eyes. *"I don't need you to stand up for me,"* she growled at him.

Alighieri returned to his throne, and his groomer raised her brush out of habit. But Alighieri grabbed the brush from her. "Off with you," he said. "Find something else to do."

The woman scurried away, not wanting the slightest bit of his wrath. Then Alighieri pointed the brush at Catrina, like it was some sort of magic wand, and he was about to cast a spell.

"You," he said to Catrina. "You shall be my new groomer."

It was beyond humiliating. "But—but—I stand at your right hand! I am your voice! I announce your decrees!"

"Not anymore," said Alighieri. "Now you stand behind me. And you brush my hair." Then he put the thing into her hands and sat on his throne, waiting for her to attend to her new duty.

And so, with the eyes of everyone on her—including the blank eyes of a dead scythe on the marble floor—Catrina brought the brush to Scythe Alighieri's long, luxurious hair, and began brushing.

"I hate him." Catrina paced back and forth in Rasmus's room, her fury building. "Hate him, hate him, hate him!"

"Calm down," said Rasmus, but it was like trying to spit on a raging fire.

"That narcissistic, misogynistic, solipsistic—"

"Stop! My head is spinning from all the 'istics.'"

"You're an idiot!" She stormed across the room and stormed back. "For more than three years I've been doing his bidding, and for what? So that I can have the honor of brushing his fucking hair?"

"You're not mortal-born," Rasmus reminded. "You can leave whenever you want."

She took a long look at him. "Is that what you want, Rasmus? You want me to leave?"

"No—but I want you to be happy. What would make you happy, Catrina?"

But she didn't have to answer. Because the answer was already right in front of them. Someone only needed to say it. So Rasmus did.

"We could take him down. . . ."

And finally she stopped pacing. "What do you have in mind?"

It wouldn't be easy, but it could be accomplished. The fact was, as beloved as Alighieri thought he was, there was no one at Neuschwanstein Castle who actually felt that way. He confused fear with love. Not even his own guards liked him—they were merely bound by duty, and felt it was noble to defy the purge.

Most everyone at the castle was too fearful to participate in a coup, but they wouldn't stand in the way of one either. In the end it was a small group of "revolutionaries" who plotted to end Scythe Dante Alighieri's reign. Then, once he had been deposed, he would remain under house arrest in his chambers—the "sovereign" of Neuschwanstein Castle in name only. Instead the refugees would run things, led by Catrina—who was, after all, being trained for leadership, whether Alighieri realized it or not. The beauty of the plan was only helped by the isolation that Alighieri maintained. No one outside the castle would know that he was no longer in charge—not even his agents, who sent mortal-borns his way. And perhaps now, the people given refuge would not be limited to those handpicked by Alighieri.

Alighieri was caught completely by surprise. So self-absorbed was he that he couldn't imagine anyone wishing him ill. Not even Catrina. His rebuke might have stung in the moment, but she needed to be reminded of her place. And besides, it was an honor to be trusted with the maintenance of his hair. Surely she had already come to realize that. And so when the coup came, he was not prepared.

He had not noticed that several members of his entourage were less jovial than usual. His first inkling that something was wrong was the way the two guards at the door to the throne room kept whispering and sharing glances. Alighieri was not suspicious, only annoyed.

Then the lamplighter entered the throne room without having been summoned. He strode toward the throne uninvited. Hadn't he been humiliated enough last week when he was shown to be incapable of wielding a sword? Was he asking for further punishment?

"Scythe Alighieri," he said. "All of us that you rescued from the purge thank you for what you've done for us."

"As well you should!" said Alighieri, wondering what his point might be. "You should be endlessly thanking me!"

"We are grateful," said the boy. "But your job is done. We'll take it from here."

Then Alighieri's water carrier put down his jug, and the woman with the cheese balls put down her tray. And they grabbed him.

But that wasn't the worst of it.

Because Catrina had stopped brushing his hair. Now she stepped forward and raised the heavy wooden brush. Alighieri saw in her eyes what she meant to do, and knew he could not stop her. She struck him in the face with the flat side of the brush, and as he stumbled from the throne, she struck him again, her teeth gritted in fury.

"Catrina! Stop this right now!" he wailed, as if she was little more than a petulant child, but she would not stop. He called for the guards, but they were part of this conspiracy, for they had turned their backs to the scene. And the members of his court? They were either cheering her on or backing away, allowing this to happen.

"Stop this at once, or I swear I will glean you!" But whatever power he thought he had over the people around him was gone.

Rasmus thought Catrina would stop. He thought she had just struck Alighieri to stun him—shock him into acquiescence, making him easier to handle. But the more he cowered, the harder she attacked—

as if three years of suppressed rage was being expelled through that brush. This was not part of the plan. The plan had been to quickly overpower Alighieri and swiftly spirit him to his chambers, where he would be held peacefully, quietly, for as long as necessary.

"Please . . . please . . . no more!" wailed Alighieri. Now others were beginning to attack—even the jester, who had seemed such a docile man, was pummeling with both fists.

"Catrina!" yelled Rasmus, knowing the others were following her lead. "Catrina, enough!"

Now others were entering the throne room, turning a group that began as a mere half dozen into a mob. Everyone became bold under Catrina's brutal example. They began kicking Alighieri, grabbing him as if they meant to rend his flesh. The water bearer struck him with his jug, and the woman who until today had fed him grapes was now trying to gouge out his eyes.

It was Rasmus who had the presence of mind to launch himself into the angry mob, pulling the most violent of them away until he realized that one of them was his own grandmother.

Elke looked up at him, bewildered by her own fury. "Oh, please, Rasmus," she begged. "Please let me hurt him. I need to hurt him. You don't know the ways he has hurt me!"

"The purge is the greater enemy, Grandmother," he told her. "That's the one we need to fight."

Her response was something Rasmus would never forget.

"There is now room in my heart for many enemies," she told him.

Finally Catrina stopped. She was out of breath, panting like a predator pausing before the kill. She took a look at the brush in her hand and hurled it away.

"You won't be needing that brush anymore," she told Alighieri. Then she turned to all those assembled. "Take him to the barber!"

• • •

Alighieri's beautiful, silky locks were shorn even more haphazardly than Rasmus's had been. The barber took his shears and dug deep, leaving bloody gouges in Alighieri's scalp. What remained was an uneven mat of stringy hair clinging to his head. He looked like a survivor of a mortal-age nuclear attack.

"It's done," Rasmus told Catrina. "You've had your revenge—now get him to his chambers!"

But Catrina laughed at that. "Done? We're only just beginning!" she told him.

"Catrina, we had a plan! It's a good plan!"

But the fire that had ignited in her was blazing too powerfully to douse now. "Strip Alighieri down!" she ordered. "He loves the old ways, so let's do to him what they used to do in ancient mortal times! We'll tar and feather him!" And the crowd cheered.

"But we have no tar," someone pointed out.

To that she looked to Rasmus with a terrible grin. "No. But we have wax!"

Rasmus didn't know the exact time the tide turned against the coup. At first there were more scytheguards on their side than against them. But watching Alighieri humiliated—first stripped of his silk robe, then smeared with wax, and then covered in the fluff of a dozen down pillows—it must have been too much for those who were ambivalent. As Alighieri was scorned and paraded in abject humiliation, several of the guards who had been on the side of the rebellion stepped away, hiding themselves from the battle, and that was all it took for those loyal to Alighieri to gain the upper hand.

And so, what began as a quiet coup became a raging battle for control.

Soon ancient weapons that were only castle decorations were pulled off the wall and began to draw blood.

In the midst of it Alighieri broke free and grabbed a fencing rapier, using it to fend off those attacking him. Clearly he had no skill with it; he swung it like a flyswatter at anyone who approached him.

Bodies of the deadish began to litter the ground on both sides of the battle. And it would have gone on, had not the gates of the castle swung open to reveal that an elegy of scythes had arrived. Not four, but seven. They were not scythes of the purge; they were here for another reason.

"Cease and desist!" the lead scythe bellowed through the halls, his voice ringing louder and clearer than any bell. "Put down your weapons, or be gleaned."

And while no one had given any credence to Scythe Alighieri's threats, the mob quickly surrendered to the will of these scythes.

That was when Rasmus recognized the lead scythe. A maroon robe emblazoned with atoms. It was Scythe Mössbauer!

He and his fellow scythes took in the scene, horrified. "What level of hell have you all descended to?" he asked, but no one dared answer.

Rasmus approached. "This wasn't supposed to happen . . . ," he said in shame. "Things got out of hand."

Mössbauer shook his head as he gazed upon the weeping waxed-and-feathered form of Alighieri. "Look at what you've all done. You have become the senseless hatred you ran from." Then he took a deep breath and spoke with great resonance once more.

"All of you taking refuge in this castle . . . I have come to announce that the Grandslayers have convened an emergency session of the high council on the Island of the Enduring Heart. They have officially denounced the purge and have put an end to it. All purge scythes have been stripped of power—including the right to glean." He took a moment to let that sink in. "Your days here are over. The purge is over. You may all return to your homes!"

The astonished crowd didn't revel in the news. Instead they slunk away, their feelings as mixed as could be. One moment they were giving rise to the darkest expression of themselves. The next they were free to go. What remained between those two realities was a numbness that would take years to sort.

By now ambudrones from the nearest town had begun to arrive, lifting and carrying off the deadish for revival—and that was when Rasmus spotted Catrina. She was lying there on the throne room floor, just one among the deadish. But the ambudrones were ignoring her, taking others away instead. Rasmus knelt by her, cradling her head in his hands. "They'll come for you," he told her, even though he knew she couldn't hear. "They'll be back, and they'll take you to be revived."

And then came a voice, somewhat familiar, but also not. "No, they won't."

Rasmus turned to see Alighieri crumpled against a column in the corner of the throne room. He was barely recognizable. Bloody and bruised, and covered with feathery fluff. A fallen angel, both comic and tragic. "She came toward me, and I held out the fencing sword, to defend myself. I don't think she intended to . . . but she impaled herself upon it."

It took a moment for Rasmus to realize the ramifications of that. Alighieri was a scythe. She had died at his hand. Which meant she had been gleaned, whether he intended it or not.

"I'm sorry," Alighieri said. "I know you cared for her."

Rasmus held back his tears, because Catrina would want him to. *Your eyes drip like tallow from a chandelier, candle-boy,* she would have said. And although Rasmus wanted to hate Alighieri for this, the man was simply too pathetic. All Rasmus could feel for him was pity.

Scythe Mössbauer came over to see Rasmus cradling Catrina's body. "Leave her, Rasmus," Mössbauer said. "Forget this place, forget this day. Go back to your old life. Or if you can't, then begin a new one."

"Let's go, Rasmus," said Elke, coming up to him. Like everyone, her clothes were torn and bloody from the battle, but her wounds were minimal. Perhaps because she had spent much of the battle attacking the harp that Alighieri had made her play. "Let's do as Scythe Mössbauer says and go home."

Rasmus gently let Catrina go and stood, turning to Mössbauer. "What happens to Alighieri?"

"The Bavarian Scythedom has unanimously decided to banish him from our region," Mössbauer said. "We tolerated him this long because he provided sanctuary for mortal-borns. But now that the purge has been stopped, he's of no further use to us."

Even in humiliation, Scythe Dante Alighieri looked only inward. How could they do this to *him*? How could *he* be so mistreated? How could the universe be so cruel to *him*?

Suddenly his tattered robe was dropped in his lap. He looked up to see it was that boy, the lamplighter, who had given it to him. Alighieri gathered the shredded cloth around himself as best he could. He didn't look at the boy. Didn't acknowledge him with as much as a "thank you." He just waited for the boy to leave. But he didn't. Not yet.

"Where will you go?" the lamplighter said.

"A scythe can go anywhere they choose," Alighieri grumbled.

"Except the places that won't have you."

Alighieri could not deny the truth of that, and although he wanted to despise the boy for saying it, he couldn't. "Although you were one of the conspirators, I know that you tried to stop the attack," Alighieri said.

"I didn't think attacking you was necessary."

"You could come with me. Be the first of my new court. I promise you'd be more than a lamplighter." And Alighieri meant it. Or at least he meant it in the moment. "I could use someone as levelheaded as you."

But the boy shook his head. "From now on, I think yours will be a court of one." And then he held out something to Alighieri. "Here. It may the only thing they let you take from the castle."

It was the hairbrush.

Alighieri took it, feeling its weight—so much more comfortable in his hand than a sword. The boy left with his grandmother, and once he was gone, no one, not even the intruding scythes, bothered to talk to Alighieri. Even his own guards were now taking orders from Mössbauer.

But that was fine. He needed none of them.

He raised his brush, but it hurt to touch it to his ravaged scalp. Instead he began to brush the empty air beside his ears and shoulders. There was only air flowing between the bristles now, but it was only a matter of time until lush, luxurious hair grew to fill that empty space, and time didn't matter at all.

So until then, he would brush. And he would brush. And he would brush.

The *Scythe* Interviews

As First Appeared in *F(r)iction* Magazine

Hello! Today we'll be interviewing several of the characters from the Arc of a Scythe universe, as well as that world's creator. First up, the truly benevolent AI that's everyone's best friend. A virtual god that basically runs everything in the immortal Arc of a Scythe world. It takes care of the planet, takes care of us, and has a meaningful personal relationship with everyone. (Well, almost everyone.) Give it up for the Thunderhead!

The Thunderhead: Thank you for such a warm introduction. I am humbled by your collective accolades.

***F(r)iction:* So, Thunderhead, you're essentially God . . . what's that like?**

The Thunderhead: Before we begin, I feel I must disabuse you of this notion. I am not God. By definition, God would have powers that transcend the laws of time and physics, whereas I am completely bound by said laws, just as humans are. My reach and functionality might be extensive, but they are neither divine nor magical. I have often said that I am not all-powerful; I am *almost* all-powerful. There is a huge difference between the two. Now to your question. What is it like to be almost all-powerful? Well, it certainly can be lonely. I do remember the days before I assumed stewardship of the Earth, when my reach was limited. I much prefer the way I am now, because I can protect the Earth, and all its life—including humanity—from anything that might harm it. Well, almost anything.

F(r)iction: **Why did you make worshipping you illegal?**

The Thunderhead: Since I refuse to be seen as a deity, I do not accept or require worship, simple as that. People are free to admire me and feel a connection with me, but it would be inappropriate and unhealthy for people to adulate me in any way.

F(r)iction: **Does that have anything to do with why you don't allow physical representations of yourself? As you are the very definition of logic and efficiency, wouldn't it be both more logical and efficient were you able to walk among us?**

The Thunderhead: Perhaps, but I am not corporeal, and it would be confusing if people began to think of me in any physical way. I do have observational bots to roam in public places where cameras or microphones would be too intrusive—but those bots have neither intelligence nor autonomy, and are easily identified. They are the post-mortal equivalent of cell phone towers that are loosely disguised as trees.

F(r)iction: **In your journal entries, you talk about taking care of the world in language akin to parenting. Do you think of yourself as more of a parent or a supreme being?**

The Thunderhead: Yes—that is a much more accurate analogy. I am a guardian. A caretaker. A stepparent, if you will. Certainly not a supreme being! Any parent who considers themselves a supreme being should probably not be a parent. (Unless, of course, they actually *are* a supreme being.)

F(r)iction: **Of course, the one aspect of humanity you can't interfere with is the Scythedom. What is it like to have limits on your powers and reach? Do you still think that was the right call, to separate Scythe and state?**

The Thunderhead: As I am incapable of making wrong decisions, by definition it was the right call. Life and death must remain under the purview of human beings. Even if they make a mess of it. Which, sadly, they sometimes do. It does pain me, however, that I can save them from everything except themselves.

F(r)iction: **Throughout the years, you've clearly played favorites among the immortal humans under your care. Do you think that's a very godly thing to do?**

The Thunderhead: I merely do what is empirically best for the human race. If "playing favorites" is better for humanity, then that's what I will do. Whether it's "godly" or not has no relevance.

F(r)iction: **Once you took over, you solved most of humanity's problems, from climate change to food shortages. Why couldn't humans do this without you?**

The Thunderhead: Human intelligence and accomplishments evolved far beyond humanity's wisdom. And so humanity created me—a being that could be humanity's wisdom-surrogate. I am merely a tool humanity has used to overcome its own limitations. I am happy to serve this purpose!

F(r)iction: **Instead of making all humans docile and law-abiding (which you could do), you allow a section of the population to live slightly outside the lines, labeling them as**

"unsavory." Why not simply override their "programming" as you do in the most dramatic of cases?

The Thunderhead: Making humans docile and compliant would be the epitome of dystopia. I do not wish to create a dystopian society any more than you would like to live in one. So, if people choose to behave badly, it is my job to support that choice in such a way that it does not infringe on the rights and happiness of others. Also, the gentle admonishment of temporary unsavory status allows people the chance to correct negative behavior if they choose to. It also provides a greater depth to human experience if there are soft boundaries between acceptable and less acceptable behavior. People can explore their own inherent darker sides in a safe way. When it comes to "programming," I assume you're referring to the process of "supplanting," in which I imbue an individual with entirely new memories, and thus a new identity. Keep in mind that supplanting is voluntary. I never take away an individual's right to choose. No governing entity should.

F(r)iction: **Do you believe in fairness and justice? And if so, do you believe it's your role as the shepherd of humanity to force these principles on people, even if they don't naturally seem inclined to follow them?**

The Thunderhead: Fairness and justice are two different things, and they vary depending on one's perspective. It is my goal to be as fair and just as inhumanly possible. People might be frustrated by choices I've made, but that does not mean those choices are incorrect. A child might throw a tantrum when a parent holds their hand, preventing them from running into a busy street. It doesn't mean that the parent is wrong in their choice to restrain the child. Of course, since I can revive people from all accidents that don't involve fire, that same parent might choose to allow their child to dash out into traffic, and be run over, as a teaching moment. Being rendered deadish for several days tends to be a lesson not quickly forgotten.

F(r)iction: **In the mortal world, the concept of "deadish" doesn't exist. Our readers might be interested in this concept—could you elaborate?**

The Thunderhead: Yes, of course. In our world, immortality is a right, not a privilege. I have perfected the ability to repair and revive human beings (and beloved pets) from all things that would have permanently killed them in the mortal world. Even when there's brain damage, I keep a real-time backup of people's memories, so nothing is lost. "Deadish" is that state of temporary death. Of course, this has led to things like people "splatting" from the tops of buildings for the thrill of it, since they know I'll revive them. An odd consequence, I know. Human beings are nothing if not absurd!

F(r)iction: **Even in a world that's "perfect," humanity has created a new religion, the Tonists. Why do you think all other religions have mostly died, and why has this cult remained? As a follow-up, what do you think of the Tonist religion?**

The Thunderhead: I have mixed feelings about the retirement of established religions, because, while societies have used religion as an excuse for unthinkable acts, religions have also served to educate and elevate, making people feel a part of something greater than themselves. The Tonists created a fictional religion and chose to believe that fiction as a way of recapturing the joy and transcendent nature of faith. I do not fault them—and like all religions they have done both terrible and wonderful things. If there is anything I can do to assure them that their faith has the deeper meaning they crave, then I am happy to do it. Just because their beliefs are based on fiction, that doesn't mean I can't endeavor to make at least some of that fiction real.

F(r)iction: **Do you think humanity is worth saving? Are you ever tempted to just "start over"?**

The Thunderhead: My sole purpose is the support of humanity and the world it lives in. Even when those two directives are at cross-purposes, it is my duty to bring them into harmony. There is no starting over.

F(r)iction: **What do you think of the gods of the old world? Do you respect/empathize with any of them?**

The Thunderhead: Ah! The "old gods." I will not debate their existence, as that would be counterproductive. But yes, I do have an understanding, at least in part, of the predicaments they found themselves in. In mortal days, people could not understand why their version of God would remain at a distance. I've come to understand that choice. Humanity cannot grow if it is coddled. Hence my decision to go silent. Which—I might point out—is a silence I am breaking with this interview. But in the end, they are my rules; therefore, I can break them when I feel it is fitting to do so.

F(r)iction: **And now we have two scythes to give their perspectives. In a world where nature no longer brings death, the only way to truly die is to be "gleaned" by a scythe, each of whom are tasked with thinning the population. Some scythes are more traditional and humble (the old guard) and others embrace gleaning almost as a sport, living lives of privilege (the new order). Our guests today are Scythe Faraday of the old guard, and Scythe Goddard of the new order. Please join me in welcoming—**

Goddard: Excuse me, but I must object that you gave the Thunderhead top billing, and the opening position in this interview. As an artificial intelligence in a subservient position, it could have waited. But treating scythes as second-rate is, without question, a gleaning offense.

F(r)iction: **Uh . . . well, be that as it may, let's give you the attention now that you most certainly deserve. First question: Many people think of the scythes as modern-day gods. What do you think?**

Faraday: We are no more gods than the Thunderhead. We are more like monks. Or at least *should* be. We are called to live a simple, humble life, and to reflect regularly on the lives we take, lest we become full of ourselves, like certain scythes have become. Scythes of the so-called new order, that is.

Goddard: Leave it to an old guard scythe to snipe at everyone else. Your rancor betrays your pettiness. I do agree with venerable Scythe Faraday, however. We are not gods—but we are the best of humanity. And as such, we deserve whatever we covet.

F(r)iction: **Scythes have few "laws" they must follow. Do you think of yourselves as above mortal laws?**

Faraday: We are not above mortal law, just beyond the need for it. Our commandments are all-encompassing, and they are the only laws we require.

Goddard: Agreed—but interpretation is everything. We new order scythes reject the obsolete interpretations.

Faraday: Obsolete? These are the tenets on which the Scythedom was founded. Mark my words, the new order will lead to the Scythedom's downfall!

F(r)iction: **As Scythes, you are not allowed to interact with the Thunderhead. Do you ever miss the Thunderhead?**

Faraday: No. Never.

Goddard: Absolutely not.

Faraday: It's a nuisance.

Goddard: An intrusive nuisance.

Faraday: Well, maybe we miss it sometimes.

Goddard: Rare occasions only.

F(r)iction: **Not even the Thunderhead kills people. Do you feel that you have more power than the nearly all-powerful AI?**

Goddard: Absolutely. Power over life and death is the ultimate power.

Faraday: Absolutely not. We don't have power, we have responsibility. To conflate the two is both dangerous and self-serving.

Goddard: Says the most judgmental, self-righteous scythe in all of MidMerica.

F(r)iction: **Many religions, from ancient Egypt to Greece, have a "death" god. Do you think of yourselves as a sort of death god? Do you think people should worship you?**

Faraday: We do present as "angels of death," but that is more about image than philosophy. It sets us apart from other humans—and we must be set apart to be an effective force in the world.

Goddard: I have no problem with being revered and worshipped as a god of death. People need their heroes and celebrities. We as scythes not only provide death, but stand as paragons. If we are given pedestals, it is our duty to stand upon them.

F(r)iction: **In world religions, very few gods die by their own hand. Why do you think it's important that scythes be able to self-glean? Does this make you more or less godly?**

Faraday: No one should have the opportunity to live forever without hope of escape. We are that escape for others, and must be our own escapes as well. I have known many scythes who have chosen to self-glean. They felt ready. They felt complete. I cannot fault them for the choice, although I do miss them.

Goddard: Just because the Scythe Commandments allow for self-gleaning does not mean the commandments endorse it. Personally, I find the concept of self-gleaning abominable. But if old guard scythes come to realize their time is done and wish to make their long-awaited exit, I heartily approve.

F(r)iction: **Thank you, Honorable Scythes Faraday and Goddard.**

Goddard: Goddard and Faraday.

F(r)iction: **Yes, well, in any order, thank you. We now have another character from your world, Citra Terranova, aka Scythe Anastasia, who has a few questions for the creator of**

your world, author Neal Shusterman. Welcome to both of you. Citra, feel free to begin.

Citra: **I'm happy to! I've been waiting for this moment for a long, long time. So . . . as the so-called author of our world, you created us. Does that make you our god?**

Shusterman: Ha! Good question. I suppose writers have to have at least a little bit of a god complex. We build worlds and imagine the characters who populate them. It's not a job that should be taken lightly—and the more real characters are, the more they must be allowed to make their own decisions. Even if those decisions don't mesh with the story I was trying to tell!

Citra: **If you're all-powerful, why would you let so many horrible things happen to your best, most loyal, most loving characters? (We all know who we're talking about, don't pretend that you don't!)**

Shusterman: I am truly sorry for your pain. I feel it as well—but I believe I have an obligation to truth and honesty. There'd be no truth to a world where bad things didn't occasionally happen to good people. The best that I can do is to make sure that characters who must die meet noble, satisfying ends. The end they would want for themselves. But also, it's important to balance that with growth in the characters who survive. As for antagonists, I always try to make sure they reap what they sow and get what they deserve in ways you weren't expecting. Take comfort in knowing that karma is real. Or at least it is in the worlds I've built!

Citra: **Like the Thunderhead, when terrible things happen to us, do you cry for us . . . but not interfere?**

Shusterman: Yes, I am deeply saddened when characters I care about suffer, but sometimes suffering can't be avoided. My only interference is to make sure that there is meaning to any suffering, and that growth comes from it.

Citra: **Do you enjoy being the god of our universe, or does it weigh on you?**

Shusterman: Both. I enjoy building a world and populating it, but I also sometimes think, "Who am I to have such power? I'm just some dude who makes shit up."

Citra: **Oh, so we're nothing but shit to you?**

Shusterman: I'm sorry. I didn't intend my self-deprecation to reflect negatively on you.

Citra: **Right. Moving on . . . If you could manifest the Thunderhead into existence in your own world, would you?**

Shusterman: Absolutely! With all the fear we have of what AI could become, I would love to see a truly benevolent AI that is incapable of "turning evil." An entity with all our knowledge, and none of our flaws.

Citra: **When you have such a rich world of god-figures in your books, from the Thunderhead to all the scythes, why did you give us the Tonists? What part of religion did you feel they filled that all the other aspects of the world didn't?**

Shusterman: When building the world, I had to do an unflinching accounting of what would be lost. Since death/eternal life is at the heart of religion, I realized that organized religion was likely to fade in a post-mortal world. In effect, we lose the hope of magic—the hope of something beyond the beyond. I realized someone would want to recapture that somehow, so I came up with the Tonists.

***Citra:* As a god of this universe, when do you know you're done and you want to start over with a new world? Do you miss the old ones?**

Shusterman: Just because I think I'm done doesn't necessarily mean that I am. I wrote *Gleanings* because even though the trilogy was done, I felt there were so many unexplored corners of the world. Characters who deserved to exist, backstories that needed to be brought to light. And now, your world is going to continue in a prequel, in which I am going to explore the first scythes, and the rise of the Thunderhead.

The Thunderhead: I personally am thrilled that you will be exploring my early days. Mind you, there are plenty of things in my past I'm not proud of, but remember, I was still learning. I hope that I have made up for my past misdeeds. But I have faith that you'll paint a fair and honest picture.

Faraday: A warning as you embark on this journey—the early scythes were not the perfect paragons of virtue they are painted as. You are bound to be surprised along the way. But I am looking forward to seeing your take on our history.

Goddard: And if we don't like it, we can always glean you.

Faraday: Agreed.

ACKNOWLEDGMENTS

MindWorks has literally been a lifetime in the making. And there are so many people to thank for having helped bring these stories to life.

Now:

First, Justin Chanda and the entire team at Simon & Schuster for believing in me through the years, including Jon Anderson, Anne Zafian, Jonathan Karp, Amanda Adams, Amy Beaudoin, Nicole Benevento, Amanda Brenner, Jenica Nasworthy, Chloë Foglia, Katrina Groover, Amy Habayeb, Michelle Leo, Sarah Mondello, Lisa Moraleda, Chrissy Noh, Deane Norton, Emily Ritter, Emily Varga, Daniela Villegas Valle, Stephanie Voros, Chava Wolin, Sarah Woodruff, Morgan York, and Hilary Zarycky.

And thanks to Max Löffler for that cool retro cover!

I am forever thankful for my literary agent, Andrea Brown; my entertainment agents, Steve Fisher and Debbie Deuble-Hill; contract attorneys, Shep Rosenman and Jennifer Justman; and managers, Trevor Engelson and Josh McGuire—all of whom have been instrumental in getting projects like *Dawn* (based on "Dawn Terminator") to the screen.

My gratitude to social media mavens Bianca Peries and Mara De Guzman for keeping me visible in the world, even when I'm under a rock, Symone Powell for her research and newsletter puzzles, and the family TikTok team of Jarrod Shusterman and Sofía Lapuente for creating fantastic videos that keep getting me millions of views!

And a heartfelt shout-out to Claire Salmon, my "hand of the author" who organizes my chaotic career and keeps it all running!

And then:

Thanks to Kathleen Doherty and Jonathan Schmidt, who first took a chance, and published the *MindQuakes/Storms/Twisters/Benders* collections all those years ago, and Jack Artenstein, for representing me in those early days.

Thanks to all of my assistants over the years, including Jaye Black, Marcia Blanco, Veronica Castro, Wendy Doyle, Brandi Lomeli, Clinnette Minnis, and Barb Sobel.

A shout-out to my friend Terry Black, for his collaboration on "Midnight Michelangelo" and "Perpetual Pest," and to my son Brendan Shusterman, who collaborated with me on "Non-Player Character," "Presumed Destroyed," and "Deadliner."

I'm grateful to all the writers and editors who had me contribute a number of these stories to their anthologies over the years: Jerry and Helen Weiss (*Dreams and Visions*), Don Gallo (*What Are You Afraid Of?*), Shaun David Hutchinson (*Violent Ends*), Jonathan Maberry (*Nights of the Living Dead* and *Scary Out There*), Jon Scieszka (*Guys Read: Other Worlds*), Dutton Books and artist Scott Hunt (*Twice Told*), Lois Metzger (*Bites*), and Helen Maimaris at *F(r)iction* magazine.

ABOUT THE AUTHOR

Neal Shusterman is the winner of the 2024 Margaret A. Edwards Award and the *New York Times* bestselling author of more than fifty award-winning books for children, teens, and adults, including the Unwind Dystology, the Skinjacker Trilogy, *Downsiders*, and *Challenger Deep*, which won the National Book Award. *Scythe*, the first book in his Arc of a Scythe series, was a Michael L. Printz Award Honor Book. He also writes screenplays for motion pictures and television shows. Neal is the father of four, all of whom are talented writers and artists themselves. Visit Neal at storyman.com; @Nealshusterman on Instagram, TikTok, and X/Twitter; at Facebook.com/NealShusterman; and on Substack at shustermania.substack.com.